All It Took Was One Shot

Terry Creegan

DEDICATION

There are a few people who have played a huge role in the creation of this novel. I am so appreciative of their help.

To Eric Austin...You were always there for me at the beginning of this journey. You were patient, so very patient when I started the journey. Fortunately, you were very directive when I needed a kick in the keister. I am so grateful. I will always remember that there are shelves in the world that one chapter completed...You are my vision of perspicacity.

To Chief Mike Zurbey...A longtime friend and a keen resource for all things related to policing. Thank you for your time and support. Any errors are of my own making.

To M.G. ...I have known you since our first year in high school. It was only later that I discovered your incredible artistic talent. Thank you for the cover page. As someone might say, "It's Dynamite!"

To Jan and Chuck...Thank you so very much for the time and patience you provided as we wended our way through the Kindle process. You are the best.

To Jeanne Marie...My beautiful, thoughtful, generous, loving wife. Thank you for listening to my endless concerns. You read and reread so many drafts without complaint. This dream would never come true without your support. I am blessed to call you HB.

ALL IT TOOK WAS ONE SHOT

CONTENTS

Confronting a mob shooting

It was 5:00 p.m. by the time the bus dropped Vincent Angelino off. The wind was biting. It meant a long trot home. Vincent was tired, dog tired. When he finally walked into his house, all he wanted to do was to lie down. His mom had other ideas. "I need you to go to the grocery store with me. We need to pick up a few things for supper." No "How'd you do at the meet?" or "How was school?" Just "Get your coat on. I need your help. You better hurry!" No arguing with Mom when she's in a hurry.

Viterio's Grocery Store was a few blocks from their home. It was in a two-story brick building that, like the rest of the town, had seen better days. Vincent could see that Viterio's was busy. He opened the door and in they went. Up and down the aisles there were greetings from friends and neighbors. Vincent's mom had worked at Cianci's Bakery for years. As a result, everyone wanted to talk to her. Vincent was getting impatient, but he knew better than to say anything.

Finally, Vincent and his mom headed towards the meat counter. No sooner had they made it to the counter when Vincent heard a pop and a gasp. He spun towards the commotion. His mom was leaning against the counter. A spattering of blood was seeping from her shoulder. Mr. De Nuncio was lying at her feet, gasping for air. Vincent turned to the front of the store. He saw a small guy with a beaked nose and zits for a face standing near the front door. The guy put a pistol in his overcoat and strolled out as if nothing happened. Suddenly the store was filled with screams. Vincent's mom had his full attention.

Mr. Viterio knelt to help De Nuncio while Vincent caught his mom just as she started to topple to the floor.

1

Vincent pulled off his scarf, pushed it up against her shoulder and shouted, "Somebody call an ambulance!" He yelled loud enough for everyone to hear. After what seemed like forever, the wail of a police car filled the air. Then, some blue suit with a beer belly raced into the grocery store with his gun drawn. A second cop was not far behind.

A few minutes later, an ambulance screeched to a halt. A nurse raced in, took one look at De Nuncio and headed towards Vincent's mom. After the nurse worked on Mrs. Angelino, she was carted off to St. Peter's Hospital. De Nuncio was headed to the morgue. It was days later before Vincent learned he was the only person who saw Mr. Zits.

A detective named Maloney limped into Viterio's just as the ambulance left. He scowled as he listened to the beefy patrol officer recount what he knew. Maloney looked around and saw a short spit of a kid with blood on his jacket standing in front of a Coca Cola display.

Maloney shuffled over to the boy. "What's your name, son?" he said in a quiet voice.

"Vincent, Vincent Angelino, sir."

"Vincent," Maloney said, "I need to talk to you. I understand you saw the shooter." Tears began to fall on Vincent's cheeks. "Let's find a quiet place to talk." They headed towards a small office in the back of the store. Maloney knew the boy needed to be handled with kid gloves.

Maloney asked Vincent to sit down. "You've had a rough day." Vincent nodded in agreement. "Can you answer a few questions?"

"I can try, sir."

"Do you live close by?" Vincent nodded his head.

"Tell me about your family, Vincent." A few minutes later, the detective asked Vincent to talk about the shooting. Vincent described the shooter. When he got to the part where his mom was shot, he started shaking. Maloney decided to end the interview for now. "I have enough information to get the investigation started," he said to himself. "How can I reach your father?" Vincent's dad worked for the county. Maloney made a call. A few minutes later, John Angelino was pulled out of a meeting. A co-worker told him to report to the director.

John was confused. "What's going on?" No one knew anything. He finally found his supervisor. "Lou, what's going on?"

"John, I got a call from the police. Detective Maloney needs to talk to you right away."

"About what, Lou?"

"John, from what I understand, Maria was hurt at the grocery store. She is headed to the hospital. Here's Maloney's number. Give him a call."

Angelino called the detective immediately. "What's going on?" Maloney told him what had happened. Mr. Angelino broke down. Once he calmed down, he wanted to know where his wife was. The detective told him. "I'm headed to the hospital. Could you drive my son there?" Maloney said he could do that.

Maloney hung up the phone. "Vincent, I'm taking you to the hospital to meet your father." They got to the hospital about 6:45. Maloney went to the information area and explained what had happened. Within a minute, an orderly took Vincent to a waiting room in the surgery

3

suite. When Vincent opened the door, his dad was pacing the floor. His aunt was trying to calm his brothers. down. It wasn't working.

When Vincent arrived, the noise level rose. He was peppered with questions. Everyone wanted to know what had happened. All Vincent cared about was how his mom was doing. "How is Mom!" His dad pulled him over to a nearby chair. He put his arm around Vincent. "Mom's in pretty bad shape. The doctors will let us know how she is doing as soon as they could."

It was well after 10 p.m. when the Angelinos left for home. Dr. Walker, their family doctor, came into the room around 9 p.m. He said that the emergency room doc stopped the bleeding and X-rays had been taken. The rest was mumbo jumbo. A specialist was being called in. Surgery was scheduled for the next morning.

"John, there's nothing more you can do," said Dr. Walker. "Maria is sedated. You are exhausted. Go home. Get some sleep." He took the doctor's advice. When he got home, he found reporters waiting at his doorstep. One look at John and the reporters backed off. The family went inside. Vincent's brothers were asleep before their bedroom door was closed.

Vincent changed into his Bosox pajamas and got ready for bed. His dad asked him to come down to the kitchen. John pulled a padded chair out from the table. "Sit down, son." Then, John got a milk bottle from the fridge and poured them both a glass. "It's late, but I need to talk to you." Vincent nodded. Then he started to cry. His dad reached over and pulled Vincent close to him. Then they cried together.

After a while, John patted Vincent's arm with one hand and held his chin with the other. "It's been a really hard day. The police told me how you took charge...putting your scarf on Mom's shoulder to stop the bleeding and then making sure the police were called. I'm so proud of you!"

"Dad," Vincent said, "Just after Mom was shot, I saw a guy put a gun in his pocket and walk out of the store. I should have yelled for someone to follow him. But I froze. I just froze!" Then Vincent started to cry again, John waited for Vincent to calm down.

"Son," he said, "The rest of the story can wait until tomorrow."

What can I tell you

Joey D showed up just after 6 pm. He looked like a shooter. He was swarthy. He had greased black hair, a pock marked face, and the eye of a killer. Marty heard someone banging at Mr. B's back door. It was loud enough to attract attention. Marty looked through the peep hole. One look was all that was needed. There was Joey standing off to the side of the backdoor stoop. Marty went to the back door and let him in.

Joey called himself One Shot, but the boss said that he was Joey D. from Hartford. By the look of him, you would think he'd come off the set of the Untouchables. He was wearing a shiny grey coat and hat, a comic book character. This guy was just like the last two bozos who came over from Connecticut. They were hare brained with a hair trigger. Killing people was apparently the only thing that set Joey apart from the others. Mr. B had talked to Marty earlier. "I'm expecting company tonight. Some guy name Joey. "Bring him to my office as soon as he arrives."

Joey walked into the house like he owned the place. Marty walked over to the stairs that led to Mr. B's office. "Follow me." There was no response. Marty turned around. Joey was waltzing around the kitchen. "You need to follow me. Mr. B's waiting to see you!"

One Shot yanked Marty's arm. "I need a drink."

"What a knucklehead!" Marty thought. "Apparently, the Connecticut folks run a different ship than we do. I have to remember to share this story after Joey leaves." Marty told Joey that he'd have to wait if he wanted a drink. Joey ambled down the stairs. Mr. B was sitting on a couch when Joey walked in. Mr. B stood up slowly, straightened his tie, and motioned for Joey to sit down. Then Mr. B walked over to the bar and poured some Campari.

"How did it go?" the boss asked.

"Smooth as silk. No problemo!" One Shot said.

Marty knew full well that Mr. B had no time for smart alecs. "This ought to be interesting."

Mr. B stood up and shouted, "Cut to the chase, you little jerk," he said. "What happened?"

Joey launched into the shooting. "I did exactly what you told me to do. For the past few weeks, I followed De Nuncio like I was his shadow. Every night, he'd leave his kid and that weirdo Mario to mind the pool hall. Then he walked to Viterio's to get some coffee and a few day-old donuts. That's what he did tonight. I waited til he went inside. There were lots of people in the store. Nobody was near the front door. Next thing I knew, he starts walking towards the back of the store. De Nuncio was all by his lonesome. I pulled out my gun and took a shot. The guy was a dead duck."

Nothing goes that smoothly, Marty thought. I better keep my trap shut and let my uncle do the talking. "Is De Nuncio dead, Joey?"

"He is! He dropped like a stone. No way he makes it."

Mr. B was amazed that all had gone so smoothly. "Did anyone see you?"

"Naw, the place exploded with screams as soon as De Nuncio hit the floor. I left right away, ran to my car, took a little detour, and then headed straight back here."

Everything Joey said was just what Mr. B wanted to hear, but there was something in the tone of Joey's voice that didn't seem right. The list of things to share with Mr. B was growing.

Mr. B pulled an envelope from his desk drawer and handed it to One Shot. He told Joey to head back to Hartford. After a few minutes of patting himself on the back, Joey left.

"Whadda you think, Marty?" Marty mentioned Joey's need for a drink.

"Mr. B, I'm concerned about the shooting itself. Something had been left out of the story."

"How do you know?"

"There is something about his story that seems fishy."

"Don't start getting highbrow, Marty! I sent you to Ithaca for an education, not for some touchy, feely crap.

The morning after

Vincent awoke to the sound of voices coming from the kitchen. He looked at his alarm clock. It was 8:30 am. He changed clothes in a flash and sped downstairs. Nonno, Vincent's grandfather, was wiping up some dishes. He was tapping his finger as he spoke to Vincent's father. In a halting voice, he asked his son how this could have happened to his daughter-in-law.

Vincent's grandmother, Nonna, was walking over to the old gas stove. She put an old red apron around her substantial waist and began to fix breakfast. When Vincent walked in, the talking stopped. Nonna pulled him to her side. "Vincente, you did good yesterday," she said in a heavily accented voice. "Sit down, have some breakfast. Then you can tell us what happened. I want to know everything." Nonna was just like his mother—you did what she asked.

For the next half hour, everyone gathered around Vincent. They all had questions about the shooting. Had you ever seen the shooter before? What did he look like? and a hundred other questions. It got to be a blur. Everyone saw that Vincent was exhausted.

"Okay, that's enough for now," John said. "It's time to go to the hospital." That was all that was needed to get the family on the road.

Everyone piled into the Plymouth Volare station wagon and headed to the hospital. St. Peter's Hospital was in Pawtucket. It was a few miles further away than the Providence hospitals, but St. Pete's was old school. Nonna had been hospitalized there for heart issues. She received great care. If it was good enough for Nonna, it was good enough for her family.

The traffic was heavy, so the ride was longer than expected. Once inside the hospital, they went directly to Vincent's mom's room. Her room was filled with bronze-colored mums. However, she was nowhere to be found. John went to the nurses' station. Apparently, the family had just missed the charge nurse's call. The surgeon had arrived a half hour ago. He decided to go ahead with surgery right away. Maria was being prepped. The Angelinos' sat down and waited.

Two hours later, Dr. Johanson, the surgeon, came out of the operating room and walked over to Mr. Angelino. They went into a nearby conference room. Ten minutes later, the family learned that the bullet had done a lot of damage. Vincent's mom's rotator cuff had been torn and her shoulder blade had a small fracture. It would take a long time for her shoulder to heal.

An hour later, Vincent's mom was wheeled back to her room. She was groggy but reached out to touch everyone. What a relief. A groggy mom was better than the alternative. A few minutes later, Detective Maloney stepped into the room. One look into his eyes and you knew right away that something was up.

Maloney motioned Mr. Angelino over to him. They stepped out of the room while the rest of the family crowded around the hospital bed. They were all jabbering. Maria smiled. Vincent's dad came back into the room and spoke to Nonna. Then he turned to Vincent. "We need to go to the police station, Son."

The detective drove Vincent and his dad to the station. When they got there, Maloney led them to a small, smelly conference room. He motioned to the Angelinos' to sit down. Then, Maloney put a small cassette recorder on the table and plugged it in.

The detective identified himself, the date and time of the meeting, and the fact that Vincent was being interviewed regarding the shooting. "Mr. Angelino, do I have permission to speak to your son?" John agreed.

Then Maloney began to ask Vincent about the shooting. Maloney didn't waste time getting to the point. "Do you remember much about the guy who shot your Mom?"

"The guy was short. His hair was dark and wavy. His nose turned up like Bob Hope's nose and he had zits all over his face."

"Vincent, have you ever seen the shooter before?

"No, sir."

"How old do you think he was?"

"He was a young guy, sir, maybe 23 or 24."

"Do you think you would recognize him if you saw him again?" Vincent nodded his head. "Son, please speak into the microphone."

"Sorry, sir. I'm certain I would recognize him."

Then Maloney asked if Vincent had seen the actual shooting. "All I saw was the gun. The guy put this handgun in his overcoat pocket moments after the shooting...like he was putting milk back into the refrigerator. Then the guy just walked away." Maloney kept up with the questions. By then, Vincent was out of answers.

Mr. B is in for a surprise

Mr. B's day always started the same way. He got up by 6:10 a.m. and headed for a hot shower and a Gillette shave. He splashed on some Old Spice, got dressed and then went to St. Rocco's early mass. There were churches closer to his home, but the Latin mass was the magnet. Mr. B was an old time Catholic. Father DiNapoli, the baby priest, always said Saturday morning mass, so it would be short and sweet. The regulars were already seated when Mr. B and Marty arrived. "Marty, let's sit in the back of the church."

Father DiNapoli sped through the readings and his sermon. During communion, Father whispered something to Mr. B. Apparently it was troublesome, because Mr. B waited for everyone to leave before he walked out of the church.

DiNapoli was waiting for him. They huddled near the baptismal font and spoke quietly so as not to draw any attention. The conversation was short. Father headed back to the rectory and Mr. B stormed to his Crown Victoria. Marty had no idea what had been said, but it was clear that there would be no lollygagging.

"Marone!" Mr. B started to sputter. That wasn't good. Marty could tell the shit would hit the fan. "Marty," Mr. B growled, "drive over to your Uncle Dino's pronto!"

They raced to Dino's. On the way over there, Mr. B noticed a phone booth in front of Augie's Barber Shop. "Pull over!" he shouted.

Mr. B went to the booth and yanked the phone off the receiver. He made a long-distance call to Hartford.

Marty could hear him through the window. "Put Cappy, on the phone!" he shouted. Thirty seconds went by. Finally, Cappy answered. "We need to meet right away. I know it's 7:45 a.m., but your boy screwed up. The details can wait. Meet me in Galilee at 11:30 a.m. sharp."

Mr. B slammed the phone down and headed towards the back seat of his car. Marty was in the dark and knew well enough not to ask any questions. "Drop me off at Dino's. Be back by 10 a.m."

As soon as Marty stopped the car, Mr. B jacked the door open, stomped along the walkway, whipped the front door open, and went into his brother's house.

Marty drove over to Front Street to get a cup of coffee. Cianci's was a little Italian joint just off the main drag. The coffee's strong and the sweet rolls are always fresh. The cafe was full. "If I play my cards right," Marty thought, "I'll learn what happened last night."

Within minutes, Marty knew what happened. Three of the regular customers started hollering about Mrs. Angelino getting shot at the grocery store. The truth of the matter was that Mrs. Angelino grew up down the street from Mr. B. The families had been close, real close. This spelled trouble.

Marty finished the coffee and drove to Dino's. A few minutes later, Mr. B got into his car. "We're out of here!" Marty drove while Mr. B fumed. Forty minutes later, they whizzed past Point Judith Pond into the heart of Galilee. Marty pulled alongside the main dock. At the end of the aging dock was a weather-beaten scow called *The Merchant of Venice*. Mr. B and the Hartford crowd used this boat as a meeting place. The dock was isolated, so unwelcomed visitors could be seen from a distance. Just what the doctor ordered.

Three men were already on board the boat. Marty jumped out of the Crown Victoria and opened Mr. B's door. "Stay here," Mr. B said. "It's bad luck for you to go on the boat."

"Bad luck my backside!" Marty started to argue. That went nowhere.

Mr. B walked to the dock. He was met at the gangplank by several members of the Hartford gang. They headed to the main cabin. Marty parked the car in an empty lot within sight of the boat and waited.

A few minutes later, one of the guys came out. His name was Gus Bernardo. He was a burly guy who took pleasure in being important. He motioned Marty to come to the wharf. The guy sneered. "Get us some chow and Java!" Marty scowled. Bernardo twisted Marty's arm until the pain became almost unbearable. "You think going to some highfalutin college makes you better than me. No way. Get going before I hurt you!"

Gus watched Marty pull out of the parking space. Then he headed back to the boat.

Marty pulled the car over about a block down on Great Island Road. "My arm's throbbing! What am I doing here? I graduated from Colgate University with a degree in Economics two years ago. Job prospects in Rhode Island were slim. But going away to someplace else meant leaving Mom in a lurch. I couldn't do that."

Marty's father had died last April. Marty decided to stick around Rhode Island for a while. Marty's mom needed to get her life back together. That had taken more time than expected. Marty began to get bored, so when Mr. B asked if Marty wanted to work for him, the answer was yes. "I'm beginning to regret taking this job. I am just a chauffeur. Advancement now takes on a new meaning—

driving a new car for Mr. B every year. This isn't what I envisioned."

After a few minutes of venting, Marty went to get some grub. There was a small cafe called the Creek Inn three blocks down from the wharf. The cafe was dingy on the outside, but the options in Galilee were limited. Marty parked right across from the café's front entrance and wasted no time crossing the street. A stiff October breeze was blowing hard.

Marty walked inside the restaurant. It was clear that this was the right place. Fishermen with scraggly beards and faded sneakers were eating in nearby booths. At the counter, there were two 20-somethings waiting to pay their bill. That delay gave Marty a chance to check the menu. There was nothing flashy about the food, but there were a lot of choices. Marty noticed several urns of freshly brewed coffee just behind the cash register. The urns were being put to good use.

A young waitress brought Marty over to a table in the back of the restaurant. "Would you like to start off with a cup of regular coffee?"

Marty nodded. The waitress came back with the coffee. "So," she said with a smile, "what'll you have?" Marty ordered food for Mr. B and the others on the boat. "That's a take-out order. I'd like to have the house special. I will eat it here."

Marty's order arrived. The waitress brought over a plate of bacon, eggs, and toast with a side of crispy hash browns. The food was as good as advertised. Marty ate quickly, picked up the chow for Mr. B and the others, paid the bill, and headed back to the scow.

Getting breakfast only took 25 minutes from start to finish. "Not bad!" Marty thought. Unfortunately, Gus was waiting impatiently. Marty took the food out of the car and walked over to him. Gus gave Marty some additional grief. Then, he took the bag of food and walked back to the boat. Marty headed to the car.

Vincent is on the run

Detective Maloney had offered to bring Vincent and his dad back to the hospital. "I'd appreciate that, Detective Maloney," John said. When they arrived at the hospital, Maloney told John that he would be in touch.

They got to the room. Vincent's mom was asleep. John wanted to stay with her for a little while. "Dad, can you take the kids back to the house? I can get a ride back home from a friend who lives nearby." Nonno and Nonna took the boys down to the parking lot. They hopped in the station wagon and headed home. As soon as they got there, Nonna went to work on the breakfast dishes. She asked Vincent's youngest brother, Stephen, to help her. Nonno, Vincent, and Vincent's middle brother Pietro, went outside. They raked and bagged leaves in the back yard. When they finished, Vincent called his best friend, Mikey, to see if he wanted to go for a run. Lunch would have to wait.

The boys met halfway between their homes. Mikey O'Day was the epitome of a runner. He was tall, lanky, and always up for a run. Vincent was much shorter than Mikey, but he ran with a much different motor than most of the boys on the cross-country team. He hated to lose and that made all the difference.

The boys started off at a slow trot. Mikey asked some questions that Vincent wasn't ready to answer. Suddenly, Vincent sprinted off. Mikey followed as best he could. They ran and then they ran some more. They raced towards the center of town and then past Jaswell's farm. At about the three-mile mark, Vincent stopped at the Sprague Reservoir, turned away, and heaved his breakfast on the shoreline. Then, he slumped down on the grass and began to cry.

"Vincent," Mikey said when he finally reached him, "Talk to me! What happened?" Vincent's tears slowed to a crawl.

Finally, he looked up. "You know my mom was shot. I was with her at Viterio's."

Mikey sat next to Vincent. "I heard a little bit about this at breakfast." It took a while for Vincent to say anything. Michael knew better than to push his friend.

Finally, Vincent told his story. "I tried to get my mother to move along when we got to Viterio's, but she had to talk with all of her friends. We would have been done shopping by the time the shooting happened if I had been more forceful. This is all my fault!"

The next thing Mikey knew, Vincent took off for the woods. Mikey tried to follow him. He searched the woods for Vincent for an hour to no avail.

Joey, where art thou

Mr. B walked down the dock about two o'clock. "It's time to head home." Marty kept quiet and waited for Mr. B to talk. Eventually, Marty learned that early that morning, Joey left for Chicago. One Shot had another out-of-town job. He would not be back for some time.

"Son of a bitch" were the first words out of Mr. B's mouth. He had told the Hartford crew what had happened in Greenville. No one was happy.

Cappy, the Hartford boss, pulled Mr. B aside. "Dante, there is good news. Joey will be gone for a while. The police won't find him. As for the shooting, I'll make it up to you. I know how close you are to Maria Angelino."

"I counted on you" Mr. B said. "You let me down!"

"I know, I know already. When you figure things out, Dante, call me. I'll help you out. No questions asked."

Mr. B knew if One Shot learned what was up, he'd be long gone. Mr. B made sure that the Hartford crew kept their mouths shut.

There was no time for chatter when they got back to town. Mr. B was meeting De Nuncio's kid the next day. They needed to go over the plan for the pool hall. Marty told Sammy and Giancarlo to come over as soon as possible. Sam was Mr. B's numbers guy and Gian had been a Marine. They knew the score. The two of them came right over that afternoon. The bottom line was that Sam was taking over the bookie business.

19

Sam came down from Worcester two months ago to help Dante figure out why the mob's take from the bookie business had fallen off. After a week observing the operation, Sam gave one of Dante's guys some marked bills to use as bets at De Nuncio's. Twice the guy placed a big bet. Both times, he lost the bet. The marked money never made it back to Mr. B. That started the ball rolling. Mr. B had someone check the safe. The guy found a huge stash of money including the marked bills! Exit stage left Mr. De Nuncio.

"Boss," Sam said when they all sat down. "I know you want this handoff to go smoothly. Does Billy know you had his dad taken out?"

"Jimmy knows nothing about the money that we found. Nor does he know that we had his father taken out."

Mr. B decided to tell Billy that he heard someone was upset about a payout. Apparently, the guy shot his father. Billy would learn that the word was out to find the shooter.

For the next hour, they went over the plan. Mr. B must have been upset because the meeting went on and on. That wasn't like him. Luckily, they finished up in time for Mr. B to go home and get ready to take his wife to the Columbus Day dinner at St. Rocco's. Marty was left to cover the phone.

Where have you been

Vincent came home about 6:15 p.m. His pants were torn and his shoes were caked with mud. His face, arms, and legs were covered with the remains of a thorny vine attack. Vincent's brother, Petey, was shooting baskets in the back yard when he saw Vincent walk towards their house.

"Vincent, where have you been? Dad's worried sick!"

Vincent could tell Petey was scared. However, now was not the time for Vincent to play "Big Brother the Comforter." As Vincent walked up the back stairs, the door creaked open. Vincent's dad was standing at the door.

"Dad, I'm sorry I'm late," he said when he saw his dad standing as if he was on guard duty.

His father spoke in a soft voice. "Vincent, I'm too angry to talk to you right now. Go upstairs and take a shower. Your grandmother has leftovers on the stove. I am headed to the hospital. I want you to stay inside for the rest of the night. We'll talk tomorrow after church."

John headed out to the car. Vincent went to his bedroom. It would have made sense to eat something, anything for that matter. But Vincent fumbled his way to the bathroom and turned on the hot water. From the shuddering sounds the pipes made, he knew it would take a while for the water to get hot.

Instead of waiting for warm water, Vincent decided that a cold shower would be a small penance to pay for his failure to protect his mom. He opened the shower curtain. The spray hit his body like a round of bullets, each one hurting more than the next. He stood in the tub and prayed for forgiveness.

When hot water began to strike, he shut off the spray and grabbed for a towel. There were no towels. Maybe that was God's way of saying that there was more penance necessary before Vincent would be forgiven. Vincent yelled for help.

A few minutes later, Nonno appeared at the door with a towel. He took a look at Vincent. His skin was as blue as an iris. He wrapped the towel around Vincent's waist. "Can Nonna fix you something to eat?"

"No," he said, "I'm going to bed." Nonno headed downstairs and Vincent headed to the bedroom he shared with his brothers. He knelt at the foot of his bed and prayed. Then he slipped between the sheets. After a half hour of tossing and turning, he finally fell asleep.

The next morning, he was up before anyone else. He dressed, went downstairs, and wrote his dad a note. "Dad, I'm sorry for what I did. I need some time to think. I got up early and went to mass at church."

St. Phillip's was five blocks from their house. By the time Vincent got there, mass had just starting. He crept into a back pew and immediately knelt to pray. He never heard one word of the homily or the blaring of the organ. The only thing he heard were the whimpering sounds his mom had made after she was shot.

Vincent's family always went to the nine o'clock service. Most of his uncles and aunts lived nearby, so there was always a passel of Angelinos at church. The children were used to being shushed during the service. That was the last thing that Vincent wanted to be a part of. He decided to stay for the 9 a.m. service, but he sat by himself in the back pew.

John was the first person to see Vincent. He turned to Nonno and pointed towards their regular pew. Then, John walked towards Vincent. He slid down the pew and knelt next to his son. They looked at each other, hugged, and began to pray. After mass was over, Mr. Angelino left the pew for a minute. He walked over to his parents and spoke to them privately. Then he turned and motioned to Vincent to come with him.

They walked to the reservoir. Not a word was spoken. They stopped beside a small waterfall and sat down by the bank of the stream. After a while, John turned to his son. "Vincent, what happened Friday was horrible! I wish I could take an eraser and wipe it all away. Better yet, I wish I could find the guy who shot your mom. The police would have a hard time talking to him after I was done with him. That's not going to happen any time soon. I feel awful. You must feel even worse. When we talked, you told me that what happened to Mom was your fault. It wasn't your fault!"

Vincent started to respond, but his father put a finger up to his lips. "Just listen to me for a second. Then I'll listen to you. We both know when Mom starts talking to her friends, it's like a freight train out of control. Not much can stop her until she runs of out of steam. I'm sure you tried to get her to get going. It was Friday afternoon. You just came back from a meet. You were exhausted, but there was nothing you could do."

Vincent was so tired that he simply shook his head. After a while, he told his dad that he froze when he saw the shooter. If he had shouted out, things might have been different. John listened carefully as Vincent recounted the entire episode. When he finished his story, John grabbed his arms and forced Vincent to look him in the eyes.

"Wouldas and couldas won't help. The gunman could have shot you, or maybe, if you left Mom, she could have lost more blood and died right then! Your mother's alive. That's all that matters. We'll help the police catch this killer. Right now, we need to focus on being strong for your brothers, your grandparents, and your mother."

"One more thing, Vincent. Running away from trouble doesn't help anyone, least of all you. Don't be afraid to come to me if something goes wrong. I will always be there for you. I was scared to death when Mikey came back and told me you ran into the woods. I went looking for you when you didn't come home. I thought you had fallen and hurt yourself. Please don't do that again. Come to me. We can talk it out. Okay?" Vincent put his head on his dad's shoulder and wept some more. Once his sobbing slowed down to a crawl, they headed home.

Relief is just a drive away

Mr. B asked Sammy and Gian to come over to his house that morning. He wanted them to take part in the meeting with Billy De Nuncio. About 9 a.m., Billy knocked on Mr. B's backdoor and was led down to Mr. B's office. After some small talk, Mr. B told Billy that Sammy and Gian were now in charge of the bookie operation. "Billy, these guys have a lot of experience running this type of business. Right now, experience matters."

When Billy heard this, he became one angry puppy. He flitted between being angry about his dad's death and disappointed that he wasn't going to be running the business. Mr. B became impatient with Billy's ranting.

Finally, Mr. B stood up. "Billy, this is the way it's going to be. You still have a job at the pool hall. Be grateful for that. I expect you to help Sammy in any way possible. If our numbers improve, you get something extra. In the meantime, I'll keep looking for the guy who shot your dad. The funeral is Tuesday. We'll be there for you. Take next week off. Then, we can figure out where to go from there."

When Billy left, Mr. B told Sammy and Gian to drive to the pool hall and get the ball rolling. Business as usual starting tomorrow.

Sammy and Gian headed right out. Mr. B and Marty followed right behind them. As they were walking out of the house, Mr. B turned to his wife and told her that he had some business to take care of. He would be home after supper.

"Sis!" Mr. B called out as he hit the front door. The next thing you know, Marty's mother, Angela, came out of the kitchen. Her shoulders were hunched and her mascara was runny.

"Dante," she sputtered. "Did you hear what happened to Maria Angelino! She was shot! At Viterio's no less. Who would do such a thing?"

With that, Marty's mother slumped into her rocking chair. Marty sat down next to her while Mr. B paced. After a minute or so, she regained her composure. She turned to Dante. "Sit down before you wear out the carpet. You seem more upset about this than I am."

"Angie, for crying out loud, she lived down the street from us when we were growing up. She ran around with Gabby. They were inseparable."

"Dante, you were in high school when Maria's family moved into the neighborhood. You were drinking beer on the corner while they were jumping rope in the park."

"Sis, Maria was like family. Yeah, I was older, but I did know what was what."

Angie's face turned red. She walked over to Dante and gave him a hug. "Sorry, I guess being your oldest sister has its downsides. I know I can get huffy at times."

Mr. B shook his head and gave her a hug. "It's been years since I've seen Maria. She'll always be like family." Then, he wondered aloud about Maria's situation.

"Dante, I got a call from Lucy Navillo. You know Lucy. She's a supervising nurse at the hospital." Dante nodded. "She told me the damage to Maria's shoulder is serious. She'll need several surgeries to take care of the damage to her shoulder. She could be laid up for several months."

Mr. B looked at Marty and then at Angie. In a very soft voice, he told Angie that he had heard a little about the shooting. "Is there anything that Maria and her family need?"

"Dante, I'm bringing a meal over to the Angelinos this afternoon. I'll talk to her husband. I'll call you tonight."

Mr. B pulled two C notes out of his wallet. "Give this to Maria's husband. Tell him to use it as he sees fit. Let me know if there is anything we can do for them." With that, Mr. B gave Marty a nod, hugged his sister and headed for the door. Marty followed right behind Mr. B.

It was blustery, so they walked quickly to the car. Marty revved the engine and put the car into gear. "Where to, Mr. B?"

"Head towards the Bourne Bridge." Mr. B had lady friend named Trixie Reilly who lived near Old Silver Beach in North Falmouth. Trixie was a pole dancer at some place in Southie. She danced on weekends. From what Marty heard, she did the trick so to speak. During the week, she was a secretary at a bank in town. Marty had heard that Mr. B owned a small piece of this bank.

Mr. B went to see Trixie when he needed to get away. Trixie was a looker. Her boobs were the size of melons and her blond hair reached her shoulders. From what Marty heard, she was as smooth as silk. No rushing allowed. According to Mr. B, this was secondary. He said she let him talk stuff through. This deal with Maria Angelino would be right up her alley. Marty's job entailed seeing, speaking, and hearing no evil, so the less Marty knew, the better.

Marty dropped Mr. B off at Trixie's. Mr. B rapped several times before Trixie came to the door. She was wearing a tight-fitting chiffon dress. Draped around her shoulders was a blue scarf that hardly covered her breasts. She reached out for Mr. B's left hand and led him inside.

Marty headed out of town. Marty had a friend who ran the Old Cape Cod Theatre in Dennis. The theatre' was old school—very comfortable, wide aisles, wide seats, and great popcorn. Marty had a "Friend Discount!" The tickets were free. "I'm set for the next three hours. I need to return to Trixie's place no later than 5:30 p.m. so we can make it back to Greenville at a decent time."

Marty got back to Trixie's with time to spare. Mr. B was in the back seat by 5:20. On the drive home, they stopped at a phone booth so Mr. B could call Angie. "What did you find out, Sis?"

"John Angelino is certain that Maria will be back to her old self, but it's going to take time for her to recuperate."

Apparently, the Angelino's insurance would cover a portion of the hospital costs. John started looking for a part time job. Losing Maria's income and facing a huge hospital debt was weighing on him. Angie told Dante that John was trying to be optimistic, but he knew the future was going to be a long haul.

"Dante," Angie asked, "is there anything we can do?"

"I'm looking into a few things, but it is too soon to say. It will take a while to nail things down." With that, Mr. B said goodbye and slammed the phone into the receiver.

Mr. B started muttering "One Shot this and Cappy that." It went on for a while. Then Mr. B told Marty to drive by Tony's Bar off Atwells Avenue.

When they got there, Mr. B headed for the back table. Marty caught Tony's eye, put up two fingers and pointed to the Narragansett tap. Then Marty caught up with Mr. B. They sat down in silence. Finally, Mr. B burned Marty's ear for several minutes. He had a bunch of things on his mind, but there were three items that stood out.

"First, I need to meet with the boss no later than Tuesday. Then, I need to get a hold of Capuano. I want to see him on Tuesday. Finally, arrange for Fr. DiNapoli to meet the principal at Don Bosco Academy as soon as possible. Did you get all that?" Marty nodded.

"Do you think I should give Dino a call?" Marty wondered aloud.

Mr. B said that he would take care of that himself. Then, he polished off three more bottles of Gansett and they hit the road to Greenville.

Joey, Joey, Joey

It was late Sunday afternoon by the time Joey arrived in Chicago. He flew out of Hartford using an alias. He was surprised to learn that he'd be flying in a small Cessna. The pilot was some old fogie named Buck. The two-seater airplane scared the crap out of Joey. He used the barf bag twice and vowed that he wasn't going to fly on a plane like that again. Once they got to Chicago, he reserved a car and then found a place to stay for the night.

The next day, Joey got up, had breakfast, and pointed the rental towards Kansas City. No more planes for him for a long while. All he had was a small tan suitcase, a wallet stuffed with dollar bills, and the name of a guy in Kansas City who needed to be called.

It took Joey twelve hours to drive to Kansas. He found a small boarding house in town. It wasn't much to look at, but it was in a quiet neighborhood with a space in the back of the house to park his ride. Joey was tired from all the driving, so he hit the hay early. "Crap, I forgot to call Cappy!" Cappy could wait.

Joey got up late the next morning and took a long, hot shower. Then he headed out for some chow. Joey had put Cappy on hold once. He decided Cappy could wait a little while longer.

Joey found a diner a few blocks down from his boarding house. He went in and ordered steak and eggs, Kansas City style, with hash browns on the side. The food was hot and the waitress was hotter. That opportunity went nowhere when the waitress heard Joey's accent and started laughing. Joey knew he had to keep a low profile, so he laughed along with her, but he was boiling mad. He ate quickly and then called Cappy.

It was eleven a.m. Hartford time by the time Joey made the call. Cappy started screaming when he found out it was Joey. Joey could hardly understand what Cappy was saying, but he knew that whatever was going on was not going to be good.

"Hold on, Cappy, what are you so mad about?"

Cappy launched into the screwup. He made it clear that Mr. B was upset to learn that a friend of his had been shot. Joey was confused. "I only took one shot, Cappy. That shot hit De Nuncio."

"What you don't know, Joey, is that the bullet that killed De Nuncio went through him and hit a friend of Mr. Bonfigore. I told you not to harm anyone else but De Nuncio! There's more bad news. Dante learned that someone might have seen you at the grocery store. Fortunately, this person couldn't give the police a good description of the shooter, so you are off the hook."

Mr. B was another story. "You need to stay in Kansas until things cool down. I'll handle Bonfigore. You do not want to meet up with him until things settle down. I will find you some additional work. Don't even think about contacting anyone but me."

Joey started to grouse about this. "Listen up. Dante has the reach to make life ugly for your family if he thinks you called them. Believe me, that wouldn't be pretty. Call me in two days. By that time, I'll have a plan. Do not get into more trouble. If you do, I won't be able to help you." With that, the call ended.

Joey didn't like what he heard. He knew life was going to be tricky for a while. Mr. B was no one to screw around with. If what Capuano said was true, Bonfigore's bookie problems would be solved. However, there'd be heat coming from the police regarding the person who had been wounded.

Joey was certain that whatever heat that was going on in Greenville meant the heat on him would be multiplied. Keeping a low profile had to be his number one priority. Then Joey called his contact in Kansas City to set up a meeting.

The contact, some mutt named Billy Dolan, wasn't happy to hear from Joey, but he agreed to meet on Wednesday at a joint in Leawood. Once that was settled, Joey drove around and found a local bar called the Big Nip just down the road from his boarding house. The rest of the afternoon was spent with a glass of Crown Royal that seemed to fill itself.

On Wednesday, Joey drove to Leawood. He felt like a big shot behind the wheel of this new Seville. It had gadgets galore. Joey arrived at Dolan's place about noon. He scouted out the neighborhood before meeting Dolan. Everything seemed to be on the level, so Joey headed towards the back door. Dolan was waiting for him. Joey walked into the room as if he owned the place. Dolan was sitting behind a small desk. A slender Montecristo cigar was smoldering in an ashtray. Dolan shook hands with Joey without standing, pointed to a hardback chair and told Joey to have a seat.

"I hear you are a guy who gets results. If you don't mind my saying so, you seem to be a little young for this job." Dolan said skeptically.

Under normal conditions, Joey would have blown a gasket, but he remembered what Cappy said about cooling his jets. "Mr. Dolan, what's this job all about."

"Okay." Dolan said. "I have a problem with a customer. A money problem. I need a convincer."

"So, you need me to get some money back for you."

Dolan nodded. "Five months ago, a friend put me in touch with a guy who needed cash to set up a liquor store. My accountant did a background check. Everything came back rosy. So, I loaned the guy the money. As soon as the liquor store opened its doors, business started to boom."

"Let me guess," Joey said with a smirk. "Your friend of a friend is making out like a bandit and you haven't seen any money. Is that right?"

Dolan was amazed. "When I spoke to Cappy, he said you were as sharp as a stick. He was right on the button! I'm out $50,000 plus interest."

"Who did you loan the money to, Mr. Dolan?"

Dolan grimaced. "I lent the money to Hank Baxter."

Dolan gave Joey the particulars about the deal. "How much time do I have, Dolan?"

"I hope you can get my cash back by next month. If that happens, I'll give you $2500 plus expenses on top of what I promised Cappy."

Joey whetted his lips at the thought of getting this bonanza. "I'll start nosing around today." They shook hands and Joey headed for the door. "This could be one sweet deal!" Joey thought.

"Joey, I need to tell you one more thing. Dolan has some relatives who work for him. They are from West Virginia. I hear they're running hooch across Kentucky right over to Kansas. These guys as mean as wolverines. They don't mess around. So, best you be careful."

Joey's face tightened. His sneer was exaggerated. "No worries, Mr. Dolan. I got a friend of mine in the car—a Smith and Wesson. That should be enough to take care of this job." He told Dolan that he'd need time to see what was going on with Baxter. "I will see you next Monday. Same time, same place. I'll have a plan by then."

Later that evening, Joey was in bed with a young whippet named Crystal. He had met her at the Big Nip earlier that night. Things progressed nicely. She worked as a stage manager for a small theatre company. Joey liked her body, but Crystal was an educated gal. She used forty cent words all the time. He needed a dictionary just to follow along That was one big drag.

"Okay, Joey," Crystal said through a plume of smoke after they had been making out for a while. "Turn over. We can start doing some carnal touching."

"Carnal what?"

Crystal tried to explain it. "Okay doll," he said with a smirk. "It's time for the real thing. I'll show you how we do this back home." Romance wasn't Joey's goal. He just wanted a quick roll in the sheets. Then he could get this broad out of here. "Carnal touching my ass!"

Help is on the way

Vincent and his dad drove home for a quick breakfast and then drove back to the hospital. Vincent's mom was asleep when they arrived. "Vincent, can you to take your brothers to the playground behind the hospital. They need to work off some energy." An hour later, the kids returned. Unfortunately, Maria had dozed off. The kids were still in a playful mood, so John decided it would be best if his folks took the kids home.

Everyone was hungry by the time they got home, so Nonna fixed a large bowl of ziti and sauce. Vincent begged off. He spent the rest of the day in his room. He was still there when John came home. Nonna was concerned about Vincent, but John decided to leave him alone. A little while later, everyone went to bed.

Usually, Vincent was an early riser on school days. He'd get cleaned up and head downstairs to have breakfast with his grandmother. When he finished eating, he'd rush out and run to the bus stop. Today, however, he slept in. He had tossed and turned most of the night. He fell asleep at two a.m. He finally got up and headed to the bathroom. John poked his head into the room. Vincent had just stepped into the shower. "I'm taking you and Mikey to school. I already spoke to Mrs. O'Day. You need to get ready, so pick up your pace."

When Vincent sat down for breakfast, oatmeal was steaming away on the stove. He got a bowl from the cupboard and devoured a huge portion. No one said a word until John walked into the room. "We need to be out of here in ten minutes, so don't dawdle."

A few minutes later, they headed to Mikey's. John stopped the car a block short of Mikey's house. He turned to Vincent. "How are you doing, son?"
"I'm okay. I'd rather stay home today, Dad!"

"This has been hard on all of us, kiddo. I know you've heard me say many times that the best way to deal with fear is to confront it right away. I learned that when I was in the service and I've tried to live that thought ever since. It's time for you to confront your own fears as hard as that may seem.

"Dad, all my friends will want to know what happened. I am not sure what to say."

John put his arm on Vincent's shoulder. "Tell them you need time before you're ready to share. If your friends are respectful, they'll understand. Mikey will make sure your friends know you need some space today."

"Mom and I are meeting with her doctor today. We hope to find out where we go from here. Once the meeting is over, I'll head to work. I will pick you two up after cross country practice." With that, he put the car in gear.

Mikey was waiting at his back door when they pulled up. He popped out of his house, raced to the car and they sped off. Vincent looked over to Mikey. "I'm sorry I left you the other day." Mikey nodded. The car was quiet the rest of the way to school.

John dropped the boys off. They headed to their lockers. As they walked down the corridor, the hallway became quiet. Vincent could see several kids pointing to him. Others were whispering. Once or twice, Vincent heard stuff like "his mom" or "shooting." It was creepy. They finally got to Mickey's locker. He hung up his jacket and got out his books. Then, they headed towards Vincent's locker.

When Vincent tried to open his locker, he fumbled with the lock. He felt all sorts of stupid. He finally got the locker opened. He hung up his coat, put his lunch bag away, and took out some books. Then, they headed to their home room.

The bell rang just as they hit their seats. The home room monitor took attendance and led the class in prayer. Then they recited the Pledge of Allegiance. After that, announcements were read and the first bell rang. Luckily, Vincent and Mikey didn't have to move. Their first two classes were held in their home room. Vincent prayed that he wouldn't be called on. He kept his head down when the teachers asked if anyone had questions. His luck ran out during his history class.

Midway through the class, there was a knock at the door. Jimmy Gaudreau, the captain of the football team, poked his head into the room. He told Brother Michael, the history teacher, that Vincent was wanted at the main office. Vincent was stunned. The only reason students were called to the office was when they got into trouble. "What did I do?" Vincent asked himself.

As soon as they left the room, Gaudreau asked "What did you do to get in trouble?" Then Gaudreau stopped. "Aren't you the kid who saw the shooting at Viterio's?"

Vincent nodded his head. "My name is Jimmy. I don't think we've met. I heard you saw the shooter and saved someone's life. That must have been scary. You were brave to do what you did!"

Vincent squeaked out an "I guess so" and pretended to fumble with a book so that he didn't have to say anything more.

By that time, they had made it to the main office. The school secretary pointed Vincent to an open door down the hall. "You can head into the room now. Brother Robert had to leave for a second. He'll be right back." Jimmy turned to Vincent and wished him good luck.

Vincent walked towards the door. He felt like he was headed towards a guillotine. Five minutes later, Brother Robert came into the room. Vincent had only seen the brother from afar, but there was no mistaking him. He was a gangly guy with bushy eyebrows and a frown that never seemed to go away. He was the school disciplinarian. Vincent had hoped that he'd never have to meet Brother Robert, and yet, here he was. Sweat beaded on his neck.

"Hello, Vincent. You seem a little nervous."

"I'm not sure what I did to get into trouble."

The brother let out a huge belly laugh. "I'm sorry for laughing, Vincent. I know many people think of me as the sheriff of this school. But my real job is to help students solve problems. I hear you are a problem solver."

Vincent was confused. "I'm a problem solver, sir?"

"First off, son, how about if you just call me Brother Robert, okay." Vincent simply nodded his head.

"There's a story going around that your mom was shot at Viterio's. Your quick thinking probably saved her life. I'd say that makes you a huge problem solver." Vincent was relieved to hear that he wasn't in trouble.

"Vincent, I called you down to see how you were doing."

It took a while before Vincent spoke. "My mom was shot, Brother Robert. I saw the whole thing" was all he could stammer as his chest began to heave. Robert pushed his chair in a little closer, made eye contact with Vincent, and just let him sob for a while.

After Vincent calmed down, Robert asked a few questions. Vincent answered them as best as he could. Finally, the room was still. "So, I gather you feel responsible for what happened to your mom. Is your mother a strongminded woman?" Vincent slowly moved his head in agreement. "Does she normally get what she wants?"

"My dad says mom can be hardheaded at times."

"Could Friday afternoon have been one of those times?" Brother Robert asked. It took a while before Vincent nodded. "I wonder if you could have done anything to get her to move more quickly."

"I guess not."

They sat through the next bell. Vincent shared a little more, much more, in fact, than he had shared with Mikey or his dad. Vincent felt comfortable sharing stuff with the brother. Finally, Robert called his secretary. A few minutes later, two lunch trays arrived at the door.

Over the past two days, Vincent hadn't eaten much. It didn't take much encouragement for him to begin inhaling food. When he finished, he asked if he could lie down for a while. He followed the brother to the nurse's office. There was a bed in the back room. Vincent went in, laid down on the bed and fell asleep immediately. Brother Robert asked the nurse to find him as soon as Vincent woke up.

At two p.m., the last bell rang. It made a clanging noise that woke Vincent up. The nurse heard a clattering of noise in the back room and asked a student aide to find Brother Robert. "You're awake," Robert said as he walked into the room. Vincent opened his eyes. "How are you doing?"

"I guess I'm okay."

"You slept for a while, son."

Vincent asked what time it was. When he learned that it was 2 p.m., he bolted upright. "I have to get to the gym. Cross country practice starts in a few minutes."

"Slow down, Vincent," the brother said. "You can go out and run. Before you go, I want you to know that you can come to me at any time, about anything."

"I don't want to bother you, Brother Robert. You have other things to worry about that are more important than my problems.

Robert waited a second before replying. "Vincent, all you need to do is ask, and I'll be there for you. You've gone through a lot. You are a great kid with a lot on your plate. Just let me know when you need to talk."

With that, Vincent was led out to the corridor. He started to run towards the gym. He stopped and turned back towards Brother Robert. "Thank you," he said. The brother smiled and pointed towards the gym. Vincent was off. In no time flat, he found his coach.

Coach White wasn't what you might expect a coach to look like. He was an older guy with close cropped hair. A tall drink of water who walked with a hitch in his gait. But Vincent knew Coach White's cross-country teams were always one of the top three in the state, right up there with Mount Pleasant High.

"Mr. Angelino, I am surprised to see you at practice!"

"Coach, I gotta be here. I guess you heard what happened this weekend. Running is the only way for me to calm down. Everything else is a blur."

"Listen, son, I guess it would be all right if you practiced today. The other guys are over at the oval running 800's. Get warmed up. We'll see what you can do." Vincent sped over to the cinder track.

A little while later, the coach walked over to Phil Hurley, his assistant coach. "What's going on, Phil?"

"The Angelino kid showed up a little while ago, Bill." After he warmed up, I had him run an 800 with some of the guys. He ran a 2:26 in the 800!"

"Are you kidding me, Phil?"

"I timed him myself. I knew he had some speed, but this is unreal for a sophomore with little training."

"I've got to see this for myself. Mr. Angelino," White shouted, "get over here!"

Vincent and Mikey were on the other side of the track. Vincent heard the coach yell. He turned towards Mikey. "The coach is calling for me. Would you run over with me? I might need some moral support." Mikey agreed. Then they jogged over to the coach.

When they got there, the coach looked towards Vincent and Mikey. "O'Day, are you Angelino's shadow?" the coach asked sarcastically.

"No, Coach. Vincent asked if I would come with him."

White had spoken with Brother Robert earlier in the afternoon. Robert brought him up to speed about the shooting, so the coach knew what was going on. As a result, White decided to let Mikey stay with Vincent.

"You're pretty quick for sophomore. I know you ran an 800 a few minutes ago. I want you and O'Day to run another one in a little while. Go do some sit ups. I'll let you know when it's time to run."

Twenty minutes later, White called them over. He wanted to see them run against the seniors. Sure enough, Vincent ran lights out. Mikey was not too far behind. Their times were eye opening. White had to look twice at his stopwatch before he looked back at "Holy Moley, Phil, the two of them! It's unbelievable."

A fist full of bad memories

Dante's brother, Dino, pulled up to Dante's place at 3:30 p.m. Dante and his wife, Benedetta, lived in a modest brown rambler on two acres of land on the outskirts of Greenville. They told folks that they like the peace and quiet of the country, but Dino knew his brother liked to keep business and family separate. Greenville was miles from the old neighborhood. When Dino finally got out of his Delta 88, he could hear a herd of cows in the neighbor's pasture. The mooing was unnerving.

As Dino started up the stone walkway that curved towards Dante's front door, he was surrounded by two rug rats. "Hey, hey, one at a time. You will get hugs and treats." The word "treats" brought immediate silence. Dino had stopped by the corner store and bought candy for the kids. He had a handful of 1000 Grand bars. "There is one for each of you. Where are Nico and Cristiana?" he shouted over the howls of "Me first!"

Their voices must have carried because his sister-in-law came around the corner with a scowl on her face. "Dino, you'll be the death of me!" Dino knew Detta didn't like his "gifts," but he couldn't help himself. Detta sighed. With that, the kids took off towards the backyard and the adults strolled up to the house.

"Where are the other two kids?" Dino asked as he gave Detta a peck on the cheek.

"Nico thinks he is the next Johnny Egan. He begged us to sign him up for basketball camp."

"Detta," Dino said, "Nico will never get taller than five feet seven."

"I know, Dino, but everybody needs to dream. We won't take that away from him right now."

Dino knew Detta could fool anyone if she wanted to. She looked like an Italian version of Audrey Hepburn with her big brown eyes, the teased black hair, and her bright sleeveless dresses. To look at her, you'd think she was the soft, cuddly type. Behind that cutesy image was one tough cookie who knew her mind. She just let out her real self to a few people.

"What about Cristiana?" asked Dino.

Detta turned towards him. "That girl has gone from a kitten to a tigress in no time flat! She's just like her father. She won't take 'no' for an answer."

Dino nodded his head knowing full well that Detta was as right as rain. "What now?" he asked.

"She came home Friday night looking like that Annie Lennox character. Her long brown hair is lying on someone's floor. To top that off, she insists on wearing these short skirts that are now in style. I know they are all the rage but not in my house. Thank goodness the girl is forced to wear a uniform at school. Fifteen years old and a mind of her own. Dante had a fit. I told him we needed to go out for a long walk. We headed out before he could gather up a head of steam. I shouldn't complain. She's doing well in school. But she is a trial."

Just then, Dino heard the whine of an engine. He looked up to see his brother on a riding lawnmower. Dante was always buying the latest gizmo, but a riding lawnmower! "Detta, what gives?"

She shook her head. "Dante and Cristiana always seem to get what they want." Dino began to laugh. Here was his brother, a skinny marink if you ever saw one, riding atop this mower. Dante's thinning hair was blowing all over the place. Then, he took a red bandana out of his back pocket and wiped his face. "What will he do for an encore?" Dino shook his head and started up with a wicked smirk that told it all.

Dante came in after he put the mower away. He had a Cubano stogie in his mouth and a bottle of Narragansett beer in his hand. He winked at Dino, handed his brother a beer, and they headed down to his office.

Downstairs was off limits to the kids, so the brothers had some peace and quiet. They headed into Dante's office and sat down next to this monster of a fireplace. Dino knew his brother thought that bigger was better, so everything that he owned was huge. From the Deere mower to his Crown Victoria, a bright blue job the size of Maine. "What gives, Dante? I get a message to come right over and I find you playing nursery man in your backyard."

"I got worked up after talking to the Boss. So, I decided to work off some energy." Dante's boss was the Mafia don in New England. Dante was his chief lieutenant. His primary responsibility was the Mafia's bookmaking business. Dino ran the family laundry businesses. He helped Dante whenever he was needed. Few folks knew of their mob involvement, not even Detta.

"What did the boss say?"

"What didn't he say! He wanted to skin me alive and feed me to the sharks. His exact words were 'How could you screw up this effing shooting?' I settled him down and promised to make it right. The boss knows about my history with Maria Angelino. Of all the people to shoot, Joey shoots our sister's best school friend. Maria was in and out of our house all the time. I haven't seen her in forever. Now I get her shot."

"What does the boss want us to do?"

"Joey better have a great excuse or he'll join De Nuncio! We need to find a way to help the Angelinos. The boss thought we should take care of the hospital bills. He's okay with that as long as we keep a low profile."

They spent an hour going over their options. Dante was meeting Cappy that evening. "Cappy doesn't know it yet, but he will be throwing a pile of money into the pot. He won't like it, but he'll do it."

"There's one more job you could take care of, Dino."

"What's that?"

"Find out the cost of a year's tuition at Don Bosco."

"Dante, Cristiana goes to Don Bosco. Don't you know the cost of tuition?"

"Detta takes care of that. I don't want to her find out I'm nosing around. Maybe we can make an anonymous donation to Don Bosco and St. Philips for the kids' tuitions. This could take some financial heat off the family. I don't want my name anywhere near this. Got it?"

Dino nodded his head. "I'll find out about the tuition. No one will the wiser."

"While I'm thinking about it," Dante said, "I will talk to Detta after we finish up. She and Viterio's wife are good friends. Maybe the Viterios can head up a community drive to pay some of Maria's hospital costs. I hear these surgeries are costly. Maybe we can make a $1500 donation. Then we can put the squeeze on some of our "friends" to come across with some dough to match our contribution. What da you think?"

"What a great idea! I think you are on to something. I'll get right on it." They headed towards the stairs.

"Dino, let me know what you find out as soon as possible. Also, could you tell Detta that I will be right up as soon as I hit the can." With that, Dante opened the bathroom door and walked in. He looked at himself in the mirror and shook his head. "You have really made a mess of this little deal!" he said quietly.

Then he came out of the bathroom and walked over to Marty. "What's up with my meeting with Capuano?"

"Cappy called. He wants to meet you in Galilee tonight— just the two of you. He'll be there a little after eight." "Marty, gas up the car. I'll have dinner with my family and then we can leave. I want to be the first one on the boat, so we should leave just before seven. No delays!"

"The car will be ready to go when you're ready to go." Dante headed upstairs. Marty stopped for a second. "Tonight's going be a really long night."

They got to the wharf at 7:30. It was dark out and the parking lot was almost empty. Marty looked around and spotted two tough guys parked in the last row of the lot. "I didn't order any backup for this meet, Mr. B!"

"I took care of this. I wanted to make sure Cappy and I would be alone. He won't be happy with what I have to say."

Normally, Mr. B waited for his door to be opened. Tonight, he jumped out and headed to the boat before Marty had a chance to get out of the car. "Stay here, Marty!" he yelled.

The two guys met Mr. B at the gangplank. They looked like they had been in a fight or two in their lives. They walked up the gangplank, turned to the right and went into the wheelhouse.

Cappy rolled into the lot at 7:50. He drove an old beater that squealed when he stomped on the brakes. Cappy was alone. He headed towards The Merchant. When he hit the deck, the boat's captain, a guy named Lenny, led him to the wheelhouse. When Cappy went in, Lenny ran towards the gangplank. Mr. B probably told him there might be fireworks on the boat. Lenny wasn't the brightest bulb on the tree, but he knew when to scram.

The lights in the wheelhouse were off when Capuano walked through the door. They flickered on and off. It was too far away to hear anything. "Maybe I'll stick close to the Crown Vic," Marty thought. "What I don't know could be a life saver in the end."

About 8:20, Mr. B walked off the boat. The hoods came out shortly thereafter. They were helping Cappy off the boat. Cappy didn't look too good from where Marty sat. Mr. B got in the car. "Let's get outta here."

When they turned onto Route 108, Dante told Marty to stop at the donut shop across from the Catholic church. "I need a cup of java." Marty pulled into the lot. "Anything else besides the coffee, Mr. B?"

"That's it." Marty went in the shop. Aside from the kid standing behind the counter, Marty was the only person there. That was a good thing. Mr. B didn't want folks to know he was in South County that night.

Marty ordered two cups of java. "Anything else?" the kid asked. Marty ordered a jelly donut. "This should hit the spot." Marty walked out to the car and jumped in. Then, they headed north. By the time they got to Greenville, it was 9:30. It had been a long day.

"Drop me off at the house, Marty. Be back at 9 a.m. tomorrow."

The next day, Marty heard that Cappy agreed to come up with $4,000 after he had "accidentally" fallen down the stairs leading to the engine room. Mr. B learned that One Shot was out west somewhere. That didn't sit too well. Cappy assured Dante that Joey would meet with him as soon as Joey made it back to Connecticut.

The first road home

Four days after her surgery, Maria was told she could go home. The doctors said that she would need one additional operation. That would have to wait until they could determine the progress of this first operation.

John appeared at Maria's hospital room the morning she was to be released. He had a big smile on his face and an even bigger bouquet of red roses in his hands. "John!" she said. "What are you doing with those flowers? You know we can't afford them right now!"

John came over to Maria's bed, kissed her on the forehead and whispered in her ear that the flowers were a gift from her church friends. Maria started to cry. A little while later, an orderly came into the room with a wheelchair. He helped Maria into the chair and wheeled her towards the parking lot. John went to get the car. No sooner had the aide opened the side door of the hospital when John pulled up to the curb. The orderly helped Maria into the car and they headed home.

Nonna, Nonno, and the boys were waiting by the back door as John drove up the driveway. The lawn had been mowed and the toys, bikes, and everything else had been put in their place. As soon as Maria got out of the car, the boys swooped in and hugged her like there was no tomorrow. Then everyone started talking. The kids got rambunctious. Nonna shouted out for them to be careful not to hit the sling that hung from Maria's neck.

For the first time in a long while, everyone was smiling. This was a time to forget the pain and enjoy the moment. The boys finally calmed down and everyone went in the house for a bite to eat. When Maria walked into the kitchen, she saw bouquets of flowers and a refrigerator crammed full of prepared food.

"Where did this come from?" she stammered. Nonna told her that the neighbors got together and signed up to bring daily meals over when they learned about the shooting. Maria slumped into her favorite chair and began to cry. Stephen, her youngest son, knelt by her leg and put his head on her lap.

Shortly thereafter, everyone settled down. Nonna came out of the kitchen holding a pan of lasagna in one hand and some fresh baked bread in the other. The boys brought some salad, glasses and a bottle of milk to the table. Nonne offered a quick prayer of thanksgiving. Then, they dug into the lasagna.

After lunch, two of Maria's sisters came over with their families. Hugs and chatter abounded. Maria started tiring 30 minutes later. John helped her up to their bedroom. The younger kids went out to play and Vincent went upstairs to study. After the women finished the dishes, the adults went into the living room.

Maria's oldest sister, Anna, a short pudgy woman with a short fuse, started in. "John, what did the doctors say?"

John shook his head. When he finally was able to talk, he said the doctor was concerned about her shoulder. "They're afraid there might be permanent damage. They won't know the extent of the damage for a few weeks. They've scheduled another operation for the end of November. In the meantime, Maria will start therapy later this week."

Nonna changed the subject. "John, I heard that you're starting a part time job. Is that true?"

"Mom, I don't have a choice. The bills are piling up and Maria won't be able to go back to work until who knows when. Willy Donatelli owns a cabbie company in town. He's willing to let me drive for him on weekends. It's not what I want, but it's something I need to do. Our neighbors have offered to help with some of the yardwork. Hopefully, that will cover us for a while.

Then Tina, one of Maria's younger sisters, told John that she and Anna were taking on some additional sewing jobs. "Any money we make will go towards your medical bills. John tried to thank them. Words just couldn't come out. Maria's family got up to leave. John hugged them all.

Later that afternoon, there was a knock at the door. Nonna went to see who was there. She found Detective Maloney standing on the front steps. "Hello," he said in a polite voice. "I'm wondering if I could speak to Mr. Angelino." Nonna told Maloney to wait for a moment. She went get her son.

A few minutes later, a weary looking John Angelino opened the door. "Detective, what a surprise! How can I help you?" "Mr. Angelino, I just need a few minutes of your time."

"Detective Maloney, Come in. Why don't you sit down next to the stove. John said. It is the warmest place in the house."

"Are you sure, Mr. Angelino. I don't want to take your seat."

"Please make yourself comfortable. Can I offer you something hot to drink? Coffee? Tea?" The detective said that tea would be great.

The kettle was still warm, so John and Maloney both had a cup of tea. John took nothing with his tea. Maloney, the Irishman that he was, added cream and sugar to his cup. After a few quiet moments, Maloney turned to John and asked how his family was doing. John was a little taken aback by Maloney's demeanor given how brusque he had been at the police station.

Maloney could see John's puzzled look. "Mr. Angelino, I want to apologize for my attitude at the station. I was frustrated. I took it out on you and your son. Your wife had been seriously injured and your son witnessed something that nobody should ever have to see. I got off on the wrong foot. I'm sorry for the way I behaved."

"Detective Maloney, as it turns out, the other day I checked up on you. My buddies at Public Works were surprised when I told them what had happened. They told me you are one of the good guys. How about if we start all over. Let's begin with you calling me John."

"Only if you call me Bill." he said with the hint of a grin.

"So, Bill, what brings you over to our house today?"

Bill began by saying that the police were stymied. "We don't have much go on. We interviewed everyone who was at Viterio's that afternoon. No one else saw the guy who shot your wife. The shooter has disappeared. The whole thing is frustrating. We are stuck in neutral. De Nuccio was killed for no apparent reason and your wife…" The last sentence seemed to stop in mid-air. "So, I'm here to ask your family for help."

"How can we be of help, Bill?"

"We need to identify this guy! The longer that takes, the less likelihood that we find him. Or, God forbid, he strikes again and attacks the only eyewitness we have."

That shook John up. "Do you think this could happen?"

"John, this guy's a stone-cold killer. He'd shoot Vincent
in a heartbeat if he thought it would save his skin."
John put up his hand to stop Maloney. "What can we do
to help you, Bill?"

"When we met at the station, Vincent looked at photos
of guys we've had previous contact with. He didn't see
anyone who resembled the shooter. We know an artist
who could meet Vincent. She's been helpful in getting
witnesses to describe their assailants. Using these
descriptions, the artist has been able to draw picures of
the assailants. If Vincent meets this artist, she can come
up with a likeness of the killer. Then we can distribute
it to folks in Greenville and neighboring communities.
Hopefully something pops."

John carefully listened to Bill's request. He was
conflicted. He could see how an artist might help
identify the shooter. However, Vincent was struggling
with the results of the shooting. "I want to be of help,
Bill. Nothing would be sweeter than to put the killer in
jail. But I am not sure that the timing is right."

Bill began to interrupt, but John put up his hand to stop
him. "Why don't we tackle this in a week or so. This
would give Vincent time to deal with his feelings. He
feels responsible for his mom's injuries. In the
meantime, you could check out the availability of the
artist. How does that sound?"

Bill wasn't happy about slowing down the process, but
he agreed to contact this artist about driving down to
Greenville next week.

Joey meets up with the Skanko brothers

By the time Thursday rolled around, Joey had the beginnings of a plan. He had scouted out the liquor store and learned that Baxter always had his boys pick up the weekly booze order at the liquor warehouse. Two burly guys with skanky beards always drove a crummy old Ford Econoline to the warehouse. The truck had big red letters identifying it as a "Wheeling Wagon!" What a couple of hicks.

Joey followed the Skanko Boys. The first day, he never got out of his car. The boys went to the liquor store early in the morning. They got a list of the liquor that was needed. Then they drove eight miles south to a warehouse in Shawnee. The boys ended up lugging a variety of cases from the warehouse to their van.

When they finished, they headed towards Missouri. They stopped at Fleming Park near Lee's Summit. They met up with another skanky guy who drove an old station wagon. This guy pulled a mittful of boxes of homemade hooch out of the wagon and put the cases in the van. Cash was exchanged and the guys went their separate ways. At that point, Baxter's boys needed to fill their stomachs. They stopped at a little place called Mae's Breakfast Nook on the east side of the city and proceeded to eat like there was no tomorrow.

Dolan was right about one thing. These boys were big. If Joey was going to stop them, he better be careful. Joey kept watch on the store for the next week. Every few days, the boys ran over to the warehouse to restock the store's liquor supply. Otherwise, not much else happened.

Joey decided it was time to give Dolan a rundown regarding what was happening. He set up a meeting for the next day. Dolan was getting nervous, but Joey thought he'd be able to calm him down. However, as soon as they sat down, Dolan started shouting.

"What is taking so long," he said.

"Dolan, Rome wasn't built in a day."

"Okay, okay. I get it," Dolan exclaimed, "I just want my dough."

Joey turned to him. "Just your dough or a little satisfaction to go along with it. Listen, you agreed to give me a few days to come up with a plan. Don't sweat the small stuff, Jocko!" Joey left Dolan sputtering.

The next day, the Skankos had a repeat performance of the first time Joey followed them. This time, the third skank followed them back to Mae's after the booze was transferred. Joey sat two booths away from them. He could have been in the next county as far as these hicks were concerned. They had no idea they were being followed. Big Bear and Booby were the guys who worked for Baxter. The third guy, Wing Nut, (where did they get these names?) was their second cousin.

Once they finished breakfast, they quieted down, but not quite quiet enough. Joey heard every word they said. Wing Nut and a friend of his had a large still near Beckley, West Virginia. No one would give them grief because Wing Nut's cousin was the county sheriff. The sheriff had agreed to help them out. However, he made sure he got his cut from the biz. The boys produced enough rot gut to satisfy the locals. The rest of the hooch was sold to Baxter.

Apparently, Baxter had customers who had a taste for the stuff. They were willing to pay good money to get moonshine on a regular basis. Baxter was getting more requests for the hooch, so he wanted Wing Nut to increase the amount he was delivering.

"How much more does Baxter want?" Wing Nut asked.

"He wants one truckload every three weeks."

"Booby, we can't make that much right now. I'll need more equipment and a bigger truck to haul the load. It will take more time and money."

"Listen up! Baxter will give you $2000 to buy the equipment and $1500 for every truckload you deliver."

There was a hint of a smile on Nut's face. "If he fronts the cash to buy a truck, you have a deal."

Booby exchanged a glance with Big Bear. "We'll talk to Baxter. We should know by the time you return to town." With that, they shook hands and headed outside.

Joey didn't need to follow them. He knew all he needed to know about the operation. Joey drove north. He stopped at Kaw Point on the Missouri River, pulled his car over to the side of the road, popped open a Bud and thought about his next step. Joey knew he couldn't count on Dolan for any manpower. Dolan was all talk and no action. Cappy made it clear that the hubbub going on in Rhode Island had created some heat, so there would be no help from that corner either.

The only help Joey could really expect would be from his old friends Smith and Wesson. He finally came up with a plan. He called Dolan. "I need a place to store some stuff." Dolan started getting out of hand. "Joey, what do you mean you need a place to store stuff?"

"Dolan, calm down. I need a place to store a truck for a few days. I'm hoping you might know someone who owns a farm outside of town. You have lots of friends in town. Do you know anyone who could help us out?"

Dolan calmed down. "I have a friend who owes me a favor. Call Tim Kincaid. Tell him I told you to call him."

Later that afternoon, Joey called Tim. Unfortunately, it took a while to connect with him. Tim owned a farm near Gallatin. He used for hunting. Deer season had ended a few days ago so Joey was able to rent it for a song.

Joey got the keys and the directions. The place was his for the next two months. Joey drove up to the farm to see what was what. It was an hour from KC. The place was perfect. It had an old barn that was set back well behind the farmhouse. The barn was dingy and rickety, but it was plenty big enough to hold Wing Nut, Nut's new truck and a few other things.

There was one problem. Joey needed to find someone who could help him with Baxter's boys. It was time for Joey to call his brother Rico. Rico worked as a mechanic at a used car dealership in Waterbury, CT. He had a wife, a young son, and a kid on the way. The car repair business had slowed down. The last time Joey spoke with his brother, he had learned that Rico was going to be laid off temporarily.

Rico needed a job. "This will work out perfectly. Rico needs cash and I happen to have cash. What a plan!" Joey called his brother. "Are you interested in making a buck or two, Little Brother?"

"If there's no shooting involved, I might be interested."

After a while, Joey hung up with a smile on his face. "This is gonna be like taking candy from a baby!"

Vincent's dilemma

Coach White told Vincent and Mikey that they would be running with the varsity at the Hope High Invitational meet. Mikey smiled from ear to ear. "Running with the varsity!" He jabbered on and on. Vincent was quiet. Mikey finally asked Vincent why he was being so quiet.

"Mikey, I need to tell you something. My mom needs another operation. That's going to cost money that we don't have. My grandfather hopes to get a part time job to help pay for the hospital bills. We need to find ways to earn extra dough. I spoke to Mr. Viterio about stocking shelves at his store. He said I could start next week. My dad doesn't like it. We need the money, so he said okay. I can't work on weekends, run cross country and keep my grades up. Something has to give. I've decided to give up running cross-country."

Mikey couldn't believe his ears. "Vincent, this is your dream come true. You are a varsity cross-country runner! You can't quit! Coach White thinks we might be able to win state with you on the team. What did the coach say when you told him you were quitting?"

"I didn't know how to tell him, so I didn't say anything. I don't want to disappoint him or let the team down. I don't see any way around it. I gotta quit." There wasn't much to say, so Mikey put his arm around Vincent's shoulder. They walked to the locker room. They showered, changed into their school clothes and took the late bus back to Greenville. It was a long ride home.

It took Vincent two days to get up the nerve to meet the coach. He saw the coach grabbing a sandwich during lunch. He went over and stood next to the coach who was

talking with another faculty member. After a few minutes, the coach finally spotted Vincent.
"What is going on, Mr. Angelino?"

Vincent stuttered at first, but finally blurted out that he needed to talk to the coach. It was clear that Vincent was upset.

"Let's find a place to talk, son." They walked to the coach's classroom. When they got there, Vincent was too nervous to sit down. "Something is going on with you, Vincent," the coach said. "What's up?"

Vincent retold his story. "I don't have a choice, Coach. I can't keep up with my schoolwork, take on a part time job, and run cross country. I need to give up something. You know I love to run, but I love my family more. I need to quit the team so I can work at Viterio's. I'm sorry to let you down." Coach White was old school, but he knew that the tough guy stuff was for another day.

He walked over to Vincent and led him to a seat in the front of the room. "Listen to me, Son. I heard a little about this from Brother Robert. He told me you saw the shooting. I had no idea about the other stuff. You aren't letting us down! No way! No one should have to go through what your family's been through. I'm amazed you've been able to keep up with school and run with the team with all that's happened!"

"Look at me, Vincent. I have an idea that I want to discuss with Brother Robert. Can you hold off from quitting the team until next week? By then, I should know if we can help your family. What do you say?"

Vincent wasn't sure what to say. After a few minutes, he told the coach that he would hold off on quitting. "Okay son," the coach said, "let's get you back to your class. I've got a vice principal to meet."

White walked Vincent to his math class. He told the teacher that Vincent had been with him. Then the coach found Brother Robert. "Do you have a few minutes?" A few minutes turned into twenty. White shared the outcome of his meeting with Vincent. "Bob, we need to do something for this family. We talk about how our school is a family. Now we need to walk the talk."

Robert stood up and told the coach to have a seat. "I'll be right back." Five minutes later Robert had Brother Allan, the school principal, in tow. Allan always reminded Coach White of a young Mr. Peepers. Wimpy looking wire rim glasses, wide eyes, and a reedy voice. That's where the comparison stopped. Allan was a bright, thoughtful guy who asked great questions and encouraged his staff to think big.

"So, Coach," Brother Allan said, "Bob filled me in on the Angelino situation. It sounds like we have a problem to solve. Do we have any solutions?"

"I have an idea we could consider. It'll take more energy than our school has to give! What if we contacted some community leaders in the area to help us put together a fundraiser tor the Angelinos." Allan and Bob nodded their heads in agreement. They spent the next hour coming up with the names of 15 people to contact. Detta Bonfigore was the third name on the list.

Help would come faster than they anticipated. The next day, Brother Allan met with his cousin, Fr. John DiNapoli. At nine a.m. Fr. DiNapoli, with his red cape and a black biretta covering his balding head, walked into the office. A diminutive woman with long black hair, a magnetic, smile and a confident stride, was not far behind.

"John, how are you? It's been a long time!"

"Too long, Allan. I'm well. Thanks for asking."

Then the priest turned to Detta. "Mrs. Bonfigore, I'd like you to meet my cousin, Brother Allan Gironde."

Allan shook Detta's hand. "Mrs. Bonfigore, I think we met last spring. If I remember correctly, you had just moved to Greenville. Your daughter was considering coming to Don Bosco. I hope everything is going well."

"My daughter is a spirited young woman. From what I gather, she is giving us both a run for our money. Just one thing before we attend to business, Brother Allan. Please call me Detta."

"Detta it will be. Why don't you both have a seat. Fr. John asked me to meet you today, Detta. How can I help you?"

Detta wasted no time on small talk. "I want to talk about Vincent Angelino!"

Brother Allan looked at her with astonishment. "God does work in strange ways," he thought to himself. "Funny thing, Detta, I was going to call you today to talk about the Angelinos."

Allan could see that Detta was way ahead of him. She had already contacted several well-connected families in her town to see if they'd be willing to assist with a fundraiser for the Angelinos. All the families were willing to help. Detta hoped Don Bosco would also agree to help.

"How can we be helpful?"

"I have two ideas for you to consider. First, I am wondering if we could use the school's gymnasium as the site for the fundraiser. Secondly, I'm hoping the school would actively promote and support the fundraiser."

"Frankly, Detta, I just had a meeting with two of my staff about the Angelinos. I understand that their medical bills are mounting. As well, Mrs. Angelino will probably be out of work for some time. I haven't talked to my Board of Directors about this, but I think they'd be willing to get involved. I just have one question. Has anyone spoken to Mr. Angelino regarding this?"

"Brother Allan, I spoke to Joe Viterio, the owner of Viterio's Market and Augie Lawrence. Mrs. Angelino is a baker at Augie's bakery. We will sit down with John Angelino once we know who is on board with this idea." "Okay," Brother Allan said, "I'll call my board chair and the bishop as soon as our meeting is over. I'll call you tomorrow to let you know if we can be involved."

"Thank you so much, Brother Allan." With that, Detta and Fr. DiNapoli shook hands with Allen and headed out the door.

Guys can be such dolts

The next morning, Detta called Joe Viterio to fill him in regarding her meeting. Joe had begun telling some of his customers about the idea. Detta was grateful that Joe was so enterprising, but she was concerned they might be getting ahead of themselves. "Joe, we need to round out our committee and talk to John Angelino before we let anyone else know about this fundraiser.

Joe understood. "I'll keep my trap shut, Detta, until I hear from you."

About 9:15 a.m., after getting her kids off to school, Detta started on the breakfast dishes. She just finished putting her mappina on the towel rack when she saw Dante and Dino come up the driveway. Once they hit the back door, Detta said, "You were out of the house pretty early today. What have you been doing?" Dante turned to his wife. "We were going over some issues at the laundromat. Business has picked up. We're thinking about buying another one up on Atwells Avenue."

Detta shrugged her shoulders. "You better stick around for a long while, Dante, because I have no head for business." Then she launched into her progress with the fundraising idea. She was talking with her hands which clearly signaled that she was into this project.

"Slow down a bit, Detta. I'm having a hard time keeping up with you," Dante said.

"I am a little excited. It feels like this fundraiser might actually happen."

"So, how about starting over, Detta. "Who have you been talking to?"

Detta told Dante about her meetings with Brother Allan and Joe Viterio. Dante squeezed her shoulder. "You've gotten off to a great start, Honey."

Dante turned to his brother. "Tell Detta what you found out!" Dino had called around and found out how much they were paying for school tuition. As well, Dino had called a friend who worked at the hospital, Dino's friend was able to find out the status of the Angelino's bill. "Couple that with Maria's lost income from work and we are talking about a huge amount of moolah!"

"The Angelinos are in debt up to their ears," Dante said with a shrug. "I'll talk to some friends in town to see what can be done. We should be able to put a good dent into this amount." At that point, the brothers headed downstairs.

Dante reached the second step when Detta said "One more thing, Dante. I overheard your oldest son teasing Cristiana about some boy at school."

Dante turned on a dime. His eyebrows twitched like crazy and his cheeks were turning bright red. "What? Who?" was all he could sputter.

"Calm down, Detta said. "Don't jump to conclusions. If you start getting upset, Cris will clam up. That would be the end of it. Let me handle this. You are good with the laundromat business, but our family goings on is my territory. Go downstairs. I will let you know when I learn what is going on with our daughter."

Later that day, Detta picked up the kids at the bus stop. Once they made it home, Detta shooed her sons upstairs to clean their rooms. "Cristiana, can you help me fix supper after you work on your homework? I had to go to church today. My meeting took longer than I expected. As a result, I'm way behind schedule."

"Okay, Ma. I need to work on some history homework. I should be done in 45 minutes."

"Thanks, honey, I knew I could count on you." Detta was keenly aware that the time would come when her daughter would snap her head off rather than help. Hopefully later rather than sooner.

Shortly after four, Cris walked into the kitchen. "How can I help, Ma?"

"The weather's frosty, Honey. I thought I'd make pasta e fagole for dinner. Can you peel some carrots for me?"

"Sure, Mom."

Once the soup was on the back burner, Detta turned to her daughter. "This morning, I overheard Nico giving you a hard time about a boy on the bus. Although I'm curious, I won't ask you any questions. Remember we are the only girls in this house. We need to stick together. When you want to talk about it, let me know. Til then, I'll keep your brothers out of the picture."

"Mom, it's no big deal. Remember last week, you finally agreed to let me ride the bus to school? I accidentally bumped into a boy. Somehow, Nico heard about it. He has been giving me a hard time. It's no big thing!" What Cris failed to tell her mom was that bumping into the boy was no accident.

Accidents Do Happen

What really happened was that Cris walked towards a seat in the back of the bus. Then she "accidentally" bumped into this cute boy she had seen at school. She thought his name was Vincent. One of her books slipped out of her hands when she pushed into him.

The boy turned to see what had happened. "Oh my gosh, I'm so sorry" he said as he knelt to pick up the book. "I must have lost my balance." His face was beet red. He avoided looking into the girl's eyes. Cristiana told him that it was an accident and that she was as much to blame as he was. She decided to introduce herself to him as he seemed to be very shy.

"My name is Cris with a "C.""

Vincent was amazed and flustered at the same time. He nodded his head and forced a smile. "My name is Vincent."

Cris said, "Aren't you Vincent Angelino?"

He wondered how this cute girl with short, short brown hair knew his name.

"Okay if I call you Vincent?"

"Yeah, I suppose so."

This girl then turned to him and said, "Can I ask you for a favor?"

"Sure," he said hesitantly. "Could I have my book back?"

"Oh no, I mean, oh sure."

At which point, Vincent tried to hand the book back to her. He was so nervous that he dropped the book again. Cris watched the book fall to the floor. Then she started to laugh. "You sure are Mr. Fumblefingers today, aren't you!"

Vincent was more embarrassed than ever. "Sorry" was all he could croak. He picked up the book again and gave it to the girl. He quickly turned away only to see Mikey. Mikey had seen the whole thing. Vincent wanted to find a hole to hide in. Nothing doing, so he opened an English book and pretended to study.

Once they got off the bus, Vincent hurried to his locker. Mikey was walking right behind him. When they got to the lockers, Vincent stood behind Mikey so that no one would notice his embarrassment. Mikey couldn't believe Vincent's luck. That girl talked to Vincent. She seemed to know who he was. But neither one of the boys had a clue as to who she was.

"I'm such a complete doofus," Vincent said. "Fumblefingers! Jeepers, a pretty girl actually talks to me and what do I do but act like an absolute idiot. I'll be the laughingstock of the entire 10th grade!" Vincent made Mikey promise not to say a word of this to anyone.

"Cross my heart" was the last thing that Vincent heard before heading to his home room.

Baxter and Joey are in for a surprise

Rico made it to Kansas City in no time flat. He wasn't excited by Joey's plan, but money was tight, so he was all in. Joey knew that Wing Nut would be driving into Kansas City in two days. He and Rico decided to "borrow" Booby's van the morning of the meet up. Nut would be all by his lonesome.

Rico and Joey bought some Halloween masks at a five and dime store so no one would recognize them. Then they drove to the warehouse. Joey parked the car a few blocks down from the building. He and Rico found Booby just outside the back door of the liquor warehouse. They couldn't believe their luck. Booby had finished loading the van with boxes of booze. On top of that, Booby was driving solo.

They boosted the van and Booby. Joey drove back to his place to drop off his car and Rico followed. Then they headed to Fleming Park. The roads were slick, so the going was slow. They made it to the regular meeting point with minutes to spare. Along came Mr. Nut. Nut walked over to the van. Flash, bam, boom, Nut's in the back of the van alongside Booby.

Nut hadn't come peacefully. Joey had to brain him with the butt of his gun to get things under control. Rico took Nut's truck and followed Joey up to Gallatin. Once Nut, Booby and the van were inside the barn, Joey left Rico in charge. "I should be back by 9 p.m. There's plenty of food and beer. Check on those two idiots hourly. It wouldn't be good if they got loose." Then Joey headed to Kansas City.

Joey arrived in the city about 3 p.m. He called the liquor store. "Mr. Baxter," he said, "I hear you are down two employees and some liquor."

"Who the hell is this?" Baxter yelled.
"No need to get excited!" Joey exclaimed. "I'm a businessman just like you. I found your merchandise. I'd like to return it. For the right price, of course."

Baxter started swearing a blue streak, all the while threatening to tear Joey limb from limb when he found him. All Joey could do was to chuckle. That stoked Baxter's anger.

Baxter started to rant. Joey cut him off. "I'm a loan shark. You borrowed fifty grand to set up a liquor business. The money has yet to be paid back. I've been asked to help you work out a payment schedule."

Baxter wasn't happy. He wanted Booby and Nut returned unharmed. He also wanted his booze. "You got my guys and my merchandise. I want them back!"

"Now, now, Mr. Baxter, all in good time. Everything has its price. I am a reasonable man."

Baxter and Joey had a phone stare down. Neither of them wanted to give in. After a few minutes of silence, Baxter asked what it would take to get his stuff back. "Let's make this easy, Mr. Baxter. You give me $50K plus $5000 in late fees and you'll get your boys back alive and well."

"What about the liquor that you stole?"

Joey started to get a little cagey. He told Baxter that he had no use for the liquor. "I did taste the stuff. Not half bad. I could get that back to you for an additional $600."

Baxter started sputtering. "I don't have $55,000 just laying around. I'll give you half now and the rest next month? Joey started to tighten up. He felt like he was getting played. He raised his voice up a notch. "You had the money to buy Wing Nut a new truck. If you can do that, you can come up with the rest of the dough."
Baxter wondered how this mutt on the other end of the phone knew about the truck. Joey took his silence as a stalling tactic. "I'll call you back tomorrow. You better have good news for me." With that, Joey slammed the phone down. "I think Mr. Baxter needs to know that I'm serious." Joey left the office, hopped into his car, and headed back to Gallatin.

The weather was blustery. Snow started to fall. The Caddy's tires had seen better days. Joey was angry and he was in a hurry, so he paid no attention to the speedometer. He spun out 20 miles from Gallatin.

Fortunately, a farmer came by on an old John Deere tractor. He called himself Thomas—blue jeans, a plaid shirt, and a weathered face covered with grey whiskers. "What happened?" Joey explained that he hit the curve too quickly and spun out. "Get in the car, son. I have a chain in the bed of my truck. Give me a second to hook it up. Then I want you to steer the car to the left when I give you the signal. Thomas started his tractor and pulled Joey out of the ditch. Joey thanked the guy and gave him $20 for his help. Thomas pocketed the money with a smile, got back on his tractor and took off for parts unknown.

Joey headed to Gallatin. This time, he was more cautious. The next thing Joey knew, he was pulling up to the barn. He got out of his car and headed towards the farmhouse. Rico was all ears as his brother recounted his conversation with Baxter. "Rico, you shoulda heard him. He was spitting nickels when I told him what he had to

71

do to get his boys back. Let's give him a day to think about this. I'll call him back tomorrow."

"Dammit, Joey! I ain't looking to stay in this backwater town until tomorrow. Folks will start noticing us."

"They'll only notice us if they see us." Joey said. "So far, the only person who has seen me was that hayseed who pulled me outta the ditch. One night here won't kill us. We got food and booze. No worries."

Joey put a mask on and went to the barn to see how the skanks were doing. He could hear them cussing up a streak. Booby and Nut were tied to a post in the corner of the barn. Joey saw that Rico had given them a blanket to keep warm. The blanket wasn't doing its job. The two men were shivering. Nut looked groggy. Booby looked worse. Booby took one look at Joey and spit at his feet. "When we get outta here, I'll find you and tear you apart, you little weasel."

Booby was a big boy. He would be a mess of trouble if it came to that. Joey laughed. "You'd be better off helping Nut instead of thinking about tangling with me. Nut looks pretty low right about now." Joey edged an oaken bucket full of water close to Booby's free hand. Then he threw a ladle at Booby and suggested that the two boys might want to take a sip or three.

"What I need," Booby said, "is some food and a toilet."

Joey headed to the door. "I'll be back."

A few minutes later, Rico and Joey decided to get Nut to the bathroom in the farmhouse. They blindfolded him. Rico led him out of the barn while Joey set a plate of food within Booby's reach. Booby nearly swallowed a ham sandwich in one bite.

When Rico came back, Booby had finished two sandwiches and a bag of chips. Rico retied Nut to the post and turned to help loosen Booby's hands. Joey decided Booby might be too much for Rico to handle so he told Rico to hold a gun on Booby. Joey cut the rope that bound Booby's hands and led him towards the barn door.

Booby turned, threw his arm around Joey's throat, and started choking him. Rico was stunned. He recovered quickly. He picked up the knife that Joey had been using and stabbed Booby twice in the leg. Booby and Joey both fell hard to the ground. Joey eyes were unfocused. Booby clutched his leg. He was screaming bloody murder.

Joey's breathing finally started to come back. He stood up very slowly. Once he got his breath, he lashed a foot into Booby's jaw. Joey reared back to kick him again, but Rico slammed him onto the floor.

"The guy's out cold. We need to bandage his leg or he's a goner. Get towels and some ice from the fridge. I'll put pressure on his leg until you come back." Joey rose slowly and weaved his way back to the house. A few minutes later, he returned with ice and towels. He dropped them at Rico's feet and began to barf.

The brothers worked on Booby for a half hour, icing his leg and using the towels as a tourniquet. In the meantime, Nut was still tied to the post with a blindfold on. He was yelling for Booby. Joey stumbled over to him, put a gun to his head and told him to be quiet. That got Nut's attention.

Blood covered Booby's leg. Rico finally got the blood to stop by twisting the towels more severely. He rummaged around the farmhouse and found some gauze in a bathroom closet. Joey was still red in the face and hot under the collar. He wanted to shoot Booby and go from there. After some coercing, Joey reluctantly agreed to bandage Booby's leg once the blood clotted.

"Joey, when the leg stops bleeding, I want you to take this guy back to where you found him and drop him off. Then give this Baxter guy a call. Tell him where to find Booby."

Joey shouted, "So, now you're the boss!"
Rico's voice was like a piece of blue steel. "Listen up, Muttonchops. I came here to help you, so don't start in on me. You're outta control. Buck up, little brother. We need to move on, get the money and then I can hightail it back to Connecticut. Nothing more, nothing less."

With that, Rico walked back to check on Booby. Joey finally calmed down. "Let's go outside and have a beer."

They walked out by the truck. They each had a bottle of Bud in their hands. Neither one said anything. Finally, Joey pushed his brother off balance. "You are right, as always." Joey told Nico that this whole mess was his fault. "I got frustrated and didn't take my time getting Booby out of the barn. Now we have a big mess."

The sun had gone down and the wind had picked up. The brothers needed to come up with a plan before they froze their asses off. They decided to put Booby in the back of the truck. Joey would drive him back to Kansas City and drop him off near the liquor store. Then Joey would call Baxter, tell him there had been a change of plan and let him know where to find Booby. The plan made sense. Joey headed back to town with Booby.

The snow had stopped falling, but the road was a mess. It took Joey over two hours to get to Baxter's. Joey backed the truck behind the store and helped Booby out of the truck. Then he stuffed a facecloth in Booby's mouth. He called Baxter's and left a message telling

74

Baxter where to find Booby. Then Joey headed over to Dolan's laundromat.

When he got to Dolan's, flames were coming out of Dolan's building. Someone had called in the fire. Firefighters were hosing down the building. Joey found a phone booth and called Dolan. Dolan started screaming when Joey told him the news. "You were supposed to get my money back, not lose my laundromat!" He went on and on. Joey finally told Dolan to meet him at the laundromat. The fire marshal would want to talk to Dolan. Dolan had to get the story straight.

Tantrums all over the place

Mr. B walked downstairs about 7:45 a.m. He asked Detta to drive the kids to school. Once she left, Mr. B lit up a stogie. Detta didn't have many rules in their house, but the no cigar smoke rule was numero uno, due, and tres.

Mr. B walked into his office and slammed the door. Marty decided to let him cool down. After a while, Marty knocked on the door. "Is everything all right?"

"Get in here!" Mr. B launched into a tirade. Detta had been out of the house a lot lately. She was working on the fundraiser. Dante had been left on his own and he didn't like it. Dante's boss was on a tear. He wanted to know what was going on with the bookmaking business. To top it off, Mr. B hadn't heard one word from Cappy.

By the time Mr. B finished his litany, he was sweating up a storm.

"Mr. B, what would you like me to do first?"

"Get Sammy on the phone," Dante said. "I want him and his pally Gian in my office right now. No excuses! Make sure they bring their paperwork for the last couple of weeks. The last thing I need is the Boss jumping all over me because I can't tell him what is going on."

"When you're done, call Cappy. Tell him we'll be in Hartford by 12:30. We need to talk about Joey. From there, we head to Trixie's. Give her a head's up." Then Mr. B headed upstairs.

Dante found Detta in the kitchen finishing up the dishes. She turned towards him when she heard the basement door opening. She could tell that he had been smoking. She started to tear into him but stopped herself when she saw the look on his face. At that point, she slipped into her demure demeanor and asked him what was wrong. He just stared at her.

Detta knew how to handle Dante's tantrums. "Honey, why don't you sit down. I'll fix you a cup of coffee." She took her time so he could settle down. She put some pastry on the table. "Here's your coffee, Sweetheart." Detta sat down next to him and put her hand on his sleeve. "You're probably upset because I haven't been around the past few days. I've been busy working on the fundraiser. I'm sorry. I'll try to spend some extra time with you and the kids over the next few weeks."

Anybody else trying to smooth talk Dante would end up with a fat lip. But Detta always hit the right notes. Dante slouched his shoulders. "Between some business stuff that is hitting the fire and you trying to get the fundraiser pulled together, I guess I got a little worked up."

"How did you get everything done around here and still havetime to work on the fundraiser?" Dante asked. "To tell you the truth, Dante, I asked Marty to help out around the house so that I could spend some time with Mr. Viterio and a few others from town. Marty seemed to be twiddling thumbs downstairs and there was a lot of work to do upstairs. I would have asked you if it that was okay, but you've been out a lot yourself. Marty became the family bus driver, cook, and nursemaid all rolled into one."

"I might have to give the kid a raise." he said amusingly. With that, he bent over and gave his wife a kiss on the cheek. "So, what's happening with the fundraiser?" Detta spent twenty minutes going over all the things that had come together over the past few days.

Just then, Marty came up and reminded Dante that the boys were coming soon." Detta, I need to go out of town on business. Marty and I are heading to Hartford this afternoon. Then I need to go up to Boston. I should be back tomorrow afternoon. I know this is last minute, but it just can't wait."

Detta put her hands on her hips and smiled. "I guess turnabout is fair play, Big Boy. I'll see you tomorrow."

Detta left for a meeting at church. As she was leaving, Sammy and Gian headed up the driveway. They went right downstairs. Marty ushered them into Dante's office. "All right, let's have it," Mr. B said. "You have been at the pool hall for a few weeks. What have you found out?"

Sammy opened a ledger and went over every angle of the business. After a fair amount of legwork, he found a huge stash of money. This was great news. "Mr. Big will be happy to hear that," Dante said. "We need to make sure that this never happens again!"

Sammy looked up. "Mr. B, we've taken care of that. We installed new protocols with the bank."

Protocols, schmowtocols. Don't give me no finance mumbo jumbo. All I want to know is that it's fixed. From here on, you two are responsible. You are telling me it is all clear. Is that right?"

"Yes sir, we have it under control."

To Sammy's surprise, Dante clapped him on the back, opened his safe, and gave each of the boys a $1,000 bonus. "Is there anything else?" Gian took over from there. He and Sammy had developed a way to keep track of the daily bets. In the past, guys who had lost bets were given time to pony up. Sometimes those bets were not repaid. Gian and Billy De Nunzio began to use some muscle to insure payments. This had added extra cash into the business.

This pleased Dante. He reopened his safe and pulled out another two hundred dollars for each of them. "Mr. Big is gonna be happy. I'll call him later this afternoon. Marty and I gotta hit the road to Hartford. It's time for you two to head back to the pool hall. Keep up the good work!"

Sammy and Gian took off. Marty was standing by the back door when Mr. B came upstairs. "I guess I better wear my winter coat by the looks of it." Dante said.

"I went outside a little while ago, Mr. B. "I took the car to the dealership to get the oil changed. The wind is swirling and the temps are dropping. You might get a sweater and a warm coat." Mr. B went upstairs to change.

An unexpected visitor

They were about to head out when a police cruiser pulled up. Marty looked out the window and turned to Mr. B. "We have a visitor."

"Who is it?" Dante growled.

"Mr. B, Detective Maloney is stopping by."

"I don't have time for that SOB!"

"Mr. B, if you give him a tough time, that might raise suspicion."

"I'll talk to Maloney. Bring him downstairs."

Maloney had followed up on every angle in the case. He'd hit nothing but thin air. He interviewed everyone who had been shopping at Viterio's that night. Vincent was the only person who saw the shooter. Maloney had begun looking at De Nuncio's pool hall business. Come to find out, the property and the pool hall were owned by Dante Bonfigore. Maloney heard rumblings that Bonfigore might be mobbed up, but that was nothing more than chatter over cups of java at the Coffee Cafe.

Over the next two days, Maloney and Freddie Masterson, one of the sergeants on the force, worked on the De Nuncio angle. Masterson checked to see if De Nuncio had any priors. Meanwhile, Maloney went door knocking. Masterson came up empty on his first go-round. There were a few parking tickets and one disorderly conduct charge, but this was old news. This search was going nowhere.

Then Masterson heard that De Nuncio grew up in Boston. He got the bright idea to call a friend at the Boston PD. Voila, De Nuncio had been picked up three times in the last six years. Once he was arrested for breaking the leg of a gang member with a lug wrench. The other arrests were for larceny. Amazingly, none of the victims were willing to cooperate with the police. Masterson called the arresting officers. Each guy was positive that De Nuncio's activities were gang related—but they had no proof.

Masterson dug deeper. It turned out that De Nuncio's dad had been involved in the numbers racket for years—from Dorchester to Worcester. He was incarcerated at MCI-Walpole in the early 70's for manslaughter. Three years later, the father was stabbed to death in his cell. Apparently, the dad had learned that one of the new inmates, a guy named Izzo, was tied to the Feds. Two weeks later, De Nuncio met his maker.

Maloney drove up to Boston to see what he could find out about the guy. As luck would have it, Maloney found his way into the rectory at St. Leonard's Catholic Church. The parish secretary, a woman named Lucia, saw his badge. "How can I help you?"

Maloney asked if De Nuncio's family had ever attended the church. Lucia pulled out an old parish directory. Lo and behold, there was a photo of De Nuncio in a cassock kneeling next to a young priest. Maloney couldn't believe his luck. "Everyone knew Luigi De Nuncio."

Maloney turned to her. "Would you mind if I asked you some questions about De Nuncio?"

"Actually, Detective, I know someone who knew Mr. De Nuncio much better than I do. You see the young priest in that photo? That's Father O'Malley. Father just retired. He is living in our rectory. I could see if he'd be willing to talk to you."

Fr. O'Malley was more than willing to share what he knew. "You understand, Detective, I can't share anything that I've heard in the confessional, but I might be of help." What a help he was. De Nuncio's father and uncle had both been involved in the mob. Both men died in prison. Luigi was left to fend for himself. O'Malley tried to help him, but the almighty dollar won out over the Almighty.

At the priest's suggestion, Maloney went to visit Giovanni Coppola. Coppola had been a drafting teacher at the local high school. O'Malley thought Coppola might have known De Nuncio. Maloney hit the jackpot. De Nuncio had been in several of Coppola's classes. Coincidentally, his best friend, a pock marked kid named Bobo, was the son of Sammy Gabbiano. For a time, Sammy was the main hit man in Boston. When Luigi's dad died, the mob took Luigi under their wing.

When Maloney got back to Greenville, he and Masterson compared notes. Maloney spoke first. "The acorn didn't fall far from the tree. Father and son were murdered at an early age. I'm not surprised we couldn't find De Nuncio's connections with the Providence mob."

O'Malley thought Luigi had become a low-level drug runner. Luigi was an order taker, not an order giver. Apparently, De Nuncio did well enough to warrant a chance to score in Rhode Island. But Maloney got nowhere when he tried to tie De Nuncio to the Rhode Island mob.

Malony thought to himself, "It might be worthwhile to meet with Bonfigore. Who knows, he might be willing to help us."

Two days later, Maloney got out of his cruiser, walked up to Bonfigore's house and rapped on the front door. Marty waited a few seconds and then opened the door. "If you are a solicitor, you've come to the wrong house," Marty said, and then began to shut the door.
Maloney stuck a leg out to hold the door open and flashed his badge. "I'm here to speak with Mr. Bonfigore."

Marty wasted no time ushering Maloney into the house. "Mr. Bonfigore is on a long-distance call. He's heading out of town as soon as the call is completed. Is there any way I can be of help?"

Maloney started to fume. He raised his voice a notch and told Marty that he was investigating Luigi De Nuncio's murder. "I want to clear a few things up with Mr. Bonfigore regarding the murder."

Marty could see that Maloney was going to get his way or else. "If you could wait here for a second, I'll see if Mr. Bonfigore has finished his phone call."

Marty went downstairs and gave Mr. B the lowdown. "Why don't we go talk to the detective?"

As soon as Dante hit the top stair, he walked over to Maloney and stuck out his hand. "You must be Bill Maloney," he said graciously. "You live next to Mike Alexander. I'm Dante Bonfigore. Welcome to my home. How can I help you?"

Maloney was stunned that Bonfigore knew where he lived. "I'm investigating the shooting at Viterio's. I need to talk about your relationship with Mr. De Nuncio."

"Marty, I'm expecting Father DiNapoli to arrive momentarily to drop off some documents. Can you watch for him?"

Marty knew this was Mr. B's way of distancing Marty from the investigation. "Absolutely, Mr. B!"

With that, Dante invited Maloney down to his office. "Have a seat, Detective. How can I be of help?"
The detective wasted no time getting to the heart of the matter. "I understand you own Willie's Pool Hall."

Dante kept his business affairs very close to the vest. He hid his surprise at learning that Maloney knew he owned the business. "I own several area businesses, Detective. Willie's is one of them."

"I was surprised you didn't express any public outrage regarding the murder."

Dante indicated that he was a very private person. He told the detective that he was aware of how hard the police force was investigating the murder. "If I felt you were pussyfooting around, you would have heard my howling from here to Fox Point!"

"I understand Mr. De Nuncio had been living in Boston before moving to Rhode Island. How did he get hooked up with you.?"

Dante lifted his eyebrows when he learned Maloney knew something of De Nuncio's past. But he kept his wits about him. "Luigi was recommended by a banker I know in the North End. He did a great job for me." Bonfigore thought his connection to De Nuncio was solid. "Obviously, Maloney had done his homework." Dante thought to himself. "I better watch what I say."

Maloney continued his questioning. "I'm wondering if you had heard any rumors about Mr. De Nuncio and his family being connected to the Boston Mafia."

Dante feigned surprise. "Are you serious, Detective? You can't be inferring that my friend, Luigi, was a mob guy. I can't believe it!"

"Mr. Bonfigore, rumors have been floating around town that De Nuncio had been killed as a result of some mob related problems at the pool hall. I'm just trying to get a handle on what might have been going on."

"I can assure you, Detective Maloney, my pool hall is not connected with the Mafia. I am as concerned as you are about Luigi's death. I am happy to cooperate in any way. If it would help, I could arrange for your people to look at our books. You're probably aware that Luigi had two people working for him, his son Billy and a guy named Tommy Barrone. I'll let them know that you might give them a call.

Maloney expressed his appreciation to Dante for his assistance. "I'll be in touch with De Nuncio and this Barrone guy in the next few days. Again, thanks for taking time out to help us with this investigation."

As soon as Dante heard the backdoor slam, he yelled for Marty. "Get Giovanni Sacco on the line right away. Our trip to Hartford will be delayed."

It took a while for Marty to track down Sacco. "What's up with Sacco, Dante?"

"Gio, we have been calling all over town trying to find you! Where the hell are you?"

"Dante, I am working on our mutual interests in Boston. I got your message, but I needed to make sure all parties were on the same page here before wrapping up our business. Sorry for taking so long. So, tell me, what is up now?"

"Before we head down that road, Gio, my guy checked to make sure we weren't having any friends listening in on our conversation." Then, Dante proceeded to describe his meeting with Maloney.

"We might have a police problem, Dante. I don't want you to say another word to Maloney."

Let's go see Cappy

The road from Greenville to Hartford winds from hither to yon. Many of the farms along the way are covered with apple trees and craggy stone fences. After seeing the fifth apple orchard, Marty commented, "Robert Frost may have driven this road once or twice."

"Is that some of your college learning?" Dante sneered. "Enough already, Smarty Pants!"

Marty shrugged. If Dante could read minds, Marty would've been out of a job. "Mr. B sends me to college and expects me to act like it never happened. Changes need to be made or I'm history!"

It took an hour and change to get through burgs like Ashford and Manchester before finally hitting Hartford. Cappy's place was located just this side of downtown. They were early, so Mr. B decided to get some takeout. He saw a small hoagie shop three blocks away from Cappy's. Marty parked the car and they went in. Mr. B didn't look at the menu. He caught the waitress' eye and waved. "We gonna have two grinders with capicola, provolone, genoa salami, lettuce and tomatoes. Oh yeah, and a few sweet peppers on the side."

The waitress, a heavy-set Italian woman with purple tinged hair, asked if the order was to go. They nodded. A few minutes later, the small talk stopped when two huge grinders were on the counter. Mr. B touched Marty's shoulder. "These are the best grinders this side of Johnston. "I'm hungry. Let's head back to Cappy's."

When they got there, Marty sat down. "Eat your grinder. I need to talk to Cappy. The less you know about this, the better!"

"Mr. B, the last time you talked with Cappy, he ended up woozy. He might cause trouble today."

"Not to worry, kiddo," he whispered, "I got someone working on the inside. Nothing will happen." With that, Dante headed into the office.

Cappy was waiting for Dante. The bruises around his face were fading, but the anger was still in his voice. "So, the boss has finally arrived!" Mr. B unholstered his gun and smashed it across Cappy's nose without even blinking an eye. "I know your cousin's well connected to my boss, but that's not enough to stop me from knocking you off right now. You screwed up with Joey and you paid for it. That's the past. Get over it. We're dealing with today right now. Put your dick back in your pants and let's get to work. Do you understand?"

Cappy nodded. He walked towards a refrigerator in the corner of the office, pulled out a bag of ice and covered his nose with it. Then he sat across from Dante.

Mr. B wasted no time getting to the point. Joey One Shot's become a problem. "This ain't gonna be swept under any carpet. The police have talked to me regarding the shooting. They know I own the pool hall. I got plenty of folks who saw my wife and me at the Italian American Club that night, so I'm covered for now. But the detective is a bulldog. He has already spoken to the Angelino kid. I don't know where that is gonna lead."

Cappy swiveled towards Mr. B. "Look, Dante, we get somebody to knock off the kid and all will be square."

"Cappy, listen up! Nothing, I mean nothing, is going to happen to that kid. I knew his mother when we were younger. She got a bullet in her shoulder that she didn't deserve. That's on me. The kid knows nothing. The only person who knows anything is Joey. I haven't talked to him. I want to talk to him. Where is this jagoff?"

Cappy told Mr. B that Joey had taken a job out of state. "Somewhere in the Midwest. Chicago, I think. I owed somebody a favor. Joey's helping someone connected to the mob. He is there to clean up a money deal that went haywire. Before he left, I told him to call me if he needed something. So far, I haven't heard from Joey."

Mr. B knew that taking on the Chicago mob would be costly and dangerous as all get out. He made it clear that Cappy better call if he heard from Joey.

"The last thing we need is for Joey to do something crazy! If that happens, I'll make sure the local police will deal with one more fatality. Do you read me?"

Cappy was in a bind. He knew how to get in touch with Joey. However, he had no intention of telling Mr. B. If Dante found out Cappy was hiding stuff, it would lead to a quick bullet.

"I'll let you know if I hear anything," he said. Dante lowered his eyebrows. His stare became intense. "I don't care what time of day it is. When you get a call, I get a call. Am I clear?" Cappy shook his head.

"At this point, Cappy, I'm speaking for the men in Providence" We want to see Joey and we want to see him fast. Nothing serious will happen if we hear from him. The longer it takes, the more nervous we become!"

Dante headed out the door towards Marty and the car. "It's time we head to the Cape, Marty. I need to spend time with my friend."

Cappy watched him go. There was no mistaking Dante's meaning. Cappy decided he better head west. "I need to find Joey before anything else gets outta hand."

Vincent gets a surprise worth waiting for

The past few weeks were a blur. Maria was getting better every day. She was bed bound, but she was able to come down for meals if someone helped her. Seeing her begin to get back to her old self helped everyone's spirits. Her cheeks were getting rosy and she was even starting to smile a little bit.

John pulled his son aside two days ago. He told Vincent that someone had made an anonymous donation to the family. The money would pay for school tuitions for this year. Vincent looked up at his father and started to sputter. "Who did this, Dad?"

"I don't know. I was as shocked as you are. I got a call from Fr. DiNapoli. He asked me to meet him at the rectory. I drove right over. Father told me about the donation, but he wouldn't tell me where it came from! That's all I know."

Vincent looked up. His dad had tears streaming down his cheeks. Suddenly, they were hugging. Vincent asked his dad what he should do about the job at Viterio's.

"Vincent, I met Mr. Viterio yesterday. I told him about the gift. He was as surprised to hear the news as we are. He said the job is still yours if you want it. Otherwise, you can stock shelves this summer. Mr. Viterio said that doing well in high school is more important than earning some money at his store."

"Dad, does this mean that I can stay on the cross-country team?" John's face lit up as he nodded his head.

Vincent started jumping up and down. He began talking a mile a minute.

"Slow down, son. You need to know two things. First, let's keep this quiet til next Monday. That will give me a chance to call Mrs. Bonfigore with the news. Can you handle that?" Vincent nodded yes. "Secondly, why don't you go upstairs and tell your mom. She's headed to the hospital in a few weeks for another operation. She could use some good news right about now. You should be the one to tell her." Vincent sped upstairs, went in his parents' bedroom and told his mother the good news

Between working on weekends and meeting with Detective Maloney, John didn't have much time to relax. However, now would be a good time to kick back and enjoy his family. He took his time walking up the stairs. When he hit the hallway, he could hear his son and his wife jabbering away. Life was almost back to normal.

John held off on telling Vincent about the police artist. Right now, his family should celebrate good news without any distractions. Vincent didn't need to worry about this until later. John went into his bedroom to share in the celebration. After a while, Maria began to tire. John suggested that he and Vincent should head downstairs and let his mother get some rest.

Late that afternoon, John pulled Vincent aside after supper. "I think you might want to call Mikey and tell him you can be on the cross-country team. Don't let on about the donation right yet, Vincent. If he asks, tell him that we came into a bit of money." With that, Vincent hugged his dad and went upstairs to give his mom a kiss. Then he called Mikey.

"Mikey, it's me. I need to see you."

Mikey started asking tons of questions, but Vincent shut him off. "I'll meet you at Jaswell's Farm at 6:15."

"Why can't we meet right now?"

"Mikey, I have jobs to do around the house before I head out." Mikey was frustrated, but he agreed to meet Vincent. Vincent went up to his room to study. He had to read a chapter of *Don Quixote* for his English class before meeting up with Mikey. Vincent was so excited about the news that he didn't get much done. Finally, he put the book down, put on a sweatshirt and headed out the door.

He raced to Jaswell's thinking he'd be the first one there. No such luck! Mikey was sitting on the stone wall in front of the farm waiting for him. "Did you get up late this morning?" Vincent asked.

Mikey wore this flea-bitten cap if he didn't have time to take a morning shower. "I was babysitting my sister last night. I didn't get up in time to take a shower," Mikey changed the topic quickly. "So, what is up? Something must be pretty important for you to put aside your homework on a school night so that we can talk!"

Vincent told Mikey the news. "My dad made me promise not to say anything about how this happened, but he told me I won't have to work at Viterio's. I can rejoin the team."

"Yowsa!" Mikey said. "That is sooo great! The state championships are a week away. If you can run, we have a good chance of winning the darn thing."

"Mikey, not so fast. First off, I haven't done any distance running lately. Secondly, I'm not sure how Coach White will feel about me rejoining the team." At that moment, Mikey took off like a bolt of lightning.

"Where are you going, you numbskull?"

"Follow me if you can," Mikey yelled over his shoulder.

By the time they reached Mikey's, they were both out of breath. They had been running at breakneck speed since they left Jaswell's. Mikey opened his back door and pushed Vincent in. Mikey's mom was wiping up the supper dishes. She wasn't dressed for company. Her red hair was up in a bun and she was covered with flour.

"Mikey! Vincent! What are you two doing here? Look at me. I look like one of those women in the Pillsbury ads." The boys blathered on about Vincent's news. "Will you slow down!" she said. "I'm having a hard time keeping up with you. Whatever's going on must be darn important. Can you each take a deep breath and start all over?"

The boys finally settled down and told her what was up. She was just as surprised as Mikey. She suggested that they call Coach White and see what he had to say. The boys were reluctant to bother the coach on a school night. Mrs. O'Day told them that there were exceptions to every rule. Then she called the coach.

She got ahold of him on the first try. She told Coach White what had happened. From that point on, she simply responded with "Aha" and "I see." Mrs. O'Day finally hung up the phone and turned to the boys with a twinkle in her eyes. "Coach White wants to talk to you. He's coming over here right now. You get yourselves some milk and sit down at the kitchen table. I'm going upstairs to see if I can look a bit more presentable."

A few minutes later there was a knock at the door. Mrs. O'Day ushered the coach into the kitchen. The boys jumped up from the table as soon as they saw him.

"Sit down, guys. I hear you have something to tell me."

Mikey's mom suggested that they go into the living room. She went to the kitchen to get Coach White a cup of coffee. "Vincent, hold off on telling Coach White anything until I return." Apparently, the boys couldn't wait. She returned to find Vincent and Mikey talking over each other as Coach White sat back trying to understand what had happened.

"Okay, let's start over! You are talking so quickly that I can't understand a word you're saying," Mrs. O'Day said. "Vincent, take a deep breath and tell the coach about your news." Vincent started choking up and couldn't get the words out. The coach reached over, put his hand on Vincent's shoulder and looked him straight in the eye. "Take your time, son, I have all night." With that, Vincent recounted his story.

"So, Vincent, do you want to run in the state meet?"

"Yes sir, if you let me rejoin the team!" It would take a lot of work to wipe off the smile on Coach White's face.

"Have you run at all in the past ten days?"

Vincent shook his head from side to side. "I haven't had time to run. Most of my free time has been spent at Viterio's or at home studying."

"Vincent, as far as I'm concerned, you never left the team," the coach said. "I never took your name off our roster. You are on our team. I only have one condition."

Vincent's face scrunched up. "A condition, sir?"

The coach leaned over to him. "You and Mr. O'Day need to put in some extra running this weekend so you can regain some stamina. Can you handle that?" Vincent looked at Mikey. They both started bobbing their heads.

"Vincent, you might try to push yourself. Do not overdo it. There's a good chance you could strain a calf muscle if you go full bore right now. That would end your chances of running in the meet. Am I clear about what you need to do?" Vincent nodded his head. The coach told them to see him before school tomorrow. Then he headed out the door.

Working together, we can get things done

Detta met Brother Allen three days later. His board had agreed to support the fundraiser. Their only condition was that the fundraiser had to be after the Christmas holidays. "I know you want to get going on this as soon as possible, but we're using the gymnasium for a lot of winter sports. The first free time would be the second Saturday in February. Detta pulled a calendar out of her purse. "That would be February 8th. I'll make that work."

Brother Allan started to smile. "Detta, you like to be ahead of the game. So, what kind of help do you need from us." "Brother Allan, it would be great if you could contact folks from the East Side of Providence and South County who might be willing to help us."

"I'll help you. I already set up a meeting with the bishop to discuss the fundraiser. He's really interested. I'll let you know what comes from our meeting."

"Timing's everything," Detta exclaimed. "We only have three months to get our ducks in a row."

Detta thanked Allan and started to leave. "One thing, Detta. Connie King, a member of my board, has a connection with a cruise company. She has talked the owners into donating a weeklong cruise for two people."

Detta just stared at him. "Oh, my goodness," she exclaimed. "You've made my day." Detta gave the brother a huge hug and headed out the door.

Detta drove back to Greenville to meet with her steering committee. She had convinced Fr. DiNapoli and Mr. Viterio to be on the committee. The newest committee member was John Petrangelo. John's family owned a Chevy dealership in Johnston. One of his sons was Pietro Angelino's best friend. John contacted Detta. The next thing you knew, he was on the committee. Detta finally got to the church. She told everyone about the cruise. Mr. Viterio's eyes lit up. "That's great!"

When they finally settled down, John had some news. He was a quiet, no nonsense kind of guy. Today, he had a twinkle in his eye. "I met with my regional manager. He knew about the shooting but didn't realize that I was helping with the fundraiser. He's willing to loan us a new Chevy Camaro Coupe for six months...we can raffle off the use of the car!

The committee was stunned. They couldn't imagine their good fortune. Detta said "I'm thinking that Dante's brother might buy a few raffle tickets for that car." Mr. Viterio turned and said. "If you are not careful, Detta, your husband might spend a few dollars on this raffle himself." "If Dante wins the raffle, we'll have a conversation about who will drive the Camaro!"

After the group calmed down, Mr. Viterio outlined their timeline. "So, the fundraiser will be on February 8th. "That seems far away, but it is just around the corner. We need more volunteers. Detta asked each of them to head up a committee. "I know we are getting close to the Christmas holidays," she said. "Everyone needs to pull their committees together as quickly as possible."

Run like the wind

The state cross country meet normally was held two weeks before Thanksgiving. However, the schedule had been pushed back due to a late season hurricane. Vincent felt a little lethargic, but he was as ready as he could be. The day of the meet, his parents drove him to school. His mom was still weak from her surgery, but she was bound and determined to be at the finish line to watch her son.

"Vincent," she said. "I couldn't be prouder of you. You've worked hard at school and at this running thing. Not to mention how much help you have been around the house. I know you will do your best today. Regardless how the race turns out, I will be waiting at the end of the race to give you a hug."

The rest of the ride was very quiet. Vincent jumped out of the car when his father came to a stop. John jerked the driver's side door open and hopped out. "Son," he said. "Wait up!"

Vincent had already hit the sidewalk. He turned towards his dad. "I know you don't want me to make a big scene right here. Just know what mom said goes for me too. Good luck this afternoon. We'll see you right after the meet." With that, John waved to him, got back into the car and headed home.

The Don Bosco cross-country team climbed into a well-used Chevy school bus and headed towards Ponagansett High School, the site of the state cross-country meet. There was no direct route to the school, so it took a while to get to there.

Vincent nudged Mikey. "I know you probably have as many butterflies as I have. My mom told me to do my best today. That goes for you too!" Mikey shrugged. "Snap out of it, Mikey. We've worked too hard to let our worries get in the way of our work today."

Mikey's eyes were squinting. "I don't want to flub up the race and hurt the team."

Vincent shook the daylights out of his friend. "Remember that you encouraged me to run in this meet. We're a team, the two of us." Then Vincent started up with the silly grin he got when he was teasing someone. "I think your problem will be keeping up with me."

That was all it took to snap Mikey out of his funk. "We'll see who beats who, you booch!" he said with a smile as huge as the school bus.

The bus got to Ponagansett a little after 2 pm. The other teams had already begun their warmups. It was blustery, so some guys on the Don Bosco team kept their sweats on. Vincent wouldn't hear of that. He pulled Mikey aside. "No sweats for us, Mikey! Nothing's going hold us back." Mikey agreed.

When the rest of the team saw what Vincent and Mikey had done, it was all for one and one for all. Everyone shed their sweats and started loosening up. Coach White pulled the team together and went over their race plan. "Okay! No rah rah talk today. Stick together as a group for as long as you can. Don't start out too fast! The weather will catch up to you. Straight and steady." Then the team knelt for a prayer. The race director blew his whistle and the team headed to the starting line hand in hand. Three minutes later, the race began.

Vincent ran the race of his life. He started slowly, pacing himself as he hit the first of three inclines. The weather and the arduous inclines forced many of the runners to fall back. Vincent looked to his right as he hit the crest of the hill and found Mikey running just behind him. Mikey yelled out, "Let's keep this pace!" Vincent pointed forward and they took off. At the mid-point of the race, Mikey began to slow down. "Don't worry about me, Vincent!" he shouted. "It's your race to win. Don't slow down for me!"

Vincent found himself racing head-to-head with the two best cross-country runners in the state until the last quarter of a mile. It got much colder. That didn't deter Vincent one little bit. He was in second place as they hit the top of the last hill. They had 200 yards to go until they would hit the finish line. Vincent knew it was time to begin his sprint. Suddenly, he felt a huge cramp in his left leg just as he had passed the lead runner. The pain was considerable. "Holy crap!" he spit out. He began to limp. "Oh no! Not now!" Vincent cried out.

Vincent willed himself to keep running. Unfortunately, the other two guys passed him before he hit the finish line. He ended up in third place. Mikey came in twelfth. The rest of their team was not far behind. The first and second place runners were from Hendricken. That was all it took for the Hendricken Hawks to win the meet. Don Bosco came in second.

Vincent and Mikey were upset with the results of the race. They knew they could have done better. They never heard the rest of the team come up behind them and carry them off to the awards ceremony. The team was screaming. Vincent's furry eyebrows started twitching. He couldn't figure out why everyone was so happy. "I lost the meet for our team due to my doggone cramps!" he said to himself. His teammates were grinning ear to ear. "What is up with that!"

The team stopped in front of Coach White. "Get those two skinny merrinks off your shoulders so I can talk to you before the ceremony begins."

"I'm so sorry, Coach, Vincent stammered once he was on level ground, "I lost the championship for us!"

"Angelino, you can be a silly nitwit sometimes. You just ran the fastest race in school history. Yeah, I saw you cramp up. That couldn't be helped. Listen up. You were terrific. You ran the hills like nobody's business. We never would have come in second place without you and Mr. O'Day."

With that, the team piled on the two boys as they started towards the podium to accept their medals. White yelled at them to get going. Vincent got up from the pile and walked towards the stage, He saw his folks out of the corner of his eye. He limped over to them. They hugged him tight as could be. They told him how proud they were. Then John pushed him towards the podium. "It's your day to shine, Vincent."

The ride back to Don Bosco was raucous. The team finally convinced Mikey and Vincent that they had done the impossible "second in the state." One measley point away from winning the whole darn thing! The team got Vincent to sing the school song. That was a bigger feat than coming in second place! By the time they got back, it was well after dark. Mr. O'Day was standing next to his car. Apparently, he had heard about the team's success because he had a huge grin on his face

Vincent was exhausted. His nerves had calmed down. The excitement of the day had left him shot. Mikey's dad gave them a hug. "I hear you did great!" he said. "Get in the car before you fall over. Let's head home."

When Vincent finally walked into his house, everyone was at the dinner table. They stood up and sped over to him. They were talking a mile a minute. Vincent saw the smile on his mother's face. That was all it took for him to reach out and give her a big hug. "Sit down, Vincent. Have something to eat," his grandmother said above all the yammering.

Everyone sat down at the table. The next thing Vincent knew, there was a bowl of pasta covered with sauce, peppers and sausages sitting in front of him. He scarfed it down while trying to answer a gazillion questions. By the time Vincent finished half of his supper, he started yawning. The excitement of the day caught up with him. His dad nudged him with an elbow and suggested that he might want to hit the hay. Vincent headed towards the stairs. He was fast asleep in no time.

The next day was crazy. When the bus drove down Academy Avenue, tons of kids were waiting to cheer for Vincent and Mikey. The first person to meet Vincent was Cris. She got to school earlier that morning so she could finish a history project. "I heard about yesterday's race. You were great! I'm sorry I wasn't there to support you," she whispered as she gave him a hug. Every kid was yelling at him, but all he could hear was Cris.

"Thank you" was all he could mutter.

The day was a blur. Back slapping, words of encouragement, and finally, an all-school assembly that focused on the team's accomplishments. Brother Allan and Coach White praised the team. "They came out of nowhere," White exclaimed. "They did a terrific job."

Then the students started chanting Vincent and Mikey's names. "Our team put on a real show, ladies and gentlemen. Mr. Angelino developed cramps during the race and still came in 3rd place with the fastest time in school history. He and Michael O'Day were spectacular." Then the coach called the entire team up to the stage. "While Mr. Angelino and Mr. O'Day were great, remember this is a team race. Here's the rest of our team. We wouldn't have come in second at the meet without each and every member of the team."

Finally, the kids headed back to class. Cris ran into Vincent near the cafeteria. "There's a dance at school tonight. My mother is driving me there. Would you like to come with me?"

Vincent was speechless. He'd never been to a dance because he couldn't dance. Now, Cristiana was asking him to go to the dance with her. Without thinking this through, he must have nodded his head in agreement because Cris said her mom would pick him up at 6:30. Then she gave him a wink and headed off to class.

All Vincent could do was to lean against a locker and shake his head. "I'm going to a dance, Yikes!"

Since the cross-country season was over, Mikey and Vincent could take the regular bus home after school. Mikey met Vincent at his locker. Then they headed towards the bus stop. "You're pretty quiet, Vincent. What is up?"

Vincent told Mikey about the dance.

Mikey was grinning ear to ear. "You're kidding me! She asked you to go to the dance. Are you going?"

"I must have nodded yes. It was kinda out of the blue. I was a space cadet. First, the kids yelling our names out at the assembly and then Cris asks me to go to the dance. I wasn't thinking straight. I'm not sure what to do. I don't want anyone else to know about this. Can we leave it alone until we get back to Greenville?" Mikey was hepped up, but he agreed to wait until they got off the bus before saying anything more.

They hopped on the bus and headed towards the back seats. Everyone was cheering. All the kids wanted to talk about the race, so there was little time to think about the dance. As soon as they got off the bus, Vincent started heading home. "Slow down, amigo," Mikey said. "We need to talk."

Vincent started to respond. He thought about it for a second, shook his head and started walking towards the center of town. His home was not too far from there. "Vincent, what are you going to do?"

"Mikey, I'll go on one condition," Vincent said. "You have to go to the dance with me!"

It took all of two seconds for Mikey to agree. "I'll see you there." With that, Mikey headed home.

Old friends can make a difference

Cappy decided he better go find Joey. Things were getting dicey. He booked a flight right after Thanksgiving. The trip was long. First, he would fly to Chicago and then onto Kansas City. He was unhappy when the pilot announced that a huge winter storm was sliding down from northern Minnesota. Cappy hoped that he would arrive in Kansas City by early that evening. Apparently, those plans weren't going to work out.

The storm arrived just as Cappy's plane landed in Chicago. After a long wait, he was told that the airport was shutting down. All the hotels were booked solid. Cappy ended up calling a gal he had known in the old days. "Renata, it's Cappy from Connecticut."

"Capuano, you never call unless there's a problem that needs fixing. So, what is it this time?"

Cappy told her that he was stuck at the airport. There were no hotel rooms available. Renata agreed to let him stay at her house for the night. "Take the Northwest-West El to the Western station. "I'll meet you there at 5:15 p.m." Connecting with Joey would have to wait.

Renata and her brothers had worked in the back office of Bradlee's in Connecticut. They helped Cappy way back when. As a result, Cappy bought her family a printing business in Chicago. The mob sent lots of business their way. Over time, Renata took over the business. Eventually,she would be set for life. At one point, Cappy dated her. That ended when she learned he was banging two other girls at the same time as he was dating her. Renata was one smart cookie. She knew which side of the bread was buttered, so she didn't make a big fuss.

But the light in her bedroom stopped shining when she learned that she was being two timed.

Renata was waiting at the station when Cappy arrived. She drove him to her house and parked her Caddy in the driveway. "Are you hungry?"

"Yep" was all she got. Renata fixed him a salami hoagie and a dry martini. Then she asked what was going on.

"Whadda you mean?"

"Capuano, you haven't shown your face in Chicago since the mob flare up in 1983!"

"Something's going on in Kansas City that needs my attention."

"Kansas is a long way from Oz, Toto," she said with that wry smile of hers.

"You're still the same pushy broad that I used to know."

"Cappy, that's why you made a play for me. You like women who'll stand up to your bluster. So, what gives?"

"I sent an enforcer to KC to settle a dispute—someone the local cops didn't know. Most of my strong arms were involved in a power play in Boston, so I had to use a new guy."

"Do I know him?" Renata asked.

"His name is Joey D. He's from Waterbury. Young, fearless, and wanting to make a name for himself. He may be in over his head. I decided to fly to KC and get the lay of the land."

"So, what's going on in Kansas City?"

Cappy laid out the situation. "Sounds like there's a lot going on." Renata said. "How about if I go with you to Kansas City? This is a quiet time of year. I could take off for a few days and help you square this up."

"Let me think about that. We can talk more after I eat."

Renata left him to himself and went out to meet a friend. She got back to her place about nine.

"I'd like it if you came with me to Kansas City, Renata. Why don't you pack your bags and call the airport to see if we can get tickets to Kansas City?" he said.

"Before we go too much further, let's get one thing straight, Buster," Renata said defiantly. "I'll go to KC with you, but I'm not sleeping with you!"

"Yeah, I got it," he said. Renata headed for the phone.

The weather had worsened. Flights were backed up for two days. There were no seats to be had. Cappy was in a rage. Renata sat him down on a leather couch. "Listen, Knucklehead! No amount of Italian swear words is going to change the situation. It's time for Plan B."

"What are you talking about, Scorpini?" She casually walked over to him and stomped on his left foot. Cappy grabbed his ankle and began to yelp. She paid no attention. A minute later, Cappy's yips diminished. "If you ever call me Scorpini again, there'll be hell to pay."

"Okay, okay!" Cappy yowled. "What is Plan B?"

Renata told him they were going to drive to Kansas City. She had watched the news. Once they got past Normal, Illinois, the snow would lighten up. She thought it would take a day to drive to Kansas City. It would be a long drive, but it could be done if they were careful. She'd make sure they were careful.

Cappy began to grumble. Renata stopped him short. "Your original plan was to take a 1 p.m. flight to Kansas City tomorrow. With my plan, we will be there by 8 pm tomorrow. You won't have to rent a car. You're riding with me. I have a newfangled phone in the car in case we have problems. That's it. Put up or shut up!"

Cappy didn't like losing control, but he had little choice. "Okay, you win," he spat out. Renata told him to put his bags in the second bedroom and get some shuteye. He limped towards the bedroom without saying a word.

Early the next morning, there was a rapping on his door. "Get your backside up and outta bed, Capuano. We hit the road in 45 minutes." He started swearing.

Renata poked her head in the door, glared at him and told him to shut his trap. "Time's a wasting, bucko." With that, she left him to his sputtering.

They were on the road by 6:45 a.m. Renata had filled two thermoses with coffee. In the back seat was a cooler filled with egg salad sandwiches, fruit, and caramel rolls. "We'll save time if we eat on the road." Soon they were headed toward St. Louis. They finally pulled into Kansas City, Missouri about 7:15 p.m. They were dog tired, so they found two rooms at the Hyatt. Tomorrow they would relocate to Kansas City, Kansas.

Even though it was late, Cappy called Dolan. That did not go well. Dolan was pissed. "You told me D'Amato could handle my problem. Now, my laundromat is history. Burned to the ground. One Shot had his one shot. As far as I'm concerned, Joey's gone. How do you plan to fix this mess?"

109

"I just drove into town. I'll find Joey in the morning."

Dolan wasn't a happy camper, but he agreed to sit tight. Cappy hung up. He suggested that they have dinner at the hotel and then hit the hay. Renata was okay with that idea. When they got back from the restaurant, Renata placed a 9 a.m. wake-up call. They slept like babies.

The next morning, they headed to Kansas. First, they decided to find a rental property that would be close to Dolan's laundromat. They stopped at a realty office and found a two-bedroom house nearby. The place was immediately available. Cappy wasn't happy to have to rent the place for a month. Renata reminded him that he had no real idea of what he was getting into. He reluctantly agreed. An hour later and $800 poorer, they were on +heir way to find One Shot.

Renata can be the real deal

It took two hours to track Joey down. They found him at the Corner Tap, a small dive not far from Dolan's place. He was with a young blonde called Crystal, He had a bottle of Pabst with one hand and fondled her breasts with the other. Crystal was so drunk that you could have poured her into the bottle. Joey looked up to find Cappy and some hot moll standing in front of him. "Whadda say, Cappy. What are you doing here?" It was easy to tell that Joey had guzzled a snootful of booze. Cappy pulled him off the stool and headed towards the door while Renata took care of Crystal.

Cappy drove to their bungalow. He and Renata coaxed Joey into one of the bedrooms. He fell asleep within 10 seconds. Then they helped Crystal into the other bedroom. She stumbled towards the bathroom with Renata right behind. A few minutes later, Renata asked Cappy to help her. They got Crystal to bed without further delay. Then they headed to the living room.

They were starved for sleep. There was no time for that. There was no food in the bungalow. Renata suggested that they go out to eat and then head to a supermarket. "Joey and his lady friend aren't getting up any time soon. Cappy and Renata drove to a barbecue place they had seen on the way back from the Corner Tap.

They didn't talk to each other until they were seated. "So, Cappy, Joey is your guy! I'm not impressed. He is out of his depth." Cappy glared at her but he didn't say a word. She paid no attention to his glare and kept right on going. "What are you gonna do now?"

"Once the dirtbag sobers up," Cappy said, "we'll drop Crystal at her place. Then, we'll have a conversation with One Shot." Cappy signaled the waitress. They both ordered scotch and ribs. Cappy didn't want to talk about Joey or anything else, so they ate in silence. Once they finished eating, they stopped at a nearby grocery store. Four bags of groceries later, they headed home.

Renata went in to check on Crystal. The girl was starting to stir. "Who are you?" Crystal slurred.

"I'm your fairy godmother, Crystal. We need to get you cleaned up and get you home." Renata began to shift Crystal out of the bed when she started gagging.

Renata yelled for Cappy. "Come here right now! I need help." They dragged Crystal to the tub. She promptly threw up. Then she started to cry. Renata told Cappy to clean up the bathroom mess. He resisted. "You either clean up the tub or the girl. Which is it gonna be?" Cappy decided that the bathroom would be his domain.

An hour later, Crystal was shoved into the Caddy. Thankfully, she only lived two miles away. Renata made it back just in time to see Cappy leading One Shot out of the bathroom. "Is everything okay?"

"Yep, I got everything covered. I'll be back as soon as I get Joey back to bed."

Cappy found Renata taking a sheet off the bed. He knew better than to smirk, so he asked Renata if she wanted a sandwich. The bedding was smelly, so she held her breath and nodded in agreement. After a while, she slunk into a kitchen chair. In front of her was a roast beef sandwich with slices of tomato and some potato chips. A cold bottle of Miller's was by her side. "Cappy, these past few hours have been draining and we haven't touched the hard stuff!"

"Hopefully," Cappy replied, "Joey is less trouble than his playmate." They looked at each other and laughed.

The long day rolled into evening. The good news was that Joey hadn't moved a muscle. At 8 o'clock, Renata let out a huge yawn. "I'm dog tired. I'm going to hit the hay. I hope we can get some real work done tomorrow. She headed to the empty bedroom and closed the door. Cappy found himself on the couch. At that point, he did not care where he slept. It had been a long two days. He had no trouble falling asleep.

The next morning, Cappy woke up to the sound of barfing. Joey was hugging the stool. Sweat poured off him like a leaky faucet. Cappy turned away without saying a word and went into Renata's bedroom. She was sleeping through the racket. Cappy headed back to Joey. "Get your arse off the pot. I have coffee brewing." Joey wanted no part of Cappy or his coffee.

The next thing Joey knew, he was dripping with ice water from head to toe. A towel was thrown in his face as he was jerked to his feet. He knew better than to open his yap. He dried off and headed to the kitchen. It took three cups of hot java before Joey could say anything. Finally, Cappy questioned him about the laundromat.

By that time, Renata had gotten up. She listened as Joey told his tale. "Let me get this straight. You boosted a truck and kidnapped two people. And one of those people was stabbed! You never even met up with Baxter! Pally, you are one dumb Wop." Cappy was fuming.

The room was still. Then Cappy started up again. "You are a hit man, One Shot. An enforcer. You aren't a negotiator. Baxter needed to see a gun in your hand. He'd get the picture right away. Now our client is livid, his business is burnt to a crisp, and Baxter controls everything. The only thing we have is a mutt named

113

Wing Nut in a barn 60 miles from here. Have I got this right?" Joey nodded. "Get back in that bedroom. Don't come back til you are sober as a stone. I need time to think."

Renata sat down across from Cappy. After a while, she turned to Cappy. "You just walked into one hell of a mess!" she said with a sneer. He glared at her. Finally, he said, "I am very aware of what this jerk dumped in my lap. Can you believe this crap?"

Renata turned to him. "Joey did okay in Greenville, but that must have been a case of dumb luck." "Cappy, I'm here to help if you want help." When he didn't respond, she suggested that they go out for a drive. "There is a World War I museum just across the river. You know I'm a history buff," she said. "Dirtbag won't be sober for a while. Going out might take the edge off."

Cappy shook his head. "We're going to some stupid museum. Eek!" he said to himself. He knew he better shut his mouth. He tossed Renata the keys and away they went. Surprisingly, the museum turned out to be very good. They wandered through the place for two hours. Then they decided to grab some food. They found a luncheonette a mile or so away. It was 2 p.m. by the time they got back to the bungalow.

Joey was lying on the couch with a towel over his head when they walked in. He sprang up from the couch with a gun in his hand. The gun was pointed in their direction "Whoa, Joey, it is just us!" Cappy shouted.

He dropped his gun to his side and swung his head back and forth. "I guess I messed up big time. I should have called you when things got out of hand. What are we gonna do?"

Renata saw that Cappy was ready to blow a gasket, so she suggested that they sit down and figure out what to do next.

Cappy and Renata sat down. Cappy pointed to a rocking chair. "Joey, sit over there. All you needed to do was to call me! It would have been a cakewalk. Now, it feels like we had a train wreck in the middle of the night and I'm the only emergency room doc on duty."

Renata let Cappy know that she was all in. "Whatever you need, you will get! Let's forget the last few days and come up with a plan."

At that moment, Cappy started screaming at Joey and they were off to the races. Renata finally stepped between them and grabbed their shirt collars. "This is getting us nowhere!" Clearly, she had a mind for order. The other two were ready for disorder. "Sit your asses down and cool off."

"Okay, I get it," Cappy finally said. "Where do we go from here?"

Renata started off. "Baxter sees himself as the kingpin. He makes the rules and makes sure they are enforced. No different than what happens in New England. Baxter sees Joey as a mug who wants to take over. She wondered what might happen if someone torched a building in Cappy's backyard. She got an earfull of crapola from Cappy about how he'd tear Baxter to pieces.

"Enough of this macho bullshit," she said. "Killing the guy and his hick country cowboys gets us nowhere—no $50k, no laundromat, and there'd be lawmen all over our tails in a November second."

Her little speech temporarily settled things down. She got up and headed to the bathroom. This was a simple ruse on her part to cool the two of them off. When she came back, she sat down with a thump. "Okay, what do we know about Baxter? Is he married? Where does he come from? Finally, where did he get his bankroll?"

Clearly, nobody knew one blessed thing about Baxter except for his hillbilly connections. Renata's business experience started to show itself. "This creep does not know us. Maybe we should put our listening ears on and find out more about him. In the meanwhile, I have a guy in Chicago who owes me big time. He investigates financial fraud. Maybe he can nose around Baxter's business ventures. Hopefully, we can get a handle on where he gets his money. It should take my guy three days to get back to us. Then we can make plans."

Renata turned to Joey. "Get your ass back up to the farm. Bring Nut back tomorrow. Blindfold this nutcase and make sure he is tied up. "Can you handle that?"

"Yeah, I can handle that. Then what?" One Shot continued to grouse.

Renata had heard enough. She went over to the counter, picked up Joey's car keys and threw them in his face. "Get out of here before I do something I might regret!" Joey was stunned. He gaped at Renata for a second and then hustled out the door.

Holy Moly! Cristiana asked you to do what?

When Cristiana asked Detta if she'd be a chaperone at the school dance, she agreed without hesitation. She knew Cristiana wanted to go to the dance, so she thought she'd kill two birds with one stone. "I can help at school and keep a watchful eye on my impetuous daughter." Little did she know that Cristiana had invited Vincent to the dance. "You did what?" she said when she learned about the change in plans.

Cris reminded her mother of all the "Benedetta" stories she heard every time she went her grandmother's. "Grandma G tells me that I'm a gentle whisper compared to you, Mom."

Detta knew it might be better to quit while she was ahead. "What time did you tell this boy that we would pick him up?"

Cris became very coy. She smiled sweetly. "We should be at his house by 6:25." Then she headed upstairs.

Detta sat down at the kitchen table and started shaking her head. She hadn't paid much attention to who they were picking up. "Oh my gosh! Is this boy any relation to Maria Angelino?" Detta grabbed the phone and called Dante's sister, Angela.

"Angie, I've been meaning to call you. This shooting at Viterio's is just awful." Angie jumped right in. "Dante and I have known Maria forever."

"Really, Angie? I don't think I have met her. Does she live in town?" Angie went from there. Fifteen minutes later, Detta had the whole story including the fact that

Maria had a son named Vincent. Shortly thereafter, Angie rang off. "Dante's going to flip out when I tell him that Cristiana asked Vincent Angelino to the dance."

Dinner was a chaotic, so Detta held off telling Dante about Vincent. Dante was going out with some friends to a hockey game, so he wouldn't be home for dinner. She arranged for Julie Perkins, their regular babysitter, to watch the boys so she could chaperone the dance.

Detta got to Vincent's house at 6:25. He was standing with his nose to the window of the side door. When he saw them pull into his driveway, he wrestled the door open and hurried to their car. Cris was sitting in the back seat when he opened the door. He handed her a red rose. "This is for you" he said shyly. Detta looked in the mirror. She could see that Cris had put on her "I got you" smile. "Thank you so much. You are so thoughtful." Detta winced a little.

"Mrs. Bonfigore," Vincent stuttered, "I also brought a rose for you. My father wanted me to thank you for all you've done to help our family."

Detta was surprised. "This is some kind of kid," she thought. She smiled graciously. "Cristiana told me all about your cross-country prowess. Your folks must be very proud of you." Detta could tell that Vincent was embarrassed when she saw his face redden. Cristiana saved the day by rattling off all the kids who were going to the dance. That settled Vincent down. Detta decided that it might be a good time to get going. She started up the car and headed to the dance.

The evening flew by. Detta was careful to stay away from Cristiana and Vincent. Cristiana had pulled her mother aside when they got to the dance. "Don't hover, Mom." Detta made sure she could watch them from afar. One of Vincent's friends had shown up just after the music started to play. Cristiana, Vincent, and his friend spent most of the night together. Vincent might be a very gifted runner, but Detta could see that he couldn't dance a lick. At that point, some of Cristiana's friends joined them and they all went out on the dance floor when the disc jockey spun "The Power of Love."

"They are pretty innocent," she murmured. Suddenly, she felt her right sleeve being tugged. Brother Allan was standing by her side. "Hi," he said. "It's great to see you. Thanks so much for helping out tonight."

Detta told him that her feet needed a rest. They walked over to nearby chairs and sat down. "Detta, I have a favor to ask. My friends call me Allan. How about you call me Allan from now on.

Detta smiled. "Allan it is. I came tonight to chaperone. It turns out that my motives have changed. Unbeknownst to me, Cristiana invited Vincent Angelino to the dance. I've tried to keep my distance."

Allan smiled. "Keeping your distance tonight might be one of the hardest things you've had to do in a long time." They laughed. Detta knew Allan was correct.

Allan quickly changed the direction of the conversation. "I hear your fundraising efforts are progressing." They spent several minutes talking about the fundraiser.

Then Allan stood up. "Thanks for all you are doing for the Angelinos," he said. "I'd better check in with the other chaperones to make sure they're doing okay." With that, he headed towards the cafeteria. Before anyone knew it, the disc jockey, was playing the last song of the night. The song was called "The Heat is Up" or something like that. Detta wasn't up on the music of the day. She finally found the kids standing near the coat rack. Cristiana introduced Mikey to her mom. "Can you give Mikey a ride back home?"

"I'd be happy to!" Then they headed west on Route 6.

When they got back home, Detta found Julie watching television. "Where's Dante?"

"Mr. Bonfigore came back to the house shortly after you left. He asked me to tell you that he had to go out of town unexpectedly. Detta was furious, but she kept her temper under control. Then she drove Julie home.

When she came back, Cristiana was sitting at the kitchen table. "I know I surprised you tonight, Mom. I hope you didn't mind my asking Vincent to the dance."

Detta put her around her daughter and gave her a hug. "Vincent seems like a wonderful young man. But next time, give me a little heads up about your plans. I know you are in high school now, but remember, to me, you are still my little girl."

She winked at her daughter. Then they headed upstairs. Detta opened the door to her bedroom and found a note from Dante. Apparently, he had to drive up to Boston for an emergency meeting. They'd be staying overnight. This was the third time in the past six months that Dante had spent the night in Boston. This was becoming a bad habit. Detta didn't appreciate this. She vowed to talk to Dante about this when he returned.

The next day brought a significant taste of the winter to come. The wind was coming in off Narragansett Bay. It was chilly. Detta could feel the cold even though she was under a down comforter. She stayed in bed for a while. Then she remembered that it was the Saturday before Thanksgiving.

Detta had been so focused on the Angelino's dilemma that she pushed Turkey Day to the back of her brain. There was a lot that needed to get done. Detta's family always spent Thanksgiving at her house. That meant nearly twenty mouths to feed and a house to clean. She looked at the alarm clock. "Oh my gosh! It's eight thirty." She sprang out of bed.

Detta put work clothes on and scampered down the stairs. Nico was sitting at the kitchen table with a book in his hand. "What on earth are you doing?" Detta knew that reading was not one of Nico's favorite things to do. He looked to his mom and told her that he had to do a book report on Robinson Crusoe.

"Guess what, Ma, this is a really cool story." Detta put aside her need to clean, sat back and reveled as Nico shared the story with her.

When he finally took a breath, Detta let him know how proud she was of him. "I want to hear more, but right now I need to start cleaning the house for Thanksgiving. Would you like to help me?"

Cleaning wasn't high on Nico's list, but he loved his mom. She hadn't been around a lot lately, so he thought it would be a great time to spend some "alone" time with her. They sat down and had a bowl of cereal. After that, the vacuum cleaner was fired up and away they went. The other kids heard the noise coming from the kitchen. They trundled downstairs shortly thereafter. They had some oatmeal. Then, they changed into work clothes and were assigned jobs to do. "It won't take long, if we work together." Detta said with a grin.

By 11:30 a.m., the living room and the kitchen were spotless. Cristiana did most of the heavy lifting in the living room and the two younger kids had picked up the toys in the family room. Detta asked Cristiana to call

Sammy's Sub Shop and order some food to go. Cris was on the phone in a hot second.

Sammy took their order. "Your neighbor, Billy Williams will deliver the sandwiches."

When Billy arrived, Detta met him at the back door. She took the bags of food and told him to wait a moment. When she returned, she gave Billy enough money to cover the cost of the sandwiches as well as a big tip for him. Billy was flabbergasted at the size of his tip. He turned and headed towards his bike. He smiled all the way back to the sub shop.

It's time to confront your fears

Across town, Vincent woke up with a start and looked at his alarm clock. "Nine a.m.!" he exclaimed. He jumped out of bed, got dressed, and headed downstairs. His brothers started giggling when he sat down at the kitchen table. They began pointing their forefingers at him. "Vincent has a girlfriend!"

That didn't sit well with Vincent. He got up and headed towards his brothers. Luckily, his father stepped between them. "Why don't you get yourself some breakfast. Nonna made scrambled eggs and bacon. There is some fresh Danish pastry on the counter. Your brothers are finished making fun of you. Aren't you, guys?

The younger brothers knew better than to say anything, so they sat down and ate their breakfast. Vincent sat down with them but didn't eat a thing. As soon as the younger brothers were finished, they cleaned their plates and headed upstairs.

Vincent's dad asked how the dance went. Vincent started to blurt out "I don't know" but thought better of it. He shared what had happened.

"It sounds like you had a good time, son."

"I did," Vincent said. "It helped that Mikey was there. He's so much better around girls than I'll ever be."

John started to laugh and then decided it might be better to choke it down. "I'm not laughing at you, son. You just made it sound so funny." With that, they both started laughing. Given all the turmoil that they had gone through, it felt good to laugh.

After a few minutes of chuckling, Vincent got up from the table and grabbed some grub. He had taken a few bites of the pastry when his dad sat down next to him. "Yesterday, Detective Maloney called. He told me that he found an artist who might be able help you remember what the shooter looked like. Maloney wants to bring her over to meet with you next week."

Vincent looked up. "I'm not sure I understand. Why does the detective want to bring an artist over to meet with me?"

John looked him straight in the eye. "He is having a hard time finding anyone who matches your description of the shooter. He hopes she can make a sketch of this zit faced guy. I told Detective Maloney that I'd talk to you about helping the police find the killer."

"Would you be there, Dad?" Vincent asked pleadingly.

"Of course. I'll be with you. I know how hard this has been for you. I'll be there if you want me to be there." After a few more minutes of discussing what he should do, Vincent decided to meet the artist if it would help the police find the killer.

John phoned Maloney. "Bill, have you been able to contact the artist?"

"Yeah, John, I spoke with her. Unfortunately, there was a death in her family. We had to put off our meeting. She can meet Vincent on Monday if that works for you."

"Bill, I spoke to Vincent. He's wary about this whole thing, but he's willing to meet the artist if it helps you find the guy who shot Maria."

"That's great news. Thanks, John," Maloney said. "I know this has been hard on your family. I appreciate your help with this. We can be at your house when Vincent comes home from school. Will that work?"

"I think so, Bill."

"Great! I'll see you then." John hung up and told his son that the artist would be coming over on Monday. After John answered all of Vincent's questions, he suggested that Vincent might want to rake some leaves in the backyard.

Maloney showed up at the Angelino's at 4:15 p.m. on Monday. Standing next to the detective was a very strange looking woman. "John and Vincent, this is MarJean McConnell. MarJean works at the Art Institute of Boston. She also assists the Boston Police Department on cases like yours. She's here to help you remember what the shooter looked like."

This woman looked like she stepped right out of a three-story apartment building in the middle of Greenwich Village. She wore a floppy purple hat with white plumes and some type of red and blue dress that hung down to her ankles.

Vincent's dad turned toward the artist. "Ms. McConnell, we've never done anything like this before. What would you like us to do?"

She turned to Vincent and started talking in this high creaky voice. "Do I need to have this big old detective stay here to protect me, Vincent?"

Vincent snapped his head around to look at her. He wasn't sure what to say. He finally shook his head and muttered "No, Ma'am, I think we can handle things."

"Vincent," she said, "I was only teasing." Vincent's eyes widened. Then he began to smile. "You were having me on, weren't you! Miss McConnell."

MarJean looked at Vincent. She had a twinkle in her eye. "Vincent," she said, "You are one sharp cookie. I guess you caught me red handed."

"So, let's sit down at the kitchen table and get to work on this sketch. Detective Maloney and your dad can go to that nice little coffeeshop I saw down the road from here. I think if we ask nicely, maybe they'll bring back some chocolate donuts. What do you think?" Vincent nodded vigorously. "Detective Maloney, could you give us an hour or so to work on this sketch?" Maloney agreed. He and John headed out the back door. With that, MarJean led Vincent to the kitchen table.

When Maloney opened the driver's side door, he turned to John. He stopped short when he saw that John's jaw had dropped a ton. John raised his eyebrows. "Is she the real deal, Bill? She seems pretty weird to me."

"She does seem weird with the clothes and what all, but the Boston PD tells me she's the best artist this side of New York City."

John shook his head in wonderment. "If you say so, Bill!" Then John went around to the other side of the police cruiser and hopped in.

They drove to the cafe and sat down at a corner table. They ordered a cup of black coffee and passed on donuts. Then they chewed the fat for a while. Come to find out that they had both enlisted in the army right after high school. That gave them plenty to talk about.

Bill and John were enjoying their time together so much that they paid no attention to the time. Bill looked at his watch. "Holy Cow, look at the time. We'd better get back."

They were out the front door when John remembered the donuts. "I can't forget those chocolate donuts, Bill." John headed towards the counter and picked up a sack of donuts Then he jumped into Bill's cruiser and they headed back to the Angelino's.

It was cold outside, so Maloney left his cruiser running. Vincent and MarJean were standing by the kitchen table grinning at each other when John and Bill walked into the house. "How is the sketch going?" Maloney asked.

"We finished that a while ago. We've been talking about some common interests while we waited for you. Vincent has a good eye for details. I think I can get something in your hands by next week."

"I nearly forgot, Ms. McConnell," John said. "Here are the donuts I promised to bring back."

"It is nearly dinner time Mr. Angelino," she said with a smile. "Maybe Vincent should keep them all." Vincent's eyes lit up at the thought of all those chocolate donuts.

With that, MarJean headed towards the front door. She turned to Vincent. "You were great. Thanks so much for trusting me. Remember to be on the lookout for Anne's sisters. Maloney caught up to her as she walked towards the front door.

Bill reached out to shake John's hand. "Thanks again for your help and your patience." Then he turned to Vincent. "Son," he said, "I hope this drawing helps us find the shooter. I know that this was scary for you. I appreciate your help." With that, he left Vincent and his dad to themselves.

John wanted to hear how things went with the artist. Vincent told his dad that as soon as he and the detective had left, "MarJean pulled a sketch pad out of her bag.

Then, she asked lots of questions about the shooter's face, his hair color. Stuff like that. The next thing I knew, she started to draw. She was amazing. She only took out her eraser four times! When she was done, her drawing looked exactly like the shooter's face."

John was amazed. "That sounds pretty cool! So, before you go on Vincent, I've got a question for you. When we came back from the coffee shop, you were grinning at each other. What was that all about?"

Vincent told his dad that MarJean had started off by asking him what he liked about school. The next thing Vincent knew, he was telling her about the state cross country meet.

"It turns out that MarJean knows a woman named Anne Hird. You probably don't remember Ms. Hird. She placed fourth in the women's division of last year's Boston Marathon. Fourth place! She has two sisters who go to Bayview Academy. They are on the cross-country team with two of Ms. Hird's sisters. We ended up having a long conversation about that. At first, I thought MarJean was kinda strange, but she turned out to be cool."

Things are in the works

The following Tuesday, Maloney met John at the City Sanitation office. "So, John, how are things going?"

"Well, Maria is beginning to regain some strength in her shoulder. We met with her surgeon. She needs another operation to put something called a fixator on her shoulder bone. With any luck, she could be back to normal in six months. The surgery is scheduled for a week from today. We're starting to feel hopeful!"

"I'm glad to hear that things are getting better. I know that you are busy, so let me get to the reason why I came by today. I met with Ms. McConnell. She said that Vincent was terrific. She thinks her drawing is spot on."

Bill pulled out a folded piece of drawing paper from his satchel and gave it to John. "Here's her drawing. It looks like Vincent's description of the shooter. I set up a meeting with the public relations officer for the Providence Police Department. He's setting up a meeting with the police beat writer at the newspaper. Also, one of my neighbors works for WJAR television. He's willing to talk to the news producer at the station. If we can get the newspaper and WJAR to run the story, we have a good chance of finding our shooter."

"Bill," John said stiffly, "I have one request. Please make every attempt to keep Vincent's name out of this story. We've enough trouble now without letting the shooter know that Vincent saw him." Maloney nodded his head before John finished his sentence. He promised there would be no mention of Vincent in the story.

Marty gets a real job

The next week, Marty drove Mr. B to Boston. Mr. B was meeting with the Boston head capo. "Marty, I want you to sit in on this meeting." Marty was surprised. "It's time for you to see how things are done at the top." Mr. B indicated that some of the mob's businesses had the potential to grow. "I think you should be more involved with our business." With that, they headed into the back room of a machine shop. Mr. B introduced Marty around. Marty got some strange looks, but nobody said a word.

The discussion revolved around the need to expand the sale of stolen cigarettes throughout New England. From what Marty could gather, the mob hijacked a trailer or two filled with cartons of cigarettes each month. Then they move the cartons to their folks who own drug stores and gas stations in New England. That idea worked swell until the state police got word of the scam.

During the meeting, there were lots of angry voices complaining about the losses being incurred. One guy hit the nail on the head. "We're losing lots of money on this. Some of our best guys are headed to prison."

Marty nudged Mr. B. "Can I have a word with you in private?" Mr. B nodded in agreement.

Dante stood up. "I'm hungry. How about we get some lunch and meet back here in 45 minutes? That gives us time to figure things out!" Everyone agreed. The room was empty in two minutes.

Mr. B and Marty headed out to a little Italian restaurant owned by a friend of Mr. B's. Once they sat down, an older guy with a huge mustache, baggy pants and a white shirt that had seen better days, limped over to them. The waiter pulled out a wad of paper and a stubby pencil. "Mr. B, how are you doing?"

Mr. B smiled. "Antonio, you're looking pretty good for an old fart."

That brought a glimmer of a smile to the older guy's face. "You want the usual, Mr. B?"

"Make that two, one for me and one for my friend. Is there any Grappa in the back room?"

"Coming right up," Antonio said with a smile that lifted his mustache to his cheeks. As soon as Antonio left, Mr. B was in Marty's face."

"So, you got a plan for me?"

"Mr. B, there are two ways to go."

"Okay, clue me in!"

Marty could sense Mr. B's impatience, so it was time to plunge right in. "We might be able to beat the police at their own game. Every few weeks, we snitch on our own guys. We make sure there are cases of cigarettes laying around in one of our warehouses. A "community minded" citizen calls the police and alerts them about the contraband. We control what they see and what they don't see."

That got Mr. B's attention. Marty continued, "We could run more product through our system if we knew where the state police might be on any given day. Wherever they go, we're somewhere else. We'd have to spend some dough to take care of the guys who were caught, but we'd be way ahead of the game." Marty sat back and wondered what Mr. B would make of this idea. The answer came immediately.

"Now that's a plan, Marty! It might just work. Good thinking! Before we head back to the meeting, tell me about your second idea."

"Mr. B, it might be time to identify state employees who are into the mob for bets that didn't go their way. There must be some folks who are into us for big money. We could pay off their debts if they're able to share information about the state's plans to deal with us."

"It would be expensive, but we'd know every step the state police would be taking. If we don't get cooperation from our reluctant informers, we'll feed them to the wolves."

"Two for two in the idea department, Marty. I think sending you to that Ivy League school in upstate New York might have been a good idea after all."

Mr. B decided that Marty should lay out both ideas when they got back to the meeting. The Boston guys were shocked. They thought Marty was just a whippersnapper. However, after Marty outlined the possibilities, it was clear that the ideas had gotten their attention. It took two days to work out an agreement. Not everyone was excited to have a young mutt lead the way, but they quickly got over that when Dante slammed his hand down on the table and told them to get a grip.

Eventually, Marty was tasked with setting up Plan A. The team needed to be in full gear within the next two months. Marty knew this was too big for one person. Most of the men who were available to help were slackers. Dante picked the two least offensive of these cowboys and told them they were on Marty's team.

Mr. B agreed with Marty's assessment. "This plan needs to get rolling."

Marty set up a team meeting. "OK guys, here is a list of tasks that need to be completed. No grousing. I want you to gather all this info by the time we meet again or there will be consequences." Marty hoped these guys would follow through with their tasks.

When the Boston meeting had finally finished up, Dante and Marty were exhausted. Two long days of meetings with very few breaks will do that to a person. They packed up and headed home. Mr. B decided to make a little side trip. Marty ended up driving Mr. B back to the Cape. Dante spent the night with Trixie while Marty shacked up with a friend who tended bar at a club in Sandwich. After a little "fooling around," Marty slept like a baby.

Oops

Marty arrived back at Trixie's place nice and early the next morning. Mr. B said he'd be ready to hit the road around 8:30 a.m. "Don't be late!" Marty was in front of Trixie's place at 8:25. Marty waited patiently.

Just after 9:30, Mr. B opened the back door of Trixie's place. As soon as he got in the car, Marty knew that something was up. There was steam coming out of Dante's ears. "What is going on, boss?"

"Marty, better for you to just drive us back home. You don't wanna know and I don't want to tell you."

Marty got the picture. Silence was golden. By the time they hit Route 195, Mr. B started to shake his head. "Marty, we got big trouble. You need to call Doc Mastriano right away. Have him meet me at that bar down the street from Augie's Barber Shop this afternoon."

Marty muffled a "Will do."

Several minutes later, Mr. B lowered his eyes and his voice and told Marty that Trixie was pregnant.

Marty was stunned. "How could this happen?"

Long story short, Miss Trixie forgot to take her birth control pill the last time she and Mr. B were together. That oops was seven weeks along. "Holy Crap! This is major league trouble, Mr. B. I'll call Mastriano as soon as we get back to town."

"I gotta get back to Providence pronto." Dante said. "The boss will want hear about our Massachusett meeting. I can meet Mastriano after that.

They pulled up to the vending business that was a front for the mob's operations. After dropping Mr. B off, Marty went to meet the doctor. Mastriano's office was down the street from St. Joe's Hospital. Marty wasted no time heading to Mastriano's waiting room. It was full of crying babies and tired mothers. Luckily, the receptionist knew Marty. Marty saw the doctor immediately. Marty found him in his office with a cigarette in his mouth.

Mastriano looked more like a vagrant than a doctor. He was a spindly guy with a bulbous nose and a receding hairline. His nose told the tale. Dante had helped him out when his taste for hooch overcame his ability to heal. Now, Mastriano was just another one of Mr. B's guys. Marty told the doc about the problem.

Mastriano shook his head as if to say, "What will happen next? I can see Mr. B this afternoon. I should be available after 4 p.m. My nurse keeps my schedule. She'll make sure that I'll be there." With that, Mastriano headed back to see his pregnant patients and Marty went back to wait for Mr. B.

Marty nursed a Coke for about an hour. Finally, Mr. B's meeting finished up. Marty drove Mr. B to his laundromat in Johnston. He and Dino met in the back office. Marty hated going to the laundromat because it always smelled like moldy detergent, but whatever Lola wants.

Dino and Mr. B spent two hours going over the details of Mr. B's meetings with the boss. During a break in the meeting, Marty managed to call Mastriano's office. When he finally got on the phone, Marty said Mr. B could meet him at the Lucky Seven near Augie's at 4:30. The doctor knew where the bar was. He promised to be on time. "Don't let us down, Doc. There is a lot riding on this."

Marty drove Mr. B to the Lucky Seven. Mr. B knew Willy, the bar owner since they were ragamuffins. He helped Willy get an interest free loan to buy the place, so Willy was always willing to let Mr. B use the meeting room in the back of his bar whenever he needed it.

The doc strolled into Willy's back room with a martini in his hand. "Dante, I hear you have a little problem."

Mr. B glared at the doc. "First thing you can do, Mastriano, is get rid of that goddamn drink. I bailed you out the last time you had a problem with booze. That's the last time you'll get my help. You need to be as sober as a stone!" The doc put his drink down right away. Suddenly, he was all ears.

Mr. B told Mastriano about Trixie. "She doesn't want this baby and guess what, Doc, I don't want to have a baby either. What can we do to take care of this?" Mastriano started fiddling with his tie. Marty finally reached over and whapped him in the face. "Mr. B needs your help, Doc. Stop being such a jerk!! What can you do for us right here, right now?"

The doctor straightened up. "I know a woman in South County. She has performed abortions on the quiet. I could call her." Marty turned to the doc. "This has to be on the QT. Call me back with the right answer."

Marty gave Mastriano a piece of paper with a phone number on it. Then Mr. B stood up and headed out the back door of the bar. Marty followed close behind. When they got in the car, Mr. B held up his hand. "Thanks for taking over. With all that happened, I wasn't on top of my game. Trixie's surprise was more than I bargained for."

Marty could tell that Mr. B was wiped out. They wasted no time driving back to Greenville. Mr. B hurried towards the back door of his home. Marty sat in the car for a while. "What in heck am I doing? "Here I am with an Ivy League education, a degree in economics no less, and I find myself being a lap dog on a leash on the one hand, and a nursemaid to a drunken gynecologist on the other. A servant no less. My friends are on the ladder of success. I'm going nowhere fast. Something better change soon, or I'm on the next train out of here."

Just who do you think you are

As soon as Dante hit the back door, Detta was all over him like glue. When Marty opened the back door, she stopped her tirade. "Marty, Dante and I need to have a little talk." She was steamed, so Marty left as quickly as possible. Detta got in Dante's face. "Where have you been? You up and leave the house. You don't tell me where you are going or when you will be back. That stuff might work with Dino or Marty, but not with me!"

Dante fumbled with an excuse. Then Detta started in on him. "You must think I'm a complete idiot. I don't know much about what you do, but I know that our laundromats won't pay for us to have a house in the country, three kids in private schools and a new car every other year. I keep my nose out of your business. I don't want to know what you do. But I draw the line when your business gets in the way of our family."

Dante tried to put his arm around Detta. She was having none of it. She glared at him and told him that she made up the guest bedroom. "I think you should sleep there tonight. We'll talk about this tomorrow after the kids leave for school." With that, she headed upstairs to their bedroom and he headed downstairs for a beer or three.

Dante had two too many beers and ended up falling asleep on the couch in his office. He didn't walk up the stairs to the kitchen until well after 10 the next morning. His head felt like a snare drum at a bad jazz concert.

Dante made it to the bathroom. Then all hell broke loose. He finally shuffled out to the kitchen and found a tall glass of ice water and some Alka-Seltzer on the table. Detta was sitting at the table with a wicked smirk on her face. "What is so goddamn funny, Detta?"

"I don't often get to see you get drunk one day and then, the next day, have a close encounter with the toilet bowl."

"If you weren't seeing double right now, Dante, you would know what was funny. You look awful." Dante didn't say a word. He put his head on the table and groaned. Detta pushed a glass of water over to him. "Drink this. Once you finish the water, I have some grape juice in the refrigerator with your name on it." Dante groaned again. He knew Detta wouldn't let up until he drank the water and the juice.

"I told Marty to take the day off," she said. "You're going nowhere but upstairs. Know this, Mr. Bonfigore. I'm very angry with you, but I can wait til tomorrow to talk to you." Once Dante finished the grape juice, Detta led him up the stairs to his own bed. When he finally hunkered down on the bed, she put a cold compress on his head. He didn't move until much later in the day when he heard voices coming from the kitchen.

Suppertime was noisier than normal. The kids were hyper. They were getting out of school for Thanksgiving in two days. Detta made their favorite meal—a big pan of lasagna, garlic bread, and a salad. The smell of food did little for Dante, but he did the best he could to put on a game face during the meal. Once dinner was done, each kid was assigned a job. Cristiana was put in charge. "I have a meeting at church. Your dad isn't feeling so hot. Try to keep the noise down. Once the jobs are done, everyone needs to hit the books. I'll be home a little after 8 pm." Detta headed out the door and Dante headed upstairs.

The next morning, Dante started feeling better. He made it downstairs in time to see his kids off to school. Detta told him that they would talk when she returned. Then she bundled the kids into her car and headed towards their bus stop.

Soon thereafter, Marty walked in. "How are you doing, Mr. B?"

Dante just nodded his head. After a few minutes of quiet, he asked Marty what had been going on. "I got a call from Mastriano. He spoke to Victoria about the abortion. She's willing to do it for a price."

"How much are we talking about?"

"Seven hundred dollars for the abortion. I knew you wanted to keep this real private—no clinic, no records, no nothing."

"Good thinking!" Mr. B started massaging his chin.

Marty knew this was a bad sign. "Is there something I missed?"

"Trixie wants some cash."

"Mr. B, we can send the boys to the Cape to put the fear of God into her."

"Marty, that ain't happening. For one thing, I like the dame even if she did make a mistake. Secondly, Trixie's hooked up pretty good with the other owners of the bank. I don't want to screw up a good thing. The bank's a gold mine. If anything happens to Trixie, my partners will start looking at me. That would mean trouble! Go to the Cape. Meet with Trixie. Find out how much she'll need to keep quiet."

They spent a few minutes catching up on issues that needed Dante's attention. Then Marty headed out. Detta came back a little while later. She hung up her coat and poured a cup of coffee. Then she sat down. Dante knew a quiet wife wouldn't be quiet for long.

"Dante, you've given me more than any husband I know. We have a wonderful family, a great home just down the road from our families, and enough money to keep us happy forever. These are things, just things. This would satisfy our mothers, but that's old school. I need more than that! I need you by my side, sharing the life we have. For the most part, you sit on the sidelines, viewing what goes on from afar. Not to mention your furtive little trips to Boston or wherever!"

"That's not true!" Dante said with some hesitation. "Give me one good example."

Detta smoothed her skirt and brushed a curl away from her eye. "When was the last time you had a one-on-one conversation with your daughter? Do you know if she likes Don Bosco? What about her feelings towards Vincent Angelino?"

"What about that Angelino kid?" Dante said. "Has he hurt her? If he's hurt her in any way, I'll pound his face into the ground."

Detta shook her head. "Dante, Cristiana likes Vincent. She really likes him! He treats her with respect even though she manipulates him." Detta went on. "Vincent is a gentle, unassuming kid. He's been more than willing to let your daughter lead the way. But he has fire in his belly. He reminds me of you when you were younger."

"Sad to say, Dante. You don't know anything about your kids." He tried to bail out of this conversation. Detta put her hand on his arm and tightened her grip. "Listen to me!" she said with a keen amount of steel in her voice. "Your kids need you. That goes double for me. Don't think I'm some airhead who's oblivious to what's going on at the Cape. There've been one too many trips up north over the past few months. Cut your losses right now or I'll cut mine! Don't think for a second that I won't follow through with this threat. You know I am good to my word."

Dante had never heard his wife speak to him like this. For that matter, he had never let anyone talk to him like this. How did she know about Trixie? What else does she know? He closed his eyes. Truth be known, Detta was right. She had given him a lot to think about.

"How about we talk after Thanksgiving?" Detta nodded in agreement. Then she gave him a peck on the cheek and pointed towards the basement. "Dino called. He needs to talk to you as soon as possible. Now would be a great time to return his call. Don't be too long. I'm going to need some help from you."

It's really nuts out there

Cappy and Renata drove up to the farm. That way, they could monitor the situation. Rico was waiting for them when they arrived. Joey introduced his brother. Rico was unhappy with the whole situation. "This has gotten out of hand," he said. "I thought I'd be in Kansas for a week. Now it's the Monday before Thanksgiving. What are we doing here?" Rico saw the grim look in Cappy's face and took a step backwards.

"What you are going to do is pack your stuff while we get Nutcase ready to go. Then we are outta here."

Rico didn't waste time heading towards the farmhouse. "What's the plan, Cappy?" Renata asked carefully.

"We'll be driving Rico back to Kansas City as soon as he packs his stuff.

"What about Mr. Wing Nut?

"He's travelling with us. I reserved a space for him in the trunk of the car. Joey can follow us in the van. We get Rico on the first flight back home. Then we drop Wing Nut off near Baxter's store. After that, Joey lets Baxter know where to find his lost and found item. Once that's done, we plan some sweet revenge."

Nut didn't make life easy for himself. He attempted to bash someone, anyone, as Joey began to untie his wrists. That led to the butt end of Joey's Smith and Wesson meeting up with Nut's forehead. Nut was down for the count. Cappy noticed that Joey had enjoyed this little brush up a little too much. Rico returned with his bag all packed. He wanted to get back to his family. Cappy told the brothers to load Nut into the trunk. Then, they headed south.

They finally made it Leavenworth. They found a travel agency. Cappy bought Rico a seat on the first plane headed to Hartford. Renata could tell there was bad blood between Joey and Rico. If looks could kill, Joey would have been lying in a funeral home somewhere. She decided to keep that little tidbit to herself.

The troupe finally made it to the airport. Cappy drove into the parking ramp. Joey pulled up next to him. Cappy jumped out of his car and yelled at Rico to follow him. They walked several car lengths away. Cappy talked and Rico listened. When Cappy was done talking, he pulled out a fist full of bills. Rico put the money in his coat pocket and headed to the terminal.

Cappy could hear Nut's moans emanating from the trunk. They needed to find a quiet little park where they could eat their lunch in peace. "We gotta hit the road. Nut's getting rambunctious. We need to find a burger joint and then we need to find a quiet park. Follow me." Joey got the message. Cappy put the key in the ignition and punched the accelerator. They got on the freeway and drove straight down I 635 towards Shawnee.

They were as hungry as bears coming out of hibernation. When Cappy saw a sign advertising Billy's Burgers, he pulled off the freeway. Billy's was just around the corner. They grabbed some food and drinks. Cappy asked if there was a park nearby where they could eat their lunch. He got directions to Pierson County Park. When they got there, the place was nearly deserted.

They found a sheltered picnic table close to the parking lot, sat down and ate their lunch. Cappy opened the trunk. Nut was still blindfolded. Cappy gripped his shirt and told him what was going to happen. "You better cooperate or else!" Nut kept his mouth shut once Cappy explained the alternatives. Renata handed Nut a burger and some fries. Eating lunch with a blindfold on was so much better than not eating at all. The weather had turned cool and the breeze was brisk, so they ate in a hurry. They got back into the vehicles about 5:30. Renata decided to take a turn driving. After a few wrong turns, she made it back to the freeway.

Renata pulled up a block away from Baxter's store. She thought it would be a good idea to scout out the area. They needed to find a place to stash Nut. They found an empty lot five blocks from the store. The lot was secluded and fenced in on three sides. Renata decided this would an ideal place to leave Mr. Nut. They waited til six p.m. By then, it was dark enough to pull Nut out of the trunk and walk him over to the lot without being seen. Wing Nut was securely tied to a telephone pole. A sock was stuffed in Nut's mouth.

"Nut," Cappy said, "we'll contact Baxter and tell him where to find you. He should be coming by soon. My friend will be in the shadow of a nearby building. If you make one sound, it'll be the last sound you ever make. Do you understand me?" Nut nodded his head in agreement. "Remember," Cappy said, "my friend is very nervous. He wouldn't think twice about shooting you."

Cappy and Renata headed back towards the liquor store. Joey was right behind them. They stopped down the block from the store. Renata found a scrap of paper in her purse and wrote a short note letting Baxter know where he would find Mr. Nut. Joey walked to the back of the store, He gathered some cardboard boxes that were lying up against the building and set them on fire. Cappy spotted a nearby fire alarm. He walked over and pulled hard down on the alarm. Then he walked away. Soon, the young man who was minding the liquor store smelled something burning. He ran out the back door to see what was happening.

Renata saw the kid take off. She calmly went into the liquor store and laid the Nut note on the counter. She then made a hasty retreat with two bottles of Jim Beam's finest under her arm. It took a few minutes before they heard the sirens. Several fire trucks headed towards them. Joey, Renata, and Cappy stuck around until Mr. Baxter arrived.

It took a while for things to calm down. Baxter went out to his car and drove off. A few minutes later, he returned with Wing Nut in tow. Shortly thereafter, Joey spotted Booby rumbling towards the liquor store. Baxter ran out and started yelling. Booby just listened. Finally, they went back into the store.

In no time flat, Baxter hurried out of the store, jumped into his car and headed south. Cappy was not far behind. They tailed Baxter to a place called Prairie Village. "Where do folks come up with names like Prairie Village?" Renata shook her head. "Cappy," she said. "This town seems like it is filthy rich. There are lots of new homes up and down the street."

"I can see that," Cappy said. "With money like this, I'm sure the police department is top notch. We'll need to keep a low profile." Baxter turned off the main road and pulled into the driveway of a two-story beauty. "Renata, write down the address of this place. We are going to be spending a lot of time in this burg."

Cristiana the Conniver

During Thanksgiving dinner, Cristiana found herself sitting next to Uncle Paulie. Paulie was her mother's baby brother. All his siblings were very successful. However, he was still trying to find his own way. He was always working on a "get rich quick" scheme. With help from Dante, Paulie bought a used car business in Greenville. The business was doing okay, but okay never seemed to be good enough.

"So, Uncle Paulie, how are you doing?" After a few minutes of meaningless chatter, Paulie began to talk about his Christmas tree business. He started this little business several years ago with a friend of his. Last year the business became profitable. Apparently, one of his employees, a guy named Ronnie, was great with people. "Ronnie just got a full-time job at the Groton shipyard. He is moving to Groton next week. I'm happy for him," Paulie said, "but this comes at the worst time for me."

Cristiana's curiosity got the better of her. She asked Paulie how he got started in the tree business in. 'Well, honey, you probably don't remember that I worked for the newspaper several years ago. I was a route supervisor. I got up early to make sure that drivers picked up their papers and got them to the readers' doorsteps. I hated that job. A friend of mine heard that I was unhappy. We started talking. The next thing I knew, we started a Christmas tree lot."

"What did Ronnie do for you?"

"I needed someone who could help us to get the word around. Ronnie was a friend of a friend. He could get along with anyone. He needed a job and we needed somebody. Voila! My partner and I decided to expand the business. We secured locations in Greenville and Johnston. Last year was our best year mostly due to Ronnie's salesmanship. It didn't take long before word got around that he was a good salesman. He got a job offer in Groton that he couldn't pass up. With Ronnie leaving, I'm concerned about what might happen to our business. We need someone to take over his job."

As Cris heard his tale of woe, an idea began to form. She wanted to know more about the business. Where it was located, what were the hours, etc. Cristiana was thinking that she and Vincent could help Paulie. This might be a way for Vincent to help his family and a way for Cris to spend more time with Vincent. The job required working on Friday nights, as well as Saturday and Sunday afternoons. This was a perfect job for a student.

"Uncle Paulie," she said, "I know someone who could help. Could you wait a few days to fill the job?"

Paulie was hesitant. "Cris, I need someone right away." He didn't realize how wily Cris could be. The next thing he knew, she was blinking her almond eyes at him. "How would it be if I worked for you. Just for this weekend. My friend's out of town til Tuesday. I could talk to him and let you know on Tuesday. What do you think?"

Paulie didn't know what hit him. He laid out a lame "Can you handle this?"

"I am sure I can. I'm a Bonfigore!"

Paulie pasted a huge smile on his puss. "Okay, you're hired." He started to get up out of his chair. Cristiana placed her hand on his arm. "One more thing, Uncle Paulie. How much do you pay for great help?"

Later that afternoon, Cris began to sweet talk Dante. She knew if he agreed to let her work at the tree stand, that would go a long way with her mom. Marty was seated a few chairs away. Marty watched with amazement as she wove her way into an agreement regarding this Christmas tree job. Cristiana made no mention of her idea to get Vincent a job.

Cristiana tapped danced around that issue. Dante wanted to know if she could handle the job. "Daddy," she said as she cuddled up to her father. "I'm your oldest child. I can handle it!"

"Okay, kiddo, if you think you can do it, go for it."

"That girl's amazing," Marty whispered to no one in particular. "It's as if Dante has fallen under a spell."

After the company left, Dante and his sons watched Dallas rolled over the Cards. Cristiana offered to help her mom clean up the dishes. Detta had been up since the break of day and she was dog tired, so she appreciated Cristiana's willingness to help.

"Everyone seemed to have had a good time, Cristiana, don't you think?"

"Even Uncle Gino was in a good mood." Cristiana replied. "He only raised his voice once when we talked about the Polish pope."

"Honey," Detta said, "there are some traditions Gino thinks should never be broken—having an Italian pope is one of them."

They giggled for a bit. Then they talked about the day's highlights. Finally, Detta scrubbed the pots, while Cris deboned the turkey. "Mom, did you know Mrs. Angelino is having another surgery this week? This must be costing a lot of money. Is your committee going to be able to raise enough to pay the hospital bills?"

"Cristiana, you know more than I do. I knew Maria needed another surgery, but I had no idea it was scheduled for this week. I guess I've had a lot of things going on. To answer your question, Cristiana, we've gotten support from all sorts of folks. I'm hoping it will all come together. Lots of things need to fall into place for this fundraiser to be successful."

"Mom, I had an idea I want to share with you."

"What kind of idea, Honey?"

Cris told Detta that Vincent felt responsible for the shooting. "Mom, you and I know he did all he could do, but he still feels responsible. He wants to earn money to help his family. Uncle Paulie told me one of his helpers is quitting. Uncle Paulie needs some extra help on the weekends."

"I was thinking that Vincent and I could work at the tree stand. Vincent is shy. I thought if I could work with him, we could make a good team. Uncle Paulie's okay with this idea. Dad is also okay with this plan. I didn't want to go behind your back. I'm hoping that you'd be okay with this."

Detta was dumbstruck. Her daughter had thought this whole project through. If they were only working on the weekends, it wouldn't interfere with schoolwork. "It sounds as if you have given this a lot of thought. Give me a day to think about it?"

Cristiana's face was beaming. "Okay, Mom!"

Later that night, Detta spoke to Dante. "Did your daughter talk to you about working at Paulie's tree stand?"

"Yeah, she did," Dante replied, "Right after the dishes were cleared. I told her I thought she could handle it, but she had to get your permission."

Detta was silent for a little while. Then she slipped her arm around Dante's waist and whispered, "Our daughter is starting to act like a young adult."

Dante noticed that his wife was wiping away a few tears. "I guess our little girl is growing up."

Let's hit the road. The malls are calling

The next day, Detta got up a little later than usual. She came downstairs and found Cristiana in the kitchen. Cris had made bacon and eggs for everyone. "What's going on? Are you taking over my job?" she said with a wink.

"My brothers were hungry, so I decided to make them breakfast. You looked tired last night. I thought you could use some extra shuteye."

"Where's everyone?" Detta asked.

"The boys are playing next door and Dad went to the laundromat. Mom, I would have made some coffee for you, but I don't know how to make it." Detta pulled her coffeemaker out of the cupboard. A few minutes later, Detta was seated at the table with a cup of coffee in front of her. Cris knew better than to disturb her mom right then, so she headed to her room to work on a book report.

The boys and Dante came back just in time for lunch. Detta wondered what they would have done if she and Cristiana had gone off galavanting that afternoon, but she kept those thoughts to herself. Luckily, Detta had made turkey soup from the Thanksgiving leftovers. Between the soup and sandwiches, everyone left the table with no complaints.

After lunch, Detta pulled Cristiana aside. "I need to start buying Christmas gifts, Cristiana. I could use your help. I was wondering if you'd like to come to the mall with me today?" Cristiana was all in on that idea. "I need to get cleaned up, Cris. How's about we leave in an hour?"

"I'll be ready," Cristiana replied with a smile.

"Dante, you are watching the kids this afternoon." Dante started to disagree. Then he found himself nodding yes after a few invisible daggers went flying past his head. "Have a great time, Honey. All will be well here," was all Dante could think of saying without getting into a deeper hole.

Detta thought she'd miss some of the post-Thanksgiving sale rush if she went shopping in the afternoon. However, they found themselves in the middle of human bedlam. Traffic was crazy. Every entrance to the mall was snarled. Folks were streaming into the mall. This might have scared some people away, but Detta was undaunted. Flying elbows might be looked down upon in some social circles, but every woman for herself today.

A trip to Filene's and then on to Jordan Marsh turned out to be more than enough for them. They had two carts full of sales items. New dungarees and sneakers for the boys, some pricey perfume for both grandmothers, and finally, games and trinkets for Detta's numerous nieces and nephews.

Detta saw a fancy cocktail dress that was on sale at Filene's. She turned to Cristiana. "You might want to drop a hint to your dad about what type of dress he could buy for his wonderful wife. Mother and daughter shared a wink as they walked out of the store.

"I think I'll talk to my father when we get home," Cristiana said with a hint of Italian humor.

"Cristiana, I have one last stop to make."

"Where are we going, Mom? I thought we were done with shopping."

Detta told her daughter that they had to hit one more store. "There's a cigar shop on the east side of

Providence that carries your father's favorite cigars. I'm going to stop in there and buy some for your father."

"Yuck!" said Cristiana. "Those things smell awful."

"Honey, someday, down the road of life, you will understand the need to do the unexpected. These stupid cigars seem to help you father relax. As long as he doesn't smoke those awful things in the house, he will be happy and, as a result, I will be happy."

When they finally headed back home, Detta broached the topic of Cris working for Paulie. "Last night, after you went to bed, your father and I talked about the tree stand. I'm concerned that you might not be able to keep your grades up. If you promise me that school will come first, then you can help your uncle." Cristiana's smile was all Detta needed to see. The trip back to Greenville was a blur of laughter and chatter.

Did you hear what I heard

Cristiana hopped out of the car after they had pulled into the driveway and brought two bags up to her mom's bedroom. Then she called Vincent. "Hey, this is Cristiana. I need to talk to you. Can you meet me at the Coffee Café in thirty minutes?"

She had been talking a mile a minute, so Vincent was slow to understand what she said. "You want to me to meet you at the cafe? What is so all fired important?"

"I'll explain it all when I see you!"

Vincent was flustered, but he eeked out a yes. Then he hung up. "Oh shoot!" he said. "I didn't even say goodbye! She's going to think that I am a complete airhead."

Vincent had been cleaning the garage for the last hour. He was covered with dirt. He rushed into the bathroom, threw off his clothes and scrubbed himself silly. Then he put on a clean shirt and his best pair of pants. Vincent was nearly out the door when his mother called out to him. "Vincent, where are you going? We are having dinner in two hours."

"I'm meeting someone down at the cafe," he said. "I'll be back in time for dinner. See ya later," he called out as he closed the kitchen door.

"What has come over that son of mine?" Maria said. She shook her head and went back to peeling potatoes. One of their neighbors, an old galoot named Sparky Arthur, had brought over potatoes and a beef roast they could have for dinner. John said that Sparky wanted to help the family out during what he had called "your family's difficult situation."

"We're lucky to have caring neighbors," she said softly. When Cris got to the Coffee Café, the frost on the window was thick. She couldn't tell if Vincent had arrived. She went in and looked around. He was nowhere to be seen. She looked at her watch. "Oh my gosh, I am twenty minutes early. What a knucklehead!!" Cris decided to sit down at a corner booth and wait for Vincent.

Joanie Bowman, a junior at the town high school, was waitressing that afternoon. Joanie lived up the street from Cris. When she spotted Cris, she came right over to her table. "Hey, stranger. How are you?"

Cris was focused on the menu, so she was surprised to hear Joanie's voice. She looked up. "Hi, Joanie. I didn't know you worked here."

Joanie gave Cris a quick hug. "Have you heard anything about Mrs. Angelino?"

Cris gave her a rundown of what was going on.

"Oh my, I knew Mrs. Angelino was hurt, but I thought it was no big deal." They talked a little longer. Then Joanie asked if Cris wanted anything to eat.

"Can I have a vanilla cabinet with two cherries?"

"Coming right up! I'll make the cabinet myself."

As Cristiana waited for her cabinet, she started daydreaming. Then she heard her name mentioned. Two elderly women were sitting two booths down from her. They were chattering away. Suddenly, Cristiana heard her name spoken again. "I'm sure she is Cristiana

Bonfigore. "She's the daughter of that mobster who bought Gardner's farm. I don't know why the police haven't arrested him for the killing at Viterio's."

Cristiana was stunned. "These old ladies are saying that Dad is a mobster. And what is this business about arresting Dad?" Her face reddened and she began to weep. Just then, Vincent walked into the café. "Oh great!" she thought. "Vincent can't see me like this." She pulled a tissue out of her purse and blew her nose just as he made it to the table.

"Hi there, Mr. Cross Country star," she managed to blurt out. "Thanks for coming on short notice."

"Cris, is everything okay? I wasn't sure what to make of your phone call." It was only then that Vincent looked at her face. "Have you been crying?"

"No, I just have a cold. Then she steered the conversation away from herself. "How about you get something to drink," she said, "then I'll tell you what is going on."

Cris waved Joanie over. "Vincent, I hear you are Don Bosco's star cross country runner."

Vincent turned beat red. "Ah, Joanie, how did you find out?"

Joanie smiled. "News travels fast at the Coffee Cafe." Vincent shook his head.

"Joanie, can you make another shake for Vincent?"

As Joanie headed back to the counter, Cris saw that one of the older women was staring directly at her. The woman quickly turned away. "I can't let on to Vincent that I'm upset. This business about Dad will have to wait until I get home."

As soon as the cabinets arrived, Cris pulled herself together. She told Vincent about her conversations with her family. "I know you want to do something for your family. I thought you might be interested in working with me at my uncle's Christmas tree stand. We'd work weekends, so it wouldn't affect school. We could make some money and you could help your parents out."

Vincent was quiet for a few seconds. He finally looked up. Cris saw the glimmer of a smile. He reached over and took her hand. Vincent wasn't quite sure just what to say. The words "thank you" slowly crawled out as he nodded in agreement.

Cristiana went off on a roll. She thought Vincent might agree, so she had begun formulating a plan on how to make this work. "We need to come up with a flyer that we pass around to our school friends."

Vincent wondered if they could post the flyer in some businesses in town.

"What a great idea, Vincent. I never thought of that!" Cris had thought of that very idea, but she decided to give Vincent all the credit.

They spent the next half hour talking about what to do next. Cristiana decided to talk to her uncle Dino about using his mimeograph machine to print the flyers. Vincent agreed to call Mikey. He's a good writer. Maybe he can come up with something to put on the flyer."

"What a great idea," Cristiana said. "How about we all meet here tomorrow to figure out what to do from here?"

She waved Joanie over and asked for the bill. "This is my treat, Mr. Angelino" she said triumphantly. "You can take care of the bill tomorrow."

Vincent had heard that "I am in charge right now, so back off" voice before, so he nodded in agreement. Cristiana left a tip on the table. Cristiana gave Vincent a little hug and they each headed towards home.

Cristiana was going to call her dad for a ride home. However, she decided that she needed time to think about how to approach him regarding what she had heard. The more she thought about it, the more upset she became. "Is Dad a part of the mafia? Did he have anything to do with the shooting?" The more Cris thought about it, the angrier she became. She decided to talk to her mother as soon as she got home to see if she could get any answers.

As Cris walked home, the weather changed. The wind was blowing from the north and the temperature had dropped. By the time she got home, she was chilled to the bone.

Detta met Cris at the back door and immediately walked her to the upstairs bathroom. "Take you clothes off right now! You need to take a hot shower." Cris didn't say a word about her concerns. She was too blooming cold to think about anything other than getting warm. She stood under the shower for the longest time. Detta wrapped her up in a warm towel, dried her off, and helped her put on some pajamas. Then she led Cris to her bedroom. A cup of cocoa was waiting for her. "Drink this slowly. It will warm you up. I'm going to get a heavy blanket from the cedar chest. I'll be right back." By the time Detta returned, Cris had fallen into a deep sleep.

She slept right through the night. The next morning, she awoke to the sound of her brothers yelling at each other.

By the time Cristiana came downstairs, everyone else had already eaten. Her dad and her brothers were doing some yard work and her mom was washing the breakfast dishes. "Mom, I need to talk to you," she said in a shaky voice.

Detta heard the desperation in her daughter's voice and went right over to her. "What's the matter?"

Cris started to cry. Finally, she settled down. She told Detta what she had overheard at the café. Detta shook her head. "I'm not sure what to tell you. I know your dad has friends who belong to the Sons of Italy. Some of them may be connected to the Mafia. But I've never heard him talk about being involved in anything like that."

Cristiana was confused. "Why would those women say such a thing?"

"I have no idea. Why don't I call your father in. You can tell him what you overheard. I'm sure he'll be as surprised as I am." Detta hurried to the back door. "Dante, I need to talk to you."

"I am right in the middle of something," he said. "Can it wait?"

"All Detta had to say was "Now!" That tone of voice got his attention. He hustled to the back door. "What's so all fired important?" he barked.

"Your daughter needs to talk to you."

Dante turned to see Cristiana's tearstained face. He threw his coat on the counter and sat next to her. "What is going on, Cristiana?" She repeated what she had heard. She spun out her story like she was handling a machine gun.

"Daddy, are you involved in the Mafia? Did you have Mr. De Nuccio killed?"

Dante was overwhelmed. "Where did this come from?" he thought. He didn't know what to say, so he simply took his daughter's hand and shook his head. That gave him a little time to recover. Finally, he told his wife and daughter that he knew nothing about the killing.

"I've asked around to see if anyone knows anything. Maybe that's what these ladies were talking about. Cristiana, I'm as upset about Maria as you are. Maybe more so. You probably don't know that my sister Carmen hung around with Marta when they were kids. I used to know her very well."

That was enough to satisfy Cristiana. Detta came over, gave her husband a kiss and helped Cristiana over to the kitchen table. "Cristiana, this might be a good time for you to have your first cup of cappuccino. Sit down while I fix a cup for all of us." They had a half hour of together time. At that point, the boys burst through the back door and clamored for some hot chocolate.

After Cristiana went upstairs, Detta turned to her husband. "Dante, you would tell me if you had anything to do with this awful business."

"I don't know much more about this than you do. I'm trying to see if anyone knows anything. So far, no such luck." Detta gave him a hug. "For a while, Mr. Bonfigore, Cristiana's story had me worried. I'm relieved that we're all on the same page." Detta took his hand and brought him over to the living room couch. They talked until late that evening.

Where in the heck is Cappy

With all the hubbub that took place on Saturday, Mr. B put the mob business on the back burner so he could enjoy the holidays. On Monday morning, however, life was back to normal. Marty arrived at the house about 8:30. Mr. B was on the phone. "Marty, get in here!" Dante motioned Marty to sit down as he continued to talk into the phone. "I know, Boss. I told you I'd connect with Capuano. I called him three times. He hasn't returned my calls." Dante's boss was yelling through the receiver. Dante shook his head as he pulled the phone away from his ear. "I read you loud and clear, Tony. I'll drive over to Hartford and see what I can find out." It was easy to hear the big boss' screaming as Mr. B was being told to find out what was up or else. Then Marty heard the phone slammed down.

Mr. B was boiling mad. "Clear the decks! Get the car ready. We are driving over to Cappy's."

Marty quickly walked back to the front office. "I'll call the pool hall and tell Sammy that our weekly meeting will have to wait until tomorrow." Mr. B was fuming as he walked up the stairs to tell Detta that he needed to drive over to Hartford.

"Okay, okay," he said to his wife, "I promised to go to your fundraising meeting tonight. I'll be back no later than five o'clock." Detta wasn't happy about this. Dante assured her that he'd be back in plenty of time. She gave Dante a peck on the cheek. Then Marty and Mr. B went out to the car and headed towards Route 6.

They got to Cappy's place in no time flat. They missed most of the morning traffic. "Marty, don't call ahead. I want to make sure we have the element of surprise on our side." When they pulled up to Cappy's front door, Marty saw two guys barking at each other in front of the building. One of the men was Cappy's number one driver. The other man was a burly guy who was shouting and pointing fingers. Marty assumed from the conversation that the other guy was unhappy that his car had been towed.

Mr. B quickly stepped out of his car and strode towards the two guys. "What's going on, Donnie? Do you need any help?"

The burly guy had a short fuse. He turned towards Mr. B. "Listen up, Meatball, this is none of your goddamn business, so why don't you and your pissant little friend over there get lost!" the big guy said as he began pushing Mr. B.

If you saw Dante walking down the street, you wouldn't give him the time of day. You'd think this short guy with a ducktail haircut and deep-set eyes couldn't hurt a fly. That was a wrong assumption. All Mr. B needed was a reason to get upset. When he heard himself being called Meatball, Dante went into action.

One punch was all it took for the burly guy to find himself lying on the ground. The guy had a black eye and a bloody nose in no time flat. Marty got between Mr. B and Burly and suggested that Burly might want to leave while the leaving was good. Apparently, Burly's ego was bigger than his ability to fight. He attempted to kick Marty in the knee. Marty swerved to avoid his kick and proceeded to step on the guy's privates. Case closed.

Donnie saw Marty nod towards the office and the three of them left Mr. Burly howling. "Thanks for the help." Donnie said. "I wasn't sure what I was going to do if that jag off had his way."

"Glad we could help." Marty replied as Mr. B guided them towards Cappy's office. Marty told Donnie to sit down as Mr. B headed for Cappy's chair.

Donnie knew something was up when he saw the glare in Mr. B's eyes. "Donnie, what's going on? We drove down here to get some straight answers. We just helped you out and now you are going to return the favor. Capiche?"

"Sure! I get it," Donnie sputtered. "Anything you want. Just name it!"

Mr. B recounted his attempts to connect with Cappy. "I haven't heard from him! I need to hear from him! You're his main man. You've been well paid to help Cappy. If he turns up dead before I get a chance to talk to him, you'll be unhappy, out of a job, and wondering when I will show up to arrange an underground meeting between you and Cappy. Do I make myself clear?"

There was no mistaking Mr. B's meaning. Donnie was visibly shaken. "How can I help?" Mr. B motioned for Marty to take over.

For the next hour, Marty and Donnie played the question game. As it turned out, Donnie knew about Cappy's whereabouts. Capuano had left for Chicago several days ago. He met up with Renata Scorpini. Donnie was under the impression that the two of them were heading towards some cattle town to see if they could find Joey.

"Who is this Scorpini woman, Donnie?" Marty asked. Donnie filled them in. Scorpini and her brothers used to live on the north side of Hartford. Back in the day, they helped Cappy. They let him use an empty storehouse to hide some art that had been swiped from a swanky home in Lower Manhattan. Cappy returned the favor by setting up Renata and her family up with a printing business in

Chicago. Then he hooked them up with some mob guys. Now they were on easy street.

Marty eased up on the nastiness. "Donnie, when is Cappy supposed to call?"

"He said he'd call me on Wednesday. Do you know how to contact Cappy?"

"Renata has a newfangled mobile phone in her car." Donnie pulled out a small pad of paper from his shirt pocket, copied the number, and handed it to Marty.

"Donnie, under no condition are you to say anything about our visit. If Cappy calls you, you call us. Do you understand?" Donnie knew the score. Marty told him to take a powder.

Mr. B started spitting out words like bees coming out of a hive. "Marty, we need to find out about this Renata woman. Phone Billy Gambucci. He's a longtime friend of mine. He lives in Chicago. You need to get the lowdown about Scorpini. I'll call Providence and let them know where we stand."

Marty went out to find a pay phone. It took a while for Marty to get some answers. "What took you so long?" Mr. B snarled.

It turned out that Marty had a hard time tracking down Gambucci. "I ran out of coins after the second call. I had to get more change."

"What did you find out?"

"Gambucci is a fount of information."

Dante almost smacked Marty. "I keep telling you, use the simple words. I feel like I'm uneducated when you throw out words like 'fount.' Enough already!"

Marty started up again. "Gambucci knows a lot about Renata. Apparently, he ran a bookie business with the Scorpinis about six years back.

"Gambucci said Renata is one smart cookie. She and her brothers helped Cappy out with some mob business. Their help caused some waves with the police. Once the air cleared, Cappy moved them to Chicago, bought them a printing business and got a few of his friends to throw them some business. Renata eventually ran the whole business. She's as sharp as a knife and as hot as a pistol. She is not someone you want to cross. She can be as mean as a pit viper.

"Dante, Cappy was sweet on her once upon a time. That ended when she learned he was two timing her. Billy thinks Cappy might still be stuck on her. Cappy showed up on her doorstep in Chicago two nights ago. Next thing you know, they were adios. Should we call her?"

Then Dante said, "Let's wait until Cappy calls Donnie. We'll he has to say."

We need a plan. This is gonna take time

Cappy called Donnie on Friday. He wasn't an apologizing type of guy, but he did tell Donnie that he had a mess to clean up. "I'll be gone for a lot longer than I anticipated."

Donnie gave Cappy the lowdown on what had been going on in Hartford. "I've been towing night and day since you left. I can't keep up with the work."

"Listen Donnie, I'll call Dante about this Kansas mess. He ain't gonna like it. I'll ask him to send his whiz kids to help you out." After a few more minutes listening to Donnie's list of complaints, Cappy signed off.

Renata was listening to Cappy's side of the conversation. She heard a little about Dante Bonfigore and wanted to know more. "What's so special about Bonfigore?" she asked.

Cappy launched into a long spiel about Dante's grip on mob action in New England. "I am close to the head capo. Dante has a lot of power in that arena. He could have me taken out in a New York minute. Folks underestimate Dante. He's a short, thin, wiry guy with eyes that could slice you in two. I learned the hard way that he is not a guy to fool around with. Dante can take you down with one punch. Bam!

"Renata, there are two things that separate Dante from your average mob guy. First, he isn't full of himself. He surrounds himself with bright people who can pull your books apart before you know it. Secondly, he is a good listener. Nothing gets past him. Once he makes a decision, he isn't afraid to act on the decision."

Cappy could see that Renata was deeply concerned. "What are you thinking about?" She asked if Joey was involved with Bonfigore. Cappy told her most of the story. He left out the part about his getting banged up on The Merchant. "So, not only do you have Baxter and Dolan to contend with, but you also have Dante on your back."

Cappy nodded. "I'm on top of this."

That didn't settle her down. "Why don't you get rid of Mr. One Shot and kidnap Baxter? He gets you the money and you pay back Dolan."

Cappy shook his head. "You're our team's brainiac, but I need Joey's muscle to get this job done. "I dragged you into this without giving you the whole scoop. I owe you an apology. If you want out, I will understand."

Renata knew that it was a difficult situation. She made it clear that she'd be with Cappy until the end.

"I am dog tired." Cappy said. "I need to get some rest before I call Dante. Can you keep an eye on Joey? If I am not up by 1:30, knock on the door."

"Maybe," she said to Cappy as she patted him on the back and then on the backside and led him to the back bedroom. Renata followed right behind and softly shut the bedroom door. Joey could wait.

It was 2 p.m. by the time Cappy got up. He saw the time and swore under his breath. He had to call Dante right away. He left Renata asleep on the bed and headed out to the kitchen. He reheated some of the morning coffee. A few minutes later, he called Dante.

"It's about time you called! I was ready to have the boss call out the dogs!"

Cappy took a deep breath and launched into the Baxter fiasco. He left nothing out. Dante was very unhappy that Cappy had known the whereabouts of One Shot without telling him, but he decided to leave that item for another time.

"So, Joey's just a young country bumpkin who shoots off his mouth as well as he shoots his gun."

Cappy agreed. Joey was not quite ready for the job. "I know I've been holding some things back from you, Dante. I thought I could take care of this on my own. If that had happened, all would be forgiven. I underestimated the situation. You can take it out of my hide after I clean up this mess."

"First things first! You seem to have your hands full. What do you have in mind?" Cappy indicated that he needed some additional time in Kansas City to scout things out. "Maybe we can kidnap one of Baxter's children. We can trade the kid for the money Baxter owes Dolan."

"Are you nuts? We're already up to our ears in trouble. Kidnapping is a federal offense."

Dante wanted to see a better plan before he'd agree to let Cappy go forward. "Cappy, you need more muscle. I am going to call in a favor from Billy Gambucci and see if he can help you. Billy lives in Chicago. He knows the Scorpinis. He has done things like this before. The only problem is that he and his wife just had a baby. Our timing is poor."

"In the meantime, Donnie needs help with the towing business. I have a connection with the Worcester crowd. I will see if we can get Donnie some help." Cappy was on board with both ideas. Dante told Cappy that he'd get back in touch by next week. With that, the call ended.

Cappy woke Renata up from a deep sleep. While she got herself together, Cappy went into the other bedroom and rustled Joey out of bed. That took longer than anticipated. A glass of ice water in his face finally did the trick. Once everyone was awake enough to connect the dots, Cappy shared his conversation with Dante.

Renata wasn't happy to learn that Cappy didn't wake her so she could listen to the conversation. Joey wasn't happy to hear himself be described as a country bumpkin.

"Enough already. It is what it is!" Cappy said. "We need to come up with a brand, new plan. The plan will include Billy Gambucci if Dante's able to convince him to help us. "We need to start planning right now. If Billy gets involved, we will include him in the plan.

They spent the afternoon going over all the possibilities. Dante agreed to see what he could find out about Baxter. "Baxter must have terrific resources to do what he is doing. His house is a real beaut. Not to mention that he has the liquor store. Getting $50,000 out of him ain't gonna come close to breaking his nut—maybe I should say his expenses because he already has a Nut." Nobody laughed except Cappy.

They took turns following Baxter for the next few days. Joey would take the first shift. Cappy made sure that Joey understood that he had to be Mr. Invisible. "I want an account of when and where Baxter travelled."

Once that was settled, Cappy and Renata went to the Hertz office. Cappy thought he should keep a low profile. He liked having expensive things. However, he selected a nondescript Ford. "We want a car that can blend in. This should do the trick." Renata agreed.

After the paperwork was signed, they went to see Dolan. They needed to find more about Baxter. How did Dolan connect with Baxter in the first place? How did Baxter make the down payment, etc.? The more they knew about Baxter's operations, the better. Having Renata ride along turned out to be just what the doctor ordered.

When they arrived at Dolan's, Renata took the lead. She defused Dolan's anger with a smile. All she had to say was "Tell me what happened, Mr. Dolan." Right away, she had Dolan eating right out of her hand. Cappy watched the whole thing unfold.

Dolan gave them all they needed to know. Baxter's father had been a bigwig with US Steel. The father had an advanced degree in strong arm tactics. He made money doing what he knew best and he passed his flair for violence on to his son.

According to Dolan, Baxter became the head of the family when his father died. "The father's death seemed mysterious. It's hard to imagine the old man was climbing trees in February," Dolan said, "but the police determined that the death was accidental. Baxter inherited a boatful of money. Most of it is tied up in some international financing deal. It can't be touched for a while. Baxter's standard of living is high, so he needed the $50,000 to tide him over."

Cappy became curious. "How do these West Virginia folks fit in?"

Dolan wasn't sure about that. "I think Baxter's wife was born in Wheeling. She and Baxter met at some fraternity party at OSU," Dolan replied. "I'm sure Booby and his pals are distant cousins of Baxter's wife."

Cappy had more questions about Dolan's connection with Baxter. Renata could tell that this was getting

171

Dolan steamed, so she quickly changed the subject. She asked Dolan about his family. That settled him down. After a few more minutes of prodding, Cappy knew that Dolan had other financial resources at his avail. Dolan had been cleared of the arson charges. So, the insurance company was willing to pay him for his loss.

"That must be a huge relief, Mr. Dolan!" Renata said.

"You can say that again. A huge fricking relief! I need to get back to my real estate company to take care of some unfinished business. Before I head back to my place, I want to say one more thing. Now that I'm getting the insurance money, I'm done with Baxter." Renata told Dolan not to worry. She'd make sure that he was out of the picture.

It's time to meet Louie and Dusty

Dante called his brother and asked if he was going to be around tomorrow. "I need to talk to you."

"I'm as free as a bird. "What's up?"

"I'll fill you when I see you. Does 9 a.m. work for you?"

"Works for me. I'll see you at the laundromat."

Then, Dante called Marty. "I need to meet Dino at his place about nine o'clock tomorrow morning. Be at my house by 8:40."

Dino was sitting in the office by the time Dante and Marty arrived. Dante poured himself a cup of java and sat down. "I need to talk to you alone, Dino. When we get done, the three of us need to talk!" he said. "Marty, give us a few minutes."

"Sure. I'll be outside. Let me know when you want me."

Dino sat on the edge of the desk. "What's going on, Dante?"

Dante shared his conversation with Maloney.

Dino's face reddened. "Let me get this straight. Maloney knows De Nuncio was tied in with the Boston mob." Dante nodded his head. "How much does he know?"

"I'm not sure."

"Maloney is like a pit bull. He won't let go if he thinks he's on to something. We need to be very careful from now on."

Dino wondered if they should rough Maloney up. "That will stir up a hornet's nest. Let's let sleeping dogs lie. If Maloney knew something, we would be looking out a jail cell window right now."

The brothers agreed to keep their ears to the ground. "I'll let you know, Dante, if I hear anything."

"That goes both ways, Bro."

Dante went out to find Marty. When Dante and Marty returned, Dante gave Dino the lowdown regarding their meetings in Boston. "Dino, I haven't had a chance to fill you in on what's going on. Marty came up with two great ideas. You need to hear what Marty has to say."

Marty was surprised. "Mr. B wants me to fill Dino in. He didn't give me any heads up. I guess an "off the cuff" version will have to do." This was not Marty's modus operandi.

"Dino, our tobacco operations are broken up into two regions. East and West. A smart aleck named Louie is responsible for the eastern area. The rest of the state is covered by a dude named Dusty. I met Louie. He's upset that he was not put in charge of the entire operation. He thinks I'm a flunky. He started giving me grief. Loser this, twerp that, etc. I'd had it with his grousing."

Marty continued, "Louie, I can call Mr. B and let him know how you feel about my leadership."

Louie went silent. He knew if Dante got involved, it wouldn't be good for his health. Louie settled down. We're now on the same page."

"So, Marty, is the other guy also a pain in the ass?"

"Heck no. Dusty is willing to cooperate. He is younger than Louie, but he is a lot wiser. Dusty know the scores. I laid out his responsibilities. He had already figured out what needed to be done."

At that point, Marty told the Bonfigores what needed to get done. "We need to figure out who is involved in our tobacco business. I'm sure there are a lot of folks who have their fingers in the pie. I need a full list of everyone involved. I want to know who we want to keep. I'm also thinking that we might let the coppers find some of our two-bit players."

Dante started shaking his head. "Are you saying that we should let some of our folks get picked up?"

"Exactly! We feed a few folks to the cops. Small fish are not worth saving. We won't get hurt because these folks know next to nothing about our operation. What they will know will be small potatoes. That will keep the cops interested."

"Are you nuts, Marty? Why do we want to keep the cops interested?" Marty knew this would be Dante's response. "Good question, Mr. B. I want to keep the cops interested. But I want to direct their interest. We give up one of our smaller operations in Pittsfield. While the state police are smiling about finding 30 cases of stolen cigarettes in western Mass., we are scoring big time on the other side of the state."

Marty had done due diligence on the project. Every question the brothers had thrown at Marty was handled easily. The Bonfigores didn't waste time throwing soft tosses. They threw Marty one fastball right after another. Dante and Dino were impressed that Marty's team had taken the time to determine which of the troopers could be the most easily swayed if the mob ended up feeding them a slug of crappy information. "This type of information would be helpful as they began to decide which locations to keep. "Nice job, Marty," was the extent of the praise that Marty got.

"So," Dino asked, "Where do we go from here?" Clearly, that was the ultimate question.

Marty indicated that there were two options. "We can continue to wait and see what the state police are up to. Or, we can be a little bolder and ruffle some feathers. I think it is time we rock the boat."

Dante and Dino were surprised to hear this forceful response. "They put me in charge," Marty thought, "so I'm going to be in charge. I am finally in a position of making suggestions on real projects and taking responsibility for these projects. I like this new Marty. If they don't like my work, so be it. I can go back to working as an overqualified chauffeur. That's not going to happen. This bird will fly the coop. For now, Dante and Dino are backing me up."

Dante finally piped up. "I want you to meet your team next week," Dante said. "Figure out the details of where we go next. I'll handle any flap from Providence."

"Oh, Trixie"

Dino, I need to get back to Greenville. I'll give you a call tomorrow." With that, Marty headed towards the car. Dante followed right behind. Marty didn't start the car right up. "I need to talk to Mr. B," Marty thought, "but I dread bringing up this 'something else."

"Marty, what's going on? Get the car in gear!"

Marty hesitated, "Mr. B, there is something else that we need to discuss."

"What the hell is going on now?"

Marty pulled into a parking lot and shut off the engine. "We need to talk about Trixie," Marty said.

"Trixie! What the hell is going on with Trixie?" Dante said with a sense of dread.

Marty took a long breath. "Last week, you told me to meet with Trixie. That didn't go well. Trixie changed her mind about the baby situation. She decided that she wants to keep the kid."

Dante exploded. "Trixie wants to keep this goddamn baby! You've got to be kidding me. That cannot happen! It cannot happen!"

"Trixie sees herself as a good Catholic girl. An abortion is not part of her equation right now. She decided to see a priest about what she should do. She came back from that meeting more fervent than ever in her desire to keep 'Cass.'"

"Don't tell me she has a name for this baby?" Dante spat out disgustedly. "My God in heaven. What next? Start the car up and turn it around, Marty. We're heading to the Cape." Marty did not move a muscle. "Didn't you hear me, Marty? Get this goddamn car going now."

"Mr. B, you took my advice about what we should do in Massachusetts. I don't give you unrequested advice very often. This situation is different. Hear me out."

Dante was red in the face. When he finally calmed down, he told Marty to say what needed to be said.

Marty took a deep breath and started in.

"If I take you up to the Cape right now, things might be said that would turn Trixie into a stone wall. That would not be good."

"What would you suggest I do, Marty?"

"You should hold off for a few days. Then we can head up to see her. You would have had time to think about how to handle this. At that point, Mr. B started to growl. "Do you want me to take you to the Cape?" Marty asked.

Mr. B shook his head. Then he raised his right hand and pointed it west. "Take me home."

"I'm not Superman, son"

Vincent missed the first day back to school after the Thanksgiving break, He and his family drove to St. Peter's Hospital Monday morning. Vincent's mom was getting prepped for her second shoulder surgery. As Maria was being taken to the operating room, she told John that she was really scared. "John, I'm afraid all these operations will go nowhere."

John looked down at her. In a calm voice he said, "You heard what the doctors told us. They are certain that once this fixator is put in, you'll be good to go. We've always trusted in God, Maria. I will ask my folks and the kids to pray with me while you undergo your surgery. Know that I love you so much." He knelt beside her and gave her a kiss on the cheek. With that, the nurse and the orderly put Maria on a gurney and wheeled her into the surgerical area.

Seeing his wife being wheeled away was a hard pill to swallow. John felt helpless, angry, and sad all at the same time. Before walking back to the waiting room, he stepped into the chapel. It was empty. He found a chair near a rose-colored window, sat down, and began to cry. His body was shaking. All he could do was think about the "What-ifs."

After a few minutes, he pushed the bad thoughts aside. "I have a fist full of kids and two parents who need me." he said to himself. "God, please be with me. I need you now more than ever. Maria, know that I am with you in spirit." Then John walked back to the waiting room. He saw that two of his sisters had arrived. He pulled his mother aside and whispered, "Mom, how about all of us spend some time in the chapel praying for Maria?" His mother nodded in agreement.

Before he knew it, his mother was herding the family down the hallway. Magdalena, John's youngest sister, had considered becoming a nun but decided against it. However, she was still very spiritual. When everyone was in the chapel, John asked Magdalena if she would lead the family in prayer. She agreed. John could see that Vincent was not doing very well. Vincent was standing all by himself in the back of the chapel. His head was cast down. There were tears in his eyes.

John got his mother's attention and nodded over to Vincent. His mother raised her left hand as if to say "Take him out of here, John. I'll take care of the others." John walked over to his son, turned him towards the door and motioned for him to follow.

"What's going on, Dad?' Vincent said as soon as they left the chapel. John made it sound as if he was feeling sad and needed Vincent's support. "Son, can you go outside with me for a little while? I need to get out of here. Maybe we can take a short walk. I don't want to be alone right now." This startled Vincent. His dad was the family's Rock of Gibraltar. Now the roles were reversed. Vincent's dad was asking Vincent for help!

Once they left the hospital, Vincent put his arm around his father's waist. They walked to a small rose garden on the south side of the hospital. John sat down on a concrete bench. Vincent followed suit. For a little while, they just sat there. Vincent wasn't sure what to say. Finally, he blurted out "What is going on, Dad? You seem pretty sad."

This was just what John had hoped to hear. John started sharing his feelings of inadequacy. "This surgery has me at sixes and sevens, Vincent. I'd like to think I can take care of just about anything. This medical stuff is completely out of my control. I think it's time for you to learn that I'm not Superman. I'm just a guy who is trying to do the best for his family. It tears me up that I'm not able to make things better. I've been so focused on your mother that I really haven't been there for you and your brothers. I am sorry if I have let you down."

John could see that Vincent's focus was no longer on his own issues. He was trying to comfort his father. John decided to keep silent and see where Vincent would go with this.

After a few minutes of silence, Vincent jostled his dad's arm. "Dad, do you remember the day after the shooting when I ran away from Mikey?"

"Yes, Vincent, I remember that day. It is a day I will never forget."

Vincent went on to tell his dad that he learned that day that he was not Superman. "I felt so alone. Life seemed out of control. I felt like I was inside a spinning wheel. Is that how you feel, Dad?"

John's inner grin was as large as the Narragansett Bay. "That's it exactly," he replied. "I guess you can understand how I might be feeling."

Vincent turned toward his father and gave him a bear hug. "Listen, Dad. You haven't come close to letting us down. Just the opposite. I remember you telling me, a long time ago, that we Angelinos need to stick together. Now's the time for us to stick together like glue. Would it be all right," Vincent asked, "if you and I went back to the chapel and shared this with our family?" John wiped tears from his eyes and nodded to Vincent. Then they headed towards the chapel.

Maria's surgeon finally walked out of the operating room. He found the Angelinos in the surgical waiting room. Vincent was the first to see the doctor walking into the room. "Dad," he said, "Dr. Johanson is here!" John was surprised to see Johanson so soon. He hurried over to the doctor and asked how the surgery went.

"The surgery went very well. Much better than I had anticipated. Everything went on without a hitch. Your wife's recovery might be much less than we initially thought."

Nonna dropped her head to her chin and started crying. "Lord, our prayers have been answered," she whispered. The doctor told them that Maria would need to have a great deal of physical therapy. With luck, she could be back to work by mid-March. The room was filled with joyful noise.

A little later, the Angelinos were able to see Maria. She was lying in bed with a contraption that kept her shoulder immobile. Maria was groggy, but she could tell by the looks on her children's faces that the surgery went well. Her hospital room was full of smiles. This brought tears to her eyes. It was clear that Maria was tired and needed some rest, so John started shuffling everyone out of the room. Then he walked over to his wife, put his fingers to his lips and then to her lips. He whispered "I love you" as Maria drifted into dreamland.

By the time the family left the hospital, it was too late to think about getting the boys back to school, so John drove everyone home. He found several boxes of food sitting on their doorstep, gifts from their neighbors. John shook his head in amazement. He knew how much pain and sadness his family had endured, but these acts of kindness left him feeling grateful and blessed.

Good news is getting catchy

Vincent walked to the Greenville Public Library. He needed to work on a book report for his history class. They were studying the Second World War. He decided to do a report on Winston Churchill. After two hours of research, he knew plenty about Churchill's "Britain's finest hour" speech.

"This Churchill character was some special kind of person," Vincent thought to himself as he headed home. "He had guts to stand up to Hitler and members of Parliament who were ready to give in to the German demands. "I wonder if I could ever do what he did when faced with such a situation." Little did he know that he would face a "Churchill" moment of his own in a few months.

The thought passed quickly from Vincent's head when he saw Mikey stepping off the bus. "Vincent, get over here. I have something to tell you."

Vincent hurried over. He could tell that Mikey was wound up. Words were coming out of his mouth faster than Vincent could comprehend. "Slow down. I'm having trouble following you!"

"Let's go to the Coffee Café. Then you can tell me what is going on." When they got there, they sat in the nearest open booth. An older waitress named Phyllis came over and took their order.

Then Mikey launched into his news. "Cristiana talked her uncle into giving us bonuses if we sold more than 600 trees. How do you like them apples!"

Vincent was astonished. "Do you think we can sell that many trees?"

"Cris and I have started working on this. Yesterday we whipped out a flyer about the tree sales. The flyer indicates that part of the sales would go toward paying your mom's hospital bill. "Today, Cris got permission from Brother Allan to pass flyers out at school. You can't believe the response! Even our teachers are ordering trees."

Vincent just sat in the booth. He shook his head in amazement. "You did all this for my family! How can I thank you?"

"You are my best friend, Vincent. Cris feels the same way. My folks have always told me that life is a gift and that friends are an extra special gift. You are my special gift."

"Thank you" was all Vincent could say.

"No thanks are necessary. That's what friends are for."

Mikey and Cristiana were going to meet up at Mikey's house after dinner to do figure out what they should do next. "Talk to your dad, Vincent. See if he will let you come over tonight." With that, the boys split up and headed home.

Vincent and his dad arrived home simultaneously. No sooner had John put his coat in the closet when Vincent pulled him over to the kitchen table. "Dad, Mikey is getting together with a friend this evening to work on publicity for the Christmas tree sale. Mikey asked me to come over and help them. Would that be okay with you?"

"Vincent, we've had an exhausting day. You can go over for a while, but you need to be back here no later than 8:15."

"I'll be back by then. Dad."
Cristiana, Vincent, and Mikey started chattering as soon as Vincent hit the O'Day's front door. "We need to get a table set up in the cafeteria tomorrow. I'll take care of that."

"Cris, that works for first lunch. We all eat during first period. How are we going to handle second lunch? Geez, Mikey, I never thought about that!"

The three of them yammered on for a few minutes. Suddenly, Vincent tapped his head. "What if I asked Joe Donatelli to help us. He took me under his wing during cross-country season. I think he has second lunch. Maybe he'd be willing to help."

Mikey grinned. "What a stellar idea, Mr. Angelino! How about the two of us talk to Joe tomorrow."

"Sounds like a plan, Mikey."

The kids were getting excited about the prospect of selling lots of trees. Cris started to frown. "What if we do get a lot of orders. I'm not sure how many trees Paulie can lay his hands on. We need to make sure that we have enough just in case sales start to pop." Cris agreed to call her uncle when she got home.

Vincent mentioned that his dad and Detective Maloney worked for the city. "Maybe they could talk to their coworkers."

"Great idea, Vincent," said Mikey. "You guys are doing great, but I am coming up empty handed."

"Mikey," Vincent asked, "doesn't your dad have eight brothers and sisters? Maybe they'd be willing to help."

"I will talk to my dad after you guys head home.

By then, it was 8 pm. The kids knew there was a lot of work ahead of them. That didn't quell their excitement. "Let's get back together on Wednesday at my house," Cris said. "That will give us time to pull things together." Vincent headed for the door. "I promised my dad that I'd be back home at 8:15. I need to scoot. I'll see you tomorrow. I appreciate all you are doing for my family."

The next day, the kids were overwhelmed by the student response. Many kids had spoken to their parents. Most of the parents were onboard about buying trees from Paulie. Kids came up to Cristiana with cash in their hands, asking her to have a tree set aside for them.

At lunchtime, Cris went to the principal's office. As luck would have it, Brother Allan had time to speak to her. She started in like a house afire. Allan could tell that Cris had her mother's style and temperament. He agreed to let the kids set up a table on the concourse before and after school. "You've touched the heart of our school with your Christmas tree idea. Let me know if we can help you with anything else."

A few more kids came up to them after the last bell had rung. Cris and Vincent quickly wrote names down in a binder, while Mikey collected money. When all was said and done, they had 25 orders on the very first day. They were gleeful. They managed to catch the bus back to Greenville.

Everyone on the bus said that their parents were going to buy Christmas trees from Paulie. As well, their parents were contacting their friends to consider buying trees from Paulie. "My uncle will need to find another source for trees!"

Once they got off the bus, Mikey started walking away. "Where are you going?" Vincent asked.
"I need to get to the bank." Mikey pulled out several $20 bills. "We need to get some change for tomorrow.

After Mikey had walked a few steps, he turned towards his friends. "Vincent, we need to get to school early tomorrow so we can set up a table and meet with kids. I'll see if my mom can take us. I will call you when I know."

That afternoon, after John had finished up at work, he went to the hospital. He was relieved to see that Maria was awake and smiling when he walked into her room. "John, my shoulder is still pretty painful, but it feels so much better than after the first surgery!' The surgeon came in earlier this morning." "What did he have to say?" John asked patiently.

"Dr. Johanson told me I could go home on Thursday if my shoulder continues to improve."

John bent down and gave his wife a tender kiss on her cheek. "That is great news, Honey! What a relief!" Maria smiled at him and nodded her head in agreement. No more words were needed. John took his wife's hand and held it for a minute. Their only communication came from the twinkles in their eyes.

Maria finally spoke up. "How is everyone doing?"

"Well, Brother Allan called me."

Maria's eyes furrowed. "Is Vincent okay?"

John told her that Brother Allan had learned that Vincent and his friends are up to something special.

She turned her head quizzically towards him. "Up to something special. What exactly does that mean?"

John took the next little while to tell his wife all about the Christmas tree sale. Maria was amazed. The more she thought about it, the faster the tears fell. Getting shot was a bummer, but Maria never dreamed that something so bad could turn out so well. Her son was growing up right before her eyes. "You know, Mr. Angelino, we have swell kids." John couldn't find words to express his gratitude and wonderment.

When John got home, Vincent was on the phone. This was new behavior. John tried not to listen to the conversation, but that ended up being less than successful. Once Vincent got off the phone, he wanted to know how his mom was doing. "It's all good, son," John said. "With any luck, Mom will come home on Thursday!"

Vincent jumped up and gave his father a hug. Vincent was as happy as he could be.

John decided to find out what this tree business was all about. "Vincent," he said, "I got a surprise today. Brother Allan called me about some sort of sale." Vincent could hear the hesitation in his father's voice. "Do you know anything about this, son?"

Vincent started to flush. "This started on Thanksgiving. My friend, Cristiana, learned that her uncle needed help at his Christmas tree stand. Cris told him she might be able to find some extra workers. She asked Mikey and me if we wanted to work at the stand on a part time basis. We agreed to work on weekends. I think I will have enough time to do my homework and work at the stand.

If it works out, Dad, I'll be able to help with some of the hospital bills. I should have talked to you about it, Dad, but I was afraid that you would say no."

John was taking this all in. His son wanted to help his family in the worst way. "This is a moment to remember," he thought. "Vincent, I'm very proud of you. Yeah, it would have been nice to know about this beforehand, but that is not important right now. Your heart is in the right place. So, tell me, is your friend any relation to Dante Bonfigore?"

"How did you know that Dad?"

"Vincent, your mom ran around with Mr. Bonfigore's sister when she was growing up. Mom has great memories of those days. She'll be surprised to hear that you are friends with his daughter. I think the Bonfigores' moved to Greenville last summer. Your mom suggested that we get together with the Bonfigores for dinner. However, that idea went by the by when she was shot."

"Wow, Dad, what a coincidence. I don't think that Cris knows anything about this. Will she be surprised when she hears this!"

John wanted to hear more about this Christmas tree idea. "So, Vincent, what is going on?"

"Well, once we agreed to work at the tree stand, Mikey and I sat down with Cris. We came up a plan on how to get the word out about the stand. The next thing we knew, our plan took off. We told some kids in school about the tree sales. Paulie agreed to give some of the profits to our family to help with our hospital bills. When the kids in school found out about this, they told their parents. Since then, the trees have been selling like hotcakes."

All John could do was nod his head. "So, Dad, we were wondering if you and Detective Maloney would let folks at work know what we are doing."

John suddenly had a lump in his throat. Words were hard to come by. Finally, John said he would see what he could do. "It's getting late, son. Let's see if we can help Nonna with dinner."
They walked into the kitchen. John's mother turned to them and asked, "Which one of you swallowed the canary?"

"Nonna," Vincent asked, "do we have enough space to put a big Christmas tree in the living room?" John stifled a laugh as he heard the word "tree" come out of his son's mouth.

Like mother like daughter

Detta was surprised when she heard Cristiana's story about the Christmas trees. "Here I am working with a ton of folks to pull together our fundraiser and you come up with a simple idea involving you and your friends. It sounds as if you've struck gold."

Now it was Cristiana's turn to calm someone down. "Mom, we're a long way from being successful! We can't get overconfident. We are taking this one step at a time." Detta wanted to find more out about the details, so the two to them sat down at the kitchen table and Cristiana outlined their plans.

It was clear to Detta that she was looking at herself in the mirror when she looked at Cristiana. "We are two peas in a pod. My daughter is an efficient organizer." Detta sat back and listened as Cristiana told her how Vincent and Mikey were spreading the word.

"Speaking about spreading the word, Mom, do you think Dad could call Fr. DiNapoli?"

"About what?" Detta asked.

"I'm hoping Father DiNapoli would put a note about the tree sale in the bulletin."

"We'd be willing to talk to Father, but you would probably get better results if you spoke to Father yourself. I'll call Father Rafferty at St. Philip's to see what he thinks about this. In the meanwhile, Let's call Paulie right now. He better scout out another source for trees. I'll also call Mr. Viterio. Maybe he and the other shop owners in town would put your flyers in their front windows."

That night, after the kids had gone to bed, Detta sat down next to Dante on their leather sofa in the living room. "Did your daughter talk to you today?"

She saw that Dante had a gleam in his eye. "Our daughter cornered me after supper. I had no idea how determined she can be."

"Like father, like daughter!" Detta replied. "Were you surprised?"

"That is an understatement. You were right. I didn't know her as well as I should. Maybe it is time for me to work on that." They sat on the sofa sharing stories for a long time. Detta started to yawn. "it's time to hit the hay," said Dante. "I'll call DiNapoli about the bulletin. This might be a done deal." Then they went upstairs.

The next morning, Detta called Paulie. He was at his used car lot. Mornings were usually slow, so he was open ears when Detta called. "What's up, big sister? I don't hear from you unless it is something big."

Detta started to laugh. "I guess you're right. I have some interesting news for you."

For the next few minutes, he listened to Detta. All Paulie could say was "You have got to me kidding me!"

"Paulie, you might start making some calls. The way Cristiana makes it sound, your Christmas tree stand might be needing a traffic cop to control traffic." Paulie said he would make some calls right away. "Paulie, let me know what you find out. Cristiana and her friends are counting on you!"

You are not working for Baxter

It took nearly a week for Billy Gambucci to make it down to Kansas City. Dante called Cappy to let him know that Gambucci was coming. "Billy will work in Kansas City for as long as you need him. So, tell me, Cappy. What's been going on since we last talked?"

"Renata and I met Dolan the other day. He gave us the lowdown regarding Mr. Baxter. Apparently, Baxter was born into money. His dad was a heavy hitter for some major corporation. I guess Mr. Baxter thinks he can fill his father's shoes. There is a trust fund set up for Baxter's family. He can't touch the money right yet. That's why he took Dolan's dough. Then Baxter started playing hard to get. So far, it has worked. Once Gambucci gets here, we will handle Mr. Baxter."

"Keep me informed, Cappy!"

Renata and Cappy took turns following Baxter around town. Every third day, they stuck close to Baxter's wife to see what her schedule was like. she was the family taxi driver/shopper. Occasionally, she met girlfriends for lunch at the golf club. It was the rare day when Baxter took on any "family" job. He was too busy having a few toots with his tony friends.

One Shot was watching Baxter's guys. Booby met Wing Nut every other week. Nut healed up quickly because he was regularly hauling hooch to Kansas. Booby, on the other hand, had a pronounced limp. His leg wasn't doing too good. Big Bear was very attentive during the unloading process. He carried a gun with enough fire power to blow a squad of soldiers away.

The liquor store was doing a bang-up business. Baxter was in the process of taking out a bank loan to buy another store. Cappy learned this little nugget from Dolan. Apparently one of Dolan's banker buddies had met Baxter a few days before. It looked as if the loan was forthcoming. All these irons in the fire might cause Baxter to trip up on the small details.

Gambucci finally arrived one week later than expected. His wife had gone into labor prematurely and he decided to stay with her until his mother-in-law could fly in from Sarasota. Billy was a lot like Dante in physique and demeanor. You didn't expect him to be a tough guy. That decision would be a major mistake. Billy was business all the way. As soon as Billy hit the front door, he wanted to be filled in regarding the situation.

"So," Billy started out, "if Dolan is out of the picture, what are we doing here?" Joey started to mouth off. Cappy slammed his fist on the table. "You are just a listener, One Shot. Keep your trap shut!"

Cappy turned to Billy. "Baxter embarrassed us. No one gets away with that. My job is to humble him and make him pay. Your job is to help us get that done."

"Okay, I can see the small picture, Cappy," Billy said, "but what's the big picture? That photo is hazy!"

Renata turned to Billy. "How long will you be here?"

"Let's say three months. My only concern is that I need to be back in Chicago to spend Christmas with my family. That is not up for discussion."

"So, Cappy," Renata said, "I started to think about Baxter and his new liquor store. If he gets his financing, he'll need to hire some extra muscle to help stock the new place, etc. As well, he'll need help with payroll and purchasing. That would get us on the inside. Before long, we would know where all the bodies were. We might start thinking about folks who could help us with these two areas."

Cappy decided that he needed a break. "We've been at this for a while. Let's knock for the rest of the day."

Billy decided to find a place to stay in the neighborhood. "There's not enough room in the bungalow to house all of us. I'm going to see if there are other rental units in the neighborhood."

They agreed to get back together for dinner. "We can all take some time to think this over. Hopefully, somebody will come up with a good idea," Renata said.

She went out for a walk. "I do my best thinking when I'm strolling through a park." She went for a drive and saw a sign for a city park. Five minutes later, she was out of her car. "It was a good thing I bundled up. The temperature must be in the forties. If I hustle, I could probably walk for three miles before I get really cold."

Renata returned at three o'clock. The wind was blustery, so she ended her walk sooner than she anticipated. Renata was carrying a cardboard tray with three cups of coffee as she walked through the front door. "I am ready to be warmed up. I thought you might be interested in java."

She laid the tray on the dining room table, pulled off her coat, and sat down. "I did some thinking while I was out walking. I like the idea of working for Mr. Baxter after he purchases his second store. He might need someone who can handle all the administrative duties. Someone who can be his assistant. It might be helpful if that person was attractive."

Cappy had been off in a daze until he heard that last comment. "What are you talking about? There's no way that you are going anywhere near that creep. I do not want you to be in the line of fire."

"Cappy, you can be so damn protective when you want to be. Listen up! We need someone on the inside. Someone who knows the ropes. Someone who can figure out where the money is. That someone is me! I have the business experience, I know how to handle people, and, if I say so myself, I am one attractive woman. I'm the whole package."

Renata could sense that Cappy was fuming at the thought of her getting involved with Baxter, so she walked towards their bedroom. "Maybe," she observed, "you might want to think this over. It has potential. In the meantime, I am dog tired. I'm going to take a nap. Wake me up in an hour or so."

It was close to 5:30 p.m. when Renata walked into the kitchen. She was surprised to see Billy sitting down next to the stove. "Where are the other two?"

Billy put his hands up. "I have no idea. I got here about 15 minutes ago. The place was empty. I stuck my head in your bedroom and saw that you were sleeping. The other two must have taken off."

Renata wondered if Billy had any success in finding a place to stay. "I spent the entire afternoon looking at rentals in the neighborhood. I finally rented a room from an elderly woman who lives several blocks away.

"The rent is dirt cheap. My room is on the first floor right next to the front door. My landlady lives by herself. She's hard of hearing so I can come and go as I please. It is a perfect set up."

Billy sat down next to Renata and asked if anything else was going on. She told him about her idea of getting close to Baxter's operation. "That's a great idea," he replied. "I was getting concerned about how much time this operation might take. If you can get on the inside, that would make life a whole lot easier."

"Cappy is not comfortable with this idea."

"That doesn't surprise me one bit. He has the hots for you. He doesn't want you to get hurt. Cappy needs to back off and take a longer look at this. From my viewpoint, your idea makes perfect sense. You got all the tools to make this work."

Just then, the front door opened. Cappy and Joey strode into the house. Cappy sat down next to Renata. Joey stood right behind him. "After you went into the bedroom," he said, "I decided that me and Joey needed some fresh air. We drove downtown and walked around for a bit. It got cold, so we went to the library." Renata looked surprised. "It was an odd choice, but it was warm inside the building. I was able to think through your suggestion. I gotta admit I was wrong. If we can get inside Baxter's operation, it would make life a lot easier. I was too protective." Cappy managed a smile as Renata and Billy took turns nodding their heads.

They spent the next week watching and waiting. This gave Cappy more time to think. He put off calling Dante until he had something to tell him. Today was the day to call him. Even though it was 6:45 p.m. EST., Cappy decided that he'd better let Dante know what was going on. He called Dante's private line and left a message. Thirty minutes later, Dante was on the horn. "You're calling late!" Dante said. "This better be good!"

Cappy told Dante that Billy had been about a week late in arriving. "He had a family emergency. Then Cappy

started talking to Dante about Renata's idea. "Dante, we tried the heavy-handed stuff. That backfired."
Dante started to spit out words. "It backfired, Cappy, because you had the wrong person involved."

"Don't I know it, Dante. But I think we have an idea that might work."

Cappy went through the bank information and the likelihood that Baxter would be starting up a second liquor store. 'He'll need help with the details. That's right up Renata's alley. I know Baxter is losing one of his employees at the first store. I think we can get a job for Renata working the counter. From there, she can angle her way into Baxter's books. If we get lucky, we might be able to grab more money than we had hoped for!"

Dante wasn't sure about this plan. He felt it would take too long to get any results. Cappy assured him that if things started to slow down, they could fall back on a more violent approach. "I did have an idea that I haven't shared with the others."

"Go on!" Dante said impatiently.

"Dante, if Baxter expands, he'll need more help to handle the rough side of the equation. Billy could fit in nicely. He can handle himself. Nobody around here knows him. The downside is that Billy would be sitting on his hands until after Christmas."

Dante thought this idea was making sense. "Send Gambucci home. Bring him back to Kansas City when the ball starts rolling. It is in your court, Capuano. Don't screw this up. If it goes south, so do you! I hope you understand exactly what I am saying." Then Cappy found himself listening to a dial tone.

Cappy turned towards the others. "Mr. B is skeptical, but he is willing to see it through, at least for a while." Billy wanted to know how he would be involved. "I don't have it all fleshed out, Billy. If Baxter does expand, he'll need more protection. Booby and Big Bear won't be enough manpower."

"Billy, I need to get a handle on that. It is likely to be quiet for a while. You should head back to Chicago. I know you have only been here for a week. I will pay you for your time. We will keep in contact. I won't need you until after Christmas. If that changes, you can come back. In the meantime, skedaddle." Billy said his goodbyes and was out the front door in no time flat.

Cappy turned to Joey. "The same goes for you. We do not need three people watching the Baxter bunch right now. Here's enough cash for you to head back to Hartford. I have your phone number if I need you. Remember, you need to keep a low profile. If Dante learns that you are in New England, we will both be needing an undertaker." Joey gathered his things and headed for the airport.

Christmas tree orders galore

The Christmas season was in full swing. Detta's kids were helping her decorate the house. Detta told them that they needed to work off some energy. "How about going outside and making a snowman. Five minutes later, the kids were bombarding each other with snowballs. Dante started heading down the stairs to his office. "Where are you going, buster?" Detta said sharply.

"I thought that we were done," Dante said.

"We are done decorating. Now you and I get to wear aprons. We need to make four dozen cookies for every member of your family. Wednesday night is only five days away." Dante hardly ever went near the kitchen. He was old fashioned about that kind of stuff. But given the brouhaha about his Boston trips, he thought better of listening to Johnny Most's play by play of the Celtics on the radio that night.

Detta had just begun to get the ingredients out of the cupboard when Cris came flying through the kitchen door. "Mom, Dad, you'll never guess what happened!"

"Slow down, Cristiana."

Cristiana went over to the coat rack and put her parka on a hook. "An administrator from St. Pete's stopped by the tree stand today. The hospital's regular source for Christmas trees can't fill their order. The hospital staff heard we are donating money from the sale of Christmas trees for the Angelino hospital fund. Since many of the surgeons and nurses had been involved with Mrs. Angelino's care, the hospital decided to buy the rest of their trees from us."

Cristiana could hardly contain her excitement. Dante, ever the numbers guy, wanted to know how many more trees they would be needing. "The hospital staff needs 170 trees! One hundred and seventy trees! Isn't that awesome? Paulie has to make a trip to Kip's Christmas Tree Farm. He knows the owner, some guy named Cliff. Paulie called Cliff. In no time flat, Cliff hooked him up with enough trees to cover the order."

Dante and Detta were grinning from ear to ear. The kids had been working hard over the past three weeks. This order was the icing on the cake. "Do you know how many trees you have sold?"

"Well, if we count the school and church orders, we've sold over 1100 trees. Before this, Uncle Paulie's biggest season was four hundred and eleven trees."

"Remind me what Paulie was going to give you for your part in this, Cristiana," Dante said. "Dad, I talked him into giving us $.55 extra for every tree over 400. That totals up to a little over $385 towards Mrs. Angelino's hospital bill."

"Wow," was all Dante could manage to say. Detta took Dante's hand and they pulled Cristiana into bear hug. "We're so proud of what you have accomplished. No one could have done a better job," Detta exclaimed.

Later that night, when the kids had finally hit the hay, Detta decided to relax. She sat down next to Dante and they watched an hour's worth of the Johnny Carson show. After a few minutes listening to Carson's monologue, Dante spoke up. "That daughter of ours is something special. I cannot believe how well she and her friends have done at Paulie's stand. They have worked their butts off. What Cristiana doesn't know is that I spread the word about Maria's situation. Some of my old neighbors in Providence agreed to pony up enough money to buy another one hundred trees. They gave the trees to underprivileged families in Pawtucket."

"You can be pretty resourceful, Dante. Cristiana shares your determination. Her efforts have been very selfless. She didn't do this to get any praise. She did this to help someone else out. That is so special."

Detta turned to her husband. "Dante, we should do something special for Cris." Dante asked her what she had in mind. "I think it would be great if she and I spent a week in New York City. Right after Christmas might be the ideal time."

"Good idea," Dante said. "I'll call my mom to see if she can help me take care of the boys while you are gone."

For the next few minutes, Detta was as quiet as a church mouse. Then she turned towards Dante. "For the last few weeks, you have been quiet and withdrawn. Is everything okay?" Dante was surprised to hear her comments. He thought he had hidden his concern about Trixie's situation. Apparently, that was not the case.

"I've been preoccupied with work. What I need to do is to leave my work issues at our front doorstep."

"Maybe you need to relax. Let's open up one of those bottles of champagne you have downstairs," Detta cooed. "Then, we can celebrate our daughter's success." Dante nodded his head vigorously as he headed towards the basement steps.

The only ball is starting to roll

The next morning was a whirlwind of activity. Detta had a meeting with Brother Allan. She and Dante didn't get to sleep until well after 1 a.m., so she was slow afoot. Detta was the first one up. She had to prod the kids to get ready. Dante and Marty had an early meeting in Providence. There was not much peace and quiet at the Bonfigore house that morning.

Detta made it to Don Bosco with minutes to spare. Brother Allan's face lit up when he met her. "I'm talking to the mother of a very successful businesswoman. You have some daughter on your hands!" Detta was overjoyed to hear his praise.

"Why don't you come into my office so we can talk?" Brother Allan knew about the work that kids had done at school, but he wanted to hear about the results. He was amazed to hear how well they had done.

"I am hoping that our fundraiser for the Angelinos will be as successful as the kids' tree stand sales. I realize this is the last day of school before the Christmas holidays, but I wanted to touch base with you so we can get a handle on where we stand."

At that point, Brother Allan indicated that the bishop had called. "Detta, he gave me the names of three priests who are willing to help! I've called them. They have already started contacting their parishioners. Everyone who was contacted had heard all about Mrs. Angelino's situation. Four families have donated some terrific gifts, including a spring yachting weekend on Long Island Sound and front row seats to a Celtics game against the Philadelphia 76'ers. The response has been awesome. How are things going on your end?"

Detta told Allan that her committee had sold over 150 tickets and they still had three weeks to go until the sales deadline. "On top of that, the Greenville Knights of Columbus have put together some great gifts including a week's ski stay for six at the Killington Ski Resort in Vermont. I need to finalize plans with the caterer and find folks who can help with decorations."

"Detta, some of our kids need confirmation projects. I think I could round up some 'volunteers' to help you."

Detta was delighted to hear this news. They agreed to get together in two weeks to finalize the arrangements. Detta hugged Brother Allan and headed towards the parking lot.

The mob business is smoking hot

Dante's meeting didn't go over so well. He met with John Iavarone. Iavarone was second in command of the New England mob. He was a short, stocky guy with a bulbous nose and a snappy smile. His smile belied his personality. He wasn't a patient man. The smile went away when Dante explained what was happening in Kansas. "Will this story have a happy ending? From where I stand, Cappy is pedaling a stationary bike. We need results. We've spent enough time and money on this damn project."

Dante agreed. "Cappy has a good plan in place. With any luck, we should get a great return on our investment by the end of February." Iavarone made it clear that this problem had to end sooner than later. Dante kept his thoughts to himself. "I'll keep you in the loop."

As Marty was about to start the car, Dante suggested that they drive over to the Lucky 7. "You need to fill me in on our cigarette venture. Let's talk this over a cold can of beer." They got to the bar before the guys at a nearby factory got off work. "So, where do we stand?"

Marty met with Louie and Dusty on Friday. "Our progress has been rocky. Once my guys understood that I was in charge, they started clicking. We now have a list of every warehouse and employee involved with the cigarette business. This morning, Dusty dropped off a list of troopers who'd be likely to jump at the small stuff. Troopers who wanted an easy collar rather than being willing to wait for a chance to catch the big fish.

"We have a small warehouse east of Pittsfield. It has enough product at to service gas stations from Pittsfield to Albany. I'll get word to a new state trooper. A guy by the name of McAfee. He's assigned to the Cheshire station. He wants to make a name for himself. We will feed him bogus information about the size of the operation.

"McAfee will find four hundred cartons of smokes and a 23-year-old kid who knows next to nothing about us. We have someone who works at the Pittsfield barracks. She will tell us when the police are headed our way. Most of product will be moved out of the building and sold before anyone is the wiser. The police get an appetizer. We get the whole enchilada."

Dante was impressed. "You have covered all the bases. I guess I am not as smart a guy as I thought I was."

"What do you mean, Mr. B?" Marty asked.

If I was really smart, I would have involved you in our operations long before now! You've done a good job. You are smart enough to come up with a terrific idea that should work like a dream. When I get back to the office, I'll get the okay to start this ball rolling."

I've been thinking about Trixie

Marty started to stand up, figuring that the meeting was over. "We're not done yet. Sit down! I've been thinking about what to do with this Trixie situation. I told you the last time we talked that we could not get involved with any type of rough stuff with Trixie. Even though I am sorely tempted to take a swing at her myself, Marty, that would really upset the apple cart. We don't need that kind of trouble!"

"Mr. B, the situation is trouble any way you look at it."

Dante wanted nothing more to do with Trixie or her kid. He liked Trixie and he enjoyed all their bedtime opportunities. However, he had a family, a good family. One family was more than enough for him. "Trixie's been a way for me to let off steam. However, she's become a distraction. What did she say when you saw her?"

"Pretty much the same thing as I told you before. Trixie enjoyed being with a bigwig. The sex was good. She made herself believe that she would be important if she could curry your favor. Now, she really wants the baby, but she doesn't want you."

Marty could tell that the news was deflating. On the other hand, Mr. B. seemed relieved. No entanglements, no baby, no sweat. "She wants to make a new start. Someplace where no one knows her or her situation. She wants some money for now and for the future. We didn't talk about specifics, I think $75k would take of her for now. Then, you have the cost of the birth, a place to stay for her to stay, and a good job. All told, we are looking at $200,000."

Dante started to smile as he thought about Trixie and this baby situation. Marty asked him what was going on. "I need to talk to Cappy. He owes me big time. I think I have a way for him to pay me back. This could be payback with a capital 'P.'" With that, they headed home.

Dante called Cappy when he got back home. "We have got two things to talk about, Cappy. First, the guys in Providence are not happy that the Baxter deal is taking so long. I know you have a plan and I like the plan. But remember that I answer to "Big Johnny." We need to get this thing in motion pretty damn soon."

Cappy understood the score. He told Dante that Billy was heading back to Chicago for Christmas. "Not much is gonna happen between now and then."

Dante reminded Cappy that he needed to watch One Shot like a hawk until this whole thing was finished. "We don't need this hot shot messing up our plans!"

"What's the second thing, Dante?"

"I have a little problem. A woman I know needs to get out of New England in a hurry. She helped me out and I want to return the favor. Kinda like what happened to you and Scorpini back in the day. I need you to sweet talk Renata into letting my friend stay at her place in Chicago for a while."

"Are you pulling my leg, Dante? You want me to convince Renata to let a stranger stay in her house for who knows how long?" Cappy's voice got louder and louder the more he understood the implications. Marty could hear one side of the conversation. It wasn't going well.

Dante's face was as red as a strawberry. Marty put his hand up as if to ask for a minute of Mr. B's time. "Cappy, I am not done with you yet. Something just came up. I'll call you back as soon as I take care of this."

Dante was not happy with Marty, and you can bet your boots that he wasn't happy with his favorite towing operator. "What the hell are you up to, Marty? Waving me to stop in mid-sentence. I was ready to lower the boom on Capuano."

"I could see that," Marty exclaimed. 'You have a whole lot on the line. This deal with Trixie is important. But, Mr. B, you know what happens when you put two cocks in a fight. At the end of the day, all you have left is feathers. You and Cappy are the cocks. You are both locked and loaded—ready to tear each other's hair out. How about giving me a try? I'll talk directly to Renata and see if I can make some headway." Dante was skeptical, but he agreed to let Marty have a go at it.

Marty redialed Cappy's number. Cappy was confused when he picked up the phone and heard Marty on the line. "What's going on? Where the hell is Dante?"

"Dante told me to talk to Renata. Put her on the phone right now!" That really set Cappy off.

Marty handed the phone to Mr. B. "Cappy isn't cooperating!" Mr. B was spitting nickels. He tore into Cappy. The next thing you knew, Renata was on the other end of the line. A little later, Marty hung up the phone. "Everything is all set, Boss!"

"What did you do Marty?" Dante asked.

"I pulled the two of you out of the equation. Cappy is a real hothead and you want things to move along without any distraction. It is darn hard to get a quick resolution with all that going on. I thought Renata might be grateful for what Cappy had done for her back in the day and, because of that, she might be willing to consider helping Trixie out."

Marty shared Trixie's story with Renata. It was Marty's lucky day. Renata knew all about gratitude. She wanted to pay it forward. Renata willing to let Trixie stay at her house in Chicago for a while. She was also willing to offer Trixie a job at her company. A twofer! Dante shook his head in disbelief. Marty's work in Massachusetts was great. This piece of magic was terrific.

"Maybe I am getting somewhere in this organization." Marty thought. "Mr. B's starting to trust my judgement!"

On Tuesday, Dante told Marty that he wanted to go to the Cape to talk to Trixie. "Can you call her and see if she would meet with me?"

Trixie was upbeat when she spoke to Marty. "Tell Dante I'm looking forward to seeing him. We need to talk!"

Early the next morning, Dante drove up to the Cape. He was got there way early to be knocking on Trixie's door, so he headed to the beach. The closest beach was Falmouth Heights Beach. The surf was up, and the sun was coming up. There was no one there except for an old guy walking an even older Labrador. Dante plopped down on the sandy beach and took it all in.

The weather was very brisk, so it wasn't too long before Dante started shivering. He got back into his car and headed north. He found a small diner three miles down the road.

Dante walked into the diner and sat down at the nearest booth. An older woman with a cigarette dangling from

her lips was standing near the counter. When Dante sat down at a booth, she walked over. She looked as if she had been around the block a time or three. "You look like an icicle, buster. Whadda you need?"
Dante started laughing. No one had called him "Buster" in a long, long while. It felt kinda good. "I need a large cup of coffee. Make sure it is black and hot."

"I'll be back in a flash." she said. "In the meantime, here is our menu. The special of the day is johnnycakes, two fried eggs, and corned beef hash. Today, Buster, I will only charge you $3.75 for our special. Coffee is included." Dante couldn't pass that up. "Add some toast and marmalade, no butter, and we have ourselves a deal." This waitress was a breath of fresh air.

Dante drove to Trixie's place. He got out of the car and walked up to her front door. It was just a bit after 9 a.m. Dante wasn't sure what type of reception he would receive. Trixie greeted him at the door. She was relaxed. "Can I come in? It might be a good idea if we talk some things over." She ushered Dante into her living room, got a cup of coffee, and sat down next to him.

"I know Marty called you last week, Trixie. Given the way things were left the last time I was here, I thought it best if I stepped back and let Marty do the talking. I understand that things went well." Trixie started crying the moment Dante opened his mouth.

"Honestly, Dante, I was as surprised as you were when I found out I was pregnant. Surprised doesn't cover it! My doctor had told me there was no way that I was ever going to get pregnant. Then this happened!" She pointed to her stomach. "I was angry and confused." Frankly, Dante, you weren't much help with all your yelling and screaming! I don't blame you for feeling angry. I was hoping for a little understanding from you."

Dante took her hand in his and told her that he was sorry for the way he treated her. "I didn't handle the news very well." Dante put his arm around her shoulder and held her tightly against his chest. Then she started to cry. They stayed in an embrace for a little while. Then Trixie started to shake and shudder.

"What am I going to do, Dante? I want to keep our child, but I have no one who can help me. My parents are dead and my brother is in no position to help me out of this mess. He and his wife are mortgaged up to the hilt. I know you have a wife and three kids in Rhode Island. There's no way you'll leave your family for me. I don't know what to do!" Tears streamed down her face.

Dante told her about his idea. She could move to Chicago and start a new life. He had found her a place to stay. He told her all about Renata. "She has a big house in the suburbs. She told us that someone helped her out of a jam. She thinks it's time for her to help someone else. She'd love to help. You can stay with her until you are ready to find your own place. On top of that, Renata has a job opening for a customer relations specialist. I know how you handle customer issues at the bank. I think this would be up your alley." Trixie's tears of frustration gave way to tears of joy.

Dante said he'd pay for the baby's birth. As well, he would give her a $100k to help her start her new life. "You're right about my family, Trixie. My wife and kids are the center of my life. They don't need to know about you or the baby. I will help you as much as I can. All you need to do is call Marty if you have any problems."

That news seemed to ease her tension. "I want you to get to know your child, Dante. I am hoping that you might come to Chicago, every now and again, to spend a little time with us."

"We'll see what happens, Trixie."

He left her house about a half hour later. He was relieved at how things had gone between the two of them. Trixie was willing to go quietly. Dante knew he had upped the ante, but if that was what it took to seal the deal, it was money well spent. "Wow, I have another kid. Who would have guessed that would ever happen!"

As Gomer Pyle would say, "Surprise, Surprise, Surprise"

Maria Angelino was released from St. Pete's five days after her second surgery. The doctors were pleased with the initial results. Dr. White stopped in just before the Angelinos were set to leave for home. He put his hand on Maria's shoulder as he spoke to John. "Mr. Angelino, I know that Maria likes to get things done in a hurry." John nodded in agreement. "For the time being, I'm appointing you as the new sheriff in the Angelino household. Your wife needs to take it easy for a few weeks. After that, if everything checks out, we can get her started on physical therapy. For now, your wife does not do any housework. Do we have a deal?"

John looked at Maria. "That'll be a tough sell, Doc, but I guarantee that she'll stay on the sidelines and coach us on what we need to do." They all laughed heartily. Then the orderly appeared and wheeled Maria down to the front door of the hospital. John went for their car.

Maria followed the doctor's orders to the T. She laid out a plan for the chores around the house and the meals. She did not touch a pot, pan, dishes, or any cleaning items. "Honey," John said a few days later, "I'm thinking you like your new supervisory position."

"I could get used to this new job," she said with a smile.

Maria's neighbors and friends continued to amaze her. Every day, someone dropped off the evening meal. Maria was overwhelmed by all the support her neighbors and friends were providing. The women from the St. Philip's pitched in and bought Christmas presents for the family. Without their help, the Angelinos would have had a sparse group of gifts under the tree.

Maria cried when her friends brought the gifts to her house. "How can we ever repay you?" Her best friend, Johanna Dwyer, told Maria that she had always been there for everyone else at church. "Now it is your time to be the recipient of support! Relax and let us be helpful." Tears of joy streaked down Maria's face.

Four days before Christmas, John got home from work and told Maria to get her coat on. He walked her to their car. Their family trailed behind. Maria wondered what was going on. "We have a little surprise for you. I know surprises are hard for you, but you need to sit back and relax. You will learn about your surprise in short order." That response only served to stir up the pot.

Maria rattled off five questions to no one in particular. She got no response. She stared at her husband. That didn't work. Finally, she sat back to see where they were going. They headed towards Route 6. It was only after they turned onto Pleasant Street that Maria figured out where they were headed.

"We are going to Twin Oaks?"

"Yes, we are." her husband said. Once they had found a place to park, everyone piled out of the car and headed towards the restaurant. Maria turned to John. "How can we afford this dinner?"

"Your old friend Dante Bonfigore is treating us to dinner, my dear." Maria's surprise was evident by the look on her face. "John Angelino! Are kidding me?"

"Scout's honor, Honey."

The wait at Twin Oaks could seem like forever. Not today. When the Angelino's walked in the front door, they were whisked to the back room. Dante and his family were already seated. Dante came over and gave

215

Maria a hug. Then he introduced his family. John and Dante shook hands. "This is very special, Dante. We don't know how to thank you."

"Your presence is thanks enough."

Vincent introduced Cristiana to his mother. Vincent made sure his mother knew Cris was responsible for the Christmas tree idea. Maria gave her a huge one-armed hug. "Vincent has told me all about you. I can't thank you enough for what you did for our family."

Cris just smiled and said "You are most welcome, Mrs. Angelino.

A waiter came in and gave everyone a menu. He asked if anyone would like something to drink. Everyone was thirsty. "What can I bring you?" the waiter asked. One person after another rattled off their choice of beverage. The waiter stood there, listening to their drink orders. He never wrote the orders down.

When the waiter headed back towards the bar, Vincent nudged his father. "Dad," he whispered, "The waiter didn't write any orders down on paper! How is he going to remember who had what?"

"I'm not sure, Vincent. I guess we'll just have to wait and see." A few minutes later, the waiter reappeared with a tray of drinks. Everyone got exactly what they ordered. Vincent was amazed. The waiter then took everyone's food order. Again, nothing was written down.

"How does he do that?" Vincent wondered.

Mr. and Mrs. Bonfigore sat at the head of the table with Vincent's parents. Vincent's mother was talking to Cristiana's father. They really knew each other. At that point, Mrs. Bonfigore started talking to Vincent's younger brother, Pietro. "So, Pietro, I understand Vincent is cross-country runner. Do you like to run?"

"Oh no, I hate running. It's boring. I want to be a basketball player just like Billy Donovan of the Providence College Friars."

She turned to her oldest son. "Nico, what is your favorite sport."

"Basketball."

"And who is your favorite player?"

"Billy Donovan."

"You guys have a lot in common." Just then, the food arrived. It took three waiters to bring the food to their table. Talking stopped and the eating began.

A little later, after most of the dinner and dessert plates had been taken away, Maria asked Detta to sit next to her. "Mrs. Bonfigore," she said, "I know how much time you have spent working with Mr. Viterio and all of the others to help our family. I am so grateful for your help."

"First off, please call me Detta and I'll call you Maria."

"Detta it is!"

"I know you and Dante's sister grew up together. Dante speaks so highly of you. When we heard about the shooting, we dropped everything to help you out. Dante thinks of you as if you were one of his younger sisters." Then they began to talk about their families. Detta could understand why folks thought so highly of Maria. She was friendly, sincere, and as genuine as the day was long. She was Detta's type of person.

"So, if I can be blunt, Maria, how are things really going for you? You have had a rough few weeks."

"It's been difficult. I'm doing well. I am in a much better place now that the second operation is over with. I can see the end of the tunnel. It is still far away, but it's getting closer. It scares me to think I might not be able to do what I used to do. I need to be patient. Everyone has pitched in without a word of complaint. And the community support, the school, you and so many others reaching out to help us. You've been a gift from God."

Detta told Maria that Vincent was a wonderful boy. "You must be really proud of him."

"We are proud of him. He is a good kid. Helpful around the house, working hard at school, etc. He's just fifteen. It is a crazy time in the life of any teenager. When you add in his cross-country successes and my injuries, it's a lot to handle. But he seems to be handling it all. You know Detta, I had no idea who Cristiana was. I knew she and Vincent were spending a lot of time on the tree sales. It was only a few days ago that I put two and two together. Let me ask you a question. I sense that Cristiana and Vincent's relationship is starting to grow. Vincent tells me that Cris is smart, sensitive, and she knows how to get things done. She's helped Vincent take risks. He thinks the world of her. What do you think?"

Detta choked up a little after hearing Maria's comments. "You don't waste time getting right to the point! I think our children enjoy each other's company. They work well together and they seem to care about each other. That's a good thing."

"I am concerned about how young they are," Detta responded, "but as long as they keep it light, I'm not going to interfere." My thoughts exactly!" Maria said. "How about we keep this conversation to ourselves."

"I think that is a great idea Maria."

"Detta, now that I am out of the hospital and continuing to get stronger, John tells me that I should get out of the house and enjoy myself a little. How would you like to have coffee sometime next week?"

"What a great idea, Maria! I'll give you a call and we can find a time to get together. I'd really enjoy that."

Going all the way. I am not stopping now

The door to Renata's bedroom was wide open. It had been open since the day Joey headed to Waterbury. Cappy was able to see Renata in a totally different light. She could handle herself well. She knew what she was doing. She might have been like that when he first met her, but he was too full of himself to notice.

They decided to celebrate Christmas in style. They flew to San Juan and rented a quiet place in the Dorado neighborhood. Sun, sand, and rum cokes were plentiful. They walked the beach every day. Renata told Cappy that they should come back to Dorado when this whole Kansas City thing was wrapped up. Cappy thought that this was her best idea yet.

When they flew back to Kansas, they kept an eye on Baxter's operations. Booby and Big Bear were bringing cases of booze to a warehouse a few miles from Baxter's home. Cappy wondered what was happening. He called Dolan. "Mr. Dolan, this is Cappy Capuano. Have you heard anything more about Baxter?"

Then Dolan told Cappy that Baxter got his loan right after Christmas. "He opened an office near his store. I hear he is looking for help with his books."

"If he's advertising for an assistant to help organize his business," Renata said. "I know someone who could step right in and help him out."

Cappy was taken aback. "You know someone who would work for that jerk?"

"I sure do. You are looking at her!"

Cappy wasn't the least bit happy at the thought of having Renata work for Baxter. He became protective. "It is too dangerous. You could get hurt."

Renata sat Cappy right down. For the next few minutes, she outlined the advantages of getting involved. She'd be in the middle of his operation. With her skills, Baxter was sure to give her more responsibility. "Once I am inside, I'll know everything that goes on. Baxter won't know what I am up to!" The more she talked, the better Cappy could see the big picture.

"I suppose it might work out. It would be helpful to know more about his operation. But I don't want you getting hurt. The past few weeks, we've had a good thing going. I must have been out of my gourd screwing around with those other women when I had you. I am hoping we can find a way to stay together."

Renata smiled, leaned over and gave him a peck on the cheek. "Why, Cappy, there is a romantic inside those old bones of yours. The last few weeks have been wonderful for the both of us. I am looking forward to spending more time with you once this operation is over."

Renata bought a newspaper. Baxter's ad was in bold print on the classified page. She headed over to his office. She started thinking about the fire they had set at Baxter's store. "I know that young kid saw me when I went into the store. He just might remember what I look like. That wouldn't be good."

Renata decided to go to the realty office that helped them find their current digs. She introduced herself to the receptionist at the front desk. Renata told the woman that she used their company to find a cute bungalow in the area. "I wanted to thank you for all your help. The place is just what the doctor ordered." The receptionist smiled. "I'm happy things had worked out."

Renata sat down next to the receptionist. "Do you have time to answer a question?"

"It's really quiet around here. How can I help you?"

Renata told the receptionist that she was thinking about changing her hairstyle. "I don't know a soul in town. I need to find a good beautician. I'm wondering If you know a stylist that you could recommend."

The receptionist thought for a second. "You might want to try the Parisian Salon over on 5th Street. It's just a few blocks down the street. Ask for Monsieur Gee. Tell him Audrey sent you."

Renata thanked the receptionist and headed off to find this Gee. The salon wasn't hard to locate. Renata went in and wondered if Mr. Gee was available. Surprisingly, his next client had just called in and canceled her appointment. "My lucky day!"

Mr. Gee came right out. He was a pinprick of a guy with wavy brown hair, a tightly trimmed goatee, and a French accent that seemed sketchy. What really got Renata's attention was his Hawaiian shirt, his tight pants, and the blue scarf around his neck. "Oh my! In for a penny, in for a pound." Then Gee walked her back to his chair. Renata had gone into the salon with luxuriously long reddish-brown hair. Two hours later, she had a short, curly cut with blonde highlights. "No one will ever recognize me now."

She jumped into her car and headed west. Fifteen minutes later, she arrived at Baxter's place. It was in a four-story office building. She walked up a long flight of stairs and found his office. The sign on the door read "Baxter Enterprises." She opened the glass framed door and walked in as if she owned the place.

Renata found Baxter sitting at a large oak desk with the newspaper sitting on his lap. The rest of the office was barren. There were no desks, file cabinets, nothing but empty space, Baxter looked up. Once he saw Renata, you could tell that he liked what he saw.

"Well, hello there!" he said. "How can I help you?"

Renata told him that she had seen his ad and wanted to apply for the job. She could tell that Baxter was more interested in her body than her mind. "What exactly are you looking for?" He had a long list of wants. When he finally took a breath, Renata said, "So, you want a Girl Friday who can answer the phone, add, subtract, and juggle hula hoops all at the same time?"

That caught Baxter a little off guard. He started to laugh. "I like a girl with a sense of humor!"

Normally, the "girl" comment would have set her off. Renata decided to keep her cool. She told Baxter that she had just moved from Ohio to be near relatives. Then she fabricated a story about her last job. "I worked for a printing company. I was the administrative assistant. I did everything the boss wanted."

Baxter liked the "everything the boss wanted" piece. It was clear that Baxter's mind was completely in the gutter. She teased him silly. "I think I have found the answer to my prayers, Renata. When can you start?"

"Yesterday, Mr. Baxter!"

"You got the job, sweetheart. I have some business to take care of tomorrow. How about you start the day after tomorrow. Be here around nine. In the meantime, I'll go out and get you a desk, a file cabinet and a used typewriter. You can buy whatever else you need when you get here. How does that sound?"

Renata started to think of Jackie Gleason's old phrase: "And Away We Go." All she could do was smile as she headed back to meet up with Mr. Capuano.

When Renata came through the front door of the bungalow, Cappy had to look twice before he said anything. "What happened to you?"

Renata could see he was surprised. She said she was concerned that she might have been noticed at the liquor store. "So," she said, "hair today, gone tomorrow."

Cappy knew better than to say how he felt about her haircut, so he simply shut his mouth.

"How did things go with Baxter?"

"I got the job."

Cappy was surprised that things had fallen into place so quickly. "Terrific. I better get Billy and One Shot back here by the middle of next week. By then, we should have an idea of Baxter's set up. Give us two more weeks and we'll have everything in place."

Renata agreed. Then she took his hand. "Appetizers before dinner?" were her last words as she led him into their bedroom and shut the door behind her.

It was well after 5 p.m. by the time they got up. They decided to take a shower together. Once they were cleaned up and dressed, Cappy wondered what they were having for dinner. "I made spaghetti carbonara last night. I thought you might like something Italian. Why don't you go find us some Frascati? In the meanwhile, I'll warm up the carbonara and fix us a nice caprese salad. How does that sound?"

Cappy murmured his agreement.

"Just one more thing, Mr. Capuano. You can go anywhere you want except Baxter's place to buy the Frascati," she said with that devilish smile of hers. Cappy was already thinking about dessert.

After dinner, Cappy called Billy. "I need you back here by Wednesday. "No later!!"

I'll be there Tuesday night, Cappy."

Joey was a totally different story. He started to whine when Cappy called. "Boss, I got a little something, something going on with a babe I knew back in high school. I'm busy. I'll try to make it back by Friday."

You could have fried an egg on Cappy's neck when he heard this line of garbage. "Joey, let's get something straight. When I say that I want you here by Wednesday, you will be here by Wednesday! Do you read me?"

Joey knew better than to mouth off to Cappy. "I'll be there by Wednesday."

When Cappy finished the phone calls, he looked over to Renata. She was standing at the bedroom door with nothing on but a flimsy blue nightgown. They had finished the whole bottle of wine during dinner. "Are you ready to take me on again, big boy?" Cappy didn't need any more encouragement as he headed towards the bedroom sheets.

Everyone made it back by Wednesday. Gambucci arrived on Tuesday afternoon as advertised. Joey was scheduled to come in late Wednesday afternoon. He didn't get in until much later that evening. His flight was delayed due to engine trouble. Renata and Cappy decided to hold off on updating them. Renata reckoned it could wait until the following day. "Things might go better if Joey gets some rest."

The next morning, everyone was at the kitchen table waiting for Cappy. He had woken up when Renata's alarm went off. However, he fell right back to sleep when she headed to the bathroom. You can only imagine the reception he received when he walked out the bedroom door a little after 8:45 a.m. Lots of "Early bird and Sleepy head, etc." were thrown towards his direction. He withstood the verbal abuse for twenty seconds. Then he told everyone to shut their traps.

Renata gave them an update as to what she had accomplished while they were away. Billy was amazed. "You're actually working for Baxter! I'm impressed."

"You'll be more impressed when you hear our plan!" She proceeded to tell them that one of her duties would be to handle all his books.

"I will be able to write checks," she said excitedly. "If everything goes right, Baxter won't know what hit him. The bad news is that Baxter won't get his hands on any of the dough for about three weeks." Renata told the guys that this extra time would give her a chance to understand his operation.

Cappy laid out the second part of the plan. Baxter had gotten the best of them the first time around. This time, Cappy wanted to hurt Baxter in the pocketbook.

"We know he is storing hooch in a warehouse about five miles from here. He probably got a sweet deal on the hooch and is stocking up ahead of time. Baxter will need extra help picking up liquor from the distributor, etc. If we could get someone who could work with Booby and Big Bear, maybe we could help ourselves to the booze in the warehouse at the same time as we take the cash. This is where you might come in real handy, Billy."

Billy was dumbstruck. He didn't understand what Cappy was getting at. Renata told him that Baxter, Booby and Wing Nut had all heard Cappy and Joey's voices. Clearly, their accents would give them away if they tried to get a job with Baxter. "Billy, nobody has heard your voice. That gives us the upper hand. Cappy tells me that you can hold your own with your fists and your gun. If you got a job with Baxter, you would come in handy if our plan went off the rails."

Billy wanted to know what he would have to do.

"If you were hired on to work for Mr. Baxter," Renata said, "you could provide him with some protection. Otherwise, you probably would load and unload boxes of booze at the warehouse. Is that something you could do? Billy assured Renata that he could handle this.

Cappy spoke up. "Billy," there is one more thing I need from you. When you get the job, I want you to keep your eyes and ears open. Do his flunkies get along? Do they have little tells regarding when they might pull the trigger if they get in a jam? That information would be helpful when we take these rascals for all they've got."

"So, Renata is working for Baxter. If I get lucky and get a job with Mr. Baxter, what are you and Joey doing?"

"Yeah," said Joey in a forceful tone, "what's left for us? Are we gonna sit around twiddling our thumbs? I've got better things to do!"

Renata could see that Cappy was feeling challenged. She knew no good would come from this. She looked at One Shot. "Joey, I know how good you are at following people. Your skills should be put to good use. Maybe you can keep an eye on Baxter—where he goes, who he sees, etc."

Cappy lifted his eyebrows as he heard Renata cozy up to Joey. She was trying to flatter this mutt. "Joey, you're the only one of us who could handle this situation."

Joey ate this up like candy. He forgot about his earlier challenges and told Renata that he could handle this. At that point, Cappy said, "We've had a long day. Let's call it a wrap for now and get something to eat. Everyone agreed. They headed back to the barbecue place for ribs and beer. After dinner, Billy went back to his place to get some shuteye. The others headed to the bungalow. Joey decided to hit the hay.

Once Cappy heard One Shot's snoring, he sat down next to Renata. "I was ready to pound Joey's face into the sand earlier this evening."

"I caught that. That's why I smothered the boy with praise. One Shot can think of nothing but himself. We need to be careful how we use this jerkoff. He could easily turn all our plans into one effing disaster."

"You and I agree. We need to watch him like a hawk!"

Renata headed over to Baxter's office the following morning. Joey and Cappy were having a cup of java when Billy poked his head in the door and said, "Is everybody up?" This was a follow up jab at Cappy from the day before. Cappy let it slide.

"Sit down. I was just thinking about you. I have an idea about how to get you a job with the Baxter bunch."

That got Billy's attention. He was eager to hear what Cappy might have to say. "Fill me in."

"Baxter and I are two peas in a pod. We both like money and we will do just about anything to get it. That usually means using brute force. Using the likes of Booby and

Big Bear comes naturally to Baxter. If he wants to grow his business, he will need more muscle." Billy nodded in agreement. He wondered where this was heading.

"Do you know anyone in Chicago who'd be willing to take a beating if there was enough money involved?" The guys Billy knew weren't interested in taking a beating. They preferred to give someone else a beating.

"Cappy, I need to give that some thought. What do you have in mind?"

Cappy explained himself "You surprise a lot of folks, Billy. They don't expect a small guy like you to pulverize the competition." Billy laughed out loud. Cappy was spot on. Most folks underestimated him.

"I wonder what would happen if we got a big galoot to go into Baxter's liquor store and start a fistfight. Maybe even with Baxter himself. That would be ideal. You just happen to walk in the store as this fricking fight breaks out. Then you can proceed to save Baxter's bacon."

Billy could see where this might be heading. He'd become Mighty Mouse for a day. The idea made sense. He could envision the set up. "I know two guys who might fit the bill," he said. "They are both big boys. You might think I'd be on the floor after one punch. However, my karate skills combined with a wicked right jab would leave them on the floor in no time."

The guys Billy had thought of were night owls, so he decided it would be better if he called them later that afternoon. "What would be in it for them?"

"Anyone who agreed to get involved would be given a reasonable share of the loot."

I need some help

The week after Christmas was a whirlwind. Every time Vincent looked around, somebody was coming by with a dessert they had made or some type of alcoholic beverage. That day a cousin dropped off Italian cream cakes and Mrs. Sullivan, their neighbor, brought over some fudge. Vincent finally figured out that bringing over something to eat was an easy way to find out how his mom was doing. The commotion was tiring her out. Finally, Vincent's aunts and uncles got the word out to everyone. "No more visitors for a while!"

Later that week, Vincent got a call from Mikey. Apparently, some of their school friends were heading over to Yawgoo Valley to go skiing on Friday. Mikey heard Cristiana might be going. He wondered if Vincent was interested in coming.

Vincent said "yes" without thinking about it. "I'll ask my dad if he can drop us off."

Then Mikey spoke up. "I'll see if my dad could pick us up after skiing."

Uncle Paulie stopped by the Angelino's house to drop off an envelope for Vincent. The envelop was full of cash. "What is this?" Vincent asked.

"I told you that I would pay you $5/hour when you worked at the tree stand. You put in 35 hours, so here is $175.00. I also added a little extra for all the trees you guys sold. Merry Christmas."

Vincent became "Fumblefingers" again when he began counting the money. There was $215.00 in the envelope.

"My gosh" was all he could say. He tried to give the money to his folks, but they would not take it.

Maria turned to her son. "Vincent, we already received a check from Paulie. The money he dropped off today is yours to spend as you wish. Merry Christmas, son."

After getting over the shock of this, Vincent asked his dad if he would take him over to Citizens Bank the following day. "Whatever for, Vincent?"

"Well, dad, I want to put some money in the bank. Mr. Genovese, the banker, told me that you would need to cosign the paperwork."

John was surprised. "I'm happy to take you. Just tell me one thing. What do you plan to do with this money?"

"I'm planning to use it to help pay for college."

John thought he had heard it all until today. He didn't know what to say except "Get in the car. We are going over to the bank right now. I want to see Genovese's face when you hand him the money."

Vincent didn't put all the money in the bank. He set aside forty dollars. Part of this would pay his admission into Yawgoo. He was also planning to buy a gift for Cris. She had done so much for his family that he decided to buy her a gift as a way of saying thank you. The question was "What should he buy her?" He had no idea.

Most of the time, Vincent was happy that he did not have sisters. This was the one time when a sister would be of help. He wasn't going to ask his mom to help him. If he did, he'd never hear the end of it. He decided to ask his aunt Eileen. Eileen was his dad's youngest sister. She just turned 22 in October. When Vincent was younger, she used to babysit Vincent and his brothers. He and

Eileen had grown close to one another. Vincent knew she was able to keep a secret.

Eileen worked at the local drug store. He called the store several times before she answered the phone. He told her that he needed her to take him to the mall. She wanted to know the details. Vincent wasn't ready to give them up just yet. "I will tell you when I see you!"

"Okay, Vincent, but this had better be important."

Eileen arrived at four o'clock on the dot. Maria was surprised to see her. Eileen came up with a cockamamie story about needing Vincent to help unpack boxes at the store. Eileen told Maria that two kids who work at the store went up to New Hampshire for the weekend. "We should be done by six." Vincent's mom was very gullible. She bought the story hook, line, and sinker.

Off they went to the Warwick Mall. Vincent filled Eileen in as they headed towards the mall. "I have a friend. Her name is Cris. She got me the job selling Christmas trees. You know how successful this was!" Eileen nodded her head. "Well," he said. "None of this would have happened without Cris. I want to buy her a gift as my way of saying thank you. However, I have no idea what to get her. This is where you come in!"

"So, my all-state cross-country nephew, you want me to be your shopping guide." Vincent started laughing out loud. It had been a while since he had laughed. It felt good.

"So," he said. "Will you help me?" Eileen told him that he had better have his wallet open because she was in the buying mood.

It took a while to find the right gift. Eileen told Vincent all the things that he needed to know regarding a gift.

The gift couldn't be audacious. It couldn't be lovey dovey. She shook her head "no" when he picked up a baseball signed by Dwight Evans. "Absolutely not." They finally decided on silver hoop earrings. Vincent wasn't sure about the earrings. "If Cris asks, tell her your cousin picked them out."

Vincent and Mikey met the gang at Yawgoo. These kids were good skiers. The best that Vincent and Cris could do was to fall on their faces on the bunny hill. They fell almost every time they went down the darn hill. After a while, this began to feel like a job, so they decided to go in the lodge and have some hot chocolate.

Cris started pummeling questions at Vincent right and left. When she asked where his grandparents grew up, Vincent sighed. "I know you love to gather lots of information, but I haven't gotten a chance to get a word in edgewise for the last few minutes. It might be my turn to talk."

"Oops," she said with a smile. "I guess I've been dominating the conversation."

Vincent was quiet most of the time. It was only when he got to know somebody that he felt comfortable sharing. This was one of those nights. He started telling Cris about the first few days after the shooting. "I felt it was my fault that Mom got shot. I know this sounds crazy, but back then, that's how I felt. My dad and Mikey helped me to see that I was not responsible for what happened, but it took a long time to accept this."

Then he talked about the folks who reached out to help his family. "So many people have been wonderful, but no one has been more wonderful than you! You rallied the community to come together and help my family. The tree stand was the talk of the town. It wouldn't have happened if you hadn't led the charge.

"I wanted to do something special for you. Something that would let you know how much I appreciate all that you have done. I thought about getting you a gift for Christmas, but I knew your brothers might tease you mercilessly if that happened. So, I asked my aunt to help me pick out a special gift for you. She is the only person who knows anything about this gift. She isn't going to tell anyone about it."

Vincent reached over the table and held her hand. He dug deep into the jacket pocket of his parka and pulled out a small box wrapped with Christmas paper. Cris' eyelashes fluttered like the wings of a bumblebee. She leaned over to Vincent and hugged the breath out of him. "Whoa! Take it easy!" he gasped. "You haven't even opened the box."

"Vincent, you silly billy. This is the nicest thing anyone has ever done for me. I did what I did because your family had gone through a lot. You needed a bit of support. I didn't expect any type of gift for helping out."

"Cris, your 'thinking of others' approach to our situation is exactly why I decided to buy you a gift. Now take your right hand out of your pocket and open up the present!"

In a flash, she ripped off the wrapping. She squealed with delight Then she kissed Vincent. "The earrings are perfect." Just then, their friends began to troop in. Vincent and Cris scooted away from each other. There was no time left for Cris say anything else.

The other kids were exhausted. That was especially true of Mikey. "My gosh, my thighs are killing me. I gotta stop." One kid after another called for a ride home. Mrs. Bonfigore was one of the first parents to arrive at Yawgoo. Cris mouthed "thank you" to Vincent as she opened the front door of her mom's car. Vincent waved just enough for Cris to notice. Then she was gone.

Two days later, the Angelino's trooped into church for the early Sunday mass. To Vincent's surprise, the Bonfigores' came down the center aisle of the church. They sat two pews away from his family. Cris turned her head, tousled her hair, and winked at Vincent. He could see his earrings were dangling from her ears. After that, he was lost in thought for the rest of the church service.

When mass was over, many parishioners headed to the parish hall for coffee and donuts. Normally, the Angelinos headed home right after mass. However, that morning, Detta and Maria started chatting. They decided that they should go get a cup of coffee. Dante found the parents a table. Then, they headed to the coffee urn. The younger kids were lined up for some jelly filled delights. Cris and Vince sat at another table.

"I never got a chance to say thank you. It didn't seem like a good idea to say anything when everyone wandered into the lodge. The earrings are wonderful."

"You're welcome. I'm glad you like them."

Cris told Vincent that she had pushed her family to come to mass because she knew that Vincent's family would probably be there. "My mom was reluctant to come, but she finally gave in. I came downstairs with some jewelry on. My mom me asked where I had gotten the set of earrings. I told her everything. All she could do was smile."

Detta and Maria were engaged in quiet conversation. The earrings were the center of their discussion. Maria was surprised to hear about this. "Detta, I had no idea that Vincent had done this. What a little munchkin he is!" Detta let on that Vincent bought the earrings as a way of saying thank you to Cristiana for all she had done for the Angelino's. "That is so sweet. I guess we have two thoughtful kids."

Then they started to talk about the fundraiser. Maria told Detta that she wanted to help. "The fundraiser is coming up quickly. There must be something I can do to help out?"

Detta thought for a second. Then she suggested that Maria could write thank you notes to the people who were coming to the fundraiser.

"Just a short note that we can put next to each place setting. We are probably talking about 150 notes. Could you handle that?"

Maria was excited to be able to help. "I could write a few thank you notes every day for the next few weeks. That shouldn't be a problem. When can I get the list of the people who are coming to the fundraiser? I'd like to be able to start on this as soon as possible?"

Detta said she could drop over a list on Wednesday.

"That would be perfect."

Where are you now, Mr. All Star?

L ater that week, Detta's committee met to finalize
plans for the fundraiser. "Joe, what's happening with
the food?"

"My best friend, Johnny Costa, owns a catering
company. We go back a long time. He heard about the
shooting. He's giving us the food at cost. That is huge."

Then John Petrangelo reported on the ticket sales. He
was smiling ear to ear. "We have sold 236 tickets. If we
sell 12 more tickets, we will net over $8000 from the
ticket sales alone! I spoke to the pastor of Our Lady of
Mercy parish in East Greenwich. This is a huge, huge
parish. The pastor has fifteen couples who have agreed
to come. If that happens, we'd clear well over $8,500!"

Detta waited until everyone else had given their updates
before she gave her report. "What I am about to tell you
is just between us chickens. So, mum is the word. I met
Brother Allan yesterday afternoon. You may have heard
the name Joe Burke. He is the general manager of the
Red Sox. What you may not know is that he graduated
from Don Bosco many years ago. Mr. Burke and Brother
Allan are good friends. They met last week.

Brother Allan mentioned our fundraiser. Apparently,
Burke had already heard that the mother of a Don Bosco
student had been shot recently. He knew about the
fundraiser and wanted to know if he could be of help.
"Joe, I have been looking for someone to be master of
ceremonies for the fundraiser."

Burke stopped him right there. "I'll be your master of
ceremonies if you want me."

The room was filled with shouts of joy. "You've got to be kidding me," John shouted. Detta raised her hands up to quiet the group down.

"Hey. I'm not finished. I'm saving the best for last." Joe Viterio wondered what could be better than this. "Mr. Burke told Brother Allan that he'd ask the Red Sox All Star shortstop if he'd be willing to come to the fundraiser."

The room was in an uproar. Mr. Viterio was jumping up and down. "My God, my favorite Italian player is coming to the fundraiser. I can probably sell another fifty tickets to my friends at the Italian Club."

Renata gains some traction, but can Palko take a punch?

Billy found someone who'd be willing to be on the receiving end of a "Billy" punch. King Palko arrived in Kansas City a week after Baxter hired Renata. Apparently, he didn't like to fly. When he travelled out of town, he took the train. He rode the rails because he could reserve an entire compartment for himself. King was a very big boy—230 pounds of pure muscle. Add a large frame to those muscles and he couldn't be missed.

King's glare was what really got folks' attention. His eyes were hidden by jet back hair that hung from the crown of his head to the middle of his cheeks. It wasn't clear what was going on with him until he swept his hair from his face. His stare was totally mean and uninviting. Billy got to know Palko when they played ball for the Buckeyes. Billy was a safety and King was an offensive tackle. Four years of pounding each other had created a weird friendship that had lasted for years.

Billy was going to be transporting King around town, so he got rid of his rental car. He bought a used Ford F series. The truck was not pretty. The faded yellow paint job and a few dents on the front bumper told the whole story. But it had two things going for it. First, it was big enough for King to be comfortable. Secondly, it had a camper that slid into the back of the truck. That would prove to be invaluable for Renata's plan to work, as Billy was soon to find out.

Billy drove to Union Station. He arrived in plenty of time. King hated being late. No sense starting off on the wrong foot. Billy was waiting near the gate when he saw Palko step out of the coach car, sling a large duffle bag onto his shoulder and mosey over towards him. They exchanged nods and a handshake. Conversation could come later. King followed Billy to the truck. They drove directly to Cappy's.

The traffic was heavy, so the trip was longer than anticipated. Finally, they got to the bungalow. Billy introduced Palko to everyone. Cappy looked King up and down. "Billy wasn't kidding. This guy is huge," Cappy said to himself. "Billy tells me you can handle yourself in a fight."

King scowled. "Listen up, Jocko! I can take of myself okay in just about any situation." Nothing more needed to be said. King's size spoke volumes.

Joey didn't know what to make of this galoot, so he kept his mouth shut. That left Renata to carry the conversation ball. She wondered if Billy had given Palko a sense of what they were up to. All King knew was that Billy needed help with a job. Renata realized that these mob guys were mostly interested in the act of doing. Figuring out how to organize themselves was a totally different story. "Good thing God made women," Renata said to herself. "Otherwise, we'd be up the creek."

Renata brought King up to speed on why they had come to Kansas City in the first place. Then she filled all of them in on what she had been doing. "I've been working for Baxter for the past week. Six days a week, ten hours a day and not having much fun. Baxter calls me his assistant. He thinks my name is Shirl. However, he insists on calling me Sugar. One day soon, Baxter will find out that sugar can be bad for you!"

Renata's job was to clean up after Baxter. The guy could hornswoggle anyone out of their own pants, but he didn't know the first thing about running a business. She was surprised that the bills had been paid prior to her coming on board. There were receipts strung all over the office,

240

no filing system, and no way to know if the business was profitable.

Then she launched into the plans for the new liquor store. "Baxter found a vacant building in Merriam. Merriam is a little north of us. There is a vacant lot right next to his building, so it offers a bit of privacy."

Cappy snorted. "Sounds like the perfect spot for a robbery."

Renata let them know that Baxter was hoping to open the new store in four weeks. "He wants to make sure that the bugs are out of the way by March 15th.

"The electricity and the heating system in the building are working. The place needs two coats of paint and some TLC, but that can be taken care of in short order. I ordered all the equipment and supplies needed for the place to be operational in time for the sale.

"Baxter is looking for somebody to work with Booby and Big Bear. He needs a brawny guy who can help with moving liquor from their warehouse over to the new store. Since the 'Booby' incident, Baxter has become skittish. He wants to beef up protection. He isn't taking any chances on having what he calls 'his West VIrginia bozos' ruin his chance to make it big.

"This is where Billy and King come in. Baxter and I are going to take inventory this week." Renata suggested that King Palko could show up and take an interest in her. "I'd take offense. In walks Billy. He sees this commotion and intervenes. He drops King with one punch. Voila, Baxter has a new tough guy in his stable."

King started to huff. "No way does Gambucci knock me down with one punch! That is total crap!"

Cappy spoke up. "You might happen to fall down if it could make you a cool thousand dollars."

King smiled at that remark. "I would take a punch from a lightweight like Billy for that kind of money."

Renata was relieved to hear King's response. It could have gotten ugly if King had become upset. Cappy and Joey took King over to the liquor store so he could see the set up. It looked like it would be easy pickings.

At that point, Renata went to Baxter's office. The good news was that Baxter had left the office shortly after she arrived. Apparently, he was meeting with a distributor to arrange an additional order of booze for the new store.

Renata finished her daily paperwork in no time at all. That gave her an opportunity to go through Baxter's bank accounts. She learned that Baxter had set up a special account for the West Virginia hooch sales. "Thirty-eight thousand dollars and counting," she said to herself. "Baxter's making money hand over fist."

Renata decided she had enough time to check out this little pot of dough. Baxter had been making bi-weekly withdrawals of twenty-two hundred dollars from this account. This was over and above his store profits. On two occasions, Renata had seen Baxter putting a wad of bills into a safe in the back of the office. She needed to pay more attention to this safe business. Getting ahold of the loot in the safe would be a nice bonus.

In the meantime, Renata spotted a memo Baxter had left for her. He wanted her to contact the business manager of the local newspaper. Baxter wanted to beef up the advertising. The memo went on to say that she should call Coot, the manager of his first store, to determine if they needed to order additional booze and beer, etc. Then she had to purchase shelving, a few coolers for the beer and a cash register for the new store. Baxter's note to Renata indicated that they would have to get up to speed quickly.

"No shit Sherlock!", Renata said to herself. "Baxter must think I am Anne Sullivan to his Helen Keller."

Cappy drove Billy over to the old store. "Billy, I know you have been there several times this past week. Let's make sure that Coot gets to know you like the back of his hand. Here's a pile of extra dough you can use to buy booze over the next couple weeks. Then we can spring our plan on Baxter."

As it turned out, the plan got off the ground quicker than expected.

Coot greeted Billy when he strolled into the store. Coot was an old codger. He had a long ponytail, a scruffy beard, and big, bushy eyebrows the color of newly fallen snow. He wore a plaid shirt with plenty of little shiny buttons. Just the type of outfit that you might see at a rodeo. Coot had his name embroidered on his shirt and he had a big old silver belt buckle that hung around his waist.

"Hey there, partner," he drawled. "My name is Coot. I seem to remember that you were in our store several days ago. You're back again."

Billy asked Coot if he had any Macallan on the shelf. "This hooch has to have been bottled in 1970."

"That is pretty spendy, partner. I don't have any in stock right now, but I could get some in tomorrow."

"I need three bottles of the stuff." That got Coot's attention right away. Billy's boss had very fancy tastes.

Coot said the scotch would be for Billy when he came back around.

Another customer came into the store, so Billy decided to walk around and see what else Coot had on the shelves. Billy ended up picking up a little bit of this and a little bit of that while he waited for Coot to finish up. The bill amounted to $150, not including the Macallan. Coot had a big flipping grin on his face just thinking about the bonus that would be coming his way.

"It looks like you are having a big shindig." Coot noted.

Billy ran on about his boss. "My boss makes a ton of money trading on the grain exchange. He likes to invite friends over to party it up. I guess I'm his water boy one day and his protection the next." Coot boxed up the booze and Billy headed out the door. "I'll be back tomorrow to pick up the scotch, Mr. Coot."

Marty makes a move on two fronts

Dante and his brother were in the middle of their weekly business meeting when Marty popped in. "Cappy's on the phone."

"I hope you have good news for me, Cappy. My boss is getting upset with how much time you are spending in Kansas City."

Cappy told Dante that Renata was working for Baxter. "She has the run of the place. She's been able to access the bank accounts. As well, she has seen Baxter's plans for expansion. I figure that this little operation will be all wrapped up in a few weeks."

Cappy went on to talk about Billy and King. "If everything works out on Thursday, Billy will be working for Baxter within a day or so. We should then have the operation covered inside and out. "Billy can handle the rough stuff. His pal, King, is enormous, Dante. Not someone you would ever want to wrangle with. We should be able to wrap things up quickly." Too bad Cappy didn't have the ability to look at his crystal ball before he made any promises. The mess was going to be much bigger than either he or Dante thought.

Dante wondered what was happening with Joey.

"I've got him in cold storage, Dante. We included him in our plans to rip off Baxter, but he won't be directly involved in the action. One Shot is not happy that he's sitting around doing nothing. But he's not getting into trouble."

Dante told Cappy to keep it that way. "We don't need any more screw ups due to Mr. Clueless' shenanigans."

"That ain't going to happen this time around, Dante."
Dante told Cappy that Marty was flying out to check up
on the progress of this operation.

"Dante, we have a full house of folks already working
on this deal. We don't need extra help!"

"You may not need Marty there, but I need Marty there.
End of story. I'll let you know when we get the flight
information pulled together."

Dante slammed the phone down. His tone was lethal.
"Cappy's britches are getting too damn big. He is starting
to tell me what to do! Marty, get your ass in here!"

Marty could tell by the tone of Dante's voice that he
meant right now. Marty was in the middle of making a
call, but the receiver went into the cradle in a hurry.

Marty rushed into the office. Dante shared the
conversation he had with Cappy. "I want you to be in
Kansas City tomorrow night. Got it? I want the lowdown
on what is happening. This deal is taking too long. I want
your impressions of the plan. How does Renata fit in?
Call me by Thursday. I got people downtown who are
upset. I need to calm them down which means you need
to calm me down. Am I making myself clear?"

Marty nodded in agreement.

"We could go down on this big time, Marty, if this isn't
handled just right. You've taken on a lot of our problem
businesses. You've exceeded my expectations. When
you arrive in Kansas City, you are going to face the most
fucked up operation we got going. I have faith that you
can make this whole thing right."

That comment produced a huge smile on Marty's face.
Mr. B saw the smile but decided to let it go. "The kid

deserves to proud of what's been accomplished." Dante decided to bring the meeting to a close. "You'll be in Kansas for several weeks. Pack accordingly."

Marty headed back to the front office. "I didn't tell you to leave, Marty. Sit your ass back down!"

"Sorry, Mr. B, I thought we were done."

"You're done when I say you're done. Understand?" Marty nodded. "You have been busy in Massachusetts. But I don't have a bloody clue as to what has been going on. Clue me in. Are we making money?"

Marty reviewed the operation. Everything was going smoothly. Marty and Louie set up two stings. One was in Springfield and the other one was near Sturbridge. There was a police barracks in each town. Marty made sure an officer at each barracks had located an "informant" who knew where cigarettes were being stored and when they were going to be moved around.

A young hood named Rocco Fontana was the key to Marty's plan. Fontana had worked for the Springfield mob for the past four years. Initially, he provided some muscle from time to time, a knuckle sandwich here or there when strong armed tactics were needed. Dusty doled out a bit of work to Rocco. It soon became clear that there was a brain under Rocco's greased ducktail.

Marty had met Rocco a few weeks previously. "Rocco seems pretty bright, Dusty. What's his story?"

"Rocco grew up in Nahant. His uncle brought him into our operation when Rocco was in high school. He did a good job for us. Unfortunately, his uncle was shot and killed during a heist. With no one to show him the ropes, Rocco's role diminished. I spotted him a year ago. I've been giving him more responsibility ever since."

Marty wondered if Rocco might be ready for some real action. "What do you think, Dusty?"

Dusty thought Rocco could step it up. The next day, the three of them met in Springfield. "Rocco," Marty said, "You're beginning to know your way around."

"It took a while to catch on. I knew the brawny side of things. It was the brain part that needed work. I'm starting to feel comfortable with both sides of the business."

Then Marty turned to Rocco. "Here's the deal. I have a big job coming down the pike. You could help us out."

"What do you have in mind for me?"

"We're selling stolen cigarettes in your area. We want to expand our business. I want the cops to think you are behind the operation. Hopefully, they will pick you up. We want them to think that they've stopped your operation in its tracks. They won't know that we are gaming them. They need to catch you in the act and then you need to serve some time."

Rocco was trying to wrap his head around this. "I'm not sure what to think. I'm not hot about spending time in the state pen."

"Here's the skinny, Rocco. The police nab you for a six month stay in the can. They see this as a big deal. While they're gloating, we'll sell a ton of stuff right under their noses. You get $15k for your time in jail. When you come out, I make you one of my lieutenants. More dough and more responsibility. How does that sound?"

It took two seconds for the light to come on. "I understand where you are headed. I'm your guy. I am all in! This is the opportunity I have been waiting for."

Marty needed a bathroom break. Mr. B indicated that it might be a good idea if they took a thirty-minute break. "I need to stretch my legs." When they got back together, Marty asked Mr. B if he had any questions. "So far, so good. Continue telling me about your plan."

"If I have this figured correctly, Mr. B, the police will think Rocco is running the Sturbridge and Springfield operations. They won't have a clue as to what is going on. We'll lose twelve thousand dollars in product plus attorneys' fees and enough money to shut Rocco up."

Dante's face reddened. "Twelve grand! We probably need to add $20k for the other expenses. You call this smooth!" Dante growled. "I don't like the sound of this. It looks like we will be losing money by the boatful! That won't go well downtown."

"I know it sounds bad. But here's the rest of the story. Dusty has been busy in Boston while we have been hoodwinking the police in Western Mass. We've moved six thousand cartons of stolen cigarettes in Southie and another nine thousand cartons on the Cape and in New Bedford are during the past month. Nobody is the wiser. If we string together three more months of this, we should be able to net $225,000."

Dante whistled softly. "That'll make the boss really happy! Are you real sure about these numbers?"

Sammy assures me that we're killing it right now." Dante's frown went away. "Sit down Marty and have a shot of whiskey with us. You done good!"

One shot turned into three shots of whiskey. They were getting up a good buzz. The phone rang. Marty jumped up to take the call. Marty came right back into Dante's office. "Dino, you need to head back to the laundromat.

249

Your gal says that one of the washers has broken down and there is water all over the floor."

"Shite," Dino said. "Marty, call Pete Petrangelo, the plumber, right away. Tell him to drop everything and head over to our laundromat. I'll meet him there. I'll call you when I get a handle on what is going on." Then Dino ran up the stairs.

Dante motioned Marty to take a seat. "I know I have been hard on you recently. We have a lot going on between Rhode Island and Massachusetts. You are doing great with all the cigarette business. Keep it up. As I move up the ladder, you will move up with me."

Dante filled Marty in regarding the mess in Kansas. "I want you to head there right away. Dino doesn't know anything about Trixie. Let's keep it that way. I want to know if we can trust Renata. Also, watch out for Joey. Cappy tells me that he's in the deep freeze. We both know him. He sneezes and someone gets hurt. I don't want him to mess up this situation. I hope we can get in and out with piles of money and booze.

"You'll be there to watch over things for me. I don't want you to get involved in the actual plan. This is Cappy's mess to clean up. I know you will keep me informed."

"I've got you covered." Marty went back to the office and made a few calls. A little later, Marty came back in to talk to Mr. B. "I'm on a flight heading to Kansas City this afternoon. I'll fill you in tonight."

Dante leaned over and opened his safe. He handed $5,000 over to Marty. "Use this as you see fit. If you need any more, let me know. I will take care of it. Make sure to keep me informed. I don't want any surprises."

"You have my word on it, Mr. B." Marty made a call and arranged to be driven to the airport by a friend. "I'm headed home to pack. I will call you tonight."

Vincent plays a new role

The second semester at school started off with a bang. Cris landed a part in the spring play. She got the role of Alice Sycamore in the play *You Can't Take It With You*. Cris was surprised that she got the role. So was her father. Detta wasn't surprised. "Dante, when Cristiana sets her mind on something, she gets what she wants. She wanted this role."

There was a ton of kids who tried out for parts. However, there was a shortage of help behind the curtains. Cris tried to draft Vincent to help the stage manager. "I don't know anything about theatre."

Cristiana was undeterred. She tried sweet talking Vincent. That didn't go very far. The one thing Cris knew about was Catholic guilt. She reminded Vincent of her work on the tree sale and how it would be nice if he would help her. Guilt worked.

Vincent was concerned about keeping his grades up. "Vincent, we can study together after play practice. You can help me with French and I'll help you with math."

Vincent got Mikey to volunteer. They spent several hours in the auditorium. Vincent started to enjoy the work. He and Mikey didn't have to memorize any lines or movements. He was grateful for that. Their work was written down, scene by scene. Vincent worked the lights. Mikey worked on the scenery. After a few days, they had their jobs under control. Life was good.

A week or so later, Cristiana overheard her mother talking to Mr. Viterio on the phone. Apparently, the committee needed more volunteers for the fundraiser. They needed folks who could make favors.

The next day, Cris asked Mr. McNally, the director, if she could speak to the company before the rehearsal began. She told him about the fundraising dinner and the need for volunteers. "What great idea! Go for it." She convinced twenty kids to help.

Vincent was speechless. "How did you manage to convince the kids?" he asked.

"Well, duh, Vincent. Did you forget how many kids convinced their folks to buy Christmas trees from Uncle Paulie? I had a ready audience."

That night Cris told her mom what had happened. Even Detta was surprised by her daughter's resourcefulness.

"I can see the girls helping out," Detta said, "but, how did you con the boys into helping?"

"Getting the girls was easy. They have been going to the bakery for years. Mrs. Angelino always gave them free samples. For guys, donuts are great to eat, but going into the bakery is another matter. It isn't manly. I had to figure something else out. I decided to have Vincent tell the boys that they would get autographed baseballs. That was all it took."

Cris decided to treat herself for all the work she had put in to get the kids to help with the fundraiser. She heard that *The Crucible* was playing at the repertory theatre in Providence. Cris decided it would be a great idea to see professional actors perform on stage. Maybe she could learn something. Cris had studied the Salem Witch Trials last year. She liked the subject matter. It seemed like going to see *The Crucible* was meant to be.

She bought three student tickets for the Saturday matinee performance. Convincing Mikey and Vincent to go was an effort and a half. "Stuffy" was the first word out of

Mikey's mouth. That almost put the kibosh on the whole affair. Cris didn't give up easily.

A few days later, she was walking down the hall at school with Vincent. The next thing Vincent knew, Cris slid her hand into his. It was the last week in January, yet his hands were clammy. He started to stutter. All he could say was "Oh my goodness." "Goodness" came out of his mouth in four syllables. Cris giggled. Then she saw Vincent's face turn bright red and realized that she had embarrassed him. Good intentions can sometimes turn sour. She turned away and went directly into her history classroom leaving Vincent flummoxed.

That night, Vincent was in a funk. He never said a word during dinner and then excused himself. He went upstairs. Maria raised her eyebrows. John shrugged in return. When everybody left the table, Maria and John decided to do up the dishes. "What is going on with Vincent?" Maria whispered to her husband.

"You got me, Honey! He hasn't acted like this since the day you were shot."

Like Father, Like Son

Shortly after seven, John lumbered up the stairs and headed to Vincent's room. A short knock was followed by "I'm busy right now." John went into Vincent's room even though he was not invited. Vincent was sitting on his bed with a large comforter around him and a few tissues strewn on the floor.

"Leaving you alone doesn't seem like a good option. Something is bothering you—almost eating you alive inside by the look of things. What's going on?"

After some prodding, Vincent shared the main event of the day. "I made a complete mess of things. Cris and I were walking down the corridor. She stopped in the middle of the corridor and took my hand. Then I turned into Mr. Robot. She's interested in me and all I do is stutter. I didn't know what to do. I messed up my chance to have a girlfriend." John wasn't sure what to say. A few seconds later, he sat down on the bed

"Vincent, have I ever told you how I met your mother?"

"No, Dad."

"It was 1966. I wanted to go to Boston University, but my family didn't have money for that. The Vietnam War was becoming a big deal. I decided to enlist in the Navy rather than get drafted.

"Anyway, some friends of mine drove me up to Brockton just before I headed out for basic training. We had this bright idea to go bowling. Someone brought a case of beer. I had a few on the way up to Brockton. Maybe more than a few. We had some fun, bowled a few lanes, and then headed home.

"We ended up at Holy Ghost Catholic Church. The church was sponsoring a dance that night. As it turned out, your mom's friends had convinced her to go to the dance. Mom was the first girl I saw. She was beautiful. Dark hair, big blue eyes, and a smile that wouldn't quit.

"Normally I would have never asked her for a dance. However, I had drunk enough beer for two people. It gave me some false courage. I went up to her and asked her to dance. She agreed. We were on the dance floor. The next thing I knew, my legs gave way and I threw up."

Vincent was shocked to hear that his father had been drunk. "What happened after that, Dad?"

"Your mom took over. My friends carried me to the bathroom. They stood watch while Mom cleaned me up. She got Bobby D'Angelo to drive me home. He snuck me up to my room without my folks knowing anything. From then on, your mom was the only girl I ever dated."

Vincent's eyes became as big as half dollars. Then a tiny giggle popped out of his mouth. John began to laugh. Vincent started to hiccup. That got them laughing harder. A few minutes later, they calmed down.

"I'm constantly amazed that your mother puts up with me. She says I'm a lifelong project. I don't know where your relationship with Cristiana is heading, Vincent. This is your first time thinking that you like someone. Remember that Cris is probably as upset about this as you are. Tomorrow, why don't you talk to her. The two of you are smart enough to figure things out."

Here goes nothing

The next morning, Vincent sat next to Cristiana on the bus. She was surprised to see him. It took him a few minutes before he could say anything. "I was a doofus yesterday. When you took my hand, I didn't know what to do or say. I froze. Nothing like that has ever happened to me. I am sorry if I spoiled your day."

"Vincent Angelino, that's the sweetest thing you could say. I was a bit spontaneous when I took your hand. I guess I get excited about something and then I am all in. You're more cautious. You let things happen in their own time rather than forcing something to happen. Maybe we both need to learn how to be more flexible."

"Vincent, I sat down with my Mom when I got home. I told her what went on. She listened without trying to tell me what to do. She thinks I went too fast and that I should apologize to you. She's right. I am sorry for surprising you like I did. I hope that you can forgive me."

That brought a smile to Vincent's face. "Cris, I spoke to my dad about what happened. He told me that we should take our time and talk through issues like this together. Your mom and my dad are probably both right."

They spent the rest of the ride talking about nothing special. Vincent told Cris that his parents like her a lot. "They think I'm too young to have a steady girlfriend."

Cris nodded in agreement. "How about we try to be good friends for now. Our new rule is that holding hands is offsides for now. What do you think, Mr. Angelino?"

"We can hold hands when we think we are ready."

When they got to school, they surrounded Mikey and started talking about the play. He quieted them down. "My mom knows all about Salem. She told me it would be a good idea if I went along. That means I better go or else. So, I am coming to the play with you."

"That's great!" Cris said. "My dad agreed to driving us to Providence."

Mikey turned to her. "You must have been pretty sure that you could convince us to go with you!"

Cris just smiled. "Guys, we can start with an early lunch and then go to the play. Maybe we could walk over to the Brown University campus after the play. I think I might like to go there for college."

"You sure like to plan ahead," Mikey said.

"I do indeed."

Saturday went off without a hitch. Dante and Cris picked the boys up. He insisted on taking them to Civita Farnese for lunch. "My treat!" The restaurant was in the heart of the Italian neighborhood. It was very busy.

The restaurant was a new experience for the boys. A older waitress came over to their table. Her name was Rosina. She was a stout woman with violet colored hair. She had a thick Italian accent. Cris and Vincent translated for Mikey. The boys decided to have meatballs and sauce with fried peppers. Cris had eggplant parmesan. Mikey was surprised that he liked the food.

When the kids got up to leave, Dante strolled over to them. He handed Cris ten dollars. "My meeting is still going strong. Why don't you take a cab to the theatre? I'll pick you up after the play is over." Cris told her dad that they were going to walk up to Brown to look around the campus after the play was over.

"Where can we meet you, Dad?"

"I'll meet you at the corner of Benevolent and Benefit at 5:15 p.m. That should give you enough time to see where the suburban big shots send their sons and daughters to college."

The kids caught a cab and headed downtown. They got to the theatre much earlier than they expected. The wind was brisk. They decided to go into the lobby and get their tickets. If they felt up to braving the cold, they could go outside to walk off their lunch.

When the kids got to the box office, a woman with short blond hair and eyelashes that were longer than her hair, waved Cris over to her station. This woman's name tag identified her as Bonnie Latour. She asked to see Cris' identification. Bonnie had an English accent, so it was hard to understand her. Cris was usually very confident. However, she was taken aback by the accent. Vincent watched the whole thing play out. Cris' confidence was waning, so he walked over and told the woman that they wanted to pick up their tickets for the matinee.

"You are so sweet to come over and help your girlfriend," Vincent blushed. Then he gave her their names.

Bonnie looked for the tickets. "Oh, my, you didn't tell me that you were on our A list. Stay right there. I'll be right back."

Two minutes later, Bonnie led a lanky, middle aged man with wire rimmed glasses over towards the kids. This man said "Hello" in a soft southern drawl. "My name is Alex. I am the artistic director here at The Playhouse.

You must be Cristiana Bonfigore. You look very much like your mother. I'm told you are a budding actress."

If Bonnie's accent put Cris off, this threw her for a loop. She stumbled through the fastest "Hello" Vincent and Mikey had ever heard. Cris was totally off her feed. Alex took up the slack. "You must be surprised to meet me. I've met your mother on several occasions. She has spoken very highly of you." With that, Cris' face turned crimson red.

Alex pretended that he didn't notice anything unusual. He swept the kids into the theatre and brought them backstage. He introduced them to the lead actors. A few minutes later, he asked one of the volunteers to bring the kids to the lobby. "Sorry, this has to be so short. Unfortunately, I need to get ready for today's production. Hope you enjoy yourself!" He gave them a wave and headed towards the stage. "Ok, people," he said. "Let's review the last scene in Act One."

"You never told us your mom knew the director." Mikey said.

"That's because I didn't know either. I'm shocked at what just happened! I forget that my mother knows just about everybody." At that point, Cristiana noticed that Vincent had a massive grin on his face. "What?"

"This is the first time I've ever seen you speechless."

Vincent and Mikey broke out into laughter. It was infectious enough for Cris to join in. Then they were escorted to their seats. They talked non-stop til the lights flashed to signal that the play was about to start.

The play was spectacular. Mikey was surprised at how little he knew about Salem. When the play ended, they stayed in their seats for ten minutes talking about the play. They paid no attention to what was going on around them. By the time, they were the only ones left in the theatre besides the cleaning crew.

They finally made it over to Brown for a look around. Cris led them past University Hall and the campus green. Mikey was impressed with the old buildings on campus. Vincent just took the whole place in. The campus felt completely comfortable to him.

Cris wanted to see the Medical school. "This is where I want to go when I graduate from college. My father will have a fit when he hears about this. He thinks people who go to Brown are highfalutin. But Brown has one of the best medical schools in New England. I need to be here." Vincent listened very intently to what Cris had to say. He was amazed by her ability to plan ahead.

Dante arrived promptly at 5:15, and they headed home. Dante asked them about the play. The kids talked non-stop. "Dad, we decided that we want to go see Salem."

Dante just shook his head. Nary a word was said about Brown University. Cris had made the boys promise not to say a word about her medical school plans.

Marty meets the gang

It was nearly forty degrees outside with a dusting of snow on the ground when Marty arrived in Kansas. This was so different from the blustery Providence weather. Cappy met Marty at the gate and they drove right over to the bungalow. Renata was at the door waiting for them. Introductions were made. Marty could tell that Renata's hello was a little stiff.

Cappy had a bundle of questions about Marty's reason for coming to Kansas. "I'm starved," Marty said. "How about we have some dinner? We can talk while we eat."

Cappy thought better than to get pushy. "I don't want to upset Dante any more than I have already."

A few minutes later, Joey, King, and Billy showed up. They had been watching Wing Nut drop off boxes of hooch. Joey got defensive when he saw Marty. "What in hell are you doing here?"

"It is nice to see you too, Mr. One Shot."

Renata ignored Joey's rant. She introduced Marty to Billy and King. "Marty works for Mr. Bonfigore. Bonfigore is Cappy's boss. Mr. B wants a firsthand update as to how things are going here. We decided to wait until you got back before giving Marty the low down." Renata went over to the stove and pulled out a large pan of lasagna. There's a huge salad and some fresh Italian bread on the sideboard. "Plates are in the cupboard. Help yourselves. I put wine and beer in the refrigerator if anyone's interested."

Cappy waited til everyone started eating before he started talking. "Do you know about the kidnapping and the firebombing of Dolan's laundromat?" Marty nodded. "I felt that we needed a new approach. This is where my friends Renata, Billy, and King come in." Cappy proceeded to talk about Renata getting a job working for Baxter. "She's been able to get the inside scoop regarding Baxter's operations as well as his bank accounts. That has put us in the game."

"Billy set up an account at Baxter's liquor store. The manager knows him by now. Tomorrow, Baxter and Renata will be at the liquor store. When Billy picks up his order, King will follow him in and make an unwelcome pass at Renata. Billy will intervene and them, he will knock King down with a punch. If this works out, I'm hoping Billy gets hired to provide protection for Baxter."

"The plan has a lot of moving parts." Marty noted.

Cappy agreed. "This isn't a sure thing. I think Renata has Baxter in the palm of her hand. Once the fight between King and Billy occurs, she'll convince Baxter to hire Billy to help out with protection. Then, we have a good chance of making off with cash and a considerable amount of hooch."

Marty wanted to hear from Renata. "I've become one of the "boys" as far as Baxter is concerned. He shared his business plan with me. I know who's working where. As well, I'm a cosigner on Baxter's checking accounts. Just yesterday I was able to get the combination of Baxter's safe. We should be able make this whole thing come together."

Then Marty asked King what he thought of the plan.

King liked the plan. He just didn't like having to take a fall, especially from Billy.

"Do you like the plan, Billy?" Billy also like the plan. "I connected with Coot, the store's manager. Coot thinks I'm levelheaded and that I know how to handle responsibility. If there's a job opening at the store, I think he'll accept my application."

Joey was the only naysayer. "I am just a bystander. This plan stinks. When am I gonna do something besides sucking my thumb?"

"Joey," Marty said, "your time will come. As for the plan, Mr. B told me to go with my gut. I think we go ahead with the fight tomorrow. Why don't you review the plan one more time? Renata and I are going out for a while."

Renata gave a "I don't know what the heck is going on" shrug to Cappy. Then she pulled her coat out of the closet and headed out the door.

"Let's get a cup of coffee, Renata." Renata drove to Augie's. It was small eatery a few blocks south of the bungalow. Marty felt right at home as soon as they walked in the door. There was a wall of fame just to the left of the cash register. Photos of Ed Asher, Amelia Earhart, and Walter Cronkite filled the wall. Marty told Renata about going to Cornell. "I was an econ major. But I also worked on the school newspaper. I love watching the news. Cronkite is one of my favorites.

When they sat down at a booth, Renata wondered how a Cornell graduate got hooked up with the mob?

"My mom is Mr. B's sister. I did very well in high school. My uncle took notice. Eventually he made some phone calls. The next thing I knew, I was on my way to

Ithaca. It was certainly an education for me in more ways than I could have imagined.

"When I graduated, I was offered a job with a management firm in Cleveland. When I told my friends the firm's offices overlooked the Cuyahoga River, they pretended to call the fire department. Then they started to laugh. They finally told me how the river had caught on fire. No way was I taking that job. Mr. B wanted me to work for him. Jobs were hard to come by. The rest is history."

A waitress took their orders. Then Renata spoke up, "I figure you wanted to talk to me in private. What's up?"

Marty filled Renata in on Trixie and her pregnancy. "For a variety of reasons, Trixie has to move away. Mr. B wants to make sure that she and her child will be well cared for. I got the sense that you might be willing to let her stay with you for a while, and when the time comes, find her a good job."

Renata was willing to help. "The mob has been good to me. About time I returned the favor."

Marty made it clear that no one needed to know about Trixie's past. "Mr. B expects a yearly report on how things are going for Trixie and her child." He would be grateful for your help. He told me you would receive a yearly stipend of $7500 dollars for your help."

"That's more than generous, Marty. I'd be happy to help Trixie out in any way I can."

 Then Marty asked about Baxter. "What kind of guy is he?"

"Baxter is a bright guy who thinks the sun rises and sets on his keister. He has the AAM disease."

"What's that?" Marty asked. "All About Me" was Renata's terse reply.

"Tell me more."

Renata kept her ears open and her mouth shut when she was at the office. She knew about Baxter's father, the contested will, and the family ties in West Virginia. She also knew Baxter paid off a city official to get his new liquor license. Best of all, Renata knew the safe's combination. "Marty, there's nearly $50k in that safe. There's another $60 grand in the checking account!"

Marty could see why Renata had done well in Chicago. She was thoughtful, articulate, and had devised a great plan. "When can we put this plan into action?"

"Today is Monday, Marty. If Billy can handle King, I'm sure I can get Baxter to hire him on. The new store opens on March 14th. We are running a lot of advertising in the local papers, so we expect a lot of business.

The new store has a huge convention order for that Saturday. We should see a significant amount of cash flowing into the checking account. Saturday should be our target date. That's less than three weeks away."

"I need to talk to Mr. B." Marty stated.

They finished their coffee and headed back. Then they heard loud voices as soon as they hit the stoop. When they opened the door, Billy was attempting to throw a punch at Joey. Cappy was lying at Joey's feet. Blood was streaming from Cappy's mouth. Then King stepped in and cold cocked Joey with one punch.

Marty helped King carry Joey to his room. They tied Joey up and gagged him for good measure. Then they returned to the front room. Joey had been drinking for the last hour. The more he drank, the more aggravated he became. Cappy tried to calm him down. He took a wicked jab to the jaw for his efforts.

Renata went into the kitchen and got a bag of ice. She headed back to Cappy. He protested vehemently. "I'm okay." Marty could see that his pride had taken more punishment than a wack to his face. He continued to squawk at Renata. "Leave me alone!"

"You say that one more time, Cappy, and I'll leave you alone permanently." He backed down and followed her into the bathroom. A few minutes later, she led Cappy to the bedroom. "He's going to lie down for a while."
Then Marty took charge. "We need to talk about Joey!"

No one trusted Joey. This was the third time Joey had blown a gasket. Alcohol exacerbated the situation. King and Billy thought Joey was a loose cannon waiting to explode. They didn't want to involve him in the plan.

Marty spoke up. "Joey is very afraid of Mr. B. If I call Mr. B about this, Joey will be lying dead as a door nail in a Connecticut alleyway. Joey and I will have a conversation when he sobers up. One Shot has a choice to make. Either he bites the bullet and does what we tell him to do or he takes a bullet in the head. Simple as that. His choice."

Let the party begin

The fundraiser was three days away. Life had gotten hectic. The number of tickets sold were way above the estimate. The committee expected over 400 people to attend. The church hall couldn't hold that many people. That was the bad news. The good news was that Detta was able to book Rhodes on the Pawtuxet for a song.

Unfortunately, that meant contacting the ticket holders about the change. Detta's church friends stepped up to the plate. The last ticket holders were called on Tuesday. The newspaper agreed to run a short notice about the change in venue. "What a relief!" Detta said as she and Maria finished up some party favors.

"I had no idea how successful this would become." Maria said. Detta could see tears in her eyes.

"You know, Maria, putting aside all the pain and suffering you've endured, there are three things to be joyful for. First, you are nearly back to full health. That is amazing. Secondly, your situation has pulled our little town together like nothing else would. Thirdly, I now have a friend for life."

Maria turned to Detta and gave her a huge hug. They embraced for several minutes. Maria told Detta that they had become as close as sisters. "I am blessed to have such a friend as you."

By the time Friday had rolled around, there was a giant collection of auction items sitting in the church basement. Dante got a moving company to lend him several trucks. Members of the Knights of Columbus loaded the trucks up with boxes of donated items.

The next night you'd think the town of Greenville had shut its doors and moved to Cranston. Pastors, elected officials, even the Governor showed up. Everyone was enjoying themselves. Nonno was standing next to the silent auction table that had the signed bat. He wasn't letting anyone outbid him for that item.

Nonno didn't know Maria had met the Red Sox player when he arrived at the fundraiser. She told him that her father-in-law was one of his biggest fans. He immediately pulled a bat out of his duffle bag and autographed a bat for Nonno. "My father-in-law will be so surprised!"

Maria asked John to divert Nonno's attention just before the auction closed. Nonno was furious. He lost the chance to make the winning bid. He was overwhelmed later in the evening when the player called him up to the stage and made a big deal of giving him a signed bat. Nonno walked on water the rest of the night.

Everyone finally took their seats. Detta thanked them for coming. She introduced the dignitaries and then asked the bishop to say grace.

"We're grateful to have Mrs. Angelino with us tonight. We ask God to bless the Angelinos and to bless the food that will be served to us this evening. Amen." A chorus of "amens" was heard throughout the room.

Detta gave the crowd a rundown about the evening's activities. Then she said, "Folks. it's time to eat!" Platters of Italian delicacies were served and devoured. Vincent and Cris were in charge of thirty kids who were bringing the food out to the serving areas.

It got a little hectic when one of the servers spilled some spaghetti on one of John's firefighter buddies. John went over to the microphone and told the crowd not to worry.

"Bill's nickname is Meatball." Everyone laughed except Bill, who gave John a one fingered salute and then gave him a smile.

About nine o'clock, John Cafferty and the Beaver Brown Band walked on to the stage. Everyone seemed to hit the dance floor. Cris, Mikey, and Vincent had finished clearing tables and cleaning up by the time that the band started playing. The kids had worked very hard for the entire night. They were looking forward to enjoying themselves on the dance floor. The music was great. Cris was getting itchy to have some fun and maybe even dance a little bit herself.

She sidled up to the dance floor to see what was happening. She stood next to Vincent's neighbor, Sparky Arthur. This old guy seemed to be enjoying himself. He bobbed his head when the band played "Layla." Cris turned towards Mr. Arthur. "This song is pretty good. Sparky looked at her with astonishment. "Sweetheart, pretty good doesn't begin to describe that song. It is one of Clapton's hallmark songs."

"Mr. Arthur, who is Clapton?"

Sparky shook his head. "Eric Clapton wrote this song."
"I see. Well, Mr. Arthur, you seem to be pretty old to be liking this kind of music."

He smiled. "Honey, I was born young and ready to have fun. Just you wait. Cafferty might pound out a little Windwood." Cris had no idea what this guy was talking about.

About 10 pm, folks were getting ready to find out who had the winning bids on the auction items, Detta felt a tap on her shoulder. Dante and a lanky black man with a guitar in his hand were standing behind her. "I have a surprise for you. I'd like you to meet B.B. King." Detta's jaw dropped. "He's in Boston for a concert tomorrow night. He is a friend of Joe Burke's. Mr. Burke told B.B. about our fundraiser. B.B. is wondering if he could play a few songs for the crowd?"

Detta was speechless. She finally squeaked out "Mr. King. We'd love it if you would be willing to play for us tonight." Dante could see that his wife was a little flustered, so he agreed to introduce B.B.

Dante and B.B. walked over to the stage. "Folks, I have a surprise for you. I know you are waiting for the results of auction. However, we just found out that B.B. King is here tonight. He'd like to play a few tunes for us." The crowd went wild. King was the hit of the evening. Everyone rushed towards the dance floor. They started jumping and clapping when King was introduced. A quiet crowd suddenly became raucous. The noise probably carried across the Narragansett Bay.

Cris was disappointed to see the Beaver Brown Band take a break so that an old guy could strum a few songs.

Sparky saw the disappointment fill her face. "Your name is Cris, isn't that right?" She nodded. "You're upset that the Beaver Brown Band isn't playing."

"I am," she said. "I was just getting ready to dance."

"Buck up, baby. You are in for a treat." Sparky told her to sit down and get ready to hear some real special music. "We are probably going to hear a song called "The Thrill is Gone." When we do, you'll change your mind. Guaranteed!" Sparky was right on. Cris couldn't believe how good this B.B. guy was.

B.B. and the band got together and played for an hour. After they played their last song, the results of the silent auction were announced. A few minutes, the place was nearly empty. Detta and Dante thanked B.B. for taking time out to share his music. "Mr. King," Detta said, "I can't begin to thank you for your willingness to be a part of our fundraiser."

At the end of the night, Joe Viterio came over to talk to Detta. He told her that this fundraiser was just the best.

Then Maria, John, and Vincent came over and hugged the Bonfigores. Maria started to say something and then she began to shudder. John put his arm around her and she started to relax. Finally, Maria told Dante and Detta how grateful she was for all the love and care that their family had received from the Bonfigores. "If you ever have need of support, we will be the first ones at your doorstep."

When all was said and done, the benefit cleared enough to pay Maria's existing hospital costs. There was an additional twelve thousand dollars to help make up for Maria's lost wages. Everyone was happy with the results. Dante's brother Dino was especially happy because he was the highest bidder for the use of the Chevy Camaro Coupe! Detta wondered if she would ever have a chance to drive Dino's new ride.

A fire storm takes over

The following Wednesday, John got a call from Bill Mahoney, "John, I need to talk to you. I've had several meetings with *The Providence Journal* and one of the television outlets. Can you meet me after work?" John wondered what had been going on regarding the shooter. "The story is a little long. It might be more beneficial for me to tell the story in its entirety."

"I'll call Maria and let her know about the meeting. You can count on both of us meeting with you."

Shortly after five, Maria and John were ushered into a conference room at the police station. Bill and another officer entered the room two minutes later. Bill introduced the officer as Lieutenant Jocelyn Devereaux. Jocelyn was the department's community relations coordinator.

"Jocelyn and I spent the entire day talking to the media. As it turns out, last week's fundraiser generated lots of interest in the community regarding the shooting. Initially, the media wasn't very interested when we approached them to help us locate the shooter. The tide has turned. The media wants to interview you."

Maria began to tremble. She wasn't sure she'd be up to meeting the press. John sensed her wariness. His reaction was mixed. He didn't want to put his family through another ordeal. However, he wanted to find the shooter and make sure that this guy went to prison. He shared his thoughts with Maloney and Devereaux. "I thought we agreed to post Ms. McConnell's drawing and that would be it."

"John, you are absolutely right. That's what we agreed upon. After we got Ms. McConnell's drawing, I asked Jocelyn to contact the media to see if they would run the drawing. By the time we got the drawing to them, the shooting was old news."

"So, what has changed?"

"The fundraiser has been the talk of the town. People from all over the state want to know more about your family. All the television stations are telling your story. That means interviews with all the media outlets."

John and Maria wanted to get their lives back to some sense of normalcy. They were not excited about reliving the nightmare.

Jocelyn spoke to them in a quiet voice. "This isn't what you expected. These past few months have been torturous. They've been filled with enormous amounts of physical and mental pain. Pain you'd rather forget than relive. I have a suggestion. A friend of mine is a well-known attorney in town. I spoke to him about your case. He's willing to meet with the media on your behalf." That was welcomed news.

Later that day, Maria received a call from Geoffrey Winslow. Winslow indicated that he had spoken to Lt. Devereaux. "She told me all about your situation. I'm sure this whole thing has been overwhelming. I might be able to help you. Would it be all right if I came over after dinner tonight to discuss this with you?"

Maria was willing to meet with Winslow if it meant the family would be able to limit contact with the media. Maria gave him directions. "I'll see you then." As soon as she got off the phone with Winslow, Maria left a message for John to come home directly after work.

Winslow stopped by as promised. The Angelinos were surprised to find that he was their kind of guy. Geoff Winslow was very down to earth and interested in learning more about Maria and John's situation. The Angelinos told him their story.

"As I see it, the media wants to get to know you and what your family has gone through. I can tell that your lives have been topsy-turvy ever since this happened. I understand why sharing your story with others would be so painful."

Geoff outlined an approach that might work. "The media will be like a dog with a bone. They won't let go of this story until they hear it from you. We might be able to set up a joint interview with all the media. I'll ask them to submit questions in writing beforehand. In that way, we can give some thought about what to say. I'll help you with the questions and I'll moderate the meeting. How does that sound?"

John thought this would be great. However, he expressed concern about paying for Geoff's time. Geoff smiled. "Don't worry. My fees have been taken care of."

The meeting with the press went off without a hitch. They held the meeting at the town hall. The place was filled with cameras, lights, and cigarette smoke. The interview lasted for a half hour. Geoff served as the moderator. He guided the Angelinos through the maze of media questions. The questions covered the whole spectrum of issues including the shooting, Maria's surgeries, and the recent fundraiser.

As the end of meeting, Geoff opened his satchel and pulled out MarJean McConnell's drawing. He stood up and tapped the microphone. "Ladies and gentlemen. I know that everyone here is shocked by the Angelino's story. There's one last thing that you can do for us."

Geoff picked the picture up so everyone could see it. "Here is a drawing of the person who may have killed Mr. De Nuncio and injured Mrs. Angelino. The police have been stymied in their attempts to find the shooter. We are asking for any help you can provide to enable the police to identify this person. Thank you for your time." The media had more questions. These went unanswered as Geoff ushered Maria and John off the stage.

Their story took off. People were interested. The police were bombarded by the press with requests for interviews. The two main questions were "Who's the shooter?" and "Who saw the shooter kill De Nuncio and injure Mrs. Angelino?" The answer to the first question was "We don't know. We are following up on some new information." Their response to the second question was "We aren't at liberty identify the eyewitness."

Vincent takes another big step

The school play was set to open in two weeks. Cris turned out to be a very good actress. The role was right up her alley. Cute, spunky girl meets good looking rich kid and they fall in love. The hitch in the giddy-up was that Alice was from the other side of the tracks. There was no need to say anything more.

Vincent liked his job. He was assistant to the stage manager. He was involved in every aspect of the play, from lighting to action. Mikey handled the props. Mikey's dad was very handy. Mikey had helped him with many home projects, so working on props was right up Mikey's alley. When Mr. O'Day learned that Mikey was going to be the prop guy, he offered to help Mikey. They really got into it. Mr. O'Day was a great help making some of the more intricate props.

Mikey and Vincent were enjoying this much more than they expected. It was hard work, but they were having fun. Every day, after play practice, they met Cris in the school cafeteria. They were able to study and get their homework done while waiting for the late bus. Not only did this transform their friendship into something special, but they all made the high honor roll. Mikey had never been on the high honor roll before. His parents were gleeful.

Everything was going smoothly until the following Monday. At the end of school, Vincent walked into the backstage area. Cris was leaning against Mr. Williams, the play's director. She was crying nonstop. Vincent ran over to Mr. Williams and asked what was going on. Williams told Vincent that Donnie Doyle, the boy who was the lead actor, had an accident and wouldn't be able to continue.

Cris asked, "An accident? What type of accident?"

"Donnie had gone skiing on Saturday at Yawgoo. He missed a turn, fell awkwardly, and broke his right leg. No play for Donnie. As you know, his backup, Jimmy Wilson, just left for California due to a family emergency. We don't have anyone else to play the role of Tony, so it looks like we'll have to cancel the show."

It took a while for Cris to calm down. She had worked so hard memorizing her lines. It didn't seem fair. Mr. Williams decided to call off practice for the day. "Put your thinking caps on. Maybe someone will come up with a great idea and save the day."

The regular busses had left by the time the kids made it to the school's front door. Cris called her mother with the news. A few minutes later, Cris came out. "My mom will pick us up at 3:30." The kids decided to go into the cafeteria and see if they could get their homework done while they waited for Mrs. Bonfigore.

Detta arrived at school right on time. No sooner had Cris opened the car door and hit the passenger seat, she began to tell her mom about Donnie. By the time Detta got to Mikey's house, Cris calmed down. She began to come up with a plan for the play.

Cris decided Vincent could take Donnie's place in the play. When Vincent heard this, he just about choked. "You want me to take Donnie's part! You've got to be kidding me! I am not an actor. There is no way that I could take on Donnie's role!"

"Now Vincent," Cris said coquettishly, "you've been watching us every day for the past four weeks. You know where the actors should stand and what their lines are. You can do this. You are perfect for the part."

Mikey knew better than to say anything, so he watched this whole scenario unfold. When Cris finished talking, Mikey thought it might be a good idea to skedaddle, so he slipped out the rear door of the car when they got to his house and ran as fast as he could towards home.

Vincent's eyes were huge. He couldn't believe Cris would suggest that he take over Donny's role. He was saved from saying any more when Mrs. Bonfigore suggested he might want to take some time to think about the idea. Just as Cris was about to add something else, Detta touched her leg. "Not now." she mouthed. Cris didn't say another word. The ride to Vincent's house was a quiet one. When Detta stopped the car, Vincent got out of the car without saying a word.

The next day at school was surprising to say the least. Cris never saw Vincent the whole day. She wondered what he was thinking. She hoped he would consider taking on the role. After the last bell rang, Cris sped towards the auditorium. Most of the cast were already seated when she got there. "So," Mr. Williams said, "does anyone have a great idea?"

An eleventh grader asked if there was time to start practicing for a different play. Mr. Williams shook his head. "Sara, there isn't enough time for the group to learn new lines. Does anybody else have another idea?

Mikey raised his hand. "Is it possible for Danny to sit in his wheelchair on stage and say his lines?"

"Now that is an interesting idea, Mr. O'Day," said Mr. Williams. "I haven't given any thought to that. It would take some major changes in how we do things. It might be possible. Let me think about that. Does anyone else have an idea?" The group was as quiet as a mouse. You could feel the tension in the air. Then, Vincent raised his hand. "Mr. Angelino, what's on your mind?"

Vincent squirmed in his seat and didn't say anything right away. "Mr. Angelino, Are you with us?"
"Hmmm, yes sir," was Vincent's response.

"So, what is your idea?"

Vincent took in a big breath. "I'd be willing to try out for Donnie's role." There was dead silence in the auditorium. Then Mikey let out a whoop. Everyone else began to jabber. Mr. Williams held up his hands. After a while, the kids quieted down. Cris sat there in amazement. Her jaw was open, but she didn't say a word.

"Mr. Angelino, I'm surprised. I wouldn't think this would be your cup of tea. What made you decide to do this?"

"Well, sir, Cris approached me after our meeting yesterday. She thought I could handle the role. I was really stunned by the idea. I railed at the thought of taking over the role. Yesterday, Mrs. Bonfigore drove Mikey, Cris, and me back to Greenville. She heard Cris tell me that I should take over Donnie's role. Mrs. Bonfigore knew that I was upset. She suggested that I go home and think about the pro's and the con's of the idea. I thought the least I could do was consider the idea.

"When I walked into my house, my mom could see that I was upset. She asked me what was wrong. She didn't buy my 'Oh nothing' response. We sat down and had a long talk. I told her about Donnie. After a half hour of listening to my meanderings, my mother finally managed to wheedle out of me what was wrong."

"So, Vincenzo," my mother said "You're afraid of failure. Do you remember when you tried out for the cross-country team and never worried about failure? You ran like the wind. Is there any difference between the one and the other?"

"I got to thinking. I finally decided that I should give it a try. If I didn't try, I would always wonder "what if? I thought that Donnie might help me learn my part. He's probably feeling bad about not being in the play. This might help him as much as it would help me. I also knew that you'd tell me if I wasn't good enough. So here I am, ready or not."

The cast and crew whooped it up. Finally, Mr. Williams raised his hands. "I think we've found someone who can handle Donnie's role. It's time for us to get back to work." With that, Williams asked the assistant director, to work with the cast. Meanwhile, Williams spent time with Vincent going over some of his dialogue in the first act of the play. The rest of the afternoon went by like a rocket ship after takeoff.

Can Billy throw a punch or what

Two hours later, Cappy woke up. He was still woozy from the shot he took from Joey. His head was pounding like a big bass drum. Renata told him to stay in bed. She would fix something for him to eat. If he felt better by then, they could go through the plan. Cappy started to swear a royal blue streak. Renata gave him the look. The sputtering ended.

After Cappy finished his omelet, Renata started off. "I'm meeting Baxter at 10:15 a.m. tomorrow so we can assess what else we need to purchase for the opening. Billy and King should get there around 10:30. Then the fireworks begin. If all goes well, Billy has a new job."

Marty took over from there. "I want everybody out of the bungalow in a half hour. I'll wait for D'Amato to regain consciousness. Then I'm lowering the boom."

"Not if I kill him first," said Cappy.

"There would be a contract on your head that wouldn't go away," said Marty. "I don't think Renata would be happy with either one of us if that happened."

All Renata needed to say was "You got that right, brother!" Her meaning was crystal clear.

Joey woke up shortly after everyone left. He was hungover and extremely moody. Marty tried talking to him. That didn't work out. Joey started out with his backtalk attitude and lots of sass. It was enough to make Marty want to gag. The backtalk continued to build up until Marty pulled out a revolver and laid the barrel across Joey's chin. That shut him up. Marty said "I'm going to talk now and you're going to listen. No interruptions. Got it?" Joey nodded warily.

"You're walking on a very thin line right now. Your job in Rhode Island has caused a great many problems. Mr. Bonfigore's unhappy. Now you decide to lay out the guy who recommended you for the Rhode Island job. Ordinarily, your actions would be cause for immediate termination—as in dead! I'm willing to give you one last chance to redeem yourself."

Marty stopped for a second and looked Joey right in the eyes. "This is your choice—straighten up, do what you are told and leave the booze alone. If you do, I will make sure Mr. B knows how you helped us out. Otherwise, your mother will see your obituary notice in the *Waterbury American*. Am I making myself crystal clear?" Joey nodded. "Nodding means nothing. I want to hear you say the words out loud!"

"You will have no more problems from me."

"I want you to monitor Baxter's West Virginia pallies. I need to know their every move. The heist will depend on their daily movements. Stick to them like glue. I want a daily report. Am I making myself clear?" Joey left Marty with no doubt that he understood what to do.

The next day, the fireworks went off as scheduled at 10:20 a.m. Renata and Baxter were at the front door of the liquor store when Coot flicked on the open sign in the front window. Coot saw Renata and Baxter standing outside the store and let them in.

"Mr. Baxter, you are right on time." They walked to the back of the store. Coot poured them a cup of coffee. Then they started to review the store's inventory. Just then, Billy popped into the store. Coot told Baxter that Billy was an important customer. "He has a big order in the back of the store. I should take care of him. I'll be back before you know it." Coot headed towards the front door

Shortly thereafter, King walked into the store. He saw Renata standing by the register. He started making a play for her. King grabbed her arm. She cried out. Baxter wasn't interested in tangling with this galoot, so he stood by and watched what was happening. Billy roared out of the back room. He went over to King and told him to let the woman go. King brushed Billy aside as if he was a piece of lint.

Baxter saw Billy tangle with the brute. "This Billy guy has no chance. He's just a squirt!" Imagine Baxter's surprise, when Billy started in with a karate move and took the thug down with one punch. The brute was convulsing. Billy was satisfied that this guy was done being a troublemaker, so he went over to calm Renata down.

While Billy tended to Renata, King got up and limped out of the store undetected. Baxter was focused on Renata. He turned around to say something to the thug, only to find that the guy was gone. "Wow, I thought this Billy guy was a goner!"

"How did you manage to get that guy down on the floor?" Billy shrugged and said he was full of surprises.

"Thank goodness for that." said Baxter. "Listen, I need someone with your skills to help us out for the next few weeks. Would you be willing to work for me on a part time basis?"

"That depends on what kind of work you want me to do and how much you're willing to pay me. I don't come cheap."

Baxter threw out a figure. Billy took his time considering the offer. He didn't want Baxter to become suspicious. "I accept your offer."

Baxter told Billy he needed to be at the store every weekday from 1 p.m. to 6 p.m. "On the weekend, you'll work from 5 p.m. to 10 p.m."

"That should work out," said Billy. He made it clear that he wanted to be paid weekly. "I have responsibilities."

"Stop by the store on Friday and your money will be waiting."

Billy walked to the back of the store, picked up his order and shuffled out the front door.

"I never would have guessed that he would take that big galoot down with one punch. This is my lucky day. I bought myself some cheap protection."

Renata smiled to herself. "If you only knew how wrong you are!"

Renata strolled into the bungalow a little after 8. Cappy was upset. "Where have you been?"

"Quit grousing! Baxter took the bait, hook, line, and sinker. Billy's hired. That is a great start. Now we need to get a few things straightened out and we will be ready for the big day."

Joey Is Recognizable

The Angelino's media event was better than anyone could have anticipated. All the television stations in town set time aside to air the Angelino's interview. Every station flashed MarJean's drawing. The stations provided a hotline number for folks who might have any information about the shooter.

The newspaper ran the story along with the sketch of the shooter. The paper went one step further. The Sunday edition included an in-depth story about mob activity in the state. They also published an editorial decrying the expansion of mob activity in New England.

The publicity that followed was enormous. The police were inundated with calls regarding the identity of the shooter. Maloney called John. "I'm coordinating our investigation. Eddie Logan is working with me. My chief assigned two additional detectives to follow up on all the calls we've received. I hope a few of these calls will generate information regarding the shooting."

The police received over 600 tips regarding the shooter. Maloney's unit narrowed the list down to 12 potential suspects. His team travelled all over New England trying to whittle the list down further. Most of the suspects were connected to the mob, so it was getting difficult to get any cooperation.

Finally, they hit the jackpot. The mother of a young woman from Waterbury, Connecticut, called the tip line. "Hello, my name is Nicolle Nicoletti. I am calling about the shooting that took place in Rhode Island last fall. My daughter, Ava, has been seeing a guy who looks exactly like the guy in the newspaper article."

The woman left her address and phone number. She said she would be willing to meet with the police. This was the third call the police had received that described the shooter as a guy from Waterbury. The other folks who called never identified themselves.

Maloney walked down to the chief's office. "Jim, we might have a solid lead on the De Nuncio slaying."

That got the chief's attention. "You have a strong lead! Give me the lowdown."

"We've received three calls describing the shooter as being from Waterbury. It might be worthwhile to drive over to Waterbury to check these leads out."

"I want you to handle this. Contact the lead detective on the Waterbury force. Give this detective a heads up about what we have regarding this investigation."

Maloney called the Waterbury Police Department. He was transferred to Lt. Dom Salvatore. Bill introduced himself and explained his role in the De Nuncio case. "I have reason to believe that one of your residents may have been involved in the shooting. We received a call from a Mrs. Nicoletti regarding our artist's drawing. She thinks she knows the shooter. I'd like to interview her. Would it be possible to assign one of your detectives to go with me when I interview Mrs. Nicoletti and her daughter?"

Lt. Salvatore was very willing to accommodate Maloney's request. "Call me back after 3 p.m. That would give me time to see if we have anybody who might be available to help you." Bill got off the phone and went right back to his chief to share the good news.

Maloney got a call later that afternoon from Sean O'Hara. O'Hara was a detective in the Waterbury P.D.

He had been assigned to help with Maloney's investigation. "Can you fill me? What is going on?"

Maloney gave O'Hara the short version of their investigation. "I'd like to interview Mrs. Nicoletti as soon as possible."

"I can meet you on Thursday. Would that work for you?"

"Thursday would be fine. I'll call Mrs. Nicoletti and see if she is available to meet with us."

Maloney called Mrs. Nicoletti right away. She was happy to meet with the police. He left a message for O'Hara. Maloney drove to Waterbury on Thursday. He met O'Hara at the police department. Then they drove over to the Nicoletti's. Mrs. Nicoletti met them at her front door. She was a short, slender woman with auburn hair that covered her head and then some. She ushered them into the front room. "Sit, sit." she said. "I'll be right back."

Two minutes later, she appeared with two cups of coffee and a tray of cookies. "Have some of these while I get my daughter." She went to the bottom of the stairway. "Ava, the detectives are here." Shortly thereafter, a slender girl of twenty or so, with big hair and a ton of makeup, walked into the room. In her hand was a Kodak photo. "Tell these officers about Joey."

Ava spent the next few minutes talking about her on again, off again relationship with Joey D'Amato. She was a fountain of knowledge. She knew where D'Amato lived, who he hung out with, etc. The only thing she couldn't tell Maloney and O'Hara was where Joey was right now. "He was here for the holidays, but he had to hurry back to his job. Joey left just before New Year's Day. He was tight lipped about his job. I have no idea where he is or what he's doing." At that point, she gave the officers the photo.

What Maloney saw was a photo of Ava standing next to a young Italian hoodlum at some Christmas party. The kid was about 5"8 and as slim as a curtain rod. He was the spitting image of the guy that MarJean had drawn. "Miss Nicoletti, you said that you knew where Joey lived. Does he live around here?"

"Well sir, Joey spends a lot of time at his mother's house. She lives on the east side." The officers asked a few more questions, but Ava was out of answers.

As the officers rose to leave, Ava wrote down Joey's mother's address. The officers headed towards the front door. O'Hara stopped. "Would it be ok if we came back if we have more questions. "I guess so," Ava said tentatively, "if it is okay with my mom." Mrs. Nicoletti said they would be happy to cooperate in any way.

The officers went back to headquarters to see what they could find out about D'Amato. Lo and behold, there was a lot of info on D'Amato. He'd been a troublemaker ever since high school. His problems with the law had escalated over the past few years. Initially, he was involved with gang skirmishes. Then he was picked up breaking into a grocery store. It went south from there

The detectives headed over to D'Amato's mother's place. Lucky for them, they found her at home. That was the only lucky thing that came their way. Mrs. D'Amato was not a big fan of the Waterbury police. Maloney knocked on the door of a two-story house that was in disrepair. Several windows were cracked and the house was in need of a paint job. A diminutive woman with pointy glasses and a wild shock of grey hair opened the door.

"Are you Mrs. D'Amato?" O'Hara asked as he flashed his badge.

The woman's eyes flared in anger. "You put my husband in his grave and you have ruined my son Choco's reputation. Get outta my yard and outta my life! I got nothing to say to you."
"Mrs. D'Amato, if we could just have a—" was all O'Hara could get out before the door slammed shut.

The detectives walked back to their car. 'What was that all about?"

"I don't have a clue, Sean, I have a funny feeling about D'Amato. He might be our guy. I know you were assigned to work with me for a day. Do you think you could spend another day on the case?"

"Let's see what I can do." They headed back to the station. Sean spoke to Salvatore while Maloney called his chief. They were given the go ahead to stay on the case for a few more days.

Bill needed to find a motel. "I told my chief that it made no sense to drive back to town at this late hour and then return to Waterbury tomorrow. He agreed to let me stay here. Is there any place you could recommend?"

Sean let out a laugh. "I have just the place for you. My sister-in-law owns a small motel just north of town. Here's Molly's number. Tell her that I sent you." Sean gave Bill directions to the motel. Bill hadn't expected to be staying overnight, so he stopped at a shopping center and picked up some toiletries and a few items of clothes. Then he found a phone booth and called his wife to let her know that he would be back in town tomorrow. Then he called Molly.

Next thing Bill knew, he was checking into Molly's motel. When he mentioned O'Hara's name, the woman behind the counter smiled. Her name tag matched her brogue. "If Sean sent you here, you must be one heck of a guy yerself."

"Is there a restaurant nearby that might be open at this time of night?"

"We live right behind the motel, Detective Maloney. We have leftovers in the refrigerator. I'd be disappointed if you didn't come over and finish them up for us." Bill couldn't say no to that offer. He was hungry and tired.

Bill knocked on Molly's door a little after seven. Before he knew it, he had a platter of roast beef and mashed potatoes sitting in front of him. He was stuffed and ready to head to his room when a slice of apple pie found its way to his plate. "We can't let you go back to your room without tasting my award-winning apple pie."

"In for a penny, in for a pound," he thought. By the time Bill was finished with dinner, he was ready to hit the hay. "Thank you so much for your hospitality."

The next day, Bill met O'Hara at a cafe several blocks from the police station. "I hear Molly sat you down for leftovers and some of her apple pie with cream last night. I thought that might happen."

Bill's face turned red. "I didn't know how to say no thank you." That brought a smile to Sean's face. Two cups of coffee later, they headed to the west side of town.

They went looking for Rico D'Amato. Rico was Joey's middle brother. Sean had called around. He heard that Rico was a mechanic at a used car dealership in town. "Apparently, Rico didn't follow in his brother's footsteps. We don't have a rap sheet with Rico's name on it. He is as clean as a whistle."

"Do you know where he lives, Sean?"

"A friend of mine bowls with Rico on Thursday nights. Rico lives a mile from his mother's house.
When they got to Rico's, Bill was surprised. His house was a small, well-kept blue and white bungalow. The front yard was well maintained. There were no junkers in the driveway or bags of trash laying near the back door. "This is not what I expected." Sean nodded in agreement. They parked on the street and walked up to the front door.

Sean rang the bell. An attractive thirty something pregnant woman answered the door. The detectives introduced themselves. "How can I help you?" the woman asked coolly. Sean inquired if she was Mrs. D'Amato. "Yes, I am Marcia D'Amato."

Sean and Bill pulled out their badges. Sean told her that the Waterbury police were involved in an important investigation. "We were wondering if we could take a few minutes of your time. We are trying to locate to your brother-in-law."

Marcia let the officers into her house. "Let's sit down in the kitchen. My two-year old is asleep upstairs, so we need to be quiet." The three of them walked down a hallway covered with photographs of a young wrestler.

When they sat down, Bill asked about the guy in the photographs. "That's my husband, Rico. He was a three time all conference wrestler in high school."

"You must be really proud of him."

"He's the only member of his family who is a stand-up person. Rico's a hard worker and one heck of a husband! Normally, I'm reluctant to talk about other people," she said, "but Joey is another story."

"I take it that you are not a big fan of Joey."

"Trouble follows Joey around like the plague." For the next ten minutes, Marcia left no stone unturned. She wanted no part of him. "He's not welcomed here!"

"Do you know where Joey might be?"

"I have no idea. He hasn't been here since New Year's. He was gone for a while this fall, came back for Christmas, and then he left. I hope he never comes back. He's nothing but trouble."

At that point, the detectives asked if Rico would be able to talk to them. At the mention of his name, Marcia froze right up. "Rico. What about my husband, Detective O'Hara?"

"We hope he might be able to shine some light on his brother's recent activities." That fell flat on its face. They asked Marcia some additional questions about Rico's whereabouts. That led nowhere. All she would tell them was that Rico was probably at work. The officers left empty handed.

When they got into the patrol car, Bill turned to Sean. "What just happened?"

"I have no idea. Things were going smoothly until we brought up Rico's name. She's afraid of something." They decided it was more important now than ever before to find Rico. He was the key to finding Joey.

They spent the rest of the day tracking Rico down. That didn't work out too well. They went to the used car lot. The only one there was a guy named Leo. "Rico was here for a while. Around eleven o'clock, he got a call. He said he had to leave for some emergency. He didn't say where he was going."

Sean suggested that they go back and stake out Rico's house. "We might get lucky and find him at home." They drove over to Rico's and spent the rest of the afternoon waiting for him. He never showed. Finally, the detectives headed back to the station.
Bill called his chief and filled him in on the details of the day. When he got off the phone, he told Sean that he could stay for another night. "We better get lucky or this whole thing goes up in smoke. So, do you think that I could stay at your in-laws' again?"

"How about I make a call and find out?" Sean said. He called Molly right away.

"I have plenty of room for Detective Maloney. Tell him that he better stay with us or I will call the cops." Maloney and O'Hara laughed at her attempt at comedy.

A deeper sense of friendship

Detta called Maria a week after the fundraiser. "Do you have time have breakfast this week? I've missed seeing you and would love to catch up."

Maria thought that would be a great idea. "I'm free tomorrow. Would that work?"

"Absolutely. I'll be at your place around 9:30."

The next day, Detta and Maria drove over to J's restaurant in Johnston for breakfast. Detta had known the owner for years. "They serve breakfast all day long, Maria. They make great waffles with fruit. Otherwise, they can make any type of omelet that meets your fancy."

When they got to the restaurant, there was one parking space available. Detta maneuvered her car into the parking space. Then, she opened the door to get out. She felt a tug on her arm. Maria asked if they could talk for a bit before going inside.

"What's going on, Maria?"

Maria started to shudder and then to cry. After a minute or so, she gained her composure. "Detta, I'm so grateful for all you've done us. You've changed our lives. However, I don't understand something. Why me? You are very well thought of in our town. You have friends in high places. People who listen to every word you say. Me. I am just a neighborhood baker trying to make the world a better place for my family."

Detta was startled to hear what Maria had to say. Finally, she turned to Maria. "For one thing, many people want me to do them favors. They aren't concerned with my needs as much as they are with how I can be of help to them. You have never asked me for anything. In fact, you've tried to keep a low profile. You're so grateful for any help you receive. I'm amazed at your strength. You had to deal with so much pain and suffering. And yet, you kept going with a smile on your face, grateful beyond belief. I see a lot of you in me.

"We've let down our hair and talked about our family struggles. We share our love for our families. As strange as it might seem, I feel like I've found a new sister— someone who takes me as I am, cares for me in a special way. You are a wonderful friend. I might be wrong, but I think you see me in much the same way."

Maria's eyes glistened. "Mary, Mother of God, Detta! That's exactly how I feel. I was afraid to say anything lest you told me some cockamamie story about wanting to help a child of God or some such nonsense. What a relief! You are the best friend I could ever imagine having." They cried for a while. Then the car got chilly, so they headed into the restaurant.

"What a busy place, Detta."

"Bob O'Hern is the owner. He and his family do a great job of making people feel right at home. Even though there was a long line of people waiting to be seated, Detta and Maria were immediately ushered to a table.

A dark-haired man with a twinkle in his eye came right over to their table after they were seated and gave Detta a big hug. Then he turned to Maria. "Hello, my name is Bob. Aren't you Maria Angelino?"

Maria was dumbfounded. This guy recognized me. "I am," she said. "Have we ever met?"

"No, ma'am. I've seen your photo in the paper." Bob told her that he had read about the shooting. "You have gone through a huge ordeal. I'm so glad to see that you are on the mend. I wanted to come to your fundraiser, but we had a large engagement party at the restaurant the night of the fundraiser. I couldn't get away.

"We're busy today. I should get back to the kitchen. I am glad to see you are doing so well. Detta, it has been way too long since I have seen you. Please order what you wish today. Your meals are on the house." He shook their hands and headed towards the kitchen.

"Everywhere I go, people have been so kind. It is overwhelming." Tears rolled off her cheeks. Detta moved her chair to be closer to Maria. "You have been on a stressful ride these past few months. Your life was turned upside down."

Maria took a deep breath. "I sometimes wonder "Why me?"

Detta had no answer for that. "All I know, Maria, is that we both trust in God. Hopefully the reason for all this will come in time."

After a few minutes, Maria wiped away her tears. "Thank you for being such a good friend. Every so often, out of nowhere, I get on this crying jag. I'm sorry."

"No worries. I am glad I was here for you. Now, how about we get some food. Are you ready?" Maria nodded. Detta got the attention of the nearest waitress.

The waitress, a young woman named Molly, came right over. Molly had the biggest bouffant hairdo Maria had ever seen. "Hi there," Molly chirped as she passed out menus. "Can I start you out with some coffee?" Detta and Maria nodded in agreement. "Two regular coffees coming up. Why don't you take a few minutes to look at the menu? I'll be right back with your coffee. Then I'll take your order."

As soon as Molly left, Maria started to giggle. "I wonder how much hairspray it takes to keep her hair in place. She looks like a double for Dolly Parton." With that, Maria and Detta burst out laughing.

Molly came back with the coffee and asked if they were ready to order. Detta wanted the waffles with strawberries and a side of bacon. "The waffles sound wonderful, Maria said, but I need to watch my weight. How about two eggs over easy and a small cup of fruit."

"I'll put your orders in right away." Molly winked at them and turned towards the kitchen.

The steaming coffee got their attention. Detta added a little bit of sugar to her cup, took a sip and smiled. "They really know how to make a pot of coffee." Then they started chattering about church and their kids.

A few minutes later, Detta asked how Vincent was doing.

"That son of mine is getting into this acting stuff! Every night after dinner, he sits down at the kitchen table and practices his lines. His brothers stay out of his way. If they disturb him when he is practicing, there is heck to pay. Vincent's all in as far as this play is concerned."

"Were you surprised when he agreed to take the role of Rick?" Detta inquired.

"Surprised wasn't the word for it. More like amazed. Vincent's always been a quiet, introverted boy. Now he is totally different. He comes down to breakfast in the morning and asks me how I am doing! He is more self-confident and willing to try new things. In fact, the other day, he asked if we could have scampi for dinner some time. My oldest son is growing up before my very eyes."

Detta nodded in agreement. "Cris is amazed at his transformation. She brought up his name on a lark when Donnie got hurt. Never in her wildest imagination did she think that he would consider taking on the role. Now she just can't stop talking about how well Vincent is doing. She tells me that he is nailing the role. You have a budding star on your hands, Maria."

Maria and Detta yakked some more about a variety of things including the new choir director at church and their kids' activities. Detta indicated that she hadn't been able to get out much during the past two weeks.

"What's going on?"

"Well, Dante's assistant had to go out of town on business. Dante had been snowed under with work, so he asked if I would help him out. I never realized how many calls that were needed to be made each day. Dante handles most of the calls, but I must follow up on a lot of stuff. There hasn't been much free time to take care of my own business. Finally, I told Dante that I am taking a vacation day today."

"Wow, good for you. What else do you have planned?"

"Dante and I are going to a dinner dance at the Cranston Country Club in two weeks, so I am heading over to the mall to see if I can find a new dress. I was wondering if you'd like to come along. I'm not very good with colors. I need help picking out a dress."

"I haven't been out to the mall in ages, Detta. I could go for a little while. My strength is coming back, but I still need to take afternoon naps. I would love to come with you if we could be back to Greenville by 2 p.m."

"We better hurry up, girl. Shopping awaits."

The Baxter plan almost works

Renata was relieved when Saturday rolled around. Everyone was on pins and needles. Cappy was more nervous than anybody because he felt Marty was looking over his shoulder. Cappy was irritable. When he got that way, most folks knew to keep their distance. However, Joey didn't read signals too well. When he started regurgitating his whine about his role in the heist, Cappy slapped him upside the head. "Enough of your whining! You'll get involved once things get rolling. Until then, just shut your yap!"

In the wink of an eye, Renata stepped between them before rough stuff could get rolling. "Both of you cool it. We don't have time for this!" Her forehead started to furrow. Her bark would turn into a vicious bite if things went further. Everyone knew what was going on and decided to find a seat.

Renata went over the plan one last time. "Does everyone understand what they need to do?" They nodded in agreement. "Okay, we'll meet at the warehouse at five p.m. There will be no screw ups. We work the plan. When we're done, everyone gets a big paycheck." She headed out the front door to meet up with Baxter.

Marty decided to call Mr. B. "So, Marty, where have you been?" Mr. B barked when he heard Marty's voice. "I haven't heard a thing from you in three days."

Marty could tell by Mr. B's growl that he was upset. "Sorry, things have been hectic."

"So, are the plans still in play?"

"We are good to go. I'll call you this afternoon to fill you in on how we made out."

"You do that, Marty, or else!"

Renata arrived at the store a little after 8. No sooner had she gotten through the door when the phone rang. It was Baxter. He was rattled. He wanted her to come over to the new store. He was concerned about having someone oversee Booby. She told him that she would clean up a few loose ends and be right over.

Renata knew her most important job was to quell all of Baxter's fears. Baxter was fidgeting like crazy when she arrived. "Where have you been, girl?"

Renata told him to give her two minutes and she'd have everything under control. "You have been on pins and needles for the last week. All will go well, Mr. Baxter. Trust me." With that, she headed towards the back room to see how things were unfolding.

No wonder Baxter's upset. Booby and Big Bear were smoking cigarettes in the back room. "I didn't think that I had to babysit you. Get your asses in gear. The liquor needs to be unloaded. We don't have the time to waste." They got up and grumbled all the way to the loading dock.

Renata went looking for Freddie, the store manager. She found him in the back room, hibernating. "What gives? You're supposed to tell the guys what to do."

Freddie shrugged. "Big Bear pinned me up to the wall. This is not what I bargained for."

"Come with me!" It was time to talk to Baxter.

She sat Freddie down and made him tell his tale. "The three West Virginians are your boys, Mr. Baxter. Apparently, they have minds of their own. I almost got beaten up by Booby after I told him to stop horsing around and get busy unloading booze."

Renata shared what she saw when she went into the back area. "I suggest we head out to the truck, Mr. Baxter. Tell them to follow Freddie's directions or hightail it back to the hills. Before you start shooting some shit about them leaving us high and dry, remember I have their paychecks. The checks amount to two weeks of pay plus bonuses. They ain't going anywhere!"

Baxter gathered the hillbillies together. He was hot under the collar. "Let's get one thing straight. Today should be a huge payday. Freddie knows the liquor business like the back of his hand. You do what he tells you to do. If you screw up again, you'll hit the road without a penny in your pockets. You got it?" They all nodded their heads. "I don't hear you!" Baxter growled.

The hillbillies responded with a loud "Yes, sir!"

Baxter was too nervous to be of any help, so Renata told him to head over to the bank and pick up the change they'd need for the store opening. When he left, Renata put up some decorations and signage. One of the suppliers came in the front door. 'Where do you want this wine display?" Freddie took over from there.

Coot and Billy were doing a bang-up business. Apparently, folks were stocking up for St. Patrick's Day. Coot called Renata. "You need to get over here. We are rooting, tooting busy."

"Things are wild over here as well. I need to stay here and help Baxter. You will have to handle things on your own. I'll call you back in an hour."

Cappy and King were twiddling their thumbs. They found a parking spot near the store. They saw the West Virginians get their comeuppance. "Baxter is going to have a snit fit when he learns that he's been taken for a ride," Cappy chortled. "The tables will be turned."

Renata met Coot at 2 p.m. The inflow of customers had slowed down to a trickle, so Coot headed out to help Baxter. "Now I need to put a 'Closed' sign in the window." She stopped for a second and looked at her "to do" list. "I'm getting ahead of myself. I need to slow down."

She went to the back room and opened the small safe in the store. There was $4,000 waiting for her there. Then, she emptied the cash out of the register and put a closed sign in the window. Renata locked the front door and headed to the bank. "Baxter will be so pissed when he finds out that 'Shirl' took him to the cleaners."

Renata met Joey and Marty at Baxter's office. "How did it go at the bank, Renata?"

"Smooth as silk. Is anyone in the office?" The coast was clear. "Okay, I'll need twenty minutes to take care of business. Watch the front of the building. Make sure no one comes in."

Fifteen minutes later, Renata came back. She was carrying a large satchel. "We are all set. Booby and his friends should be back at the open house by now, I want you to meet King at the warehouse. Start loading the truck with booze. I'll meet you as soon as I can." Renata headed to the bungalow. She wiped down the counter tops, the refrigerator, and the bathroom. It was 5 p.m. when she finally packed up her car and headed to the warehouse.

The getaway plan should have been flawless. Who would have thought Booby and his friends would come back for more booze? They arrived just as Joey lifted the last case of Seagram's on Billy's truck. Wing Nut pulled his revolver and started screaming at Joey to put the booze down and raise his hands to the sky. Marty and the others were in the warehouse when they heard the yelling. Cappy ran to the backdoor and slipped out while King and Billy headed towards the open doorway.

Cappy crept behind Nut. "Drop your gun!" Chaos ensued. Booby and Big Bear started shooting. Then Joey, Marty, and King started shooting. A few seconds later, the shooting stopped. Marty saw three people on the ground moaning. Nut and Booby had been shot. A sigh of relief soon turned into utter horror. Marty turned towards the warehouse and saw Cappy leaning against the warehouse door. He was barely conscious. He had been shot twice. His pants were stained with blood.

Marty ran over to Cappy. Marty knew Cappy needed medical attention. "Joey, help Cappy into the truck!" Billy and King ran over to see if they could be of help. Marty shouted. "Make sure the hillbillies won't be able to do anymore shooting!"

Renata pulled up. She saw Cappy being loaded into the back seat of the truck. She slammed the car into park and jumped out. She didn't need to know what had happened. "Billy, you and King get Nut and his friends into the warehouse. Then let's get outta here."

Instinct overtook fear. They pulled Booby into the warehouse. He had a shoulder wound that didn't look too serious. Billy told Joey to grab some rope and tie Booby up. "Then rip up his shirt, stuff some of it against his shoulder, and put the remainder in his mouth." Billy and King pulled the other hillbillies into the warehouse. "These guys aren't seriously injured, King, so we can just tie them up and leave them here. They should be okay."

Renata went directly to the truck to assess Cappy's condition. She saw that Marty had put a makeshift tourniquet around Cappy's thigh. That would slow the bleeding. She gathered the group around her. "Here's what we are going to do. Billy, we'll drive Cappy to Chicago. Marty, take my car and head to Canada. Joey's going with you. He has ties to Dolan. That would not be good if the police got a hold of Joey. King, take Cappy's car and follow us." King wasn't happy about driving, but there was no other option.

Joey started complaining about going to Canada. Renata headed him off right away "Listen up, numbskull. I don't have time to argue. You need to get as far away from here as you can. You shot Big Bear. I don't think they will forget that. So get going!"

"Marty, once you have Joey settled down, give me a call. Here's my number. I hope to be back in Chicago by midnight. We will plan from there." Renata jumped in the truck and took off. King was right behind her.

Some guy named Chooch helps out

Maloney was able to stay another night at Molly's motel. However, another huge meal and two whiskeys later were more than enough to help him get some sleep. The sun was shining on his face when he began to stir. Maloney squinted at his watch. When he saw the time, he jumped out of bed and headed to the shower. "Oh my God. I overslept!" It was well after 9:15 when Maloney finally pulled up to the police station.

Sean started to laugh when he saw Maloney. "You must have had a taste of Ireland's finest last night." Maloney motioned for Sean to lead the way back to his office. "Bill, you look like you need some Java." Maloney needed two cups of coffee before he was able to talk.

"Here's what we do. Let's see if Rico made it to work today. I have a feeling that he was involved in some of Joey's shenanigans. If that's true, he could take it on the lam." Bill agreed. A few minutes later, they arrived at the used car lot. They headed to the office. One of the salesmen said the owner, some guy named Chooch, was running an errand. When Maloney asked to talk to Rico, they learned that he had called in sick.

Bill decided to dig a little further. "Has Rico been working pretty steadily over the past few months?"

The salesman told them that business had slowed down. Rico and another guy were laid off for a few weeks. "Rico came back to work two weeks ago." The detectives thanked the salesman for his time and headed to their car.

"So, Sean, what do you make of this whole thing?"

"It seems pretty convenient for Rico to be taking today off work. We might want to slide by his house. I'm afraid our talk with his wife might prompt D'Amato to head for the hills." With that, they headed over to Rico's place.

They got there in time to see Rico putting a few pieces of luggage in the backseat of his Ford. "Why don't you get out here, Bill. Maybe you can circle behind the neighbor's house just in case Rico starts to make a run for it when he sees me pull into his driveway."

Sure enough, Rico started sprinting towards his back yard when Sean pulled up. unfortunately, he ran right into Maloney. "Mr. D'Amato, fancy meeting you here." Rico tried to shake loose, but Bill had him firmly in his grasp. Sean ran over to help with Rico. "Mr. D'Amato, I think the three of us are headed back to police headquarters. We want to ask you a few questions concerning a gangland killing in Rhode Island." At that point, Sean read Rico his rights.

Rico was too upset to think about keeping quiet. You could hear him proclaiming his innocence from three blocks away. "I don't know nothing about any gangland hit!"

Just then, Rico's wife scrambled out the backdoor of their house. "What is going on here?" she yelled when she saw the detective holding Rico. "Rico, don't say a thing. I'll call our attorney and have him meet you at the station." Bill ushered Rico into the back seat of the patrol car and they headed back to the station.

A few minutes later, Rico was cuffed to a table in one of the conference rooms at the station. Bill and Sean left him alone for a little while. Maloney could see that Dino was sweating profusely. "What do you think, Sean? Is it time to question him?"

Sean headed into the room. Bill watched the scene play out through a two-way mirror. Sean went through the legal mumbo jumbo. All Rico could do was to blather on. "I know nothing about any murder."

"I have a few questions I need to ask you, Rico."

Rico shook his head. "I want to talk to my lawyer."

"Life would get a lot easier, if we could clean up a few questions we have about your brother." Rico wasn't talking to anyone except his lawyer.

A weary looking guy with a mop of wiry hair and a Fu Manchu mustache approached the desk sergeant. "My name is Louis Jacobi. You are holding Rico D'Amato. I'm his attorney. I'd like to see my client immediately."

The desk sergeant called O'Hara. "D'Amato's attorney was in the building."

"I'll be right out." Sean turned to Bill, "D'Amato's attorney is here."

"That didn't take long," Bill declared.

Jacobi wasn't the belligerent type. However, he made it clear that no further conversations would take place until he had a chance to talk to his client. Sean led Jacobi to the conference room. "I need some time alone with my client."

"Mr. Jacobi, I'll be back in a while to check up on you."

Maloney pulled Sean aside. "It might be wise to give Rico's boss a call. Maybe we can pick up some information about Rico's comings and goings."

"Great idea, Bill! Could you take care of this? I need to meet with my chief about D'Amato."

Bill called the used car dealership. Chooch, the owner, had just come back from running errands. He was willing to talk to Bill, but it had to be face to face and it had to be far away from the dealership. Chooch chimed in, "Joey is a wild man. I need to be careful. Joey can't find out that I've been talking to you. If he does, I'm a dead man."

Maloney agreed to meet Chooch at a nearby restaurant. Maloney found Sean in the chief's office. "I'm heading out to meet Rico's boss."

"O'Hara and I still have a lot to talk about. Take a radio with you just in case something weird happens."

Bill arrived at the restaurant a little early. He was lucky to find a parking space. A few minutes later a candy apple red Chevy truck with an "All American Auto" sign on the door pulled into the parking lot. A geezer opened the truck door and slid off the front seat. Chooch had told Bill to look for a middle-aged guy with a hat. "I'll be easy to spot."

One look at this guy and Bill knew that the years hadn't been kind to him. He looked to be on the north side of 60 rather than being 45 years old; he looked like a used car salesman—dark purple shirt with a black tie. His hair hadn't seen a comb in a month. The only snappy things about him were the red suspenders that held up his pants.

Bill introduced himself. They went into the diner, grabbed a booth, and ordered coffee. As soon as the waitress left, Bill started right in. "I get the sense that Joey is not someone to tangle with!"

"You bet your sweet ass. D'Amato would pistol whip you without hesitation. He's one scary customer."

Bill wondered if Chooch had seen Joey recently. "I have not seen him around town lately. That's a good thing."

"I'm trying to find Joey. He might know something about a case I'm working on. Nobody has seen him for a while. I'm hoping to talk to him."

"Good luck with that!" Chooch spat out. "I wouldn't believe one word that comes out of D'Amato's mouth."

"Is Rico anything like his brother?"

"Absolutely not, Rico is a hard-working, down to earth guy. His word is the gospel truth. If he tells you he will have a carburetor installed in the hour, you can set your watch by it."

"If he's that good, why did you lay him off?"

Chooch started to wring his hands together. His business had fallen off. "My other mechanic has been with me for seven years. He is as good as Rico. I told Rico that I had to lay him off for a few weeks. Rico understood. He told me he'd be ready to come back to work at a moment's notice. That was five weeks ago. I called him up two weeks ago. His wife said he was out of town."

"Tell him to get his ass back into the shop."

"Rico called me a few hours later. He said he would return as soon as possible."

"Did Rico mentioned what he had been doing during his time off?

"All he said was that he went out west."

"Anywhere specific?"

Chooch scratched his chin for a second. "Let me think. All I remember is that the town had great barbecue."

"Could it have been Kansas City?"

"Yeah, that's right. Rico and I talked about how the Royals had the second-best Italian ball player ever to play the game. Steve Balboni. You must have heard of him. What a slugger!"

Bill knew that this conversation could go off the rails if he didn't intervene. "Did Rico say anything else?"

"I think Rico might have met up with his brother for a few days, but I can't say for sure."

Then the conversation headed south. Bill needed to get back to the station. "Thanks, Chooch, for meeting me."

Chooch looked right into Maloney's eyes. "Listen, Detective, you have got to promise me that you won't say anything to Joey about our conversation." Bill nodded and then headed out the door.

Dante, where are your loyalties

Dante and Detta were heading out for the first performance of *You Can't Take It With You*. Cris had left three hours ago. The last thing she said as she headed out was "Mom, Daddy takes his time getting ready. Please make sure he isn't late."

Detta got on Dante's case. "Dante," she yelled. "You need to hustle! We will not be late for this performance!"

A few minutes later, Dante came downstairs. He was wearing a dark blue shirt, a vee necked sweater and white pants. Detta shook her head. "Follow me, Buster." Detta made Dante change into a nice grey suit and tie. Dante wasn't happy about that. The only thing he was happy about was that Cristiana had let her hair grow out. "Dad, my character would never wear her hair short." He knew better than to open his trap. It would only get him in trouble.

They were about to head to Providence when the phone rang. It was Marty. Dante told Detta he was going downstairs to take the call. "Hang up the phone as soon as I pick up the receiver."

She scowled at him. "Five minutes is all you've got! Nothing is more important than being at the school play to watch Cristiana."

Dante listened as Marty retold the events of the afternoon. "How bad is Capuano hurt?"

"Billy and Renata staunched the bleeding, but he's still hurt bad. Renata's in the backseat of the truck with Capuano. Billy is driving. I guess they are 45 minutes from Des Moines." Apparently, Renata had called a friend of hers. This guy was a surgeon who knew how to keep his mouth shut. He gave Renata instructions about what to do with Cappy for the time being. He also gave her the name of an ER nurse in Des Moines. She'll check on Cappy. If he can travel, Renata and Billy will head to Chicago. The surgeon will take care of Cappy once they get to Renata's house."

"Marty, I have something important to take care of tonight. I should be home by 10:30. Call me as soon as you hear from Renata. We can talk more then." With that, Dante slammed the phone down and shook his head. "This is becoming one goddamn disaster."

Detta was waiting for Dante at the top of the stairs. She had already put her suede coat on. She could tell by Dante's expression that something was seriously wrong. "Do you want to tell me what that was all about?"

"One of my guys got caught off guard. Somebody got hurt. I didn't get all the details. I'm going get a call later tonight. I'll need to take it, so we won't have much time to stop and chat when the play is over."

That got Detta's attention. She went from concerned to apoplectic in the space of three seconds. "This is your daughter's time to shine. You will be there for her tonight, Dante, or else!" He decided to go along with his wife, but he knew he had to take Marty's call. The ride to town was stormy. Detta was on pins and needles. This business with Dante had galled her. She let him know it.

They got to Don Bosco in plenty of time. When they walked into the school, they met some friends from St. Philip's. Everyone except Dante was chatting up a storm.

Just then, the Angelinos walked into the foyer. Detta went over and gave Maria a big hug. Then she gave John a peck on the cheek. The next thing John knew, the women were engaged in a heavy-duty conversation. John knew where this was headed. He would become the forgotten husband. He meandered over to the cafeteria and talked to a couple of guys who were on his bowling team.

Maria was on a roll. Right off the bat, she told Detta that she had gone back to work. "I'm only working five hours twice a week."

"How is that going?"

"I'm tired when I finish my shift and I need a nap at the end of the day, but it is wonderful to get back to work. I almost feel like I'm back to normal. There was a time when I thought I'd never be able to do anything and now, I am back to work. What a great feeling!"

Maria started talking about Vincent and how he was handling this acting thing. "I can't believe the change in my son. He is so self-confident. He started quoting some sign he had seen in school. "Mom," he said, "if you think you can, you can."

"I had to ask him to explain it to me. Now, this phrase has become our family motto. Vincent has worked so hard on his role. Cristiana has been such a big help. She's spent a huge amount of time working with him. Vincent thinks the world of her. She's helped him to conquer his fears. I am grateful that Cristiana has been there for my son."

Then the bell rang to let the crowd know that the play was soon going to start. "We better find our husbands before the lights go down."

The play went off without a hitch. Vincent and Cris received standing ovations. Once the curtain went down for the final time, the Angelinos and the Bonfigores went backstage to find their kids. The actors reverted back to being teenagers. They were jabbering on and on about the play.

Mr. Williams raised his hands and his voice. He was finally able to quiet the kids down. "Listen up. We have another show tomorrow night. You did a great job tonight. You'll need to get some rest if you are going to duplicate tonight's performance. Get out of your costumes and find your ride home. Be back here by 5:30 p.m. tomorrow. Be prepared to be great."

Detta knew it was going to take a while for Cris to get dressed. Dante was itchy to get home. Detta told Maria that Dante needed to get right back home. "Could Cris and I hitch a ride back to Greenville?"

"Sure, we can squeeze you in. We aren't going to get a chance to talk. Our kids have a lot to talk about."

Dante was pacing back and forth in front of the stage. Detta wasn't sure what was going on, but whatever it was, it was important. She walked up and touched his shoulder. Dante jumped and let out a swear word. He turned on a dime and was surprised to see his wife standing next to him. His scowl softened. "You scared the bejeebers out of me!"

"I have no idea what's going on with you. You've been at the play, but you are a million miles away. Whatever happened must be important. John and Maria will give us a ride home. Why don't you see if you can take care of whatever has gotten you twisted up like a pretzel?"

Dante didn't need to be asked twice. "I'm sorry for being such a doofus. A few things have become pretty rocky. I need to straighten them out. Thanks for understanding." He gave her a kiss and headed home.

Tell me a little more about Cappy

Dante burned rubber all the way to Greenville. He nearly got a ticket for speeding in Johnston. Fortunately, the cop had done some work for Dante a few months back. As a result, he didn't give Dante a ticket.

Dante opened his back door just as the phone rang. It was Marty, "What the hell happened? I thought the plan was foolproof."

Marty laid out the situation. "We were doing fine until the hillbillies came back to the warehouse. They caught us off guard. All hell broke loose. They started shooting and we fired back. I hit one of them in the shoulder. The other two were also hit, so that put an end to the shooting. Unfortunately, Cappy was shot during the fracas.

Dante was livid. "I don't give a rat's ass about those country bumpkins. What about Cappy? Go back to the beginning and tell me what you know!"

Marty went over everything that happened from the time they got to the warehouse. Renata and Billy started pulling away. "All I know is that Cappy's hurt pretty bad. Other than that, I know next to nothing."

"Have you heard anything more from Renata?"

"An ER nurse agreed to check on Cappy's condition. I'm assuming they are in Chicago by now. I called Renata when we got to Minneapolis and left a message for her to call when she could. I haven't heard from her. I'm assuming that getting no call is a good thing."

Dante shied away from putting any more pressure on Marty to hook up with Renata. "Let me know as soon as you hear anything! In the meantime, is there anything else I should know about?"

Marty told Dante that they got away with a boodle of cash. "There must have be over $100,000 all told. That included the money Renata had lifted from Baxter's safe, the money in the cash register, and the receipts that Renata was supposed to have deposited from the open house. On top of that, there is ten thousand dollars of booze in the back of the pick-up."

"That's all well and good, Marty, but I'd give it all back if I had known that Cappy was going to be shot. We have had our differences, but in the end, Capuano is worth twenty folks like One Shot. I hope he will be okay. Speaking of the devil, what is going on with Joey?"

"He's been a huge pain in the keister. I pulled him off the front line because he was too head strong. His ego kept getting in the way of his judgement." Marty told Dante about Joey's drinking. "He was getting wasted on a nightly basis. That led to some fighting. We gave him mop up jobs for the last few weeks. That didn't sit too well with him. He pouted and drank way too much. However, Joey was great when bullets started to fly. He saved my bacon at the warehouse. He was fearless."

This was worrisome to Dante. From the beginning, Dante felt Joey's explanation of the Di Nuccio shooting seemed too convenient. "This guy has a huge ego. That concerns me. I think he should stay in Canada. I got a tip from a friend of mine. The police found someone who identified Joey to a tee. One Shot needs to stay away from New England until things cool down."

Then Marty and Dante talked about the cigarette operation in Massachusetts. "Frankly, the operation's

318

going better than expected. Your guys are doing a terrific job. However, they don't have your smarts. I need you back here to make things happen. The sooner, the better. When can you make it back to Rhode Island?"

Marty thought about it for a second, "I can call a travel agency first thing in the morning and see about flying back ASAP.

"See if you can get back by the day after tomorrow," Dante said. "I have a funny feeling that things are going to heat up much quicker than either of us had anticipated."

"What about Joey? What do you want me to do with him?" Dante was interested to hear if Marty had any suggestions.

"Well, Thunder Bay is a sleepy town. Not much is happening right now. I have most of the money that you gave me when I headed west. I could give Joey five thousand dollars for starters. Joey could probably make that amount of cash go a long way."

"Do it! Tell Joey that he needs to keep his head down for a month or so. Lay it out as sharply as you can. He cannot get in trouble with the Thunder Bay police. He needs to be a stand-up guy. By the time he heads back here, things should have blown over. Let him know that when he does come back, I'll make it worth his while if he follows these instructions to the letter."

"I'll pass those instructions on. I will try to get out of here. The way the schedules are, it might be rough trying to get back home by tomorrow. I'll stay overnight in Detroit and head to Rhode Island the next day."

"Okay. Let me know if you hear anything from Renata. Call me right away." Dante hung up the phone. "I need a drink." He poured himself a whiskey and downed it in one swig. "Shit, shit, shit!"

Two drinks later, he headed upstairs. Then he heard a car pull up to the house. Cristiana bounced into the kitchen. Detta was not too far behind. "Daddy, what did you think of the play? Wasn't Vincent just the greatest?" Before Dante could open his mouth, his daughter was off to the races. All he had to do was smile, nod his head, and say "Ah" every fourth sentence.

Detta finally broke the spell. "Cristiana, this has been a day to remember. You nailed your part, Honey. Everyone was terrific. You are really wound up. I want to hear all your stories, but that'll have to wait til tomorrow. Mr. Williams said everyone needed to get a good night sleep." Cristiana started to argue with her mother. Detta simply shook her head and pointed to the stairs. "I will be up in a few minutes, sweetheart."

Once Cris made it up to her room, Detta started in on her husband. "So, were you able to get everything squared away?"

Dante shook his head. "A couple of mistakes led to one big headache. I can't get into it right now." Dante walked over to Detta and put his arm around her waist. "I'm sorry for upsetting you. My head was up my arse. Thanks for getting a ride home."

"Dante, why don't you head up to our bedroom? You look exhausted. Once I get Cris settled down, I think I'll find you snoozing away." It didn't take long for her to confirm that her assessment was spot on.

The next day, Cris was up bright and early. "What in heaven's name are you doing up so early? It is barely 8 o'clock in the morning. I thought you would sleep in on a Saturday morning."

"Mom, today is the anniversary of Vincent's grandmother's death. He wants me to bike to the florist shop with him. He needs help picking out flowers that he can lay on her grave. I said I'd go with him."

Detta was amazed at Cristiana's transformation from a whiny eighth grader to a responsible young woman. "That's very sweet. You seem to like Vincent a lot."

"Well, Mom, we are not like boyfriend/girlfriend, but we do like each other. I'm not ready for a serious relationship with anyone."

"My sisters and I are taking Grandma to the mall today. Her birthday falls on Holy Saturday, so we are having a little party for her after church. Everyone is coming here for her birthday."

"Mom," Cristiana whispered, "you'll be surprised to know that I remembered that. I thought I would order a dozen red roses for her when we go to the florist shop."

That took Detta by surprise. She walked over to Cris and gave her a hug. "Honey, you are something else."

So, Rico, what really went on?

Maloney headed to the police station. Rico was still talking to his attorney. "So, Bill, did you learn anything important from your meeting with this Chooch character? Maloney went over his interview with Chooch. "The best I can gather is that it seems as if Rico might have been with Joey for a few days in Kansas City."

"Really! When did that happen, Bill?"

"Rico made it back to Waterbury about ten days ago. Chooch isn't sure, but he got the impression that Rico and Joey spent some time together recently."

"Did Chooch say anything else that might be of any value to our investigation?"

"That's about it. But if Rico spent time with his brother, Joey might have given him a heads up about what he was up to. This information would be real helpful."

Bill and Sean walked towards the conference room. Jacobi came out to greet them. "My client is willing to talk to you. I'll be with him during the entire interview. Any questions about his stay in Kansas City are off limits." That was fine as far as the detectives were concerned. With that, they all went into the conference room.

"Rico, my name is Detective Maloney. I work for the Johnston Police Department. This is Detective O'Hara. He works for the Waterbury Police Department. We're investigating a murder that occurred in Rhode Island last fall. I'd like to ask you a few questions about this murder."

"I don't know nothing about any murder that occurred in Rhode Island. I haven't been in Rhode Island for over ten years," Rico said with a startled voice.

Maloney could see that he had ruffled Rico's feathers. "I don't have any reason to believe that you were involved with this murder." That seemed to mollify him. "Rico. Is Joey D'Amato your brother?" Rico nodded hesitantly. "Mr. D'Amato, you need to speak into the tape recorder."

"Joey D'Amato is my brother."

"The talk around town is that you are very different from your brother."

"What's that supposed to mean?" Rico spat out. Jacobi leaned over and attempted to calm his client down. A few seconds later, Rico seemed more relaxed.

"Rico," Maloney continued, "I checked your record with the Waterbury Police Department. Your record is as clean as the driven snow. When I mention your name to folks in town, they have good things to say about you. I can't say the same for your brother."

That got Rico talking. "Joey always had a chip on his shoulder. My dad had big plans for him. Dad thought Joey could work at Electric Boat. My Uncle Pete knew someone who worked there. Joey could have had a great job. But he wasn't interested in working for EB. He wanted more excitement. He saw my dad wheeling and dealing in the neighborhood. Joey wanted to play in that game. He always looked for the easy way to make a buck. Nothing else would work for Joey."

"When Joey turned down the Electric Boat offer, my dad turned a cold shoulder to him. From then on, Joey had to prove himself to everybody. Fast cars, good looking girls with no brains, and friends who were always in trouble. So I guess my brother and I are different."

"Rico," Maloney said. "I hear you were laid off a few weeks back."
Rico followed the same script that Chooch had given to Maloney. "Yeah, business slowed down at the garage, so my boss had to lay me off for a couple of weeks. I came back to work two weeks ago."

"What did you do while you were laid off?"

"A little of this and that. My wife's expecting any day now, so I helped around the house. Maloney's voice became edgier and his grilling intensified.

"Is that all you did during your time off, Rico? I got the sense that you might have left to see your brother in Kansas City." Rico reached for the glass of water. Maloney saw Rico's face blanch as soon as Kansas City was mentioned. Maloney could tell that any talk of Rico's visit to Kansas City was causing tension. Rico looked over towards Jacobi for advice.

"Detective, I thought we had a clear understanding."

Bill thought over his response for a second. "Mr. Jacobi, I have no interest in what activities Rico might have been involved with in Kansas City. However, I am interested in learning if Joey had mentioned what he had been doing prior to Rico's arrival in Kansas City."

Jacobi turned towards Rico and let him know that it would be okay for him to answer this question. Rico was quiet for a second. "All my brother told me was that he worked on a couple of big jobs back East before he arrived in Kansas. He didn't say anything specific about his work. All I know is that Joey has been away from

Waterbury for the past four months. Other than that, I know nothing about what he has been doing."

The detectives stepped out of the office. "We aren't going to get anything more out of D'Amato. He's told us all he knows." Sean agreed. They headed back to the room. "Rico, we are releasing you. If you think of anything else about Joey's activities, call me." Sean gave D'Amato one of his cards and led him out of the room.

Once Jacobi and D'Amato left, Bill and Sean went back to Sean's office. "Sean, I need to get back to Rhode Island. My boss is taking off for a well-deserved vacation. I am filling in for him. Do you think your chief will let you stay on this case for a little while longer?"

Sean nodded affirmatively. "The chief thinks we are on to something big, Bill. I am pretty sure I can stay on this case for another two weeks. Hopefully, something will break loose by then."

"That's great. It might be helpful if you could scout around town. There might be others who knew about Joey's whereabouts over the past few months."

Sean agreed to follow up on that idea. "I'll call you if I hear anything about Joey's whereabouts." They shook hands. Then Bill headed straight for Route 6.

Just who do you think you are, Joey Jerkoff?

Renata called Marty. She was exhausted. She filled Marty in on what had happened. The words crawled out of her mouth. "The good news is that we got Cappy here just after midnight. We pulled into a rest stop near Holt, Kansas, and managed to stop the bleeding. Then I called Louis, a doctor friend of mine. He's helped me with some 'business' injuries in the past. He put me in touch with a nurse who agreed to help us for the right price. She met us at a hotel south of Des Moines. She worked on Cappy for a half hour. She stabilized him. Then we hightailed it to Chicago."

"What is going on now? How is Cappy?"

"Trixie arrived at my place last week. She's a Godsend. She let the doctor and his nurses into the house. They turned the dining room into a surgical area. The doc removed the bullet in Cappy's thigh. Cappy has an excellent chance of making a full recovery. Then she started to cry. "Sorry," she said, "This has been incredibly stressful."

Marty wondered if they could trust Louis to keep his mouth shut. Renata pulled herself together. Louis was in her debt. "I've saved his bacon more than once. I know he will keep his trap shut. The nurses also know how to keep mum, especially given what we paid them."

Renata wanted to know where things stood with the Rhode Island mob. "I talked to Dante. He knows all about Cappy. I'll call him as soon as we finish up so I can update him. I'm in Thunder Bay right now. I'm headed down to Detroit this afternoon and then on to Rhode Island."

"What about Joey Jerkoff?"

"Joey is staying here until things cool down. Mr. B thinks that this would best for everyone concerned."

"I'm assuming this means best for everyone except for Joey. I can't imagine that he's liking this option one bit."

"Joey doesn't know anything about the plan. I am certain he won't be the least bit happy. He will have to like it or else. The 'or else' could be a deadly option. Listen, I need to get going." Marty gave Renata Mr. B's phone number. "When I talk to him, I'll tell him that you will call him with an update. Thanks for all you've done. I don't know where we'd be without you."

It was time for Joey to face the music. Marty had called Renata from a telephone booth a few blocks away from their motel. It was a hike back to their place. Marty opened the door and found Joey lying on the couch swilling some Canadian Club. "Jesus H. Christ!" Marty shouted. "Give me that damn bottle, you moron!"

"What's your problem? We are miles away from Kansas. No one knows us here. Yesterday was crazy. I think I deserve some time to kick back and relax a little."

"I have seen you relax, Buckaroo. You start drinking and then all hell seems to break loose. The last thing we need right now is to draw attention to ourselves. The best thing we can do is to keep a low profile!"

Joey started getting into a snit fit. "I can handle myself!"

"You will have every opportunity to do that."

"Whadda ya mean by that?"

"I spoke to Mr. B. He wants me to head back to Rhode Island tonight."

"That's really great!" Joey said. "Thunder Bay is one step away from the polar bears. I can't wait to get out of this burg and get back to some home cooking."

"You aren't coming with me, Joey. Mr. B wants you to stay here for a while. That is a direct order. You are staying put in Thunder Bay until Mr. B says otherwise."

"Are you nuts? There is no way that I'm staying here by myself. What possible reason is there for me to stay in this flea bag of a town?"

Marty told Joey about the media hysteria that was going on. *"The Providence Journal* and all the television stations have been showing a drawing of the man who apparently shot Di Nuccio. This has generated a boatload of interest. The drawing bears an incredible likeness of you. Mr. B doesn't want you anywhere near New England. You need to stay out of sight."

Joey was stunned. "Say that again!" Marty retold the story. "There is no way anyone saw me in that flea-bitten grocery store. I went in the front door, shot the guy, and left right away. There must be some mistake!"

"There is no flipping mistake. Some guy saw you at the grocery store that night. The police are over this like a bear in a honeycomb. Dante heard that a detective was nosing around Waterbury. Your name was mentioned as a person of interest. If you show up, who knows what might happen? It would not be good for any of us!"

Joey was livid. "We need to find the person who saw me and put a bullet in his head. Easy as that. I can go back to Rhode Island right now and handle it myself."

"Mr. B thought you might say that. He told me that under no circumstances are you to set foot in New England until you hear from him. That is a direct order. If you come back, Mr. Bonfigore will kill you himself. He told me that he has things under control. Deal with it!"

Joey shook his head in disbelief. "So, I'm supposed to keep a low profile in this godforsaken town for who knows how long. What a complete joke! Exactly what am I supposed to do for money? And, oh by the way, just how long am I supposed to stay here?"

Marty pulled out a wad of cash. "Here's $5,000 for starters. That should tide you over for a month or so. By then, things should cool off. Then you can come home. Here are the keys to the car. I'll send you some more cash as soon as I get to Rhode Island. In the meantime, you need to find a place to stay. You might be here for a month or so. Lastly Joey, you need to keep a low profile here—a very low profile. Do you understand me?"

Joey understood where he stood. He was on his own. There would be no help from the mob. Joey knew he had to agree to Marty's conditions, at least for the time being. Otherwise, he would have a neon sign on his back that read "Shoot me right now!" in bold letters. "Yeah, I get it. I need to disappear for a while."

Marty packed a bag and called a cab. When the cab pulled up, Marty told Joey to call in three days. "I want you to have a place rented. Then I can send you some money. I should know how Mr. B wants to handle this situation." There was nothing more to be said. Marty walked out and got in the cab. "Where are you going?" asked the cabbie. "I am going to the airport."

Joey went back to the hotel and started guzzling Canadian Club. Within a half hour, he had a good buzz on. "There's no way I'm sitting in a fleabitten rental waiting for a call from Mr. Goomba's assistant. I will wait until the additional money arrives. Between now and then, I'm gonna come up with a plan. Any plan Bonfigore and Marty come up with will be of help to them—it sure won't help me.

Everyone is in for a surprise

Later that night, Renata called Dante. She gave him the lowdown about what had taken place.

"Yeah, Renata, Marty told me all about it. What I want to know is how Cappy is doing? Is he going to be okay?"

Renata was surprised by the tone of Dante's voice. She could tell that Dante was concerned about Cappy. "My doctor friend stopped by today. He says the next two or three days are going to be rough. If Cappy can make it through this stretch without any complications, he should be home free."

The phone went silent. "Mr. Bonfigore, are you still there?"

Dante muffled a "I'll be right with you." After a while, he said, "Renata, you know that my relationship with Cappy has been rocky. But we go way back. There's no one better than Cappy when the chips are down. This business in Kansas. He took it on the chin for me. I won't forget that."

Renata was taken aback. She thought Dante would be livid about Kansas City. But he was really concerned about Cappy's well-being. "When he's up to it, I'll tell him what you said. Dante, can I speak to you freely?"

"Go for it, Renata. I like folks who aren't afraid of me."

"Dante, we made off with over $100,000 in cash and $10,000 or so in booze." Dante wanted to know about the expenses they incurred. "Between the house rental, buying a used car and a truck, and some other incidentals, we probably spent $8000. That doesn't include the cost of getting there, etc. As well, I'm giving my doctor friend four grand for taking care of Cappy. That leaves us with about ninety thousand dollars."

Dante was impressed with her ability to think on the fly. "So, Renata, you were there the entire time. You saw what everyone did. What should I give them for their work on the job?"

Renata was taken aback. Dante was asking her for her advice. "Well, Billy and King were a ton of help. Without their fight at the liquor store, I don't think we would have been able to pull this whole thing off. Their act convinced Baxter to hire Billy. They were stand up when the bullets began to fly. They deserve at least four thousand dollars each. As for Marty, no one worked harder to make things turn out right. Marty was great."

Dante stopped her in mid-sentence. "Don't worry about Marty. I'll take care of Marty. What about Joey?"

Renata thought for a second. "What do I say? Okay, in for a penny, in for a pound!" she thought. "Joey's a young punk who sees himself as a gangster. He was helpful at times, but for the most part, he was trouble waiting to happen."

"That's what I expected. I'll take care of Joey. That leaves you and Cappy. What should I do for you?"

"I don't know what to say. We did what needed to be done. Except for Cappy getting shot, it all worked out."

"Well, Renata, you aren't giving yourself enough credit. I think the two of you put this whole thing together. Here's what I want you to do. Dole out expense money to whomever deserves it. Then I want you to pay off this Louis character, as well as Billy and King. After that, I want you to send me $32,000. The rest is yours."

Renata started to calculate. Suddenly, she was dumbstruck. "Mr. B, did I understand you correctly? You want me to keep about $50,000 as our share of the pot?"

"You heard me correctly, Renata. You did yeoman's work finding the right people to do the job, and then pulling it off. You deserve the money. This is my way of saying thanks." Dante could tell that Renata was about to cry. He told her that he had a meeting to go to. He hung up the phone just as she burst into tears.

Who in the hell are you?

Dante was about to head to his office when he heard someone pounding on the door. Normally, Detta would handle this, but she had gone over to the church. "I'm too busy to find out who is at the door. If it is important, they'll come back."

He started towards the office. The pounding continued. "What is going on?" Dante lumbered up the stairs and looked out the window. There was a black guy standing on his doorstep. The guy was memorable. Not only was he wearing a paisley raincoat and a bright neon blue shirt, but this guy had Marleyesque dreadlocks hanging to his shoulders. He was whacking the door with his fist as if his life depended on it.

Dante opened the door. "Who in the hell are you and what do you want?"

The guy sashayed up the stairs one step at a time and said one word that stopped Dante in his tracks. "Trixie. I'm looking for Trixie." Dante's eyes almost popped out of his head. He was stunned to hear this looney tune say Trixie's name.

Dante tried to regroup. "Who are you?"

This guy pulled a card out of his shirt pocket. "Wilson P. Greystone!" Dante glanced at the card. This guy was a private dick. "I happened to be in the neighborhood and wondered if you knew where Trixie has gone to."

Dante started sputtering. He told this character that he didn't know anybody named Trixie. Then he tried to close the door.

The private eye grabbed the door handle and flung the door open. This guy was stronger than he looked. "Mr. Bonfigore, my middle name is Perspicacious. Wilson Perspicacious Greystone. My mama likes to read the dictionary. Perspicacious means that I am plenty smart. As it happens, Trixie's brother, Paul has been trying to contact his sister. She's nowhere to be found. Paul hired me to find his younger sister. Trixie has up and left Cape Cod. No forwarding address, no nothing."

"So, what exactly does this have anything to do with me?" Dante sputtered.

"Now, now, Mr. Bonfigore, I know I look like a little black weasel, but give me some credit for finding you. You probably think Trixie kept quiet about her pregnancy. Unfortunately, her big brother, Paul Revere Reilly, the former New England middleweight boxing champ, noticed the baby bump. He was able to wheedle information out of his sister. Amazingly, your name came up. Paul helped me out with a small problem a while back and now I'm returning the favor."

"I figure you don't want the neighbors to hear our little ruckus right on your front step, so why don't we have a civil conversation. By the way, I hear you are handy with a Smith and Wesson. Doggone if I don't have a fondness for one of those myself, so let's be peaceful."

Dante let Greystone in. He knew Detta should be home any minute. He didn't want her to hear about his escapades. "Okay, so I know Trixie. How can I help you?"

"Now that is the spirit. We don't want to have word get around that you're about to have a fourth child."

Dante started to get angry. "If you are thinking of blackmailing me, Mr. Greystone or whatever you call

335

yourself, I can assure you that you and every living relative of yours will die a slow death if that happens."

"Now, now, we are getting a little harsh. Remember P stands for perspicacious. My attorney has a document in his office that identifies all the information regarding your paternity issues. I bet the police could put one and one together if you got careless. So, stop beating around the bush and tell me where Trixie is."

Dante knew when his balls were about to be hung out to dry. He told Greystone that he needed to make a few calls. "I want to hear from you by tomorrow. Trixie's brother is getting concerned. You have my card. Call me. I think we can settle this without having to involve your wife in any of this naughty business."

Greystone slipped out of the house and drove away just as Detta came up the driveway. "Who was that?" she asked. Dante muttered, "A guy asking for directions."

Dante went down to his office to give Trixie a call. "I had a visit from Wilson Greystone today. Your brother hadn't heard from you. He sicced Greystone on me."

Trixie chuckled. "I would love to have seen you mix it up with Mr. Perspicacious. Wilson is cute in a corny kinda way. Those dreadlocks are something else."

"Maybe he is cute to you, but his teeth are as sharp as a razor. So, is it okay if I give him your phone number?"

"He must have put the hurt on you. Yeah, tell him that I will call my brother."

Their first trip to Snake Den Park

Vincent ran to Cris' house on Good Friday morning. There was no school due to the Easter vacation, so he was going to have lunch at Cristiana's. It was awfully quiet at the Bonfigore's when he arrived.

Cris had finished making egg salad and tomato sandwiches by the time Vincent knocked on the door. "Aren't you the early bird. This isn't like you."

Vincent told her that his mom and grandmother were preparing food for Easter dinner. "My brothers and I had jobs to do around our house. Pietro was getting on my nerves. I knew I couldn't take it much longer, so I finished my chores quickly. Then I headed over here."

"You are too funny, Vincent. I'll have to remember to be noisy when I begin to tire of your company. Then I can move on to somebody who might be more interesting."

Vincent gave her little shove in the back. "Now, what guys do you know who are more interesting than me?" "Oh, my, I believe you're getting jealous. I didn't know you had it in you. Okay, so how about you and I have some of these tasty egg salad and tomato sandwiches. Mom went to the A & W on Putnam Pike and brought home a huge jug of root beer for us. We better have a glass of soda before it gets flat."

When they finished eating, Vincent wandered over to the bench where he had left his windbreaker. Cris noticed that Vincent was holding a gift bag. "What do you have there?"

"Oh, a little something I found the other day while I was helping my aunt shop for Easter gifts."

"You were helping your aunt shop! Aha, I see. That wouldn't be your Aunt Eileen, the very same aunt who helped you buy a wonderful Christmas present for a certain girl I know."

"You know," Vincent exclaimed, "I'm starting to experience some terrible memory loss. I don't remember who this present is for. It might be a gift for my mother. I better set it by my wind-breaker so I can remember to take it home." Cristiana tapped his head and then started to put on her sad face. Vincent began to laugh out loud. "Oh, my goodness. That tap on my head brought my memory right back. This gift is for you."

Cris looked at the package. "What is it?" she asked.

"This is something you might need."

She wasted no time tearing off the wrapping paper. What she found was a pair of bronze-colored barrettes made in the likeness of two legs wrapped together.

"You are probably wondering about the significance of these barrettes. Maybe I should explain. I know you grew your hair out for your role in the play. My aunt took me to this specialty shop that sells barrettes. I saw these and decided that I had to buy them for you."

Cris hugged him like there was no tomorrow. Words were hard to come by. "I guess we are both fortunate," Vincent exclaimed. "Do you remember the first day we met? I couldn't believe that you talked to me. You've helped me to gain confidence in myself. Now, I am a risk taker. That's all due to you. A while back, we decided to hold off becoming boyfriend/girlfriend. We weren't ready then. I think we are ready now. Will you be my steady girlfriend, Cristiana?" Cris jumped into Vincent's arms and hugged him to pieces.

They talked nonstop for about an hour. That ended when Cris' brothers came through the back door. "Hey Vincent," Nico said, "how are you?" Before Vincent could respond, Cris told them that she and Vincent were going for a bike ride to Snake Den Park.

"Really," Nico said, "I didn't see a bike in the yard."

"So, Nico, Vincent's getting ready for the spring track season. He ran over to our house. Would it be okay if he borrowed your bike? I'll do all your chores for the next two days if you could let him use the bike." Nico tried to get Cris to sweeten the deal. That didn't go far.

"Okay, you have a deal."

Cris knew that Snake Den Park was one of Vincent's favorite places to go to. It was only a few miles from her house. Much of the park was set aside for open space. Vincent enjoyed the trails that wound their way through groves of oaks and maples.

Cris and Vincent bundled themselves up and biked to the park. It was nearly noon by the time they arrived. The weather was brisk. The sky was overcast, the temperature was 51 degrees and there was a hint of rain in the air. Vincent thought it might be better to go along the woodland trails. There were clusters of oak trees along the trails that would cut the wind down to size.

The trails were rutted, so they walked along the trails. Vincent stopped a one hundred yards from one of the trails. "This is my favorite trail in the entire park."

Cris was confused. All she saw was a huge stand of trees and shrubs. "What's so special about this spot?"

Vincent took her hand and led her to a nearly invisible opening between the bushes. "If you go through here, you'll understand."

Fourteen paces in and a few tree branches in the face later, Cris saw several mid-sized boulders brushing up against a much larger boulder. "Oh my goodness, you would never know that the boulders were here."

"That's not the special part. Follow me just a little further down the trail." He led her up the path to the smallest of the boulders. As soon as she got there, she knew what was so special about the place. "This boulder is enormous. Look at this view. You can see everything for miles. I had no idea that this was here."

"I come here when I need to get away. It is quiet and peaceful here. Besides that, the boulder is so big that I can lie down on it and no one would ever know that I was here. It is like having my own personal hideout. Now, it'll be our personal hideout." They spent the next two hours enjoying the peacefulness of the day.

Shortly before three, Vincent told her that they better head back to town. Vincent's mom wanted him to get back home in time to go to the four o'clock church service. Cris was disappointed. "Don't worry, I'll make sure we come back again." Little did Vincent know that they'd be coming back sooner rather than later.

Joeyeee, they say you killed somebody

Joey lasted in Thunder Bay for three weeks. He was bored to tears. A packet had arrived a week after Marty left for New England. It contained $1500. Joey had plenty of money, but nowhere to spend it. His only friend was Jack Daniels. He had been seeing a lot of Jack over the past two weeks. The bars in town were full of guys who steered clear of strangers. That left Joey with four walls and a black and white television that needed an antenna to get the stations in town.

A few days later, Joey called his ma. He had to call her collect. He was surprised when his mother accepted the call. Joey started to talk, but he was immediately cut off by his mom's tinny voice. "Joey!" she shouted. "What did you do? Your picture is all over the newspapers. I can't go anywhere in town. Folks look at me as if I was a piece of dirt." She ranted on for a while. Joey had no flipping idea what in the hell she was talking about.

She finally stopped to catch her breath. Joey was overwhelmed. "Ma, slow down. What are you talking about?"

She started to howl. "Joey, they say you killed someone. Did you kill someone?" That got Joey's attention.

Joey wheedled the details from her. "Someone saw you shoot this De Nuncio guy. Joey, where you been? Someplace on Mars? He was shot in a grocery store. There was a witness. This witness had someone draw a likeness of the shooter. The drawing is the spitting image of you—the pimples, the hair, everything."

"Ma, I had nothing to do with this. There must be some mistake."

"Tell that to my neighbor, Eva Cortone. This is all she talks about. I listen to her yammerings every day and every night. She tells me how awful it must be to have a criminal for a son. I can't believe this is happening!"

"Ma, calm down! This is a stupid mistake. I'm out of town right now. I should be able to get home in three days. I will drive to your place. Then we can straighten this thing out."

"Joseph, that's the last thing you want to do! The police have been camped out in front of my house for the past week. If you show your face in town, the police will arrest you on the spot."

His mother started talking about the killing. Joey snapped. "Shut up and let me think!" A minute later, he spoke to her "If the police are that interested in me, they might be listening to our conversation. Why don't you drive over to your sister's place. I will give you a call.

Joey called his mother a few minutes later. She picked up the phone right away. "Does Uncle Tony still have a cabin near Burr Pond State Park?"

"I'm sure he owns the cabin, Joey, but nobody has been up there in years."

"Call your brother. See if you can use his cabin for a few days. Tell him you're spending hours on the phone answering a boatload of questions. You need a break. Find out where he leaves the spare key. I'll call you tomorrow." Then Joey hung up the phone.

Joey was worried. If the police found someone who could identify him, he would be spending the better part of his life in a cell at the Rhode Island maximum security prison. That wasn't going to happen. He needed to figure out what to do.

Joey went over every step he had taken leading up to the shooting. He was certain no one had seen him at the market. But, if what his mother had told him was true, he missed something bigtime. Joey had to find out who had identified him. He needed to make sure that this person would be taking a one-way trip to a mortuary. That wasn't going happen if he stayed in Thunder Bay. He had to get back to Connecticut.

No one connected to Mr. B would be of any help. For all Joey knew, Cappy could be as dead as a doornail. Mr. B probably had a contract out on him. Joey thought, "Marty knew where I was and wouldn't think twice about sending someone across the border to cap me."

The more he thought about this, the more he knew he would have to take care of this problem on his lonesome. The sooner he took care of this, the better. He finally called his mother back. "Joey, I have the key to the cabin. You cannot come to my house. I will meet you somewhere else. Where are you now, Joey?"

"Ma, the less you know about where I am, the better. I will leave tomorrow. I will call you when I hit the Connecticut state line. We can figure out where to meet when I get closer to home."

Joey tossed and turned the entire night. Any stray noise had him reaching for his gun. He got up early the next morning and went to a little restaurant two blocks down from his place. No sooner had he sat down when a chatty waitress named Ginger poured him a cup of coffee. "Do you need a breakfast menu, stranger?" Joey stared at her with a glare that would wither most folks.

"No," he snapped. "Just give me some scrambled eggs and hash browns. I want the eggs cooked well."

Ginger left the table in a hurry. "This guy is one crazy dude!" she said as she hurried back to the kitchen. It didn't take long for her to come back with his order. She left as quick as she came. Joey choked down the eggs and barely touched the hash browns. He threw money on the table and stalked out. Ginger was happy to see this jerk head out the front door. "Good riddance!"

Joey needed to get to back home pronto. "I can't fly. "Who knows if the police have staked out the airport?" He had seen a used car lot seven blocks down from his apartment. The weather was colder than a witch's backside, so Joey went back to his place and threw on a sweater. Then he jogged to the lot.

A little later, Joey was driving off with a light blue 1976 Nova SS. He paid a little more for the car than it was probably worth, but the low mileage and the large engine made it worth all the bread he shelled out. Joey drove to his apartment, packed up his belongings and began his trek to Connecticut.

Thoughts of retirement

Dante headed to Providence to meet with Mr. Big. Before he left for the meeting, he asked Marty to check on Cappy's progress. "Mr. B., it's an hour earlier than here. It's way too early for a call."

"I forgot about the time difference. See if you can talk to Cappy directly. Find out if he needs anything."

Marty called Renata shortly after 9 a.m. central standard time. Trixie answered the phone. "Trixie, it's me, Marty. Mr. B wants a run down on how Cappy is doing."

Trixie launched into a spiel about Cappy's health. "He's doing better than the doctor expected. His gunshot wound is healing and his collapsed lung is finally recovering. He's beginning to get testy. I had to slap him upside the head three different times to keep him in his hospital bed. It hasn't been pretty."

"Can I talk to him?"

Trixie hesitated. "Renata has told me to discourage any conversations for the time being. The doctor's concerned about his blood pressure. It is still pretty high."

"Okay, can I talk to Renata?"

"She drove to the drugstore to pick up a prescription. She should be back shortly."

"Trixie, have her call me as soon as she gets back. It's important." Trixie assured Marty that she would let Renata know about the call. She rang off before Marty could say anything more.

Renata returned a few minutes later. She was exhausted. She had been sitting up with Cappy every night since they came back from Kansas City. Sleep had become a luxury. Trixie pulled Renata aside just as she was heading into Cappy's room. "Renata," she said, "Marty called a little while ago wondering how Cappy was doing."

Renata's face turned red. "Everyday I get a call from Rhode Island. It's either Marty or Bonfigore wondering how Cappy is doing. Those bozos must think I have nothing better to do than to keep them updated. Taking care of Cappy is a full-time job. Don't they get it?"

Trixie gave Renata a hug. "Why don't you go in and comfort Cappy. I'll call Marty. From now on, I will be responsible for any info they want regarding Cappy."

"Thanks, Trixie. You are a sweetheart."

Renata went in to see Cappy. He was just starting to wake up. His pajamas were stained with blood from his chest wound, but the blood had dried. "That's a start." She bent over and nudged him. His eyes snapped open. She told Cappy about Marty's call.

That shot Cappy into a rage. It was all Renata could do to quiet him down. "Cappy Capuano, calm down and listen to me."

He started to interrupt her. Suddenly he experienced serious pain. "What the F?" he said, as he looked down towards his right arm. There were two feminine fingers clamped on his arm. The pain brought tears to his eyes.

"Listen to me, you moron, or the pain will get worse instead of better." Cappy shut his trap immediately. Renata took a deep breath, bent over, and kissed him.

His surprised look would have been comical if anyone had been around to notice.

"I thought you were going to smack me upside the head."

"Sometimes, I wonder what I see in you. Sit up so I can put an extra pillow under your back. Then I want you to listen to me. Keep your trap shut 'til I say you can talk."

Renata started in. "I left Connecticut years ago. I didn't have a choice. The police were getting closer to the truth and I needed to find another life. Back then, you were a young, two timing, son of a bitch. I loved you and hated you at the same time. I needed to leave for any number of reasons. You helped me get away and get connected. That is why I agreed to help you."

Renata rested her right hand on Cappy's shoulder and gently rubbed his neck. "Sometime around Christmas, I fell back in love with you. You can be a fiery, middle-aged mobster at times, but you can be as tender as any man I know. I love you for it. I want to marry you and have a family with you. Yes, that means kids! I want our lives to have the happiest of endings. That can only happen if you leave the mob and stay in Chicago with me. I don't want to worry about someone shooting you. Do you understanding what I am saying?"

He was stunned. His mouth opened, but no words came out. He lifted his hand and tried to touch her. Renata took his hand in hers. "My timing is bad, given what you have been going through, Cappy. I love you."

He finally got a word in edgewise. "The past few months have been a royal headache. I'm tired of taking orders from Bonfigore or giving orders to schmucks like Joey. The only good thing that has come of my time in Kansas City is you. I was a jerk in the old days. I was full of myself. You helped me become a different person. All I want is to make you happy. How about we get hitched as soon as I get out of this bed?"

Renata started to weep. "Are you sure?"

"I'm as sure as sure can be."

Renata leaned over and kissed him. Her tears fell on his cheeks. "What about Bonfigore?" Renata said apprehensively.

"Call Dante. Tell him I'll call in a few days. I know he's concerned, but the commotion is doing me in. Tell him I am getting better and that I appreciate his concern, but I need some quiet time right now."

"Cappy, he won't like this one little bit."

"Renata, whirl your magic wand a few times. You can make it right as rain. Dante will understand."

Whoa, am I a steady date?

The second semester at Don Bosco sped by faster than Superman. Vincent and Mikey were excelling in school. Vincent was good at math and science and Mikey could write up a storm. They studied together. Their grades attested to their diligence. Most of the tumult of the fall had gone away. Occasionally Maloney would come by and talk to Vincent's dad about the investigation. Otherwise, life was back to normal.

Coach White pulled Vincent and Mikey aside one day and asked if they were interested in running track that spring. Mikey smiled at the coach and told him that they had been running on their own for the past few weeks. "We'd like to be on the team if you will have us."

The coach was relieved. "Practice starts next week Monday. I'll see you on the track." Then the coach headed towards his office

"How about we get a few miles of road work in after school?"

"No can do, Mikey. I promised Cris that I'd help her with her science homework. I'm headed to the library right after the last bell is rung."

Mikey looked up with a smirk on his face. "You two are making a habit of getting together. Anything I should know about, lover boy?"

Vincent and Cris hadn't told anyone about going steady. Mikey was quick to notice the change. "Mikey, we are working on schoolwork. Nothing more!"

Mikey shrugged his shoulders and gave Vincent a sneaky grin. "Okay, partner. Whatever you say. How about running before supper?"

"That's a great idea." They agreed to meet at St. Philip's for a run after Vincent got back from school.

Vincent walked to Cris' locker after the last bell had rung. She saw that he had a grim look on his face. "What is wrong, Vincent?"

He told Cris about his conversation with Mikey. "I guess the jig is up. I thought we were doing a good job of keeping our relationship under wraps."

Cris smiled. "Are you still okay with being steady?"

"Sure, I am okay with that. You are the best."

Cris could tell he meant what he said. "Maybe, we should tell everyone we're going steady. My dad will have a conniption when he hears about this, but he will get over it. What do you say?"

Vincent smiled at the thought of telling everyone what they had probably guessed by now. "I am okay with this if you are."

Dante was going out to a meeting that night. Cris figured it would be better if she told her mom about Vincent without having her dad around. Cris lingered in the kitchen after her brothers went upstairs. "What's up, honey?" her mom asked when she noticed that Cris had been drying the same glass for the past five minutes.

"Mom, can we talk?"

"Absolutely!" Detta exclaimed.

Words spilled out of Cris' mouth like bullets fired from a machine gun. She told her mom the whole story. "So, Mom, what do you think?"

"You've found a great guy. Vincent is bright, conscientious, and keenly interested in you. Some folks might question whether it is okay for you to be dating. Those folks don't know you like I do. What I know is that you feel comfortable talking to me. That feels right. Hopefully we can keep that going. Don't be afraid to come to me, Honey."

Detta stopped and looked Cris in the eye. "There is only one problem. And it is a big problem."

"Mom, are you talking about dad?"

"Cris, your father is old school all the way. He likes Vincent a lot. I've heard him say that Vincent is a great kid. That tone will change when he finds out that you're going steady. He'll want to send you to some Catholic boarding school in Australia."

That garnered a smile from Cris. "What are we going to do, Mom?"

"We aren't going to do a thing. This is on me. Keep this a secret. I will find the right time to tell your father what is going on." Cris was relieved to hear her mother's supportive comments.

The next two days leapt by. Everyone was busy. Little League tryouts, church meetings, etc. Finally, Dante and Detta had some quiet time together. Dino and his wife had invited the kids out for pizza and a movie. Dante and Detta had a quiet dinner at home.

Detta prepared Dante's favorite meal, shrimp scampi with roasted tomatoes and asparagus spears. She pulled out a bottle of Vermentino to have with dinner. "You're treating me like a king," Dante said. "I'm getting nervous. When you pull out the scampi for dinner, you are up to something. What do you want?" Detta started flashing her eyes at Dante. Then she started to coo.

Two hours and a little bedtime later, Detta told him what was going on. "Before you go off like Mount Etna, let me fill you in." Detta shared her conversation with Cris. "I know what you are going to say. Your daughter is too young to be dating. It is safe to say that you would feel the same way if she was going on her first date at the age of 32."

Dante's brow furrowed. He started to say something, but then he thought better of it. Detta decided to wait him out. It took several sips of wine to slow Dante down. "Tell me why this is a good idea."

Detta had a list of reasons why they should let Cris go steady. "I think reason number one will be enough. Your daughter is just like her father. She has street smarts, she plans things out strategically, and she knows how to get the best out of a situation. I think she can handle this. If you give it some thought, you'll agree with me."

"I need a night to think about this. Why don't we go out for breakfast? We can talk about this without having the bambini around."

"You got yourself a deal, big boy. Now come to bed. It is time to get under the covers."

A one-on-one conversation with Mom

It took Joey four days to get back home. He took the northern route back home. Joey thought this would lessen the chances of being picked up by the police. His front tire blew 50 miles from St. Ignace. Joey found out the hard way that there are very few folks in the Upper Peninsula and even fewer places to get a tire for his car. After 30 minutes, he finally hitched a ride and got a tire jockey to help him out.

Joey finally made it to the cabin. His mother was waiting for him. That was good news. The better news was that she brought a boatload of food. Joey was exhausted, so, as soon as he emptied his car, he hit the sack. His mother took over from there.

The cabin was just what the doctor ordered. It had all the creature comforts. A bed, an indoor toilet, and plenty of dried wood for the stove. On top of that, his Ma brought him a case of Narragansett beer.

Joey woke up ten hours later to the smell of spaghetti sauce and peppers. He wandered out to the kitchen. There were some meatballs cooking on the stove. Joey hadn't been too hospitable when he first arrived, so he decided to give his mother a hug and a kiss. That went a long way towards breaking the icy stare that she had given him when he walked into the kitchen.

She started in on him about the shooting. She was firing words at him, one right after another. He finally put his hand over her mouth and whispered "I love you" in her ear—years of experience told him that this was the only way to shut her up. She put her head on his shoulder and started to cry. "I am so worried about you." Joey held her until the tears dried up.

His mother wanted to talk about the shooting. "Ma, we can talk about this. But first, I need to hit the bathroom."

"Okay, do your business. I'll have some coffee waiting for you. Then we'll talk."

Joey knew this would happen one way or another. Better to get it out of the way right away. "So, the police are hounding you!"

"That doesn't begin to cover it." Patrol cars are going up and down the street. Neighbors are continually being questioned. My friends are disappearing by the minute. No one wants to have any part of me!"

Joey put his hands on her shoulders. "Ma, I did nothing. You have to believe me." That seemed to ease her discomfort. "I've been away for months. I haven't seen any reports about this murder. What do you know?"

She told him all about the killing. Joey knew his mother well enough to know that she made the least relevant item of news become a frontpage article on the *New York Times*.

Once she finished, Joey silenced her. "Let me get this straight. Last October, some woman and her son were shopping in a grocery store in Greenville, Rhode Island, when a guy was shot. This guy ended up at the morgue. "Have I got the story right so far?"

"That's what I understand."

Joey started in again. "The only person who spotted the killer was the kid. He gave the police a description of a guy who looked like me. "Ma, it wasn't me."

Joey's mother started to cry. "This has been a horrible nightmare. I was afraid you got involved in something terrible. But now, I know you are telling me the truth." Joey knew he had hornswoggled his mother. She was such an easy touch. "Everything will turn out okay, I promise. I need to see some people in Providence so that I can straighten this out. But I can't go anywhere right now because of that picture in the paper. Somebody is bound to recognize me.

"Here's what you can do. Drive to Torrington and buy electric shears and a razor. When you come back, you can shave my head. Between my shaved head and my beard, no one will recognize me. Then I can head over to Rhode Island." Joey's mom was skeptical, but, in the end, she agreed to help.

When she got back to the cabin, she shaved his head. "You're right, Joey. No one will recognize you!"

"That's the idea." Then they sat down and had a bite to eat. When they finished, Joey's mom decided to head back home. "The police might get nervous if they can't find me." A few minutes later, she was on her way back to Waterbury.

Detective Joey at your service

The next day, Joey got up and had something to eat. Then he headed to Rhode Island. Normally, it would take about two hours to get there. Joey decided to take his time. "I don't want to get pulled over by a cop." He finally stopped at the Blue Bell Restaurant in Greenville to get a bite to eat. It was too early for the dinner crowd to start coming in. That was exactly what he had in mind. Joey figured he'd have a better chance of getting information if the restaurant wasn't going full blast.

A young woman with long legs and hair to match met him by the cash register. Her name tag read Marsha. Joey could tell right away that this gal could help him. She flashed her eyelashes and called him Hon. She had been around the block a few times. Her wink was telltale. Joey knew if he played his cards right, Miss Marsha was going to be dessert later in the evening.

"I've been on the road for a while." Joey piped up. "I missed lunch, so I'm hoping to get myself an early dinner and two cold bottles of beer. Then, maybe I can find a place to bed down for the night."

Marsha jumped all over that. "Well, I can help with the first two requests, Hon." He put on his "I got you" smile. Then he asked her if she had any specials on the menu.

"It's your lucky day. We have two specials. Veal scaloppini, or Steak Marsha." She began to giggle. "Tomorrow, Abigail is the lead waitress. So, the special will be Steak Abby."

Joey rolled his eyes. "The chef is quite the comedian." Marsha giggled some more. "Why don't I get you a bottle of Narragansett. Then you can look at the menu."

Joey chose the steak special with a side of new potatoes. He also asked for a side salad with blue cheese dressing. "Why sure, Hon."

When Marsha asked about dessert, Joey said he would love Baked Marsha. "I'll be off by ten. "Let's see if you are still awake by then!" She left to greet a new customer. Joey smacked his lips.

The night was very entertaining. They went up to her apartment and had a few beers. Then she told Joey about the shooting. He heard all about Vincent Angelino and his family. After an hour of playful sex, Marcia nodded off to sleep. Joey found what he was looking for. "Tomorrow, I'll scout around Greenville."

The next day, after breakfast, Joey drove around the town. He got a room at a small motel down the road. Marsha had told him where the Angelinos lived. He scouted out the neighborhood. He headed back to the motel and hit the hay. He got up later that afternoon and headed for Angelino's house. About five thirty, a kid jogged up to the Angelino's. Joey started to smile. He pointed a finger at the kid. "I got you now, kiddo."

For the next two days, Joey took in the lay of the land. He'd been in Greenville once before. However, his focus was on the pool room. This time he figured out the best way to get out of town once he took care of the kid. Joey got lucky again. He ran into Marsha at a neighborhood bar. The next thing he knew he was spending another night with her. He learned that Vincent was going steady with Bonfigore's daughter. "This is my lucky day."

It's time to smell the roses, Dante

Dante had been calling Trixie every day so he could keep abreast of Cappy's condition. It took a lot of wheedling, but Dante was finally able to talk to him.

"Hello, Dante. It has been a while."

Dante was relieved to hear Capuano's voice. "Hello, Cappy. You got us a bit worried. I am glad to hear your voice. How are you doing?"

Cappy gave Dante the low down about his condition. "It has been a tough few weeks. The doctor wasn't sure if I would make it. I guess I'm not ready to see the gates of hell."

Suddenly, Cappy developed a violent cough. Renata tried to wrench the phone from his hand. Cappy was having no part of that. They argued for a minute or so. A few seconds later, Dante could hear Capuano tell Renata that he was all right.

"Sorry about that, Dante. I'm still trying to get better."

"I understand. You have been through a lot. It'll take time to get your health back. Your towing business will be waiting for you when you return to Connecticut.

There was a moment of silence. Then Dante heard Cappy mutter something to Renata. Finally, he got back on the line. "Dante, I gotta get something off my chest."

Cappy took a deep breath. "I'm not coming back. This has been a huge kick in the pants for me. I nearly died. I don't want to test fate anymore. Renata says this is my Carpe Diem moment."

"What the F is a Cap the Dime moment or whatever?"

"Dante, it's time for me to smell the roses. I had a good run. I did a good job for the mob. Now I need to get out while the getting is good!"

This shook Dante up. He hadn't expected this. "Cappy, you've been through the wars. You know what it is like. Why don't you give yourself a few weeks to relax and work on getting better? Marty can take care of all the stuff in Hartford. When you are ready to return to work, you can come back."

Cappy wasn't having any part of that. "Listen, I don't want to sound like I'm not grateful. But my answer is "no"! Way back when, I had a chance to be with Renata. I screwed that up royally. These past months, I have come to understand that Renata means everything to me. Couple that with my being shot, and I am absolutely sure that now's the time to say Adios.

"I will say this, Dante, you are right on the button about Marty. In the beginning, Marty was a young mutt whose tail wagged at everything you said. I have come to respect Marty. You couldn't have picked a better person to replace me. Marty has the ability to take on any crumbling project and get it to work the right way."

Dante tried to dissuade Cappy from leaving. Cappy was undeterred. "Dante, I'm ready to hit the trail. You know me well enough to know that I won't rat on the mob. In the future, if there is a way that I can help you, I will be there for you. But I need to get out. My body has taken a beating. I am lucky to still be alive. I have enough money to keep me going for a good long while. Somebody can take over the towing business. Whomever you pick will be ten times better than me. I hope you understand where I am coming from."

Dante digested what he had said. "Okay, if that is what you want, I'll talk to the Boss and see that everything is taken care of. As far as the towing business is concerned, I'll make sure you are compensated. Our relationship has been rocky at times, but that's behind us. I'm appreciative of all you have done. If there ever comes a time when you need something, no matter how small, call me. I will always be willing to help you out."

Dante knew it was time to cut the cord. He told his friend to take care. "Thanks for everything, Dante." A few seconds later, Dante slowly hung up the phone.

Joey's back in town. Time to get the posse

Saturday morning, John Angelino started walking towards the back door. Maria asked where he was going. "I'm heading to the Blue Bell. Bill Maloney wants to fill me in regarding the investigation."

"Aha," Maria said, "Our family has a lot going on today."

"How is that, Maria?"

"Your dad's taking our younger sons to the zoo. Vincent is biking with Mikey and Cristiana. They're headed to Snake Den Park. And I'm going shopping with Detta."

"We are busy today!" he said as he walked out the door.

John drove over to the Blue Bell. When he got there, the parking lot was full. "What a busy place!" He went in and started looking for Maloney. The next thing he heard was his name being called out.

Dante and Marty were just sitting down for breakfast. Dante waved John over. "Long time, no see. How ya doing? Sit down and join us."

John shook his head. "I'd love to Dante, but I'm meeting with Bill Maloney to talk about the investigation." Just then Maloney came in and walked over to them

Marsha was working the early shift. When she came out of the kitchen, she saw Mr. Angelino and Mr. Bonfigore. She walked over to them. "Hey guys," she said, "I was just talking about you two the other day."

Dante looked at her quizzically. "You don't say."

Marsha said she met a new guy in town who was asking about Dante. Dante's spine started tingling. "This guy, Joey, had come in for dinner. We got to talking. He had heard about a kid named Angelino who was a great cross-country runner. I told him all about Vincent. I mentioned that your daughter was dating Vincent."

"What did this guy look like?" Dante sputtered.

Marsha could see that something was terribly wrong. "Is there something the matter, Mr. Bonfigore?"

Dante was ready to blow his top. "Is the party room available, Marsha?" Dante asked. She nodded hesitantly. "Maloney, follow us." Dante took Marsha's forearm and headed towards the back room. Everyone else trailed behind.

When they sat down, Dante continued questioning Marsha. "You never answered my question. What did this guy look like?" Marsha was getting upset. She started to cry. She had never heard Dante get this upset.

Dante filled Maloney in on what Marsha had said. Then, he repeated his question. "What did he look like?" Marsha told them that Joey was about 5'8," slender, and bald as bald could be. "He had plenty of zits."

Bill could see where this was heading. Dante was about to lay into her again when Bill stepped in. "Dante, let me ask a question or two."

At that point, Marty pulled at Dante's elbow. "Back off, Mr. B. I know you are really upset. I can see where you are headed. You need to act like concerned father right now rather than a mob boss. Maloney might be able put two and two together." Dante backed off.

Maloney asked Marsha if she had ever seen the drawing of the guy at the grocery store. Marsha went white. "Oh, my God, Joey looks like the guy in the drawing. I didn't put two and two together. What have I done?" she said just before she collapsed. Marty ran out the door and told a waitress to come into the back room. "First, get me a wet towel. Then you need to call for an ambulance. We have a medical emergency on our hands."

Dante tried to call Detta. She had apparently left for the morning. John had the house phone in his hand. He was talking to Maria. Maloney could hear the sense of fear in John's voice. Finally, Maloney took control. "John, do you know where Vincent might be?"

"Vincent, Mikey, and Cristiana are biking at Snake Den Park. Dante had a fit when he heard this. "Jesus Christ!" he shouted. "Joey could be there right now."

Maloney had never seen Dante in such a state. He was shaking like a leaf. The look in his eyes was deadly. Maloney motioned the two of them over to him. "We don't know where this character is. Go back to your homes pronto. I'll send a patrol car to make sure the guy isn't hiding near your property. Now get outta here." Then Maloney called his chief.

John sped out of the room. Dante pulled Marty away from Maloney. "Do you have a piece, Marty?"

"Sure, Dante!"

"The police will only have a sketch of Joey. You know what he looks like. Head over to the park right now. If Joey is there, stop him any way you can. No one threatens my family and lives to tell about it. I don't want Joey to be able to say anything to anybody." Then Marty raced out the back door.

A shot in the dark

The kids couldn't have picked a nicer day to go for a ride. The sun was out in full force and there was no breeze to speak of. Vincent and Mikey raced to see who could get to the park first. They left Cris far behind. She wasn't happy. By the time she reached them, they were lying on the grass soaking up some sun.

Cris got off her bike and snatched two handfuls of dirt. She sauntered over to the guys and sprinkled dirt on their faces. "Hey! What's going on?"

"Listen up, you dumbbells. We were going out for a nice, leisurely road trip, not a race at Seekonk Speedway. You raced off and left me in the dust. I'm not happy!" The guys started apologizing.

Spring had come early this year. Red and yellow tulips were clustered a stone's throw from where the kids had stopped. Vincent thought it might be a good idea to take Cris' mind off the ride, so he suggested that they walk towards the trails.

Joey had followed the kids all the way from Bonfigore's. He kept a fair distance from them so as not to draw any attention to himself. Several families were walking around the tulips, so he decided to stay in his car. "No one will see me here."

"Dante's damn daughter, this Vincent kid and his buddy will get tired of the stupid tulips and start biking the trails. The trails are the perfect spot to take these kids out. No muss, no fuss. They are far enough away from the farm that no one will be able to see me. Then I'm outta here for good."

Joey saw the kids heading towards the trail. He waited til they were near the trailhead before starting his car. He parked about 200 yards from the kids. Joey noticed that they had stopped to get a drink. He jumped out of his car and pulled his gun out of his windbreaker. The girl was in his sights. "This is perfect!" Joey steadied himself, aimed, and took a shot at the girl. Just as Joey shot, Cris tripped on a rock. Mikey reached out to stop her fall. The bullet caught him in the arm.

Vincent heard the shot and then heard Mikey scream. He looked back. A guy was aiming a gun at them. He recognized the guy. "Holy Crap! Mr. De Nuncio's killer is shooting at us. Run towards the woods right now!"

Joey cursed at himself for missing the kill shot. Then he heard Vincent say something about De Nuncio. That shook him up. As a result, he missed seeing the kids run for the trail. "Oh shit!" He took another shot, but it hit nothing but the bushes.

Cris made it to the trailhead. Vincent was helping Mikey run towards her. "Are you okay, Mikey?"

"I got shot in the arm. It hurts like crazy. But my legs still work."

"Cris," Vincent yelled, "Run to my favorite spot. We'll be right behind you." They heard Joey take another shot at them just as they ran down the wooded trail.

Joey was pissed as heck. "I missed them from short range." He started running towards them. He stopped and took another shot. "Missed again! Son of a bitch!" he screamed. Joey knew he was trying way too hard. "Take your time, you asshole!" That calmed him down. He had never been in the park before, so he decided to move slowly. The last thing he wanted was for these pissants to jump him.

The kids made it to the small clearing in the trail. "Cris, lead Mikey up to the top of the boulder and stay there. This guy will never find you."

"What about you, Vincent?"

"I'll lead him away. I'm plenty fast. This guy will be cautious. I can get away from him before he knows what hit him. Go to the top of the boulder. Don't make a single sound. I love you both." Then he sped down the trail before Mikey or Cristiana could say another word.

Marty got to the park just in time to hear a gunshot. Then Joey screamed. Marty made it to a clearing without being noticed. Joey was walking towards the trailhead. "He's holding a gun. This isn't good!" Marty said.

Joey decided it would be better to stay off the trail. He might be able to surprise these twerps. He was having difficulty locating the kids. Suddenly, Vincent popped out of the trees about a hundred yards ahead of him. "Now I have this kid right where I want him!" Then he aimed his gun directly at Vincent.

Vincent heard a stick crack. He ducked down to avoid being hit and slipped on some rocks along the side of the trail. The next thing he knew, he heard someone shouting. "Vincent, are you okay?"

Vincent was totally confused. The voice sounded familiar. "Is this the killer trying to draw me out into the open?" Vincent decided to keep quiet. Ten seconds later, he heard the voice again.

"Vincent, it's Marty Nicosia, Cris' cousin. You can get up off the ground now. There's nothing to worry about."

Vincent couldn't believe his ears. Cris' cousin was calling out to him. Out of the corner of his eye, he saw

Cris and Mikey coming out from their hiding place. Cristiana ran over and hugged Marty. Vincent started to shake. He tried to get up, but he lost his balance and fell to the ground. He opened his eyes a few minutes later.

There were all sorts of people in the clearing. Most of them looked like police officers. Cris saw that Vincent was awake. "What is going on Cris?"

She pointed towards the copse of trees. "This guy was about to shoot you. Marty shot this jerk. Nailed him in the head. The guy is headed to the morgue."

Vincent didn't see Mikey. "Where is Mikey?"

"The police showed up just after the shooting started. They called an ambulance when they saw Mikey. The medics took one look at him and put him in the ambulance. He's headed to the hospital." Vincent wondered how this could have happened. "I was only out for a second or so!" Cris started to smile.

"Vincent, you hit your head on a rock when you fainted. You've been out for a while. Dr. Jones should be here any minute." Cris heard voices and turned to see what was going on. "Speak of the devil, here comes the doctor. Vincent's awake," she shouted.

"You took a nasty fall." Vincent looked at the doctor with a grimace. "Oh, Dr. Jones. I'm okay. I just have a little headache." He tried to stand up by himself and became woozy.

"I think you should go to the hospital just in case." She called for another ambulance.

Maloney arrived at the park about the time that the medical examiner had arrived. The doctor was directed to where Joey was lying.

Marty and the kids get grilled

Maloney found the officers who were first to arrive on the scene. They shared what they had learned about the shooting. "Did you speak to Marty?" The officers did talk to Marty. They asked a few questions and decided that Maloney should be called. Maloney thanked then. "I'll take it from here." Then he went over and got Marty out of the squad car.

He started in on the Miranda warning. Marty stopped him in mid-sentence and immediately waived any rights regarding the situation. They spoke for 25 minutes. Marty outlined Dante's directions.

"How did you know it was this Joey guy?"

"Detective Maloney, I was with you at the Blue Bell. I heard Marsha give you a description of the guy and I saw the drawing of the shooter on television. When our meeting ended, Dante asked me to find Cris. I drove to the park. When I got there, I saw the kids heading towards the trail. Then I saw the shooter. He was standing on the hillside. Then he started shooting."

Maloney stopped Marty. "Let me get this straight. You saw the kids walk towards the trailhead. Before you had a chance to call out to them, this guy walked towards the kids. Is that right?" Marty nodded in agreement.

Maloney asked about the actual shooting.

"I saw this guy point his gun at the kids. Then he took a shot at them and hit Mikey. Then the kids ran. The guy matched Marsha's description. The guy followed the kids. A few seconds later, he pointed his gun at Vincent. There wasn't time to wait for the police. Something had to be done. I ran towards the shooter. This character lined up to take a shot. I pulled my gun out and squeezed the trigger. I got lucky."

Maloney went back over Marty's story. He seemed satisfied with the answers. "Marty, one of my officers will drive you to the station. We need to interview any other witnesses. I'll contact the State's Attorney General's office about this. I will see you when I return." Then, Big Hank McArdle, an officer at the scene, walked Marty back to the squad car. Then they headed to the station.

Maloney had two officers check for any additional evidence. "Look for shell casings near the shooter."

Maloney spoke with Dr. O'Brian, the medical examiner. He asked O'Brian if he would be working on Joey today. "I have a meeting at St. Pete's in an hour. The soonest that I can get to this case will be tomorrow." That wasn't what Maloney wanted to hear.

When Marty got to the police station, one of officers asked if Marty wanted to make a phone call. "You bet I do!" The officer pointed to a phone on a nearby desk. Marty dialed Mr. B's private line.

Dante picked the phone up. "Who in the hell is this?" he shouted. "Mr. B, it's Marty. Calm yourself down and listen to what I have to say."

"OK, Marty, what's going on?"

"Cristiana and her friends are safe, and Joey's as dead as a door nail." Mr. B wanted more information. He started shouting. Marty began to yell back. It took a while before Dante calmed down.

"I'm at the police station. They're holding me. I need some legal counsel pronto. Can you make a call?"

Dante understood immediately. "I will call John Monroe. He is my personal attorney. He's as smart as a whip. He'll know what to do."

"I have to hang up now." Marty hung up before Dante had a chance to say thanks for keeping Cris safe.

Maloney headed over to the hospital. He needed to talk with the kids about the shooting. Maloney found the Angelinos in the surgical waiting room. He walked over to John. "How is Michael doing?"

"Well, you know that he was shot. The bullet was very close to the ulnar nerve. It is taking a while to remove it. If everything goes well, Mikey will be out of the hospital in a few days.

"John, I was hoping to interview Vincent."

"I'm okay with that. But you know he fell and hit his head on a rock. He has a concussion. I think he is fine. You need to stop if you see that he is losing it."

"Absolutely!"

Then they walked over to Vincent. John told his son that Detective Maloney had a few questions about the shooting. "Can you handle this, son?" "Sure Dad!"

Just as Maloney was about to take Vincent to a nearby room, Dante rushed into the waiting room. Detta was a few steps behind. They ran over to Cris to see how she was doing. Detta put her arm around her daughter and started to cry. "Are you okay, Honey?"

"I'm okay, Mom."

Dante noticed Maloney and Vincent were walking out of the room. "Where do you think you are going, Maloney? I need to talk to you." Dante shouted. "Marty's in jail for no reason."

"Mr. Bonfigore, I'm in the middle of a homicide investigation. Marty is in police custody. My job is to collect information regarding the shooting and send it to the legal beagles in Providence. They'll decide if Marty will be held over for trial. Right now, I need to interview Vincent. After that, if you give me permission, I'll interview Cris." Then Bill escorted Vincent out of the room.

They walked to an empty conference room. Maloney pointed to a chair in the corner. "Vincent, make yourself comfortable." Vincent sat down. Then the detective asked how he was doing?"

"Well, my head is pounding. Otherwise, I am okay."

"You've been put through the wringer!" Vincent nodded in agreement. "So, I suppose you know why I am here."

"You want to talk to me about what happened at the park."

"Exactly."

Maloney took a tape recorder out of his satchel. He told Vincent that he was recording their conversation. Then Vincent gave Maloney a step-by-step accounting of what took place. He was very thorough. His recollection was a mirror image of Marty's description. Vincent had no doubt that if Marty hadn't shot D'Amato, then D'Amato would have shot him. Maloney had heard enough.

"Vincent, you've done a great job sharing what you saw. Head back to the waiting room. I'll be right behind you."

Dante was talking to Maria when Bill entered the room. "Mr. Bonfigore, I need to speak to you." Bill asked if he could interview Cris by herself. That idea went nowhere. Maloney tried to dissuade Dante from sitting in on the interview. Dante was completely within his rights to be present. That was unfortunate. The interview would take a different course if Dante were present. There was nothing else to do.

The interview went surprising well. Cris' responses mirrored Vincent's. Dante sat quietly during the entire interview. It was only when the interview was completed that Dante spoke up. "Cristiana, would you please go back to the waiting room. I'll be there in a minute. I need to talk the detective."

When she left the room, Dante closed the door and looked at Maloney.

"How can I help you, Mr. Bonfigore?"

Dante launched into a huge snit fit about Maloney's decision to hold Marty at the police station. There was no way to appease Bonfigore. Maloney listened patiently while Bonfigore went on and on about how Marty had achieved what the police had been incapable of doing. Finally, Maloney had enough.

"Mr. Bonfigore, I've followed the letter of the law during this entire investigation. If I had done otherwise, the investigation would have gone down the tubes. I know Marty has been at the station for the whole day. That couldn't be helped."

"Maloney," Dante barked, "when will Marty be released?"

"There is no way of telling. We need to interview Michael O'Day. I hope to accomplish that tomorrow. I need to confer with the medical examiner and get the ballistics report. Then I will meet with the State's attorney to review the case. This could take several days. In the meantime, Marty will stay at the station." There was nothing left to say. Maloney headed out the door.

Maloney called Marty's attorney. He told Monroe the status of the investigation. "I know Mr. Bonfigore is upset. That can't be helped. There's no way to appease him."

"Thank you, Detective. I assume you'll call me regarding Marty's status."

"Mr. Monroe, you will know when I know."

Monroe headed over to the police station and gave Marty the news. "You need to spend the night at the station. We need to verify O'Day's story.

"Thanks for letting me know, Mr. Monroe. Could you do me a favor and let my mom know that I am all right?"

"Count on it, Marty."

Maloney spent the next morning talking to lawyers. He met with the city prosecutor. Finally, a state attorney named Williams showed up. Maloney and Williams spent the afternoon reviewing the case. They wrapped up about 5:30 p.m. "Detective, If Nicosia's account matches O'Day's, you can cut Nicosia loose."

"O'Day had surgery yesterday. I can meet him tonight. if his accounting differs from Nicosia's, we can always reignite the investigation. Otherwise, I'll cut Nicosia loose."

Maloney called Marty's attorney. He told him the status of the investigation. "I know Bonfigore is upset. That can't be helped. There's no way to appease him."

"Thanks, Detective, I'll talk to Dante. Then I'll head to the station to give Marty a heads up."

Maloney interviewed Mikey. His story was identical with the others. Maloney informed the state attorney and was told to let Nicosia go. It took an hour to get the release forms signed. Dante waited patiently.

Finally, Marty and Monroe walked out of the station. They breathed a sigh of relief. Dante walked over to them. They jabbered on and on. Marty was exhausted. "It has been a long day Mr. B. I'm ready to head home."

Dante nudged Monroe. "Thanks for everything. I owe you big time."

Dante and Marty walked to the parking lot. "Listen up. Detta and I are very grateful for what you did. I won't forget how you saved Cris' life. I'm indebted to you."

Marty got into Mr. B's car and slumped into the passenger seat. They were both completely worn out. Dante headed to Marty's place. He stopped right in front of the apartment.

"Before you head in, Marty," Dante said, "I have two things to say. First, you did one hell of a job. My daughter and her friends would have been goners if you hadn't taken care of business with D'Amato."

At that point, tears began to fall onto Dante's cheeks. "Get yourself out of here, have a glass of wine, and relax. I'll see you tomorrow morning."

Marty opened the door to get out and then turned to face Dante. "So, Mr. B, what was the second thing you wanted to say to me?"

"Oh that," he said with the hint of a smile. "You don't shoot so bad for a girl." At that point, Marty headed towards her apartment.

The End

ABOUT THE AUTHOR

Terry is a native of Rhode Island. He received a B.A. from Providence College and an M.S. from Southern Illinois University. He resides in Florida in the winter and goes back to Minnesota for the other six months. This is his first novel.

Made in the USA
Middletown, DE
14 April 2021